A PLACE WHERE DREAMS WERE LOST AND RECOVERED OR FOREVER DESTROYED . . .

BARON ALFRED DE ROCHEFLEUR—The patriarch, a hot-tempered magnate who would sacrifice anything—even his beloved daughter—for his own desires.

ANNE—The heiress, a shy, large-boned girl whose blind passion for one man led to a hideous mistake . . . and a scandalous *ménage à trois*.

CHARLES—The poor cousin, tall and blond as a Greek god, who would get back his family's fortune in the bed of one woman . . . and the arms of another.

AMELIA—The Viennese beauty, rich and flirtatious, who ran from Hitler's fires into a blazing affair with a ruthless married man.

ALEXIS—The heir, the courageous Resistance fighter, who didn't know the family secret that could cost him a dynasty . . . and his life.

Books by Monique Raphel High

THE FOUR WINDS OF HEAVEN
ENCORE
THE ELEVENTH YEAR
THE KEEPER OF THE WALLS
THY FATHER'S HOUSE

THY FATHER'S HOUSE

Monique Raphel High

A DELL BOOK

Published by
Dell Publishing
a division of
The Bantam Doubleday Dell Publishing Group, Inc.
1 Dag Hammarskjold Plaza
New York, New York 10017

Dell ® TM 681510, Dell Publishing,
a division of the Bantam Doubleday Dell Publishing Group, Inc.

ISBN: 0-440-20129-2

Reprinted by arrangement with Delacorte Press

Printed in the United States of America

Published simultaneously in Canada

June 1988

10 9 8 7 6 5 4 3 2 1

KRI

Dearest Grisha, my husband . . . this book is for you. For all the midnight walks we took hand in hand, discussing strategy and characters. For all the hours you spent proofreading in a language that isn't your own. For all the cups of tea and the late-night snacks you concocted to keep me going. For your unending, ever-growing, and life-inspiring love.

"This is my beloved, and this is my friend. . . . Thou art all fair, my love; there is no spot in thee."

(Song of Solomon, 5:16; 4:7)

ACKNOWLEDGMENTS

———————◆◇◆———————

A book is a writer's child. This one was blessed with two caring fathers. From its very conception, two men have been backing me with their support, their ideas, and the publishing houses each represents. I wish to thank Mark Barty-King, of Bantam Press in Great Britain, and Charles E. Spicer, Jr., of Delacorte Press in New York, for being "with me all the way" in this endeavor.

As a rule, publishers are not a writer's best friend. Mark, you have provided the salient exception: You are a very good friend indeed. Since the beginning of my publishing career you have given me your gentle understanding, your professional expertise, and a mirror image of myself as an author that made me strive more than ever to match your good opinion. Because of you, I have never had that sinking feeling of being stranded alone, not knowing where to turn for my next project: your resourceful words have brightened many a fearful moment. It is a privilege to be published by your company.

As for you, Charlie, on the eve of your departure from Delacorte, words come more easily from my pen than from my mouth. I am overcome with emotions: the sense of personal loss because you are leaving battling a deep feeling of gratitude for our five years of close cooperation, and, underscoring all else, a true, abiding friendship. You have worked with me on three books, giving truth to the statement that when an editor works well with an author, the result is a joint effort that, like a child, reflects both parents. How could I not love you for the understanding you have always had of me as a creator and as a human being?

I want to thank you both for lending me your ears, across oceans and continents. For never putting off speaking to me, even when you were swamped with work and other emergencies. For helping me to forge my identity through these books . . . and especially through this, our new "baby," *Thy Father's House.*

* * *

No book can hope to see the light of day without the active involvement of a good literary agent. Mine is the best. Roberta Pryor has encouraged me, prodded me on, at times given me a severe talking-to during the creation of this novel. Creative people can sometimes be difficult to deal with, and Roberta, since 1980, has known exactly how to get the best out of me while remaining a wonderful friend at the same time. I'm very grateful.

Another bright, professionally excellent woman has worked with me on the manuscript—my new editor, Emily Reichert. It's difficult at best to take on somebody else's project, somebody else's author—and somebody else's headaches. Yet, when Charlie Spicer left Delacorte, he handpicked Emily to "inherit" my book . . . and me with it. Emily bounced enthusiastically on the bandwagon and put in countless hours of absolutely superlative work. Emily, thank you. You have proved to be every bit as good as Charlie had promised!

Not every human being views his own life as an intricate game of chess. Some of us like to be impulsive; others claim that their luck is just a matter of chance. But, as an ever-curious observer of people, I have noticed that the most powerful individuals in Western society—the knights of industry who control the world—are set apart by the fact that they take nothing for granted . . . not a single action, not a single reaction. To them, life is a series of moves they have planned long in advance, gauging their opponents' strength and trying to second-guess their hidden intentions. In fact, so cleverly do they plan their moves that the very joy of living is often left unnoticed by the wayside. . . .

My friend Lev Alburt, U.S. national chess champion, can foresee his adversary's moves ten steps ahead. But in his case, it's just a game. If he loses, he can still go home and laugh the next morning. Those who consider life to be their game of chess, stand to lose everything—but if they're very careful, they might gain an empire and a dynasty. To them—the knights of industry who control the world—each move is an intelligent gamble that is no laughing matter. To them—it means life itself. . . .

"There are fathers so unnatural that the whole of their lives seems to be devoted to giving their children reason for being consoled when they die."

Jean de la Bruyère: *Les Caractères*, XI, 1688.

"He who governs himself according to what he calls his principles may be punished either by one party or the other for those very principles. He who proceeds without principle, as chance, timidity, or self-preservation directs, will not perhaps fare better; but he will be less blamed."

Michel Guillaume Jean de Crèvecoeur:
Letters from an American Farmer, XII, 1782.

"One's cruelty is one's power, and when one parts with one's cruelty, one parts with one's power."

William Congreve: *The Way of the World*, II, iv.

"My mother says that he is my father, but myself I do not know, for no man can know who was his father."

Homer: *Odyssey*, I, c. 700 B.C.

PROLOGUE

The quiet, majestic avenue, paved with uneven cobblestones, spoke of forbidden trysts and clandestine intrigue, as if the ghosts of long-dead kings of France—Saint Louis IX, Francis I, and, finally, the Sun King, Louis XIV, still haunted the town. The enormous castle, begun by Louis IX and eventually abandoned by the Sun King for the more sumptuous Versailles, lay hidden behind its decorous, well-ordered French garden, shaded by chestnut trees. Yet, one felt its presence. Opposite the garden a flat, one-and-a-half-mile walk gave way to a riotously flowered bluff planted with fruit trees. And below, the River Seine, moved by Nature's erratic moods, wound its way gray, bright blue, or mysteriously opaque, the steady current its one constant attribute.

The afternoon sun played hopscotch over the cobblestones, dappling them ocher and burnt sienna. It ventured as far as the façade of the imposing mansion of red brick and white stone, then retreated, as if in awe of its two square turrets. Of all the old homesteads that bordered the avenue, this mansion stood the proudest, topped with gray slate, impassively guarded by a huge sculpted doorway depicting a crown of laurels with an imperial *N* at its center. Within its strong walls, Napoleon had rested before setting forth to hunt the fox in the neighboring forest.

Beyond the carriage entrance was a charming garden with pebbled walkways, trellised arbors, and strangely shaped beds of multicolored flowers. Because the afternoon was already half spent, the August heat had somewhat abated. Among the cheerfully disposed, fashionably attired guests, the butler in his tails and starched shirt seemed to be the only one perspiring, as he passed around a silver tray of petits fours.

At the center of the party, a portly, middle-aged gentleman, his stomach quivering with laughter, was attempting to juggle two oranges from hand to hand, while a dozen onlookers tittered around him, teacups raised in mock salute. But the entertainment, and the spectators' attention, were actually intended to amuse a much smaller individual. For this elite gathering was in fact a child's birthday party. Holding on to the hand of his grandmother, a tiny boy in a sailor suit shrieked his delight. He was a beautiful child, with a delicate, heart-shaped face dominated by deep blue eyes; below the sailor cap, golden curls tumbled gently to his small shoulders. Out of breath, the juggler pleaded: "Enough, Charlie boy?"

A tall, dark man in his thirties stood off to the side contemplating the scene. Next to him was a young woman only a few years his junior. Her full figure was properly set off in a high-waisted tea dress of soft teal linen, its sleeves bouffant at the shoulders and tight over her forearms, its long skirt clinging to her shapely hips. Her eyes, though a paler blue than the small boy's, were similar enough to draw comparison, and her own blond pompadour had the same bronze highlights as his curls. As she watched the juggler and the child her expression seemed both attentive and anxious, as if, in the midst of motherly concentration, other thoughts kept intruding.

"You're very lucky, Yvonne," the man beside her said. Raising her eyes to his, she shuddered slightly. For some reason his tone of voice annoyed her.

"I know. Charles is a wonderful, bright child. But you're about to have one of your own, Alfred," she countered.

"I'd like my child to be exactly like yours." He smiled, but his dark eyes remained unrevealing. Then he laughed. "But that can't be, can it, Cousin? Sonia, my wife, is almost as dark as I am: the typical Russian Jewess, with black hair and pale gray eyes. You made a lucky choice, marrying a German: your child had to be light, like both you *and* your handsome Wilhelm!"

"You're only half making sense, Alfred," she said, a trifle curtly. "Russian, German—what difference does it make? We're all Jews, from the same roots, aren't we? Our ancestors came from the same ghettos, in France, Spain, or Bavaria. And those who thought they were escaping by fleeing to Mother Russia, ended up in identical ghettos in the Pale of Settlement. Your Sonia's and my Willy's people spoke the same Yiddish, years and years ago, and regardless of the color of our children's hair, their backgrounds are the same, aren't they?"

"Damn it, Yvonne, must you always ruin my clever speeches with that dreary logic of yours?" Playfully, he pulled a curl from her pompadour and twirled it lightly around his finger. Then, more gently, he added: "Or is something else the matter?"

She faced him, suddenly cold, rubbing her hands over her arms. "It's just that Willy hasn't come downstairs yet, and the guests are all waiting. What could be keeping him in the house so long? Mama's held the cake back till the last minute. It's not fair for him to be this late for Charles's birthday party. After all, we have only *one* child!"

"Stop fretting," Alfred said, but instinctively he turned to gaze at the guest room windows on the second floor of the house. Yvonne and her husband, visiting for the summer from their home in Berlin, had been given the grandest suite for their stay. Alfred sighed, admitting that she was right: the habitually punctual Willy now seemed conspicuous by his absence. Oh, well, he thought. Parties like this were meant for women, children, and the old folks; he himself was growing a bit bored with all the games and amusements. The little boy, Charles, was chasing one of his grandfather's oranges across the lawn; his excited laughter chimed through the garden. Yvonne bent down and caught her son in a quick, impulsive hug, burying her nose in his soft hair. For a moment nobody spoke as they watched mother and child, and Alfred recalled Keats's "Ode to a Grecian Urn," the present caught forever, joy materialized and preserved for eternity. The thought sobered him.

The lovely moment was abruptly shattered by the sound of a gunshot exploding from behind one of the windows on the second floor. But before anyone had a chance to react, a chorus of church bells broke out, heralding the changing of the hour. It was four o'clock, on the first day of August 1900. And in the perfectly landscaped garden behind the emperor Napoleon's hunting pavilion, a dozen people in colorful party attire remained frozen in place, shocked into silence, aware that something tragic had just occurred.

The small, delicate boy, Charles Lévy, did not understand. But an instinctive fear had penetrated him, and in later years he would know that on his second birthday, a shadow had crept over his childhood, marring it forever. His was the first movement, as he ran to his mother; and his was, for a moment, the only human cry that sounded in the garden.

BOOK ONE

Opening Moves

CHAPTER I

Baron Alfred de Rochefleur studied the gold crest on his signet ring. In the dim winter sunlight one could just barely distinguish the timeworn outlines of a roughhewn rock and the strong, bristly head of an open thistle. A sturdy flower, the symbol of endurance and perseverence. Alfred ran the tip of his finger over the emblem that his family had taken as its own more than two centuries ago. The rock and the flower: the preservation of the Family, the continuation of this clan, this *dynasty* that today ranked among the first tier of Jewish families in Europe.

The rock and the flower. And *La Folie,* of course. For every great family had to be drawn together by a powerful centripetal force that could bind each member to the others, ignoring the passions of the heart: love, hatred, fear. With the de Rochefleurs, business alone was not sufficient motive: by now the family "empire" had stretched out to encompass diverse and varied holdings and investments. But La Folie . . . Napoleon's Folly—the house that had witnessed so many births, weddings, deaths—La Folie was strong enough to draw each of the de Rochefleurs back to his or her childhood roots.

There are so few of us left, Alfred thought, gazing at the ring. Just he himself, in Saint Petersburg, Russia; his sister, Barbara, Countess von Guttman, in Vienna; and Yvonne Levy, their cousin, who still resided at La Folie. Their grandfather's will had been quite definite: The family estate would pass from eldest son to eldest son. By rights, Alfred should have been its master. He should have been in the Parisian suburbs, enjoying a stroll through his garden . . . instead of being *here,* in this harsh, godforsaken land.

The rock and the flower, and La Folie. No one would ever strip him of his family name, the way he had been stripped of his patrimony. But I shall get you back, he thought fiercely. And when I take you back, I shall never let you go. . . .

Alfred de Rochefleur laughed dryly. Men spoke in such absurd clichés when they were in love. But for him the family estate was so much more important than a passing fancy for a beautiful woman. La Folie *meant* the Rochefleurs, just as much as the crest on his old ring did. Its regal façade symbolized how far the family had come since the boy from Swabia, Gabriel Blumenfels, had taken the first step on the road to wealth and power.

Who would have predicted that a sixteen-year-old Jewish boy, born in the ghetto of Ulm in Swabia in 1694, could have set in motion such a powerful chain of events that his own descendants would one day possess a mansion built by an emperor? Napoleon's Folly, that most beautiful of homes, that most accursed of patrimonies. . . .

Alfred sighed, wondering why, in 1916, family affairs had reached this critical point. Three adult heirs, one house, and too few offspring to carry on the name and tradition created by the patriarch Gabriel. Created against all odds, like a stubborn flower pushing its way up through a hard rock. . . .

* * *

Alfred's father had told him the story many times. He could imagine the scene of young Gabriel Blumenfels in his tailor shop, yearning for a better life, wanting to *be somebody.* Gabriel had married the rabbi's daughter and started a textile mill with his wife's slim dowry. Several strong sons were born to them, and each of them had worked together to turn their father's dream into a reality, pushing themselves into the lumber business, setting money aside so that *their* sons could purchase an old coal mine, gambling it would still yield. . . . And finally they had started a modest little bank and moved the family to Paris, the city of light and hope. There they hoped that the strong stain of Swabian prejudice would fade in these new, cosmopolitan surroundings.

But once a Jew, always a Jew. Only the name had changed: "Blumenfels" was neatly gallicized into "Rochefleur." The advantage in Paris was that money purchased culture. In the nineteenth century the Jewish Blumenfelses, who had heretofore spoken only the Yiddish dialect, learned French as it was spoken at the courts of Napoleon and Louis XVIII. They learned to follow fashions and to appreciate the arts. They consolidated their wealth and married their daughters to sons of yet more firmly entrenched Jewish businessmen. When the Rochefleur bank made a discreet loan to Louis the Eighteenth, allowing him to cover an embarrassing debt incurred by his mistress Madame du Cayla, the family was rewarded with a title. Henceforth, every male offspring would be a Baron de Rochefleur.

And so a dynasty was established in the first quarter of the nineteenth century. By the 1850s the de Rochefleur family was firmly established in the Jewish aristocratic elite, whose enormous wealth unlocked all doors, even those blocked off by prejudice. Like the Gunzburgs in Russia and the Rothschilds in Germany, theirs was a dynasty that had broken through national boundaries: behind the scenes in every government in Europe, their influence was felt, though never flaunted. Speaking through the intricate network of their banks, the de Rochefleurs exerted subtle control; and heads of state, always afraid of economic reprisals, listened carefully. The de Rochefleurs knew they were feared, held in some awe, and respected; and for them, this was enough. They never hoped to be *liked,* for they understood that the invisible though ever palpable barrier of religion would always separate them from their peers. Those they controlled might fawn upon them, and their gold might purchase any imaginable luxury: but as soon as their backs were turned, all pleasantries ceased, and there would be whispers about "the hated Jews." No matter: these whispers, after all, carried no hint of power. For the de Rochefleur name had come to symbolize the indestructible banner of clout.

Alfred had clear memories of his grandfather, Baron Charles Jacques René de Rochefleur. During the reign of Louis XVIII, it was Charles's father, Armand, who made the propitious loan that had won the family its title. Baron Charles had consolidated his position during the tenure of Louis Philippe from 1830 to 1848. Charles was a tall, stately man, his prominent nose and his Vandyke beard giving him the appearance of an elegant German rabbi. Alfred had stood in awe of him as a little boy.

Charles had purchased a venerable mansion on the rue de Tilsitt, around the Barrière de l'Etoile, but his Swabian blood yearned for open country and fresh air, and so he started to look for a suburban home as well. Three had been proposed to him: the château of Maisons-Laffitte, whose layout was not to his taste; the palace of Malmaison, where Napoleon I had resided with Josephine (Charles found it too drafty); and, finally, the rather modest red-brick hunting lodge in Saint-Germain-en-Laye, near the old Renaissance castle with its moat and forest. Charles had picked the lodge over the others for its charm and its location.

We can't change our roots, Alfred now reflected. The wide open spaces in the hills of Swabia, its lush green forests, had found an echo in the landscape of this peaceful suburb of Paris. Charles had fallen in love with the immense woods that bordered the English garden in front of the old castle. The town itself consisted of narrow, winding roads with picturesque names: Bread Street, Hall Street, and the Street of the Old Butcher Shops. Beyond Market Square stretched a beautiful residential area.

Across from the castle lay a straight road, one and a half miles long, named the Terrace. A wrought-iron gate protected passersby from slipping down the steep cliff that overlooked a dozen small towns and Paris itself in the far distance. In the springtime the entire cliffside was alive with scented fruit trees in full bloom. Charles, who liked to hike, had decided that although the hunting lodge lacked the prestige associated with Maisons-Laffitte or Malmaison, the walk through both the forest and the Terrace quite overcame other mundane considerations. He had purchased La Folie and set to work to remodel its interior.

Napoleon had loved this old lodge. His staff called it "La Folie" —their emperor's folly—mostly as a joke. He had made a habit of retiring there before a campaign, to allow his mind peaceful reflection in a serene atmosphere. His staff had thought it a haven for him and affectionately remarked that he loved it the way a man loves a woman.

Charles understood Napoleon, and La Folie became *his* folly, *his* retreat before difficult maneuvers at the bank. A financial emperor had replaced the short man with the tricornered hat as master of the hunting lodge in Saint-Germain. But Charles wanted La Folie to be a family home: unlike his predecessor, he'd brought his wife along, as well as his two strapping sons, Henri and Guy. The boys went riding with him in the forest on their thoroughbred Arabian stallions, while his wife waited for them in the gallery, her hands busy with her embroidery, her eyes darting from her agile fingers to the comely view of the garden beyond.

La Folie possessed two wings, the main and the servants' quarters, separated by a huge carriage entrance that went all the way to the garden behind the house. Three floors and a huge attic were topped by two square turrets and afforded space enough for all of Charles's household to move in for brief holidays.

On the ground floor Charles had set up the reception rooms and the dining room, large and square and hung with raw silk. Glowing faces portrayed by the Old Masters stared down at the family from the austere walls. The glass-encased gallery at the back overlooked the garden with its trellised arbors and pretty white gazebo.

The second floor, with its imposing high ceilings, had been remodeled as living quarters for Charles and his wife, Sarah, and their butler and maid-in-waiting. The third floor was turned into twin suites for Henri and Guy and for their private tutors. Charles had particularly admired the plain, sturdy mahogany furniture of Louis XIII, and had lightened the decor of his country home only in the boys' rooms and his wife's boudoir. He'd respected Napoleon's wish and kept it mainly a man's house, giving Sarah free rein in the Paris mansion to balance out the injustice of his autocracy at Saint-Germain.

Alfred had no trouble recalling La Folie as it had been when he himself had been growing up, for it had changed hardly at all since those days. Except that it had fallen into a mournful state of disrepair, like a well-remembered first love unexpectedly encountered after thirty years. His grandfather Charles had loved the house more than Henri, Alfred's father, had. Of Charles's two sons, Guy had appreciated it more, though perhaps only because he had liked the idea of leaving his wife and daughter there alone while he took the coach into Paris to meet his mistresses. La Folie, of late, had been anything but a man's retreat. It had become the symbol of two women's suffering, of their penury, and of the tragedy that had exploded when a gun's trigger had been set off in 1900. . . .

It wasn't difficult to summon up images of his father and uncle as they had been as boys. Alfred had heard all the stories and seen portrait paintings of the family. Henri, older by two years, had been good-looking in a quiet sort of way: dark-haired, gray-eyed, with finely honed features, a rather short, thin boy. Guy's looks had been flamboyant even then: his red-gold hair caught the sun's rays, and his eyes glowed a special peacock blue; he was tall, strong, and, though still a teenager, already virile.

Alfred had been told many tales of his uncle Guy's extravagant behavior: how he had impregnated one of the maids, and, that same winter, his Latin tutor's daughter; how he would spend his entire allowance in a single day, having red roses sent to a girl he'd glimpsed at a bar mitzvah or walking to church with her governess; how he never would study and had therefore been turned away

from every European university. On the other hand, Henri had
been received by the universities with open arms, winning awards
from both Göttingen and Oxford in the fields of law and international economics.

While studying at Oxford, Henri met the David Sassoons, one of
the leading families of London, whose ancestors had made a colos-
sal fortune in India. Furthermore, they were observant Jews. One
of the Sassoon daughters, Anne, made a lasting impression on
young Henri. She was reserved and poised, with a face more dignified and refined than actually beautiful. Within a year, they became
engaged; and after receiving his diploma in the summer of 1865,
Henri de Rochefleur married Anne Sassoon in the magnificent syn-
agogue in Hampstead, under a *huppah* of interwoven orchids, lilies,
and baby rosebuds. Their wedding was the event of the year in
European Jewish society just as, in the fifteen years that followed,
their marriage became known for both partners' loyalty, strength,
and unswerving love.

Henri and his bride settled in Paris, moving into the second
story of Charles and Sarah's house on the Barrière de l'Etoile. In
1866, Anne gave birth to a son, whom they named Alfred. Five
years later a daughter, Barbara, was born.

Meanwhile, Guy was living downstairs in the same mansion, in
elegant bachelor's quarters especially segregated from the rest of
the household. And there he held court for his friends, dragging in
all the tattered, impoverished, debauched elements of society from
the Clichy and Montmartre neighborhoods to add spice to his parties.

Since Charles couldn't turn his second son into a professional
man, he decided that it would at least look more respectable if he
could marry him off and turn him into a family man. But which
upstanding family would have allowed Guy to court their daughter, let alone marry her? Charles realized that none of the eligible
debutantes would come close to Guy; and so he looked beyond, at
moneyed American heiresses and well-named families' poorer relations.

And then he found the perfect woman. Jeannette Fould bore one
of the most renowned names in Paris, for the Foulds rivaled the
Rothschild and de Rochefleur names among French Jews. But
Jeannette's father had been on the "poor side of the family" and
had made some bad investments to boot. Jeannette's dowry was
very small, and although she was pretty in a traditional fashion,

and came from such a formidable clan, her power to attract an eligible bachelor of her own background seemed remote. Until the day Charles picked her out for his son.

When Charles arranged Guy's marriage to Jeannette, the two young people had known each other hardly more than a few weeks, and had never been alone. But to remain in his father's good graces, Guy knew that he'd have to give in and "settle down." Jeannette saw only that her fiancé was good-looking, and that somehow she'd been saved from becoming a cloistered old maid.

It wasn't until after the wedding that Jeannette realized the sort of man she had married, and then she wondered if perhaps spinsterhood had not been underrated. After she became pregnant almost at once, Guy began disappearing early in the morning and returning late at night, long after Jeannette had gone to sleep. She'd married a de Rochefleur, but one who carried no prestige and spent all his father's money on his own pleasures, a handsome rake who hardly remembered she existed. To keep her from total solitude, at least she had a kind sister-in-law in the same house, and the birth of her baby to anticipate.

When Yvonne was born to Guy and Jeannette, in 1872, Barbara, Henri's daughter, was one year old. Henri had been prospering in his father's business, while Guy continued to do nothing but play. With Jeannette's dowry, the young man had purchased several racehorses, but none had yet won a race, and it seemed as if he had invested in the wrong commodity.

Charles had practically retired by then. His wife had passed away and, despondent and lonely, he had moved lock, stock, and barrel into La Folie. Guy decided that his father needed looking after, and so he sent his wife and daughter to the country house and had Jeannette "take care of" Charles. Henri sighed with exasperation and turned his back on the whole lot of them, concentrating on acquiring further assets. His father allowed him free rein, knowing Henri would accomplish a great deal of good in the banking world; and he allowed Jeannette free rein at La Folie, knowing she would be kind to him and leave him alone.

And so the years went by. Now that Guy's family had moved to the country, the three children saw each other only on holidays or during summer vacations. In any case, Alfred was six years Yvonne's senior and had shown little interest in his cousin. And then, suddenly, Anne de Rochefleur died of pneumonia. It was 1880 and Alfred was a boy of fourteen, Barbara, a plump nine-

year-old. Their father sent them to La Folie to be cared for by their
aunt Jeannette. It was then that Alfred's attachment to the old
hunting lodge was cemented, and he began to envy little Yvonne.

What a princess she had seemed, all golden and pretty, compared to Barbara, his overweight sister. The princess of La Folie,
the mistress of the house, while he and his sister felt like guests
walking on eggs because she lived there and they didn't. At that
time he hadn't known of Charles's will, hadn't known that Yvonne
wasn't supposed to inherit the splendid family estate. *He* was, Alfred, the only son of Charles's older son. . . .

Alfred would never forget the day he learned how his own father
had betrayed him. His grandfather had quietly passed away in
1882, becoming the third occupant of the family vault at the Montparnasse Cemetery. Alfred's father had taken him to a morning
minyan at the Temple de la Victoire, and afterward they'd met his
uncle Guy at the Café Weber for breakfast.

Outside, a light drizzle was fogging the gray autumn morning.
Guy strode into the café with his habitual good humor. Alfred
liked him; one couldn't help liking Guy, with his pleasant demeanor, his jokes, and his self-deprecating manner. Here was a
man who never pretended to be anything but what he was: a buf-
foon, an unfaithful husband, a wastrel who had never accomplished a single thing "of substance." But how he enjoyed life!
Henri, the good banker, the devout Jew, had never done one unexpected thing in his entire existence. Alfred saw the differences between the two men, and, recognizing them, couldn't help but look
with indulgence at his "wayward" uncle.

Alfred at sixteen was a rather quiet boy. He sat still and gazed
around him, taking in the sad expression on his father's face with
the nonchalance of the young, for whom all side issues, all "grown-
up" problems, weighed equally unimportant.

"I can't afford to keep supporting a second family," Henri was
saying. "The expenses at La Folie probably triple my own expenses
at rue de Tilsitt."

"But you're not entertaining anymore, Henri," Guy countered.

"Jeannette doesn't entertain either," Henri replied, his voice just
barely ironic.

"So where do you suppose the money's going? Do you think
perhaps the accountant has made a miscalculation?"

"Our accountant never miscalculates," Henri answered dryly.

"Well then . . ."

"Well then, *nothing.* Hear me out, Guy. Our father's will was very clear: I am to run the business and administer your trust fund. You are not to receive any direct benefits from your side of the inheritance. Papa knew you'd waste it all in a month's time if you ever laid your hands on it. But this arrangement hasn't been working out. Every month, your expenses exceed the amount of money I send you. Your trust fund is already operating in the red. I've had to reimburse it from my own moneys."

"What are you about to suggest?" Guy asked pleasantly.

"You and your family have been living in *my* house. Are you even aware of this, Guy? *You and Jeannette have been residing in a house that belongs to me.* And at the same time, I've been sending you money from my own pocket."

Henri seldom yelled, and never lost his temper; but when he became tense and angry, as he was now, he would speak with icy tones that underscored that very emotion he kept so tightly controlled.

Guy began to shift in his seat, awkwardly rubbing his hands together. He glanced at his nephew, and Alfred felt his embarrassment and pitied him. At the same time, he was interested and astounded by the news that his uncle wasn't the owner of La Folie. How was this possible?

"There comes a point of reckoning in every man's life," Henri continued. "You and I have come to ours, Guy. I don't want to keep perpetuating an unfairness. Our father supported you; I made the business grow. Now I'm supporting you, and you've been living in my house. What's my benefit, in your opinion?"

Guy hadn't answered. Henri pushed on relentlessly: "I've had enough! All our lives, I've worked and you've spent. I've had to take care of you, and you never once lifted a finger to help yourself. You were a burden I never expected to bear for such a long time. And so today, I'm cutting you off."

In the silence that followed, Alfred felt himself growing hot with embarrassment. Why am I here? he wondered. Why did Papa drag me along to witness Uncle Guy's humiliation?

As if reading his thoughts, his father said: "La Folie is mine, and should one day be my son's. I wanted him to know every detail of what is about to pass between us. He must know, so that he will understand why I'm doing this."

"Are you going to throw us out?" Guy asked, his face all at once pathetic.

"No. That would be unfair to Jeannette and Yvonne. Do you ever stop to consider them, Guy? I'd like to cut off all your funds, force you to take stock of your life and perhaps make some timely changes. But you know I *can't*. I have to send you the check from the trust fund, but I also know that if I did no more, your wife and daughter would end up totally destitute, without a roof over their heads. I've given the matter a lot of thought, and can see only one solution: to give you La Folie, and then forget you ever existed, wash my hands of you completely!"

"What do you mean?" Guy asked, bewildered.

"You don't have two sous to rub together. Your trust fund is operating in the red. You will never set money aside to provide your daughter with a dowry suitable for a Baroness de Rochefleur. And I will not continue to plow away for both of us! I'll hand the house over to you, Guy, and instruct my accountant to send you monthly checks from your trust fund. But from now on, you can forget you ever had a brother. You'll never see another franc from my personal holdings, no matter why you may need it. Do you understand?"

Alfred stared at both of them: at his furious, outraged father, who had never once raised his voice . . . and at his miserable uncle, mopping his forehead with a silk handkerchief, avoiding both their eyes. . . . And he felt as if, surreptitiously, someone had plunged a long, slick blade between his ribs. Had he heard correctly? La Folie *should have been his one day*? And now Henri had passed it to his brother, simply to avoid having to augment the income from Guy's trust fund? Had years of unfair burdens suddenly made Henri lose control of his mental faculties? The de Rochefleurs were among the forty richest families in France— didn't that imply that a trust fund could be immeasurably stretched before any effect would be felt by other members of the clan?

"I've always loved La Folie, Papa," Alfred said, for the first time breaking into the confrontation. "It's not right that you should give it away, just like that."

His uncle stared at him, as if to say: *Et tu, Brute?* Henri looked at his son and replied sternly: "It's not right that an injustice be perpetuated till the end of my life. Guy must learn to manage his own affairs, and the only way that this can ever happen is if I put him in control of the house he lives in. Otherwise I'll end up being dragged in to save him from the mess he creates, as I've always been."

"Then why not buy another house—somewhere, anywhere—for Uncle Guy and Aunt Jeannette?"

"That old house would only be an expensive burden, Alfred." Henri sighed. "In a few years, you'll be taking over my position and will be in charge of all of our family's affairs. You'll be as busy as I am, if not busier. What would you do with such a house, too far from Paris to be convenient for everyday living, and too close to be an adequate holiday resort? You'd end up having to sell it, as I would have if Jeannette, Guy, and Yvonne had not taken up residence there during Papa's lifetime."

"That's not true!" Alfred stood up, blood pounding in his head. "I'd—I'd . . ." But he wasn't able to find the right words. He hadn't known the magic configuration of speech to change his father's mind.

So he hadn't said anything. With his father's stern eyes upon him, young Alfred stammered something unintelligible and dropped back into his chair like a punished schoolboy. His uncle looked at him with compassion, as if to say: He's closed both our mouths, hasn't he, boy?

And that was how the country estate had gone from Henri's hands to Guy's, from being the very symbol of the de Rochefleur power to a sad token of dispossession and punishment. To make a moral point, Henri had degraded his brother by withdrawing *his own son's* just inheritance!

Then and there, stared down by the cold gray eyes of the head of the de Rochefleur dynasty, sixteen-year-old Alfred promised himself that he would never work for his father. This was the only way he could even the score between himself and Henri, meeting pain with pain and injustice with vengefulness. You have sold my birthright for a mess of potage, Alfred thought, rage entering his heart and making him feel hatred for the man whose esteem he had always sought. Well then, so be it. *But I shall find a way to earn it back, and from your grave, you will regret this day. . . .*

* * *

Alfred de Rochefleur tugged on his silk bow tie and looked out over the sea of faces in the ballroom. He was still a stranger here, after so many years, and now it made him uncomfortable to be hosting his daughter's debut in a city so far from his own home. Saint Petersburg was deceptively familiar because, in high society, everyone spoke his language, French. But apart from that he felt totally out of his element and yearned for the quiet, serene beauty of Paris, which he had left behind for good twenty years ago.

Bitterness began to take hold of him again, the way it did at the most unexpected moments. He'd run away to spite his father, to pay him back for having so nonchalantly handed over La Folie to his uncle Guy years before. He'd made a quick decision to court Sonia Aschkenasy, a rich young Russian heiress who had come to Paris in the winter of '95, and he had followed her back to Saint Petersburg to marry her in '96.

Sonia had been slender and pretty then, with pale gray eyes, black hair, and translucent skin. She was still delicate and beautiful, although of course she was forty now, and illness had sharpened her features. Alfred had been attracted to her, but there was more to it than that. He'd also been excited by the fact that she had come from such a distant country, one that sounded half barbarian, half mythical, with a history of grandeur and culture side by side with unchecked, primordial lusts. A country rich in exoticism, filling him with dreams and fantasies of never-ending forests and palaces capped with bulbous domes that narrowed into delicate, faerie spires that pricked the purple skies overhead. . . .

Yes, Alfred thought, Petersburg was a sumptuous city. Its palaces resembled nothing he'd ever seen in western Europe. Their rounded cupolas were like silent laughter, and the colors he saw here were bright, a pathway of violent contrasts and hues. Petersburg was magnificent but frightening, for he had come unprepared, his Parisian control in strong opposition to the abysmal nadirs and exalted peaks of the Russian national character.

Sometimes, in the afternoon, on the way home from his father-in-law's offices, he would ask his driver to take him through the city. The reassuring clip-clop of the horses soothed him from the day's load of pressure as the carriage rolled through the quays, bounded on one side by a parapet of granite and on the other by the vast, dark Neva River, more than half a mile wide.

Even his own daughter was a Russian, he thought, looking at her. Anne, he had named her, after his mother; here they called her "Anna," "Anya," "Annushka." Foreign-sounding, sentimental names. She *was* sentimental: sensitive, shy, afraid, but the kind of timid girl whose passions were held at bay only because the opportunity to unleash them had not yet presented itself. Nor should it have: this winter of 1916, she was only sixteen. He wished he'd been able to keep her a child just a little while longer. . . .

Normally, young girls didn't "come out" at sixteen. In Petersburg, some of them were presented at seventeen, or they waited for the usual age, eighteen, the way they did in Paris. But because of the war, many formalities had been dropped. Anne hadn't wanted a lavish debut, but her mother was insistent. And so, in spite of the fact that most members of the elite had considerably reduced their social life, paring it down to the bare minimum out of respect for "the men at the front," an exception had been made for Anne. Her mother was ill, and her friends had forgiven her for indulging in this party, understanding that her days were numbered. It hurt Alfred to think that the doctor had given him so little hope. Sonia had suffered from heart trouble since childhood, and now her delicate health had deteriorated to the point of danger.

Alfred had married into the Aschkenasy family, which, fifty years before, had been permitted by Tsar Alexander II to migrate from their native Odessa to the capital, Saint Petersburg. Very few Jews were ever allowed this privilege . . . even today. The Aschkenasys were very rich and had lumber mills and gold mines in Siberia, which Alfred now managed. But they were nothing like the de Rochefleurs. His mother-in-law, to Alfred's mortification, still had her head shaved and wore the traditional wig of Orthodox women, and spoke Yiddish at home.

His wife, Sonia, and her brother Evgeny, had been sent abroad for an excellent education that had given them sophistication. But still, Alfred thought, Sonia had never dreamed of becoming a baroness. He'd always felt a tiny edge of superiority toward her, which had resulted in her becoming insecure and clinging.

Had it not been for Anne, Alfred might even have yearned to break loose and head sooner for Siberia, an area he hated for its bone-chilling cold and its desolate devastation. He'd studied engineering in Paris before his marriage, and now he supervised his father-in-law's gold operations, hating everything about it.

Tonight the grand ballroom was filled with elegant people, in shimmering evening attire. Everyone in Petersburg had come to pay their respects to the granddaughter of Yakov Aschkenasy, the Jew whose lumber kept their fireplaces working day and night during the freezing winters. Alfred felt an acute atmosphere of anti-Semitism in this city, where one never discussed religion openly. The lines were drawn, and no Jew, no matter how rich or well brought up, could cross them.

As Alfred gazed out at his guests he felt the war acutely, in spite of the seeming abundance of fine food and liquor, and of the finesse of the ladies' clothing. But these were yesterday's gowns, yesterday's jewels. And the young men were either on leave from their regiments, proudly displaying their medals and ribbons on their uniforms, or they were the ones left over: the only sons, the elder sons, the sons of widows, and those suffering from chronic ill health.

Anne was standing awkwardly to one side, twisting a ruby ring round and round her finger. Alfred looked at her and frowned. She wasn't pretty, like her mother, nor did she resemble him. Both he and his wife shared a finely chiseled look that their only child had failed to inherit. Anne seemed more like a peasant girl than a Baroness de Rochefleur. She was of medium height, with large bones, heavy hips, and full breasts. Her brown hair, though thick and lustrous, was totally straight, and needed hours and hours of the curling iron to punish it into form. Already, wisps of hair were making their escape from her elaborate pompadour.

Dressed tonight in silks and satins, she wore a skirt of lavender crinolines held together by pannier drapery and whalebones. All wrong, somehow, Alfred thought. She should have worn a simple, flowing garment to emphasize the striking outline of her strong young figure; now she looked absurd, as though wearing somebody else's hand-me-down.

But I'll make her marry the right man, Alfred thought, suddenly choked up with love for his dear, homely daughter. He walked peremptorily over to Anne, and said, "Princess, it's time you and I had a waltz together to show these young dolts how a Frenchman moves his feet!"

*   *   *

"Anna Alfredovna . . . what a marvelous gown!" Marie Zagat exclaimed. Marie was the daughter of a well-known Jewish biscuit manufacturer, but it was rumored that her *real* father was in fact a general close to the Tsar. She was a very pretty girl, blond and green-eyed, with a tiny doll's figure. Beside her, Anne felt like a huge plow horse facing a dainty Arabian thoroughbred.

"You know, I haven't had a new gown made for two years. Mama says it's obscene to spend money on ourselves, when our sons and brothers are freezing to death on the battlefront," Marie added.

"It's how I feel, too, Marie Victorevna," Anne replied, blushing. "But you see . . . my mother . . ." She pulled on a cuticle and brought the mistreated finger to her lips, tasting blood.

"It's so wonderful to dance again," Marie commented. "I've grown so tired of volunteer work." Her eyes swept over the immense ballroom, where crystal chandeliers reflected thousands of rainbow hues over the fine silk walls.

"What kind of relief work have *you* been doing?" Marie asked. "I've been helping Mama mail packages to the front."

Anne felt her cheeks grow warm with embarrassment. "I wasn't allowed to join any groups," she mumbled. "You see, my mother wanted me to finish my education first. . . ."

"Of course! How stupid of me! You're only sixteen. I had forgotten." Marie's eyes drifted over the room again. She laid a light hand on Anne's forearm and whispered, "I'd better go. I promised Grisha Nelidov I'd give him at least three waltzes, and here comes one now!"

Anne watched her sail off into the distance, and shifted her stance. Her feet were aching, and the whalebones of her corset were making deep ridges in the flesh around her ribs. Let this ordeal be over soon, she prayed, touching her forehead to brush away the sweat.

"Stand up straight, Annushka." Anne started, and turned around. Her mother, always so upright and elegant, stood facing her. Sonia looked pale and ill, but still so beautiful in her gown of gray silk, highlighted by rows of seed pearls interspersed with amethysts. Somehow, Sonia's beauty always made Anne feel guilty: a woman like that deserved a daughter more in keeping with her own image.

"I'm sorry, Mama."

"Just make sure you look as if you're having a good time. Your father spent thousands of rubles on this party, to make certain that your coming-out ball would draw all the best people. It's up to you to attract the eligible bachelors in this city, and what do I see? Marie Victorevna has five or six men dancing attendance on her, while you have none!"

"Mama," Anne said, her voice trembling slightly. "Marie is two years older than I am. I don't know anyone here, except for a few girls . . . daughters of your friends, like her! And besides, there aren't many 'eligible bachelors' around these days. Most of them are in the army."

"The good ones found a way to avoid all this foolish fighting. Just look around you! The room is full of handsome, wealthy men, many of them Jewish. The older girls will introduce you: it's your debut, and that's why I invited girls like that Marie. Making friends is so easy, darling." Sonia sighed. "You have everything to offer them: your social standing as a Baroness de Rochefleur, your father's money, your grandfather's millions. Why should anyone turn you away?"

"I'm neither charming nor pretty," Anne cut in hastily, avoiding her mother's eyes. "I don't know how to speak to people the way you do, or the way Marie does. One's either born attractive, or one isn't!"

Sonia stared coldly at her. "Your attraction is your breeding, and your family connection. Look at your aunt, Barbara de Rochefleur! She weighed over two hundred pounds when she was married off to Count Louis von Guttman in Vienna. And you're not nearly so overweight or awkward."

Anne's eyes filled with tears, and she turned aside and stared down at her shoes. Go away, *go away, Mama!* she thought. Go away and *die,* the way everyone says you're going to die. *I wish you were already dead!* Anne could feel herself shaking with anger.

"I've arranged for Baron Vladimir Rykovsky to take you for the next waltz," Sonia was saying, her voice low but insistent. "His father owes Alfred twenty thousand rubles, heaven knows—"

Anne wheeled about, her face red and splotchy, tears welling in her eyes. "I don't want Vladimir Rykovsky!" she cried, her voice beginning to break. "He smells of garlic and he belches on the dance floor. And I don't want you or Papa to arrange anything for me, or marry me off the way Grandfather did to poor Aunt Barbara! I'll find my own man . . . my own husband . . . and he'll be someone I'm in love with, not someone who just happens to owe Papa a lot of money!"

A thin smile spread over Sonia's face. "That, my love, remains to be seen," she replied stiffly. "You'll marry a man with money and status, and if he smells of garlic, all the better! Then you shan't have to fight off other women all your life!"

Abruptly, Anne turned her back on her mother, holding up the hem of her lavender gown so that she might run more easily out of the room. *Dear God,* she thought, tears blurring her vision. *I wish I*

could just lie down and die, or that Mother would die, now, before I
have to go through another night like tonight. . . .

* * *

In the bitter cold, Alfred de Rochefleur rubbed his arms to warm
himself, but that didn't help. Just weeks ago he had been dancing
with his daughter at her debut, in the ballroom of his apartment in
Saint Petersburg. But as soon as the fine linens and hand-blown
Lalique crystals had been put away, old Yakov Aschkenasy had
ordered him to pack for another lonely voyage to the Arctic regions of the Lena River. And so Alfred had sped across the frozen
hinterland in his troika, muffled to the ears, each day bringing him
farther and farther from civilization.

An entire continent now separated him from his loved ones. He
felt the icy Siberian wind piercing through the pelts of his astra-
khan coat, and through his gloves as well. He was sure he was
coming down with a nasty chill: his forehead felt hot and sweaty.
Silently he damned his father-in-law for sending him here, and
wondered whether, subconsciously, the old man didn't hate him.
Convicts—murderers and traitors—were sent to Siberia; the countryside was filled with them. He'd even met some, distinguished
scholars who had once plotted against the Tsar, and they'd shared
a few glasses of Vodka. And he'd thought that even they did not
merit the harshness of a Siberian winter.

It made no sense to be looking for gold nuggets at this time of
year. Alfred strode over to the riverbed of the Lena, cursing under
his breath. During the summer the task was an easy one. His men
simply dragged the river with huge, closely woven nets so that the
smallest nugget could be gathered up and brought to the surface.
Now the Lena lay completely frozen, and the men had been attacking it with pickaxes. A bloody waste of time, Alfred thought, his
teeth chattering.

He wondered what Anne and Sonia were doing in Saint Petersburg, and pictured them in the drawing room of the apartment on
the Galernaia, his daughter at the piano in a red velvet dress, his
wife doing her embroidery on the Louis XV sofa. A wave of longing washed over him.

Why had he decided to stay in this brutal country? He was a
Frenchman, yet here he stood in a land that had conquered his
most formidable countryman, Napoleon, by the rigors of its winter
and the insurmountable expanse of land. Alfred directed his steps
toward his most trusted foreman, a Jew called Aron. For some

reason Alfred liked this man, perhaps because unlike the other *muzhiks,* Aron didn't drink and didn't waste his time telling moronic jokes or laughing at others'. And he spoke a clear, crisp Russian that Alfred could understand, for he'd had eight years of schooling in his shtetl yeshiva.

"Well?" Alfred called as he approached the foreman. "How's it going?"

Aron, a tall, thin man with a beaked nose and a receding chin, shook his head. "It's very tough, Baron. Some of the nuggets are so tiny, they're no more than grains; and they're embedded in the ice so that it's almost impossible to separate them from the rest of the frozen matter. We're going to have to bring in half the river and melt down hundreds of pounds of wastes in order to garner the smallest amount of gold. And the men"—he made a sweeping gesture with his arm—"are cold, and tired, and growing impatient."

Alfred could feel a slight tremor of fever pass through him, and he clenched his jaw. Then he turned around, to scrutinize his men. He didn't like what he saw.

"Tell them to get back to work," he said curtly. "I want those pickaxes swinging to the tune of one-two-three, because I have news for you, we're *all* cold as hell! This isn't a national fair, this is business. I'm not going to pay one extra kopek to any imbecile who's standing around, waiting for the ice to melt by itself at his goddamned feet!"

Aron coughed. "It's not as simple as all that, unfortunately. You know how hard it's been to round up healthy men during a war crisis. We've got mostly older ones, Baron, and their strength gives out more quickly. They were up at five this morning; it's now one o'clock, and most of them are too hungry to continue. I gave them a little break and told them that they could have their lunch in an hour. I could have let them eat right now, but I knew you'd be displeased when you saw how little was brought in today and yesterday."

Alfred sighed. "Let them have their lunch. But they're going to have to work harder when they come back. You tell them I said so. There's nothing more disgusting than a lazy Russian peasant, except maybe a hundred lazy Russian peasants. You know damn well that I bribed the authorities to slip me as many of their healthy young recruits as they could—so don't pretend we've got nothing but a pack of weak old men working here!"

The fingers of both his hands were hurting him with frostbite, and he felt thoroughly chilled. "I'll be gone one hour," he told Aron. "Make sure that when I return, all the men are hard at work. If I see one who isn't, I've a mind to make an example of him to all his fellows."

Aron smiled, but his tone was ironic. "The Baron wants to go home, to the lights of Petersburg. The sooner the better."

Alfred smiled too. "Wouldn't *you,* if your family were there?"

"I don't have a family," Aron replied. His hazel eyes were unreadable in the white winter glare. Then he saluted. "I'll take care of the men, Baron. They'll do fine."

* * *

Alfred was lying on his cot in the workmen's hut when the shouting awakened him. His hands and face were numb with cold, and his teeth started to chatter. At first he wondered if this terrible noise was the tail end of a dream, but as he sat up he realized that the shouts were coming from just outside the hut. He felt his heart begin to hammer.

And then, before he could rise and gather his wits about him, the door was flung open wide. He found himself staring into the bloodshot eyes of a teenage boy, and then the eyes of other faceless men who were pushing their way into the hut. How many were there? Twenty? Thirty?

"We want more pay!" the youth—apparently their leader—said angrily.

Another man spoke up—an older, more composed individual. "We want to go home, Baron. We've been working twelve hours a day for the last three weeks, and we're exhausted, and underpaid. We've told all this to Aron. Without a raise, we're quitting—all of us!"

Alfred stared at the speaker, a gray-haired, plain man who walked with a slight limp. He recognized him, and thought he remembered seeing him drinking in the village tavern the night before. "If you didn't have a hangover, Vanya, you'd shut up and get back to work," he said, hoping to bring down the sense of hysteria that hovered in the air. "I'm warning all of you: get back to work immediately."

"And if we don't, Baron?" It was the wild-eyed youth again—the leader. "What will you do to us? Behead us? Even in the Tsar's army, Russians don't kill other Russians!"

"I'm going to pretend you never said that," Alfred replied quietly. "When I stand up, I expect this door to be closed, and all of you will be outside, on your way back to work. Is that clear?"

He could feel the fear creeping through his body, tensing every muscle, but he had to stay calm and display only the utmost calm. He stared unflinchingly at the young man, racking his brain to remember his name. Ah: *Kolya*. That was it. Always a slow worker and a troublemaker.

The young man stared back, and Alfred read naked hatred in his eyes. The goddamned wretch should have been on his knees, thanking him for having saved him from being sent to the front. . . . But gratitude was something he'd probably never felt.

Savages, all of them. Alfred hated them with a virulence that surprised him. He hated them for their ignorance, for their terrible stench, for the wet vowels of their language, which was so foreign to his own clean, precise French. He should never have come to Russia.

Why had he been such a fool, running away from his father? He should have stayed in Paris and accepted the loss of the manor, and remained close to everything he loved. But no—like many young hotheads, he had decided instead to prove to Henri that he would become a success on his own merits . . . a greater success than Baron Henri had ever dreamed of being, riding the coattails of old Baron Charles. Now, looking back, Alfred realized what a grave error in judgment he had made. And he was paying for it in spades.

Alfred didn't like the Aschkenasys. They treated him the way these workers did: with diffidence and distrust, understanding that *he was not one of them*. He was an aristocrat, and his in-laws represented new, unpolished wealth that hadn't had time to acquire breeding.

But the prestige and pay that his father-in-law's business afforded him were hardly negligible. He wasn't about to jeopardize his position by allowing this scum to see through to his fear. "I'm going to stand up," he announced, his voice crisp and cold and even. "And when I do, every last one of you will be out of here, on your way back to work."

As he rose some of the older workers slunk off; but not Kolya. "We're not afraid," the young man called out.

"What exactly is it you're after?" Alfred demanded. "I've given you extra time off for lunch. I've always been fair, expecting no more than a twelve-hour day in return for decent pay. *Now* what do you want?"

"We want the goddamned kike, Aron, to give us a lunch break at twelve o'clock, every day. And we want him to stay off our backs. We're doing a good job, but he's never satisfied. At night, he comes into the tavern to check up on us. That's none of his business: we're not drinking on the job!"

"If you're hung over, it becomes his problem—*my* problem," Alfred retorted. A veil seemed to have fallen over his eyes, and he stood very still, like a statue of ice. But below the surface, every nerve was quivering, on fire. "I'm just doing my job, and the harder you make it for me, the worse off it's going to be for you. My patience is wearing thin, Kolya. I have orders. If the men cause me any trouble, I will see to it that they're punished. So, once again, I'm going to ask that you be a good boy and take your men off my doorstep, and return to work."

"We want a raise in pay, Baron," another man stated, emboldened by his leader's defiance. "You heard Vanya before! We deserve more money when it's dark outside, and when the blizzard blinds us hour after hour. Even soldiers get treated better than *this*!"

"There will be no raise," Alfred replied, clenching his fists. "You aren't going to be rewarded for impudence."

"Then you can find other workers," Kolya shot back, throwing down his pickax. "We'd rather fight the Germans!" Immediately, three others followed suit. The wind was howling in through the open door, bringing snow and debris into the workmen's hut, but in the silence that ensued, Alfred became aware of some sort of commotion outside. He straightened his stance and strode decisively to the doorway, pushing two men aside in order to get a glimpse of what was taking place.

Outside Alfred saw three young ruffians pinning Aron against a thick tree. Suddenly, all his pent-up rage exploded, and adrenaline shot through his body, filling him with outrage. These drunken peasants were actually threatening his foreman with bodily harm . . . ! "Now you've really done it," he said, his voice sharp and icy as steel. "This is a matter of principle: you push him, it means you're pushing *me,* and I can't let *anybody* get away with that."

"Aron's a kike; he's not even a Russian!" an old man shouted.

Halfway out the door, Alfred came to a complete stop. His eyes shone like cold black marbles. "Aron is a Jew, like me, and like the Aschkenasys who pay your wages," he said with a voice that trembled slightly, like a tightwire, and the men on either side of him stepped back in fear. "I'd remember that if I were you, you dirty, filthy, ignoble bastards: The only good man around here is Aron. Now, let me through!"

As Alfred started to run, the cold hitting him like a gigantic, tingling slap, his head reeling from the shock of the wind's power against his body, he heard the mumbled words: "'Baron,' my ass. He's nothing but a kike himself—that's all!" An image intruded into his mind. He was twelve; Barbara was seven. A tall, gangly German boy was teasing her, calling her a pig, a fat, ugly Jewish pig. Alfred had grown very hard inside, everything coiled together, ready to spring, his nerves ragged, his skin burning. He'd told the boy to shut up; he'd spoken very quietly, like a gentleman. And then he'd pounded him to a pulp, until the boy's parents had separated them. He'd broken his nose and two of his ribs. And he hadn't felt a single twinge of guilt when, two days later, his governess had told him that his victim had been taken to the hospital, with a hemorrhage that could have been fatal. Alfred had thought, Good; that's what he deserves. And he hadn't cared about the police when his mother had wept and told him that if the German boy had died, charges would surely have been brought against him for brutality. The bastard had called his sister a fat, ugly Jewish pig. He'd deserved to die.

Now Alfred felt the acid churning in his stomach, and for a moment nausea obscured his vision and threatened to turn the world topsy-turvy. He'd have to send for the doctor tomorrow, for he was quite ill, but this was not the time to think of that. He lurched forward, caught his breath, and collected himself; but the anger continued to propel him forward, toward Aron. *They'd called him a kike . . . ! He hated them!* At that moment, he was twelve again, in front of the German boy, and pain, frustration, and anger were propelling him forward, his mind filled with blood lust.

When he reached the tree trunk, he saw that the small group had grown in size, and that at least one hundred workers were surrounding them, watching expectantly. On one side stood Aron, with his three assailants; and on the other, the disheveled Siberians, their wind-whipped faces aglow with anticipation at the scene that was about to be played out before them. The pigs! Alfred was sure that his fever had soared, but he paid scant attention to the chills that shook him. He pushed the men away from Aron and grabbed him roughly by the arm. There was a cut on his cheek, and a bruise below his eye.

"Which one of you did this?" Alfred demanded of the workers.

Silence echoed eerily. Alfred was no longer afraid, although all around the foreign faces of the *mujiks* stared at him like a hostile battalion. The Siberian wind roared in his ears, and he raised his voice, asking once more: "Which one of you did this?"

"It's all right, Baron. I'm not really hurt," Aron said softly. He reached out and touched Alfred's sleeve. "Everyone's tired and cold. Why don't we forget this?"

Hadn't Barbara said something like that, that time, years ago? *Don't hurt him, Alfred.* But she'd been wrong. It hadn't been a question of his hurting the boy; the boy had hurt *her,* had hurt all of them, had impugned on the dignity of the de Rochefleur family and their religion. Alfred shook his head angrily. "If we allow these bastards to get away with this now, then tomorrow they'll feel free to kill you . . . or even me. No, Aron, we can't forget this. They're no better than cattle: they have to be hurt before they know to be afraid."

"Respect and fear aren't the same thing, Baron," Aron said.

"Oh, yes, they are. You respect whom you fear. And since you seem to be too soft to understand this, I shall have to show you." His eye rested on the bold young-speaker from the hut. "Kolya, *you* tell me who you think did this to our foreman. Your word will be good enough; these men already consider you their leader."

A hushed murmur of dismay spread through the ranks of the workers. Kolya moved forward, and coughed. "I can't tell you. I wasn't there, so I don't know. These men are all my brothers: how can I unjustly accuse one of them?"

"Do *you,* therefore, accept to take the blame, then?"

Kolya's face paled. "No. That isn't fair either."

"It is to me. Come here, boy. Walk to the tree trunk and put your hands behind your back." Alfred pushed Kolya ahead of him, prodding him with a kick at his legs. When they came to the tree, Kolya had no choice but to lean face forward onto the trunk and to place his hands behind him. Then Alfred loosened his belt and started to whip him: first his legs, then his head, for the rest of his body was protected by heavy layers of clothing. Frenzy and rage made Alfred's actions fierce, and he knew he was out of control, that he was whipping his adversary as though his own life depended on how hard he could swing. Kolya let out a huge wail, and blood spurted from behind his ear onto the white snow. The men were strangely silent, and only a lone eagle screeched in the wilderness.

And then two or three men broke from the ranks and rushed toward Alfred and Aron. Alfred wheeled around, his face bathed in sweat. The expressions on the men's faces frightened him. He thrust his hand behind his right hip, reaching for the small revolver he kept hidden there. He heard Aron cry out: "No, Baron! You don't need that!" and then Alfred felt himself being thrown to the ground, his face pushed violently into the snow. He was suffocating; ice shards were burning his skin. With all the strength he could muster, he threw off his attackers and staggered to his knees. The gun was still in his hand, and he was clutching it tightly.

Alfred raised the gun and pointed it at Kolya, who was holding his wounded head. He aimed it at the boy's stomach, and pulled the trigger. As Kolya fell, holding his bowels, which were spilling out of him, a terrific din erupted in Alfred's head, sweat pouring from his pounding forehead. He dropped the gun and pressed his hands over his ears.

The goddamned bastards had called him a kike. Or was it Aron they had called a kike? No matter. The boy, Kolya, had to be responsible: he had been their leader. And rebellion must be crushed at once, or a revolution could start.

"That was a mistake, Baron," Aron was saying to him, his voice almost a sob. "You should have listened to me, and let it go."

As the vomit rose Alfred could only remember the German boy, and his own feelings when he'd been told about the hemorrhage. He'd thought: *I wish I'd killed him.*

But now he wasn't twelve years old, and he'd *really* killed a man.

He was a Jew in a Christian land, a foreigner, an aristocrat among angry peasants. And now he was also a murderer. He'd have to rely on the power of his money, and old Yakov Aschkenasy's, and hope to God that he would never be prosecuted. For here he was the underdog, and, far from the cupolas of Petersburg, the denizens of this Siberian wilderness would think of him only as the Jewish assassin of one of their own. . . .

CHAPTER II

Beyond the tall, frosted windows of the military hospital, the city of Vienna gave off a hint of its prewar glory. Amelia von Guttman paused to glance out over the rooftops, down at twisting medieval streets of the Old City. Between the Old and the New Cities she could see the magnificent boulevard of the Ringstrasse, studded with ornate ministries in the baroque style. Among them, not far from the Opera, her mother's house displayed its three long stories of immaculate sandstone.

She sighed, and turned back to the large hospital dormitory, where row upon row of iron cots stood around her like so many white coffins. She tightened the psyche knot that held her black hair up, and tugged on the sleeves of her uniform. She was exhausted, her lithe young body aching and sore. She'd been on her feet since ten o'clock that morning, and it was now two-thirty in the afternoon.

Amelia took a deep breath and walked over to the large tin coffeepot to pour two cups. Adding a teaspoon of sugar to each, she brought the coffee over to one of the cots in the middle of the room and set the cups down on the wobbly wooden table beside it. She sank down into the metal chair by the bed and looked compassionately at its occupant.

What a sad, sad thing it was to watch someone her brother's age feeling such pain. The twenty-one-year-old lieutenant who gazed up at her had a thin face, with huge brown eyes like bowls of hot chocolate. "How are you feeling?" she murmured gently, leaning over to prop his pillow up. She put one of the cups in his hand and made certain his fingers had grasped it properly before she let go.

"I'm going to die, Fräulein Amelia," he replied, his voice low but resigned. "The doctor tells me that gangrene has set into my leg and thigh."

"Then he'll just have to get rid of the gangrene, won't he?" she said matter-of-factly.

"He's going to amputate the leg."

Amelia felt a jolt of horror rush through her and tried not to let it show on her face. Thank God her brother Richard was stationed at the Vienna headquarters, where he'd been given a job processing other men's orders to the front. He was in no danger, unlike this poor young soldier. It was the winter of 1916, and things weren't going well for the emperor's armies.

"You'll be fine, Otto," Amelia stated, taking the patient's other hand lying limply on the blanket and squeezing it. "I'm here. I won't let anybody hurt you anymore!" It was their own private joke, that she was his good fairy and had magic powers to ward off all further evils.

The lieutenant, weakened by severe wounds and the ordeal he had gone through, strained to stare at her earnestly. She bent down closer to spare him the effort. "Fräulein Amelia," he whispered. "You have the most beautiful face I've ever seen. I'm in love with you. If I survive . . . will you marry me?"

Amelia drew back, surprised. But then she recalled other such proposals she'd received from condemned patients, five to be exact. She kept hold of his hand and smiled. "I'm sure everything will be all right," she murmured. "And yes, of course, I'd be proud to be your wife, Otto. But now"—she glanced around—"if I don't move on to someone else, my supervisor will yell at me and take away my next coffee break."

She kissed him lightly on the lips, then stood up to leave. In the doorway she could see her mother, the Walkyrie of the hospital volunteer staff, her two hundred and fifty pounds blocking the door frame. Amelia raised her small hand to get her mother's attention, and hastened over to her. Because now she felt the urge to cry, and to be comforted herself. Lieutenant Otto Krauss, like the other five soldiers before him, wasn't going to live through the night.

* * *

Dowager Countess Barbara von Guttman had always been, even in her own wry perception, an oddity. As a little girl, she had been ridiculously overweight, and the only one who hadn't laughed at her had been her cousin Yvonne, a year younger than herself. (After all, Yvonne had grown up so isolated and deprived that she'd probably not even realized Barbara's abnormalities.)

Barbara had grown into an obese adolescent with voluminous

breasts and a huge midriff, oblivious to the pastimes of girls her own age. She'd cared about one thing alone: playing her piano. Her mother, Anne Sassoon de Rochefleur, had passed on an ardent love of music to her child. In fact, the great Paderewski pronounced her a prodigy, and Barbara had possessed but a single wish, and that was to become a concert pianist. But fate had dealt her an unexpected card: As she was the only daughter of the powerful banker Henri de Rochefleur, her hand had suddenly been petitioned in marriage all the way from Vienna by the equally wealthy and powerful Count Helmut von Guttman on behalf of his son, Louis, who had never seen her.

And so, to merge two financial empires and to retain the strong Jewish heritage important to both families, Barbara, already in her twenties, had been married off to a virtual stranger. Louis had been handsome as a Greek god; his fidelity to his rotund, six-foot-tall wife had lasted three days . . . just time enough for his fascination with his wife's hair (black, smooth, shining, and, when let down at night, reaching all the way to her ankles) to wear off. But he'd taken Barbara back to Vienna and had settled her into the "castle of spun sugar," as Amelia's British nanny had once called the family's palatial residence on the Ringstrasse.

After that, Count Louis von Guttman had spent very little time at home. Long enough, however, to produce an heir in 1895, Richard. Then had come three miscarriages and another son, who died of the scarlet fever. By the time of Amelia's birth, in 1900, Louis had given up his wife's bed and practically moved in with his mistress, an opera singer who had already borne him two illegitimate sons.

Barbara hadn't really cared. She made the best of her existence, and of her disappointment in having given up the dream of a professional career. Known as an eccentric about Vienna, but a very rich one, she had befriended three chamber musicians from the Vienna Orchestra, and the four of them played together twice a week in the large music room she had set up for them at the von Guttman *Schloss*. These gatherings meant far more to her than a faithful husband.

She loved her children, but had had no idea how to bring them up, and so a long succession of private tutors and governesses had amplified the huge von Guttman staff. Barbara breathed a sigh of relief and let them all do whatever they wished with Richard and Amelia. Somehow, her son and daughter both had managed to learn fine manners, to speak various erudite languages, to ride to the hounds, and to dance intricate steps at the cotillions.

The year the war started, Louis had died of a sudden heart attack. The hysterical opera singer had shown up at the von Guttman *Schloss,* demanding a settlement for her two sons. Barbara had calmed her down with a hot toddy and a letter to an exclusive boarding school in Switzerland, and sent her home with a large check and a portrait of Louis in a silver frame. "How can I mourn a man who was only home six times . . . half an hour for each child I conceived?" Barbara wrote her cousin, Yvonne Lévy, with her customary brand of undaunted candor.

Amelia adored her mother, and valued her straightforward honesty. Now, troubled over the lieutenant's proposal, she hastened toward Barbara, and, catching up with her in the long, badly lit corridor, she said without preamble: "Mama—tell me something. . . . Why do they propose to me and *die*? What is there about death that makes a man want to ask a woman to *marry* him?"

"I don't know why you're asking *me.*" Barbara shrugged. "No man ever proposed to *me* in person." She expected a chuckle but received instead a wan, forlorn smile. "They want a reward for struggling to stay alive. And what lovelier reward than a fresh, pretty girl like you?"

"But they must realize that I'm not serious. I haven't even had my debut . . ." She wanted to add: I'm just a child, but then she thought, That's not true either. The war has made me grow up, and I've skipped the age when girls get courted with roses and champagne, when young men come calling. Nobody with any sense of decency would even consider having a debut, a good old-fashioned coming-out ball, while the emperor's troops are being slaughtered on several fronts. How, then, could a self-respecting woman think of love—of being in love—without also feeling ashamed of her own frivolity?

"You're punishing yourself for sins you haven't committed," her mother remarked, reading her thoughts. "You're different from me, Amelia. You're feminine and charming and attractive. Many men will want you; many men will fall in love with you. What you must do is let your own feelings guide your behavior. You have to act on the strength of your convictions."

Words, words . . . But I have no experience, Amelia thought as her mother kissed her and then gently pushed her back toward the infirmary. And why do they all tell me I'm so beautiful?

She was curious, and stopped in the rest room for a minute to examine herself in the thin, cracked mirror on the wall above the washbasin. *Beautiful* was Sarah Bernhardt, or Karsavina, the Russian ballerina. What Amelia saw was a heart-shaped face with translucent pale skin, a generous mouth, a small, upturned nose, a well-defined little chin, and large blue eyes. Yes, her eyes *were* nice, a deep cobalt blue like the blue in a peacock's fantail, ringed with thick, curling lashes.

Like her mother, she was honest. And so she turned away, satisfied and a little excited by what she had just seen. She was a very pretty girl, and that, probably, was why those poor dying boys always wanted *her* and not the other nurse's aides as their reward for staying alive.

Mama thinks that many men will want me and that their love will be easy to come by, she told herself. But I don't want an easy conquest. What *I* want is a man who isn't so easy to win over . . . one whom *I'*ll have to go after, with all my might . . . with the strength of my convictions.

To go after true love the way the boys were going after the enemy . . . what a marvelous dream! Her cheeks suddenly bright with color, Amelia, Countess von Guttman, walked resolutely over to the large tin coffeepot to pour out a few more cups for the wounded officers.

*　*　*

Amelia felt herself growing tense with excitement; it was always that way before a hunt. The thrill mounted right inside her body, causing tingling sensations in her fingers and toes, and a kind of throbbing in her muscles. She loved riding, the fun of the chase through forest and glen. What she could easily have lived without, of course, was what happened once the fox was caught.

The von Stecher estate, outside Vienna, was surrounded by woods and hilly terrain, and represented one of the most extensive pieces of private property near the capital. This spring of 1917, while the Allies scored victories at sea that equaled the Central Powers' impressive gains on land, virtually no social life had existed for the "young, smart set." The young men came and went according to their orders, and it was almost impossible to plan an event that would find members of one's own group all home together at the same time.

Countess Anna von Stecher, "Nanni," was a few years older than Amelia, but they had become friendly through the war-relief effort. Nanni's husband, Karl, had just returned home on leave from active duty on the high seas. He and Amelia's brother, Richard, had become friends in spite of the von Stechers' being devout Catholics. Amelia felt a moment of awkwardness as the blond, bone-thin count strode over to greet them; she was conscious of being seventeen and inexperienced, compared to Nanni and the "older," more sophisticated young married women.

"My dear Richard! Welcome, welcome! And the incomparable Amelia . . . what a pleasure to feast my war-sore eyes on you!"

She blushed, thinking, Why must men weave such complicated tales just to say hello? But she smiled, tilting her head to the side: men loved to look at her when she played half shy, half provocative. She'd discovered that at the hospital.

And then everything began happening at once. Three young officers helped her to mount Mufti, her tawny Arabian, and she lightly pressed her thighs around his sleek girth, anticipating the pleasure of the gallop to follow. The young officers were filled with talk about the United States' recent declaration of war against Germany, and how Nicholas, the tsar of Russia, had just abdicated. Amelia found it all very boring.

"I have a cousin in Saint Petersburg, but we've never met," she said, in order to fill an expectant pause. The young men were looking at her with polite expectancy, as if it were her turn to speak.

"Then I guess she's already left the country," one of her admirers supposed. "Life isn't going to be safe for the aristocracy in Russia. . . ."

Amelia shrugged and shook her head. "My mother and my uncle Alfred haven't seen each other in ages," she admitted. "And to me, Russia seems . . . well, like the United States, or China: too far away to be real."

She looked out toward the hillside, and shuddered with nascent joy. The crisp air smelled of new leaves and wild berries, and she could feel the sun caressing her skin. Amelia heard the young officer ask her something about her cousin and he seemed to be waiting for an answer, but she was bored and restless.

And then she saw *him,* sitting alone, astride a nervous black stallion: a tall, erect man in uniform, older than Richard—maybe twenty-six or twenty-seven—with a long face and very definite narrow features and black eyes. Medals gleamed in the sun, pinned below his collarbone. She turned briefly to the young man at her side and, pointing with a thrust of her small chin, asked: "Lieutenant von Banheim, who is that man?"

"Him? Oh . . . that's Peter Habig. You know, the haberdasher."

She *didn't* know. The name was vaguely familiar, but she had trouble placing it. A *haberdasher?* What would a man of that sort be doing *here,* at the von Stechers'?

"Would you like me to introduce him to you?" the lieutenant asked, his tone half ironic.

Seriously, Amelia nodded. *Peter Habig . . .* Ah, yes! Now she remembered. The elegant *maison de couture* that specialized in sporting outfits. Hadn't her mother ordered her boots there? Amelia couldn't help laughing. "He's not really a 'haberdasher.' But yes, bring him over. I'd like to meet him."

Amelia's eyes were on Habig. She ran her tongue lightly over her lips. What a terribly attractive man, so dark and brooding, all alone, like Heathcliff in *Wuthering Heights.* Not actually a handsome man, but nevertheless . . .

"*Gnädige Frau . . .* delighted, I'm sure."

He was there before her, mounted on his huge stallion, a half smile playing over his gaunt features. Amelia hated chubby men with baby faces. This man had . . . character. "*Are* you?" she asked, surprised at her own sudden boldness. "Delighted, I mean?" And she gave him her smile, half timid, half engaging, and sat back in her saddle to watch him.

His hand had reached to clasp her small one, but already he was releasing it politely. She could tell nothing from his eyes. "Well now, *Gräfin,* all Vienna is already at your feet. Why would you have me join the legion of your attendants?"

She laughed. "Who told you that? About 'all Vienna'?"

Peter Habig was still smiling, but Amelia felt a seriousness behind the pleasantry. It intrigued her. "I simply guessed," he replied.

His answer astonished her. She'd expected to hear the names of young men whose wounds she might have dressed when they'd been brought to the hospital earlier that year. She wondered whether to feel flattered or insulted by his direct, unembroidered reply. "Then . . . tell me *why*?" she asked.

"Because you're beautiful. And because you love to play with young men. And because young men love to find a girl like you, eager to play the social game to perfection, as I'm sure you do."

"Now I *am* insulted," Amelia retorted, her cheeks reddening. "I'm no longer a schoolgirl, you know, Herr Habig. And I'm not an inconsequential social butterfly. I've been a nurse's aide at the hospital for over a year!"

"The beautiful *gräfin* also pays her dues, I see." The man's black eyes were troublesome, their irises almost as dark as the pupils. Why was he taunting her? What had she done? She'd been polite . . . charming, in fact. Other men always fell all over themselves when Amelia acted charming. But this one—this *haberdasher*, for God's sake . . . !

Her nostrils flared as she attempted to control a rising anger. "I don't know why you're making fun of me, but I don't like it. What do you have against me, Herr Habig? We've only just met!"

He raised his eyebrows, and cocked his head to the side. " 'Against you'? Why, nothing, nothing at all. I'm flattered that you wanted to make my acquaintance. You're a stunning young woman, *Gräfin* von Guttman. Your eyes are incredible, like the Aegean Sea on a clear summer day. It isn't *you* that I resent. On the contrary, if you were a few years older, I'd give these young clods a good run for their money. But it's your *attitude* that galls me—it's the chic thing to do, you see, to bandage the wounded. Last year it was care packages for the prisoners of war; this year, it's nursing. While we poor dolts are fighting for a cause few of us ever comprehended, but for which we seem doomed to give up our lives!"

His cheekbones glowed red, too, with excitement. She looked over his uniform: the navy. Yes, of course, that explained his bitterness. . . . The galling defeats . . .

"Doesn't everyone understand Sarajevo?" she asked.

"Aha. *Sarajevo*. The magic formula for war. A madman kills a member of the imperial family and suddenly millions of young soldiers are being sent out to avenge the bloody deed."

"What makes that such an unreasonable sequence of events?" Amelia demanded.

"Had a poor fireman's son been killed, or a farmer's brother, do you suppose anyone would have cared to bring *his* assassin to heel? Let's be serious for a moment, *Gnädige Frau*."

Amelia could feel tears threatening to spill. "I detest politics!" she cried. "Why couldn't we just have a civilized conversation?"

Habig looked at her, his large eyes suddenly devoid of bitterness, totally serious, composed, sad. "Because, sweet, innocent *Gräfin von Guttman*, the world no longer is a civilized place to live in."

She stared at him, shocked. Peter Habig bowed slightly and prodded his heels into his horse's side. Before she had time to realize that he'd taken his leave of her, he was gone. She shook her head, mystified and angered. Her eyes followed him as he approached a group of laughing young matrons on horseback, and then he was lost in the crowd.

Beside herself with humiliation, Amelia clenched her fist and struck her leg in fury. What was it he had said—that *haberdasher*, that uncouth socialist in a naval officer's uniform? *If you were a few years older* . . . What did he take her for, at seventeen? A silly *child*?

He thinks I'm spoiled. He thinks we're *all* spoiled.

But if he didn't approve of her group of friends, why had he accepted Nanni von Stecher's invitation in the first place?

"Who were you talking to just now?" Richard asked, cantering up beside her.

Amelia sighed. Habig had also told her that her eyes reminded him of the Aegean Sea. . . .

"No one important," she stated. "Tell me, aren't they about to release the dogs?"

To her enormous relief, the sound of bugles cut off her brother's reply. She took in a breath of pure, earthy spring air and more than willingly gave in to her pent-up excitement. Only now, strange to say, there was yet another layer to it, a deeper thrill that teased her senses. Peter Habig was nowhere to be seen.

Amelia von Guttman spurred Mufti on and thought, To hell with you, then, you supercilious "older man!" Just let's wait and see how soon you're able to forget my eyes!

CHAPTER III

Charles Lévy turned to look at his mother and, as always, felt a pang of anguish. It was the spring of 1917, and at forty-five, Yvonne hardly seemed her age. Women like her were supposed to be "old," yet her figure was still slim and firm, and her bearing, proud and regal. He particularly admired her long, slender neck unmarked by age lines, and her pale blond hair, always piled on top of her head, demurely. She was a remarkable person, a woman who had experienced almost no happiness of any kind, except when she was painting at her easel. This made him feel, among other emotions, guilt. For without him, she might have been free to remarry.

"What are you thinking about, darling?" Yvonne asked, standing still. They had been synchronizing their steps, slow and easy, by the lakeside. Dusk had already thrown its lilac veil over the mountains all around the placid waters of Lake Geneva.

Charles took her hand and ran the pad of his index finger over her delicate knuckles. "About how unfair life is," he replied.

So that was it. Yvonne couldn't help feeling a pang of guilt. By marrying Wilhelm Levy, a German, she herself had taken on German citizenship. And so, of course, their son had been born a German national. Now this small formality, which had meant nothing to her at the time, had come back to haunt them. . . .

"Oh, we don't have it so bad," she countered. "As soon as this bloody war is over, we'll be able to go home again."

"Somehow that makes me feel ashamed. All my life I assumed I was a Frenchman, just like everybody else around. Then, to discover, when the war started, that we were really German citizens—it galls me, even to remember! I'm ashamed at the thought of going back. How will I ever face my friends?"

Yvonne sighed and looked away, over the shining surface of the enormous lake that stretched out forever to a mountainous distance. And as he watched her expectantly Charles wondered, once again, why tragedy had been trailing her all her life, and what kind of man, in fact, his father had been.

He'd learned the story in bits and pieces, mostly by picking up odd phrases of other people's conversations. How his grandfather, Baron Guy de Rochefleur, had squandered most of his fortune on bad business ventures and on high living, while his grandmother, Jeannette, had tried to make do with what little she had in her home outside the city, at La Folie. How his mother had grown up a "poor little rich girl" in the luxurious mansion with its garden and stables: a Baroness without two gold coins to pay for a coach ride into Paris; sleeping in an emperor's quarters but having to wear her obese cousin Barbara's outdated dresses, taken in. Never going on holiday unless other rich relatives (her uncle Henri) paid for the trip, out of a sense of charity. And finally, a seventeen-year-old Yvonne coming out in society a year early, tagged on as an afterthought to Barbara's debut; coming out into a society to which she would have no further access, being poor when it was considered impossible to marry unless one's dowry was well padded.

Yet, even while recognizing his grandfather's irresponsible, indeed *unkind,* behavior toward the two people Charles held dearest in the world, his mother and grandmother, he couldn't hate him. He loved the old man. Memories flooded him of games they'd played together when Charles had been little; of being initiated into manhood by his grandfather, taken along to his men's club and being encouraged to smoke his first cigar. Of the pride Guy had taken in the young boy, pride that Charles's father should have felt, had he been alive.

What sort of life would we all have had, if Wilhelm Levy hadn't shot himself? Charles often found himself wondering.

He knew very little about his father's family, whom he hadn't seen since his mother moved back to France after the suicide. The Levys, a Jewish family from Munich, had once been very rich but were the victims of a tremendous swindle ten years before Charles's parents married. Their manager had stolen most of their fortune, then taken off for South America leaving them virtually destitute.

Charles's grandparents had possessed just enough money to send their son, Wilhelm, to law school. His parents had hoped that with his good looks and infinite charm, he would be able to bestow his

distinguished family name on one of the city's rich heiresses. But
destiny had propelled Willy onto a different road. While vacationing in Paris, a friend had brought him to visit La Folie.

Yvonne had told Charles the story. She had been standing under
a trellised arbor, trimming a recalcitrant vine, when she heard a
Teutonic voice behind her. She turned, and blushed, seeing the
young man. Charles's father was tall, with broad, proud shoulders
and flaxen hair of an almost white hue as the sunlight fell upon it.
A devastatingly handsome man, with sensitive blue eyes. Charles's
mother felt embarrassed in her gardening clothes, gritty cloth
gloves still covering her hands.

"They tell me you're the belle of the manor," Wilhelm had said
in his accented, clipped French. "And that perhaps you would
show us around your most charming little town?"

Yvonne felt a little afraid of this exotic man, and of his obvious
pleasure in looking at her. He had taken her for a walk through
Saint-Germain, and the following day he sent her a basket of fresh
fruit and chocolates. He had come calling, very proper in his linen
suit, his posture erect, like an officer's, his manners impeccable.

Willy had been amusingly formal about everything. One night,
he came to dinner at La Folie, and when Yvonne saw him to the
door at the end of the evening, he looked her in the eye and asked,
seriously: "Mademoiselle, would you permit me to kiss you?"

As his Parisian holiday was coming to an end, Yvonne waited
expectantly for him to propose. She was sure she was in love with
him. The proposal came after a night at the opera, where they had
seen *Carmen*. Willy took Yvonne's hand and bowed over it, clicking his heels in the Prussian fashion. He said, earnestly: "I find that
I cannot continue my life without you. I cannot imagine returning
to Munich without a promise of marriage from you, Mademoiselle
Yvonne."

"Well then," she replied, standing on her toes to reach him. "My
promise is yours to pack into your suitcase. I hope you won't have
to declare it at customs!" And she planted a quick kiss on his lips.

"Grab him while he's eager!" Charles's grandfather had declared, laughing heartily when his daughter told him of Willy's
proposal. And he had taken the young man aside and whispered,
"I wouldn't wait if I were you. Frenchwomen are known for their
ability to change their minds on a moment's whim!"

And so the engagement had been formalized, then and there.
Willy was thrilled at the prospect of marrying his pretty French

girl before returning home. And Yvonne's uncle the banker, Baron Henri, who had cut off his brother Guy a number of years before, had taken pity on the young couple. Unexpectedly relenting from his hard stand against his brother, he opened up the family coffers: a dowry, albeit a modest one, had been brought out, and a wedding staged at La Folie. And then Willy and his bride took the train back to Munich, and a year later Charles was born. That had been in August of the year 1898.

She only knew him for three years, Charles thought, anger rising against the dead man, as it did every time he thought of him. Yvonne and Willy had their three years together, and then they came to Paris for the summer, and Willy shot himself at his son's birthday party. Charles had to turn his back on his mother so that she would not see his face as he thought about his father's suicide. Wilhelm Levy had cursed his son with a fatal shot, had made certain to mar every year of Charles Levy's life thereafter. For not a birthday would go by that everyone present would not remember August 1900. What a legacy indeed!

Young Charles had taught himself never to appear weak in front of his mother. Yet was it fair that only women were allowed to weep?

He knew that she was proud of him, of his achievements at the university, where he was studying engineering. He also knew that people considered him particularly handsome. He was tall, well built, with golden hair like his mother's and with her wonderful dark blue eyes, like lapis lazuli. But his high cheekbones and his strong mouth were not Yvonne's, they were Willy's. *I wish that nothing about me were a link to him,* he thought with despair. I have my life in front of me, a promising career, my mother's good name. I could make it all work out, Mama . . . *everything* . . . for you, for myself, for Grandfather and Grandmother. So we would never have to ask Uncle Henri for a single franc. But even then, *he* would continue to pursue me, to haunt me like some mysterious ghost. My features will always remind me of him, every morning when I look in the mirror. And then I'll have to think about his death, over and over again.

Why, Papa? Charles asked silently. Why did you commit suicide? What terrible secret broke you down, that you had to ruin my mother's life? Why, Papa—*why*?

* * *

The summer he turned sixteen, in 1914, Charles's grandmother had booked them into a small *pension* in Lausanne, at number 5, rue des Cèdres. It was a large, low white house surrounded by a garden that, though medium in size, was well landscaped: tall old trees shaded the lawn and flower beds, and tortuous paths wound their way past thickets and a trellised arbor. Charles thought it gave the illusion of being part of a park, with that same quality of peace to it that conveyed enchantment. At La Folie he had often experienced this feeling, as if the day's angers, frustrations, and injustices were suddenly washed away by a silent, invisible nymph there to watch over him.

It was in this peaceful resort that they had been caught at the outbreak of the war. Charles had never paid much attention to the formalities of citizenship and nationality; his mother had been born French, and his father, German. Charles had always believed that in actuality he was entitled to both nationalities, although his mother and he had carried German passports. He'd simply considered himself French, for after his father's suicide, he had not again set foot on German soil.

Then, suddenly, two days after his sixteenth birthday, his mother had dropped her head in her hands and wept. "We can't go home," she'd told him. "When I married your father, I naturally assumed his nationality. You and I are both German citizens . . . enemies of France."

Charles's anger at his father had multiplied; now he knew for certain that he would never, under any condition, forgive this man he couldn't even remember for having left the two of them in this terrible predicament.

Charles's grandparents, already in their early seventies, had refused to return to Paris by themselves. Baron Henri had somehow managed to pull some strings and unblock funds for the four of them to continue living at the *pension*. And Charles had enrolled at the prestigious Ecole Nouvelle de Lausanne to finish his schooling.

It was Charles who first suggested that they become Swiss. In 1915, his last year at the Ecole Nouvelle, he had begun to add up the lies the German government was perpetrating through its news bulletins. Yvonne, along with three other foreign women trapped in Switzerland by the onset of the war, had become nurses at the train depot, and every night they would get together and discuss the latest stories they had heard from the lips of the Allied wounded. And these stories hardly jibed with German propaganda.

Life in Lausanne was hardly unpleasant, and the war seemed one layer removed, as if it were occurring in some far-off continent rather than right next door. Charles often felt ashamed that he was not "doing something," yet what could he, as a German national, have done? For he believed that the Germans were in the wrong, and still, in his heart and mind, he thought and felt like a Frenchman. The fourteen years he had lived in Paris, under the impression of being French, mattered to him far more than the incidence of his birth in a country he had not visited after the age of two.

Yet the French had declared that no German national would ever again be granted citizenship. Eventually, when the war ended, he and his mother would want to return to Paris. As *Germans?* What if another war were to occur? It made sense to change nationalities as soon as possible. They would become Swiss.

An attorney, Maître Legrand, explained to them that Switzerland granted citizenship only to those who had owned land there for at least two years. Yet the Swiss were known to sell reluctantly to strangers. There was, he told them, a small terrain near Geneva, stony and sterile, which changed hands every two years for the purpose of naturalization. And so Yvonne had sold a few oil paintings, and Baron Guy had traded in his diamond cuff links, so that Charles and his mother might put up the money for this crucial purchase. Now it was simply a matter of time before they would be granted Swiss citizenship.

Charles wondered what his school friends were doing now. Which of them were pilots, which were infantrymen? I alone am having to sit out this damned war, he thought bitterly: I alone had to be born a German.

*   *   *

A large table had been set up at the spot where the greatest view of Lausanne and Lake Geneva could be seen from Sauvabelin Hill. Leafy trees were planted close to each other around the table, protecting several benches with their shade. This area, at the edge of the forest, was called the Signal.

"Well, children," Jeannette said. "We'll take the cable car and meet you at the top of the hill in just a few minutes. And then we'll have tea at the hotel."

Charles smiled. His grandmother always called anyone younger than she "my child." His mother smiled too; by now this was an old family joke.

But it pained Charles to look at them, these two dear people who found it an effort now to take even a ten-minute walk. His grandfather, especially, seemed very old now. Charles held him firmly under the elbow, helping him into the small cabin of the cable car. Guy wheezed and coughed. Jeannette climbed in after her husband.

Charles loved his grandmother with a quiet devotion that she felt and knew how to appreciate, for they were kindred spirits, both of them realistic, practical, and sparing in outward demonstrations of their personal feelings. He loved the way she protected his mother, yet never patronized her or made her feel dependent.

Jeannette de Rochefleur had become an expert at trimming the luxuries from her own suburban existence, and the only time she ever allowed herself a somewhat freer rein was when it came to summer vacations. Then, to Charles's amusement, she would take out the maps, atlases, and guidebooks she had collected over the years, and proceed to outline three months of pure pleasure for the four of them: herself, his grandfather, his mother, and him. Though even then she was cautious, unwilling to abandon her role of family purser.

She was unostentatious in her tastes, and preferred the restful atmosphere of little towns in Switzerland to the more lavish resorts of France and Germany. She particularly enjoyed Lausanne, built on a hillside, with its parallel streets, each one of which was charmingly uneven.

Behind the university stood a high cliff, the Sauvabelin; Jeannette usually rode up by cable car with her husband, sparing themselves shortness of breath, while Charles and his mother would take the brisk, invigorating twenty-minute walk that their youth allowed them. Once at the top, one could see a panorama that swept the entire lakefront area, Lausanne at one's feet, Ouchy farther down, and on the opposite shoreline, Evian, Thonon, and the tall mountain range that crested with the Mont Blanc cluster, its various peaks outlined like a houndstooth pattern on the backdrop of the azure sky.

As Charles stepped out into the afternoon sunshine, Jeannette and Guy looked at each other, and she thought: We've been together nearly fifty years. "For better or for worse." Long ago she'd stopped dreaming, and had simply accepted reality. She was married to a man who had never done anything with his life. They hadn't shared the same bed for nearly thirty-five of those fifty years, but still, he'd given her Yvonne, as well as some measure of amusement. Did she love Guy? Perhaps, though it was more likely habit, and habit brought comfort when one was old.

Jeannette peered out the window and saw Charles and his mother begin their hike toward the Signal. She'd made reservations for tea at the hotel at the top of the hill, and wondered if they would serve that wonderful peach jam she and Yvonne liked so much. How sinful, in times of war, to dream this way of food. . . . And then the sliding door shut, and she felt the cable car jerk forward as it began its ascent.

She was fussing with Guy's collar, which seemed to be bothering him, when the man at the controls at the foot of the hill noticed something was wrong. The cable car was wobbling back and forth, back and forth. He called his assistant, and they stared anxiously out the window. "It's not the car. It's the wire cable," the assistant said.

"Stop the mechanism, then, and bring them back down at once!"

Jeannette and Guy felt the jolt, and looked at each other. The old woman laid her gnarled fingers over her husband's hand, and felt him trembling. "We seem to be going back down," she said, furrowing her brow.

But they were moving at high speed, and now all the people inside the cabin were shifting in their seats, looking worried. "Perhaps they can't control the car," a man said.

Jeannette's mouth was dry. How long had they been up? A minute? Two? The car was definitely out of control now, going faster and faster down the hill. It would soon be over, and then the engineers would fix the trouble and send them back up. "Don't be concerned," she said to Guy. "It will take Yvonne and Charles twenty minutes to walk, and we'll still arrive before them."

Guy turned to her, his blue eyes strangely intense in his pale face. The car was now hurtling through the air, as if a giant had given it a vehement push downward. Jeannette saw the main cabin on the ground, could even distinguish the two faces of the engineers peering out at them.

And then, suddenly, it was over. The small cable car crashed into the side of the ground cabin, which shattered with the force of its momentum. Glass was flying everywhere, and bloodcurdling screams resounded in what had once been the small control house at the foot of the hill.

Jeannette's hand lay over Guy's, and hours later when they were extricated from the debris, her head was found on his breast, her neck slashed; but they found no evidence of serious wounds on his body, and it was assumed that he had simply died of shock, instantly.

The next day, when Charles found the write-up of the accident in the local newspaper, it had already been relegated to an inside page. In the sea of continuing wartime casualties, the death of his grandparents had been washed on shore like so much flotsam. What difference had they made in the world? he wondered. Their lives had touched his mother's, and his own—but that was all.

My life is going to matter, Charles decided, pressing his fingers over his swollen eyes to make sure no further tears would escape. My life is going to affect the world, so that, when my death comes, they will all say, *He made a difference.*

And then he rose and covered his mother's shoulders with a shawl, and went out to speak to the funeral director.

CHAPTER IV

Anne clenched and unclenched her moist hands. Since morning she had been pacing the floor of the enormous dining room of the de Rochefleur apartment on the Galernaia. Distant rumors of street fights had reached her ears through the servants, and now she felt the worry growing inside her. Although her impulse was to look outside to see if she could spot any commotion, she didn't dare open any windows, for it was November—a cold, bitter, and raw November 7, 1917—and she had to block out the Saint Petersburg winter chill from her father's home.

Anne felt alone. Since her mother's death in January, she had spent most of her time by herself. In the beginning she felt relief. A guilty relief that her oppressor had finally died, allowing her space to live and breathe as she wanted. But then she had noticed that this space seemed unending—rooms vaster than mausoleums, ceilings like vaults—and she felt entombed within the huge apartment, like a tiny fly caught inside a gigantic bell jar, knowing that outside lay life but not understanding how to break away to freedom. Invisible bonds held her inside, and she felt panic growing almost uncontrollably.

She wondered what was holding her back. Had she imagined Alfred's disapproval, so strong that it had paralyzed her will to socialize? Sometimes another young woman called Anne on the telephone or sent an invitation to a tea or to the ballet. Sometimes she went, but most of the time shyness held her back. Anne was afraid to dress up and go out, to mingle with those who laughed and chatted naturally. After all, hadn't her mother, Sonia, told her over and over that the only friends she could attract were drawn only to her family name?

Anne wanted none of this; better to stay home alone than to be paraded on the arm of a so-called friend whose father just happened to be partners with hers or, worse yet, to owe hers money.

The political situation had been steadily worsening since the Tsar's forced abdication in March. Alexander Kerensky's Provisional Government, constantly undermined by a disorderly Soviet of elected officials that fed on an ever-changing public opinion, had recently freed those Bolshevik leaders it had held responsible for the riots of July.

Anne and her father had been vacationing in the Crimea and had not witnessed the summer's excitement firsthand. At that time, some sailors, soldiers, and armed workmen had attempted to take over Saint Petersburg, but the Preobrazhensky Regiment had checked their progress and contained the slaughter. But now Kerensky had signaled his helplessness by letting Trotsky out of jail, and Lenin had emerged from hiding. Anne's father had gone to his study in a very black mood, predicting terrible bloodshed and speaking of moving back to France.

Baron Alfred hadn't been the same since he'd returned from Siberia for the last time, before Sonia's death. Anne had never asked him what happened that winter of 1916, a year ago now. But she had seen him withdraw even more deeply into himself, and had heard the rumors. People said that there had been a riot by the riverbed, and that her father had killed a miner. In Saint Petersburg they had called him "the murdering Jew," and some of their old friends had conveniently "forgotten" to include their names on their guest lists. The servants had whispered ugly things behind Anne's back. . . .

"Baroness! Anna Alfredovna!"

Anne whirled around to face her young chambermaid, Manya. The girl was gesticulating, her face red with excitement. "The Bolsheviks have thrown the Vor-Parlament out of the Palace of Mary!" she cried. "And they're shelling the Winter Palace!"

"Where's Papa?"

"The Baron has just ordered the coachman to make ready the victoria. He's in his study, gathering all his private papers!"

"His private papers? Then . . . are we leaving town?"

"I don't know, Anna Alfredovna. I only know what the baron's secretary told the cook."

"Get me my long mink coat," the young woman commanded, suddenly chilled to the bone. There were riots outside, and her father had forgotten her again. Whatever his plans were, he hadn't bothered to let her know any part of them.

She looked at Manya, and noticed that the girl's black eyes were glowing. The Bolsheviks weren't *her* enemies—they were on *her* side, fighting against the wealthy and the titled, fighting against all the Alfreds and the Annes who had wielded the power over the previous centuries. Anne felt alone and wretched, but there was little time to indulge in self-pity. "For God's sake, *move!*" she cried, and finally Manya scampered away.

Anne went to the window and stared nervously outside. She heard noises and screams through the double glass panes but could still discern nothing out of the ordinary. And then, just as Manya was returning, Anne saw them at the end of the street: a horde of disheveled, angry men brandishing bayonets and rifles. Anne's eyes widened in horror, and no sound emerged from her throat. She took the proffered coat and slid her arms through its sleeves, like an automaton that could not think but had to act.

"Are they coming, Anna Alfredovna?" Manya was asking. She seemed happy and a bit defiant.

Anne didn't answer. She moved past the servant girl and ran down the corridor to her father's study. The door stood wide open, and she could see him fumbling with the combination on the metal safe hidden behind the Vermeer portrait. Today, Alfred didn't seem to care who might see him push the canvas aside and pull out Sonia's diamonds and rubies, the emeralds and lapis lazuli that now legally belonged to Anne. His back was turned but his gestures were hasty, almost panicked.

"What are we going to do, Papa?" she asked, coming up behind him.

Without stopping what he was doing, he said, under his breath: "We're going to get the hell out of here! Ivan is going to drive us to the Finnish border, and from there we'll arrange transportation to Paris. Get your things, Anne. Whatever you value above all—your furs, your clothes, your books—but only the things you won't be able to replace in France!"

"There's nothing that special," she stammered.

"Then wait for me downstairs, and take these with you!"

He was looking at her, and in his cold, handsome face she read the anxious fear. Anne held her arms out to receive the jewels her father was grasping clumsily. Her knees were trembling as he loaded her down with shimmering strands of necklaces, tiaras, and bulky, ornate bracelets.

I need you to look after me, she told him silently. But he was already busy with a new task, pulling out sheaves of papers from the vault. *Nobody's ever looked after me,* she thought bitterly, clamping her jaw shut to stop her teeth from chattering.

Then, all at once, the world crashed around them. The silence was shattered by yells and shouts as six strange men, hirsute and menacing, burst into the room pointing guns at Anne and her father. From the corner of her eye she could see Manya in the background, dancing on her toes and laughing. One of the men addressed her father: "Hand all this over, Baron. It's ours now. Give it to us or we'll splatter your brains all over that painting!"

Anne couldn't move. One of the men, leering, strode over and pulled some sapphire necklaces right out of her hands. What did they want? she wondered desperately. Were they planning to kill her and her father?

Then, suddenly, Ivan, the maître d'hôtel, appeared at the door. He was pointing a gun at the man who had grabbed her mother's jewels. Anne heard a shot, then a second shot, and then a third. The horrible sounds reverberated throughout the room. She was so frightened that she almost could not move her eyes and take in what was happening.

A man, all bloodied, was lying at her feet, his hands still entangled in Sonia's necklaces and bracelets. Ivan lay sprawled by the door, his uniform marred by a splash of scarlet dribbling down his stomach. A man was holding her father down, but two others lay dead on the ancient Chinese rug. Manya was screaming hysterically, jumping up and down like a marionette with springs in her arms and legs. . . .

Anne felt her knees turn to water and reached out to grab the back of an armchair. Her father was struggling with his assailant, but he was being badly beaten. She knew that he kept a small pearl-handled revolver in the safe. And so she ran for the safe, plunged her hand inside, and pulled out the gun—just as two men burst through the doorway. Anne's fingers tightened over the revolver, and she aimed and pulled the trigger. One of the men fell on top of Ivan; the other stood blinking, surprised into inaction. She aimed once more, her head totally empty except for the pinpricks of fire that were sparking at her temples. She felt dizzy, nauseous, as she fired right at the second man's throat.

"Anne!" her father was shouting. *"Anne!"* But suddenly the room was tipping to the side, and she felt tremendously light-headed. She turned, dropping the pistol, and saw that Alfred had knocked down his aggressor. Her father's face was pale and drawn, like the face of a ghost, or a death's-head.

Anne felt herself beginning to lose consciousness, felt her arms and legs lightening to a feathery weightlessness. Alfred was holding her up, taking her in his arms, rushing past Manya into the hallway. Anne tried to lift her head to ask where he was taking her, but the effort was too great. Stars twinkled before her eyes, and she felt herself slipping down, down, through a breathless eddy and into a vacuum blotting out all other reality.

Her last thought, as she relinquished all will and mastery over her mind and body, was that she had never been so totally afraid, so completely overpowered by the fear of death. She'd killed two men: *she had killed two men!* And then the world disappeared for Anne, and she fainted in her father's arms.

* * *

Anne pressed numbed fingertips to her aching temples, and stole a look at her father's stern profile. I've shot two men, she suddenly remembered. She had fallen into a deep, perturbed sleep in the large victoria, and now, awakening, she was flooded with vivid images of what had happened in the house on the Galernaia. I saved Papa's life, she thought, a searing pain ripping through her; I saved his life, but still he doesn't love me. . . . I shall never do enough to fulfill the dreams he had of me before I was born.

Where did I ever find the strength to pull the trigger, and how did I know how to make the gun work? Papa, why don't you tell me how pleased you are?

"I don't feel bad about those men," she murmured, amazed at her own lack of emotion. She felt strangely detached, as though she existed outside herself and was watching, from a distance. Was this natural, or was she totally without conscience, a freak?

Her father turned to her. His face suddenly appeared ashen, its muscles slack. "I killed a man, last year, in Siberia" he said, his voice strangely toneless. "He was threatening my foreman's life. I had to do it. I didn't feel bad until much, much later. The man I killed had been so young . . . ! But you needn't ever feel remorse: if you hadn't shot these men, they would have murdered us both, the way they murdered Ivan."

"Are you glad I did it?" she asked timidly.

Alfred sighed, his handsome face pale and worn. "Glad? What a question. It was them or us. But now we'll both be considered assassins. I just want to cross the border into safety, and book passage to France."

Anne pushed the curtains aside and looked out. The countryside was a bleak, uniform white, all the trees weighed down with fresh snow, the village houses practically eclipsed from sight. "Where are we?"

"We've been traveling a day and a half," her father explained. "You've been asleep or unconscious. We're going toward the Finnish border. We'll be there soon."

"Who's driving?"

"The only servant besides Ivan who didn't go over to the Bolsheviks. The stableboy, Sasha."

Anne closed her eyes. She still felt faint, and dizzy. But now she was also aware of being hungry. No wonder, if she'd been out cold for almost two days.

"Do we have anything to eat, Papa?" she asked. And wondered why she felt so calm, after all that had taken place.

* * *

The carriage came to an abrupt halt, and Anne heard one of the horses whinny. She heard Sasha jump down from the driver's seat, his boots crunching on snow. Then he was beating on the window, and her father opened his door. A freezing wind blew into the carriage, and she heard Sasha shouting above it, "We've got trouble, Baron! Border patrol!"

Outside, Anne could discern a night sky, the distant twinkling diamond stars. Alfred was getting out, and so, hugging her fur coat, she unlatched her own door and stepped down. The wind caught her hair and whipped her cheeks, but she pressed forward toward the two men.

In the distance, perhaps a hundred feet away, she could see hooded men with long rifles. Beams of light from a guardhouse illumined the landscape. "They'll let us through," Alfred said. "They're Kerensky's men, aren't they? The Bolsheviks haven't penetrated this far from the capital, have they?"

No one answered him. The men with rifles were so close that Anne shivered from head to toe, and not from the chilling winds. Sasha called out: "Hail, Comrades! Will you let us pass the frontier?"

Two of the men had plodded through the snow and reached

them. Anne saw only their eyes, for they were heavily scarved and cloaked, to protect them from the wintry elements. Their armbands were crimson, the color of fresh blood: even in the dim light of the crescent moon and the distant beams of the guardhouse lanterns, she could tell the hue.

Her legs couldn't move. They were marching on her and her father, with their red armbands. Bolsheviks. Anne stood paralyzed, terrified as she had not been in her own house when their assailants had burst in on them. Here, it was worse: they were standing in the bitter cold, night shadows disguising the panorama and casting a foreboding chill over everything.

"Greetings, Comrades!" Sasha kept repeating.

The two men stopped, inches away from Anne and Alfred, their rifle butts practically in their faces. "Let's see your papers," one of them demanded.

Alfred held out two passports. The first man took them, flipped through them, and threw them into the snow. "No good!" he called out in a harsh, guttural Russian. "These were made by the Tsar's people! We can't let you through!"

"Where are Kerensky's men?" Alfred asked.

"Long dead. We got here this morning. The Provisional Government has been overthrown—or hadn't you heard?"

Anne couldn't feel her fingers and her toes. She was a block of ice, frozen by terror and the wind. "You are nobility, enemies of the people!" the second man shouted, pointing his rifle at her father. "We've been ordered to seize anyone who tried to cross to Finland on a tsarist passport! Enemies of the state!"

"We'll pay you well," Alfred said, digging into his coat pocket and coming up with a handful of bills and coins. "We're nobodies, just private citizens wishing to return to their French homeland. Let us through, I beg of you!"

The first man laughed. "Through to jail, you mean. Baron Alfred de Rochefleur, we know who you are. You killed one of our brothers last winter, in Siberia. We were told not to shoot anyone coming through on a tsarist passport—our people in Petrograd want to have the pleasure of locking you up themselves, then chopping you into little pieces! You are under arrest!"

Anne felt someone holding her up from behind, steadying her body as it began to sway, her knees buckling. "You are both under arrest!" the man called out. And then he laughed once more.

Sasha, the stableboy, was laughing too.

* * *

All night long, Anne shivered and trembled in the small jail. The straw on which she was lying smelled of vomit, and horse's piss. She'd believed that the de Rochefleur name would be strong enough to save them, like a magic password. But the revolution was on. Russia no longer belonged to her father and his cronies. A mad band of robbers and looters had taken over, in the name of Lenin and Trotsky and the workers of the land. She wasn't sure who Lenin was, but he was their new leader.

"Up, you Jewish whore!"

Anne looked up, into the black eyes of a fat woman she had never seen before. "Where's my father?" she asked, her voice trembling.

"They've taken him back to Petrograd. But look at you—you're not even pretty. You're a dog, in a fur coat!" The woman rocked back and forth, laughing. Her mean eyes narrowed to slits. "And you're going to give me that coat, aren't you? *Are*n't you?"

Anne nodded, her teeth chattering.

"Your papa can't help you now! No one can help you. You're to stay here, in custody, until your father turns over the jewels to the state! And then, of course, we'll make mincemeat and suet out of you, my precious. You wait and see!"

They're going to kill Papa, Anne thought. And then they'll kill me too. She struggled out of her coat, and let it drop to the floor of the jail. The woman was cackling wickedly. "Hand it over nice and polite," she ordered. "Go on—do as you're told!"

Anne obeyed meekly, and thought, I'm going to die of cold, if they don't kill me first.

* * *

Anne had never felt so isolated in her whole life. She had been in the small jail for more than one month, and every day the woman and the two men who had arrested her and her father would come and threaten her with imminent death. Why didn't they kill her? What was holding them back?

What had they done to her father?

She tried not to spend time thinking. When she thought too much, she would start to cry, remembering how she had shot the two insurgents in Petrograd. Fear would make Anne's stomach knot up, and she would hug herself and crouch on the straw, rocking back and forth like a terrified animal.

Sometimes she remembered her mother, and her childhood. She

had hated growing up in that household, but now, looking back, it had been a reassuring time, a time of plenty, if not human warmth. As terribly as her mother had treated her, nothing quite compared to the life she had been ekeing out here in this jail in a nameless small town on the border of Russia and Finland.

Her father had been taken back to Petrograd in custody. Would she ever see him again? And if not, would these people ever let her out? The woman, Marina, joked with the men and drank vodka with them from the bottle, and afterward she would belch and tell stories that raised the small hairs on the back of Anne's neck. Stories of men and what she'd done with them. Anne looked at the two men, the ones who had arrested her, with increasing fear after Marina's stories. Would these men . . . ?

But, so far, nothing. Marina taunted her with insults, but no one seemed to know that it was Anne who had shot the two Bolsheviks in the apartment.

It was already December, and Anne was wearing three sweaters, all thrown into her "cage" by vicious Marina to keep her alive, or she would surely have frozen in this miserable cell. But why were they trying to keep her alive? Bolsheviks weren't known for their gentle natures. Anne was sure that Marina had killed before, in cold blood. Then why not kill her?

They're waiting, she decided. But for what?

And then one morning the two men stood before her and Marina pulled her roughly to her feet. "Where are you taking me?" Anne asked, frightened to death.

"We're going to escort you across the border," one of the men replied. "Your father is already there."

"But—"

"No questions. Just put on your jacket and let's go."

In total silence they trudged through the deep snow, and Anne's feet, in her boots, felt painful stabs of cold. But it appeared that the man had been telling the truth. They were going to cross the border. Anne walked between the two Bolshevik guards, and suddenly she was pushed through barbed wire, and she saw her father in the distance, waiting on the Finnish side. Why had they let him go? And her?

Alfred was calling to her, and she started to run, breathless and suddenly anxious. She could tell that he hadn't shaved in days. She hadn't had a bath since November, and it was almost Hanukkah. Anne ran and caught her foot on a small piece of snowy driftwood, and before she could stop herself, her body was hurtling to the ground, her head crashing down on the snow and hitting a piece of brittle ice that slashed her cheek open.

"Anne!" her father called. *"Anne!"*

Her face bloody, the breath knocked out of her, Anne struggled to her feet. Her father was running toward her, and then it was over, he was holding her, hugging her, and she was sobbing into the lapels of his coat.

"Papa, Papa," she cried, but he was throwing her down into the snow, throwing her facedown, hard, his own body covering hers. Anne closed her eyes in terror, and he hissed, "Keep down. They're trying to kill us now!"

She heard shots: one, two, three. And then, abruptly, nothing. Alfred was pulling her up beside him and pointing back toward the Russian side of the barbed-wire fence. "I suspected they would try to get us after the ransom payment," he told her.

"What payment?"

"They held me for six weeks in the Fortress of Peter and Paul. They know our name, Anne. Everyone knows our name. They wanted money from the de Rochefleur banks. They need money."

"But it's the war!"

"Our bank in Paris wired them the money."

She was breathing in deep gulps, tears streaming down her face. Was it really over? The men across the border had stopped shooting, just like that. "They can't be bothered with us now," her father said, his voice exhausted and drained. "They gave it a try so they could tell their superiors how well they followed orders. But now they want to go home to their wives, and to their vodka. We're free, Princess, free to wait in Finland until the bank wires us the money for our trip to France."

So, even in the midst of the revolution, the de Rochefleur name had worked its magic. Anne wiped her tears with the back of her sleeve and looked up into the treetops at the overcast sky. What would the future hold? she wondered. Paris . . . where she'd come as a tiny child, for a few visits to her grandfather Henri.

"I don't remember Paris," she said. "Just my grandpa, that's all."

"And our family estate, La Folie. You remember the beautiful old house with its pretty garden?"

Anne shrugged, suddenly so tired that nothing mattered beyond the need for sleep. An estate? A garden? She recalled very little.

They hadn't stayed there long, had they? A few hours recaptured through the haze of memory.

"I'll remember it when I see it, Papa," she told him.

* * *

Anne looked timidly into the living room. A blond woman was sitting in the slightly frayed damask armchair, beautiful and proud, her long swan's neck supporting a head held high, plaits of white-blond hair coiled over its crown. So this was the true owner of La Folie. . . .

Anne sighed. She liked the old homestead, and felt at peace there among the once beautiful furnishings. She liked the graceful garden and its neat paths and flower beds. After the trauma she had lived through in Russia during the November revolution, the superb simplicity of La Folie had soothed away her fears and made her nightmares ebb away.

She and her father had arrived in Paris six weeks after their nerve-racking exodus from Russia. At first they were obliged to stay in Finland, awaiting funds, for Alfred had reached the border with empty pockets. Nothing was left of the Aschkenasys' immense fortune. But the de Rochefleur banks still functioned, and Baron Henri was dead. Legally, therefore, Anne's father stood at the head of an even greater international fortune, and the banking empire belonged to him. The funds had been wired by his men in Paris, and Alfred and Anne arrived there in February 1918.

Later they received the shocking news that Yakov Aschkenasy and his wife had been brutally murdered in their Petrograd palace, which the Bolsheviks had sacked and looted. Anne felt a momentary horror, then grief and loss, all of which disappeared in a haze of gratitude that she and her father had managed to escape a similar fate.

Anne seldom thought about the men she'd killed. She wanted to forget, and being at La Folie helped. Alfred had moved back there to give her a chance to recuperate. He'd told her the history of the beautiful mansion that had belonged to her grandfather Henri; how Henri had handed La Folie over to his irresponsible brother, Guy, without so much as consulting Alfred, his only son. He explained that La Folie belonged to Guy's only heir, Yvonne Lévy, who was living out the war in Lausanne, Switzerland, with her son, Charles. Since the house had been boarded up and Yvonne would not be returning until the end of the war, Alfred had decided to stay there with Anne, temporarily. And now it was December

1918, and "temporarily" had stretched to ten long months. La Folie was *home* to Anne and her father.

The only difference now was the presence of Yvonne and Charles Lévy at La Folie. On November 11, an armistice had been declared, and the hostilities that had shaken a continent had ceased. Barely two weeks later, Yvonne and Charles returned to Paris and set up house in a modest *pension*. But until today, when Yvonne had come to see Alfred, Anne had seen nothing of her Swiss cousins.

Anne couldn't remember Yvonne, though when she'd been little, she had surely met her. Now, looking at the blond woman sitting there with her father, Anne thought: What a strange family we are, all of us strangers.

Her father sat in his wing chair, smoking and gesticulating with his cigarette. "How are you and Charles possibly going to pay for the upkeep on this place?" he was saying. "It's a monumental expense. You're not thinking, Yvonne!"

The woman poured herself a cup of tea, and added cream and sugar before replying. Tilting her head to look right into Alfred's eyes, she stated coolly: "My son graduated second in his class at the college of engineers in Lausanne. I believe he'll find a good job here in Paris, now that the war is finally over. We shall manage our affairs quite nicely, Alfred. And besides, I'm going to have a one-woman show at the Leponnier Gallery next month. That ought to sell a lot of paintings."

Alfred laughed mirthlessly. "My dear Yvonne, you really are a dreamer, aren't you?" he said softly. Yet his eyes were hard. "It costs thousands of francs to heat this mansion, and thousands more to pay for gardeners and household servants. There are a dozen young engineers for every available job! As bright as Charles may be, Lausanne is only a small town, and being second will hardly impress Parisian firms looking for talent. As for your show . . . have the Leponniers drawn up a contract yet?"

Yvonne took a dainty sip of tea. Anne admired how she was handling her father. Had Anne been in her place, her hands would have been trembling and she would now be spilling tea all over the monogrammed linen. "Madame Leponnier has given me her word on the matter. I'm not worried. So, you see, Charles and I shall need to move back as soon as possible. I need the space to work on some paintings I'd like to finish in time for the show." She smiled. "Of course, Alfred, you and Anne don't have to move away on our account. You're welcome to stay here until you can find the right place for yourselves in Paris."

Anne thought: *The perfect place is right here. I love living here!* She felt the cold shock of displacement, of being thrown out, as in Russia, into an unwelcome no-man's-land. But clearly she and her father were the interlopers. Yvonne Levy was within her rights: the old homestead belonged to her, no matter what Alfred said. No matter Anne's attachment.

"I'd like to see Annie," Yvonne was saying. "Isn't she planning to join us for tea? Charles will be arriving any minute, to pick me up. They haven't seen each other since they were very small, have they, Alfred?" Yvonne's voice was smooth and cultured, as though by switching topics she had also neatly changed gears into neutral territory.

Oh, God, Anne thought, Charles, the cousin I can't remember! I don't want to meet him. I want to skip the whole ordeal and go back up to my room and read—

"Anne, darling!" Her father's voice broke into her thoughts. He'd seen her. Now there could be no retreating. Anne plunged ahead, wringing her hands helplessly, her eyes downcast, avoiding Yvonne's clear blue gaze. Let this be over quickly, she told herself miserably.

* * *

Anne's hand moved to her throat, and remained there. She could feel herself blushing, and the conscious part of her mind told her to stop staring. But somehow she just wasn't able to take her eyes off her cousin. Charles Lévy was the best-looking young man she had ever seen. He was tall—at least six feet two inches—and his face was like a Greek god's. Blue eyes framed in dark, curling lashes, a small snub nose, and lips that were just thick enough to make one want to be kissed by them. Anne blushed with shame at her own thoughts, wondering what *he* might be thinking of *her*.

Anne was almost eighteen now and had not yet felt such an overpowering sense of attraction toward a man. Her friends in Saint Petersburg—Petrograd—had often discussed their suitors, but Anne listened silently, with nothing of her own to add. She'd felt embarrassed, hearing their stories. Marie Zagat had kissed at least ten or twelve boys—*men*—and had described how Count Boris Ovtchinnikov had left her trembling from head to toe. But had the Count's lips been as appealing as Charles's? Lips like rose petals, soft rose petals . . .

"Anne," Yvonne was asking, evidently repeating something Anne had missed. "Do you still like candied almonds as much as you did when you were a little girl?"

"Y-yes.".

Anne, choked with timidity, examined her hands and twisted one of her rings round and round on her finger. Now her father was speaking. "So, Charles, my boy, tell me about looking for work. How has it been going?"

Older adults had an absurd habit of talking down to younger people. Immediately, Anne felt embarrassed for Charles. She looked at him and saw him smile back, briefly. He'd understood her sympathy, and was responding. Her heart began to soar.

"I've had a lot of rejections," he replied honestly. "Everyone wants to see a résumé of my previous jobs. It's a vicious cycle: I can't find work because I haven't held a position somewhere else first. And I'm not sure I know how to circumvent this problem."

Alfred gave Yvonne a piercing look. Then he asked Charles, "Perhaps you'd consider clerking for me, at the bank?"

Anne was mortified. Now her father was nailing down Charles's coffin, in front of her, in front of his own mother. But Charles merely smiled. "Thank you, Cousin Alfred. But I'd prefer to work in my own field. Don't worry, something will surely come up soon."

"I'm hardly the one who should be worried," Alfred said haughtily.

In the frosty silence that ensued, Anne stirred the sugar into her tea and wondered whether Charles had a steady girlfriend. She cleared her throat. Everyone was staring at her. How would Marie Zagat have started off speaking?

"Charles," she asked. "Have you been enjoying your social life in Paris?"

He appeared surprised that she had actually dared to express herself. "Mother and I don't have much of a social life," he answered pleasantly. "We didn't in Lausanne, and we've only recently arrived here. I think we'll both feel a great deal more secure once I have a job. Then I'll be able to think about the theatre, the opera, all the worldly pastimes."

"And have you been doing the rounds of postwar parties?" Yvonne questioned her.

Anne shook her head. "I . . . I haven't wanted to. I . . . don't know anyone here."

"Yes, it must be quite a cultural change from Russia." Yvonne laid a delicate hand on Anne's arm. "My dear, anytime you feel like visiting somebody, or going to a museum, or attending a ballet performance, please call me. Charles will just have to make an effort to relax a little, and escort both of us newcomers around town!"

"I'd be glad to," Charles declared. And then he rose, a little aloof, a little tired. "Mother, Don't forget we have an engagement this evening. We shall have to take our leave now of Cousin Alfred and Anne."

"So soon?" The words escaped from Anne before she could control herself. Then, stammering with embarrassment, she added: "I've—it's been—fun. . . ."

"Indeed it has," Yvonne agreed. "And so we shall repeat this performance. Good night, my dear. Good night, Alfred."

Moments later they were gone. Anne leaned against the heavy front door, her heart pounding. She remembered her debut, and Baron Vladimir Rykovsky, who had belched three times while twirling her around the dance floor. The man her mother had picked out for her. What would her mother have thought of Charles?

He's our cousin, Anne thought. Is it wrong to feel so attracted to him . . . ?

"Yvonne is in for a hard time," her father said, walking into the hallway and lighting a candle on a small side table. "There won't be any show at the Leponnier Gallery, and Charlie boy won't find a job."

"Why not?" Anne asked, suddenly afraid.

Alfred turned to her, and in the glow of the soft candlelight, the sharpness of his features sprang out against the wall in grotesque caricature. Although he was smiling, his expression conveyed anything but friendliness.

"It's simply my prediction for the day," he answered, shrugging. "Take it or leave it, Princess."

And then, casually, he patted her on the back of the head.

* * *

Charles shifted uncomfortably in the upright leather chair and faced the florid older man behind the huge Empire desk. "I see that you did very well at school in Lausanne," his interviewer admitted. "Your specialty was heavy machinery?"

Charles nodded, his throat dry. "I designed a machine to facilitate the manufacturing of metal gears for auto parts."

Jean Laffitte sighed. "And how do you suppose such a machine could be of use to us at Meyer Frères? We're in the business of building railway cars, not private automobiles."

Charles could feel his palms beginning to sweat as he opened his briefcase. He extracted some folded paper and laid it neatly out on the desk in front of the personnel director. The large blueprint took up half the space on the oversize desk. "We're entering a phase of industrial history when everything is going to become more and more specialized," he explained. "The field of engineering design will have to go along with this general trend. A heavy machine that turns out refrigerator doors, metal tools, car parts regardless of detail will soon be obsolete. My machine is designed to manufacture auto gears more quickly, and with less expense. A similar one could be designed for train gears."

The director pinched the bridge of his nose, and scrutinized Charles. "Do you have any experience in the railway industry?"

Blushing, Charles shook his head. "But I'm a quick study."

"'A quick study' . . . Young man, I don't think you have a realistic concept of the postwar business world." The director looked down at the blueprint, and pushed it aside. "This design is no doubt good. But we at Meyer Frères, and, I dare say, at almost any major French company, cannot afford to train new designers at this point. Orders for more railway cars are piling up on our desks. It's already May—six months since the armistice was signed! We are rebuilding our country, monsieur, and we are in a hurry to get on with this task. I suggest that you try one of the smaller cities— perhaps Montpellier, or Rouen—and apply for a position with a less important firm. They are proceeding more slowly there, and might have time to train you."

Charles opened his mouth, but the director was already rising. The young man could feel himself redden to the roots of his hair; his fingers trembled as he folded up his blueprint and put it back into the briefcase. When he looked up again, Laffitte was standing, plump and proud, his hands at his sides. Charles hesitated, then extended his right hand. "Thank you for your time."

"Good luck to you, Monsieur Lévy," Laffitte replied. But he did not take Charles's hand. Instead, he looked at his wristwatch and cleared his throat.

* * *

Marguerite Leponnier smiled. "Really, Madame Lévy, we understand how you must be feeling."

Charles blinked, amazed. "You 'understand'? Madame Leponnier, you promised to give my mother a one-woman show, and now you're telling us that she isn't going to have one . . . and you're saying you 'understand'?"

"Well, my husband and I had no idea that Count Dobrynin would consent to let us exhibit his Chagall collection. It's unfortunate that the time we had set aside for your mother's show falls the same two weeks the Dobrynins will be in Paris. They're elderly people. The revolution has upset their lives, and since they moved to London they haven't traveled much. We have to accept their terms or our gallery will be passed over once and for all by the great collectors of western Europe."

"Of course, madame," Yvonne said softly. "One can't compare the honor of showing Dobrynin's Chagalls with my simple watercolors. But perhaps you might consider me at some later date?"

Madame Leponnier inclined her head. "Naturally. And I *do* have a piece of good news: There's been an offer on the small gouache, *The Encounter*. I had it in the window a few weeks, just for exposure, and a famous collector immediately asked that it be set aside for him. I took it down, of course, because it's far better publicity to adorn the walls of someone well known, even if the price is modest, than to pocket a somewhat larger sum of money from a sale to a nobody!" She licked her lips, demurely hesitant, and waited for an answer.

"How 'modest' was this man's offer?" Charles asked, his voice clipped and cold.

"Well now, monsieur . . . it was two hundred francs."

Charles paled. "Only two hundred? But it's one of Mother's best! You yourself thought so!"

Marguerite Leponnier sighed. "You're right, my dear. The only problem is, nobody is familiar yet with your mother's work. She's a virtual unknown. And two hundred francs for someone starting out isn't such a bad offer."

Yvonne's voice was hushed. "We'll take it, won't we? I mean—"

"Certainly. My husband will be glad to make you out a check for the balance: one hundred twenty francs. The rest, as you realize, will be the gallery's commission."

"May I ask . . . who wants to buy it?"

Charles stared at his mother, dumbfounded. The expression on her face was so openly eager, so slavishly accepting of the slightest crumb of recognition, that he wanted to turn away from her, to avoid his own pain at witnessing this. "Mama," he murmured. "For two hundred francs, does it really matter who the buyer is?"

"It always matters to an artist," Yvonne replied, her voice somewhat cool. "Doesn't it, Madame Leponnier?"

"Indeed it does. And in this case it happens to be a most distinguished man. Perhaps you've met the Baron Alfred de Rochefleur? Surely you've read about him? He owns and manages the Crédit Industriel."

Incredulous, Charles leapt out of his chair. "Alfred? *Alfred* reserved the right to buy your gouache, for *two hundred goddamned francs*? I can't believe it!" His face was red and he glared at Yvonne. "He took *The Encounter* out of circulation on purpose! He wanted to make damn *sure* you wouldn't get a better price for it, that sly manipulator! But *why*? Why did he bother?"

Madame Leponnier blinked, taken aback. "Monsieur Lévy, I beg you, calm down! I see you do know the Baron. But clearly, you've misjudged him: he's such a thoroughly decent man, such an absolute gentleman—what else can I tell you? He's been one of our patrons for a year now, since he and his daughter moved to Paris."

Charles took a few steps, facing the gallery owner. "Do you realize what an absurd situation you've helped to create, madame? Aren't you even aware that my mother's maiden name was 'de Rochefleur'? Alfred is her cousin! And he's one of the wealthiest men in France! If he had truly fallen in love with Mother's work, he could have purchased it for what it's worth! Or else he should have had the morality to leave it alone, for another collector to buy at its proper price!"

Yvonne jumped up, placing an urgent hand on her son's forearm. "Darling—"

"Don't you 'darling' *me!*" he broke in, furious. "This is the epitome of humiliation! Don't you see, Mother?"

Yvonne raised her head and gave him a frosty stare. "I don't see anything of the sort. My cousin liked one of my paintings and made a reasonable offer for it to Madame Leponnier. We're in no position to refuse, are we, Charles? I am, as Madame has graciously pointed out, a mere beginner on the Paris art scene. With this in mind, I'm quite ready to accept Alfred's offer."

The words died in Charles's throat. Marguerite Leponnier

looked anxiously at Yvonne. "Really, Madame Lévy, no offense was intended, I'm certain of that—"

"And none was taken. Thank you for your time, Madame Leponnier."

Yvonne, her back erect, swirled her coat about her and started to walk to the door. Charles stood staring at the gallery owner, dismayed and in shock. Madame Leponnier coughed delicately, embarrassment painted over her birdlike features. At the door, Yvonne called out, "Well, Charles? Shall we go?"

It wasn't until they were both outside that Charles was able to express himself. "How could you have allowed this woman to treat you so condescendingly?" he cried. "And don't you see how Alfred has made you the fool of the art world?"

"I don't see it, no," his mother answered. "In his own fashion, he's trying to help us. And God knows, we need all the help we can get, to pay the bills that are piling up!"

Charles looked at his mother and noticed how her chin was trembling. Then he felt ashamed. Deeply ashamed that, for whatever reason, he had been unable to find a job. That Alfred de Rochefleur had made a humiliating offer for a painting his mother had put hours of love and care into creating. That Yvonne had no choice but to accept this offer . . .

Something had to begin going right for them, he thought, anger pumping through his body. His luck had to turn . . . and soon. It simply *had* to.

* * *

Yvonne paced the floor of the oak-paneled office of the president and general manager of the Crédit Industriel. One entered the building through a modest carriage gate on the rue Saint-Florentin, although the offices overlooked, on the other side, the more glamorous rue Saint-Honoré, not far from the Place de la Concorde.

The de Rochefleur family had owned the building since the days of Baron Charles, but leased out the lower stories. On the ground floor stood the celebrated restaurant Au Grand Vatel, and on the second, the workrooms of the couturier Creed. Henri had kept the third and fourth floors, where he set up his office and those of his key employees. Rather than flaunt a forefront on the rue Saint-Honoré, he preferred the greater privacy of the side-street entrance on 6, rue Saint-Florentin.

And now Alfred presided over the intricate network of European bank operations whose headquarters his father had established in Paris under the aegis of the Crédit Industriel. Yvonne was in such turmoil as she paced in front of the large windows that she remained totally unmoved by the beauty of her surroundings.

"I wish you would calm down," her cousin murmured, his voice low and soothing. "Young engineers, I warned you, are having a devil of a time finding suitable positions these days."

"It's just that we can't hold out any longer," she declared, stopping in her tracks and looking at Alfred. Her eyes were tired and bloodshot. "I've tried every art gallery in town. No luck."

"What exactly do you want from me, Yvonne?" Alfred asked, leaning across his desk and staring at her intently. "A loan? A long-term bond, perhaps?"

Yvonne shook her head, pressing her eyelids closed so that the tears that shamed her could be held back. She let her shoulders rise, then drop, helplessly. "I've never been in such a situation. I'm not even sure what to ask for. And I don't like having to ask for anything. . . ."

"Well now, we're family, aren't we? Who else do we have, besides my sister?" Alfred leaned forward to underscore the meaning he was trying to convey. "Actually, you're closer to me than Barbara, Yvonne. Barbara and her children have been off in their own world for so many years. Vienna is so far away, after all."

Alfred rose from behind his desk and pulled out a comfortable brown suede armchair for his cousin. Her face, which had been vulnerable with pain, suddenly became remote, wary. She sat down wordlessly in the proffered chair and waited, her hands folded in her lap.

Alfred scrutinized her, circumspectly. "Yvonne, my dear, there *is* something I can do. You and Charles have been living way beyond your means at La Folie. For myself, the upkeep of that property would be nothing, a drop drained from the ocean. I'd like to take it off your hands . . . and pay you handsomely for the land and the house."

Yvonne leaned back into her chair and examined Alfred. Her blue eyes flicked from his eyes to his mouth, then down to his hands. Finally she said, "I don't want to sell my father's house, Alfred. I want to have it for my son. It's his only patrimony."

"Charles is a bright young man; he'll make his own way! And meanwhile, do you think you're helping him by beggaring yourself to pay the expenses on La Folie? What he needs is the money to travel, to dine out, to invite young ladies of good family to the theater or the symphony. He needs a decent wardrobe. You *do* believe that he should marry well, don't you? Then do what's truly right! Sell me La Folie."

Yvonne's face suddenly flushed, and she bit her lower lip with an unexpected fierceness, betraying angry frustration. At length, she faced her cousin once again. "You've always resented Uncle Henri's gift of that property to my father," she declared, her voice deceptively even. "You've held it against me, and against Charles. It would be so easy for me just to hand it over, and to take whatever you're about to offer. But Uncle Henri *planned* for us to own it. He knew that without it, Charles and I would have nothing to call our own, that we'd be at the mercy of every blackguard and ne'er-do-well in town. This way, at least, we're landowners, gentry. My son has property. If I let La Folie go, we'd have a little bit of money for a short while, that's all. We'd immediately have to purchase an apartment in town, and the furniture to go with it. How much longer before we'd be penniless again, begging for your help?"

"Charles will have a job soon."

"Really? And how much do you suppose a young engineer can earn? I think that if we just hold out a little while longer . . . Providence will help us. There *is* a God, Alfred! Charles will find a job, and if we keep La Folie, we shall be able to live modestly on my son's income. He and I need very little."

Alfred sighed. "All right, Yvonne. That makes perfect sense. But the question remains—how much longer do you think you and Charles *will* be able to hold out without having to declare bankruptcy? Remember why you came to me in the first place! *You have no other option!* If you sell me La Folie, I shall set up a trust fund for you that will keep you going for the rest of your life. You will not have to depend on Charles for support, nor on gallery owners. And who knows? I might even know of a firm or two that could use a good young designer, starting out—"

Yvonne stood up, her nostrils flaring. "You've always been in a position to throw in a good word for Charles!" she said, her voice still low, but trembling now. "But until now you never had the need to help him! You're a bad man, Alfred, a very bad man. Only now you're holding all the cards, and I can do nothing to fight you. Take La Folie!" she cried. "Take it, and do with it whatever you choose! I'll accept the trust fund, because there appears to be no other alternative! But take it, knowing that I hate you, and that I see you for what and who you are: an opportunist without one ounce of loving-kindness in his soul!"

Alfred brought his right hand up over his mouth, to hide a half smile. "Really, now, Yvonne, you're overreacting," he demurred. "You're not being fair or realistic. I'm trying to help you . . . as you asked me to."

She took a linen handkerchief out of her bag and pressed it against the corners of her eyes. "I'd like to get this transaction over with as soon as possible. You have me where you want me, so let's end this ordeal right now."

"As you wish," he replied evenly, ringing for his secretary. But he could scarcely contain the nervous exhilaration that had been building inside him. After all these years, he was about to redress the wrong done to him by his father's careless gesture, and he thought, *Finally* . . .

* * *

Charles tried to control his impatience as Jean Laffitte took his time adjusting the cuffs on his sleeves and settling a pair of spectacles on the bridge of his nose. Finally he spoke. "The reason we've called you back, young man," Laffitte announced, "is that a position has opened up in our drafting section. We'll be needing a junior designer starting on Monday."

Charles felt a surge of tremendous excitement rush through his body. He broke into a smile; then, witnessing Laffitte's disdainful appraisal of his demeanor, he restrained his enthusiasm and simply said, "Thank you, sir, for thinking of me."

The personnel manager sniffed. "You'll have to thank Monsieur Meyer himself for this. The order came from *him* to hire you."

Charles blinked. "But I've never met him."

"Apparently he knows of *you.* In any case, you're to report on Monday to the main draftsroom. Your salary will be modest, to begin with: it's our policy to put our trainees on a six-month probation at minimum wage."

"That will be fine, Monsieur Laffitte," Charles replied. He could just imagine his mother's happy face when he told her. Even a junior designer's minimum wage, within a major industrial firm, would be sufficient to carry the basic expenses incurred every month at La Folie.

* * *

Yvonne heard her son's joyous call even before she saw him striding in with two bottles of Dom Pérignon champagne. She had been sitting, lost in thought, by the French windows of the gallery that overlooked the once graceful garden, now sadly kept down to a bare lawn. When Charles walked into the room, he cried, "Why haven't you turned the lights on, Mama?" and automatically flicked on the Pigeon lamp that burned with alcohol on a small side table. Its raw white light made her blink.

"Tonight we're celebrating! I've finally found a job!" he announced, falling into one of the lounge chairs and kicking off his shoes. "All our problems will be over as of next Monday! I'm starting in the main drafting room of Meyer Frères."

But Yvonne's face was pale and drawn, and instead of rejoicing she looked ready to burst into tears. "Why aren't you more excited, Mother?" he inquired, suddenly worried.

Then she stood up, wringing her hands and looking away. "Because this has happened four hours too late! I . . . I couldn't think of any other solution! I *had* to go to Alfred . . ."

"What on earth do you mean, Mama?"

She flicked her tongue over parchment-dry lips, and looked him in the eye. "We're going to have to move, Charles. Alfred will be taking over La Folie. I *had* to let him do it! We were destitute!"

Charles stood up, his features starting to register shock. "You did *what*? *Why*? Couldn't you have waited even one day?"

"We'd both been waiting for six months now. Our savings were depleted, eaten away. . . . He's going to pay me every month, a lot of money, Charles, from a trust fund that he'll maintain for the rest of my life. You're never going to have to worry about me anymore, son. I'll be completely taken care of."

Charles pounded his fist down on the mantelpiece, and a glass paperweight jumped an inch into the air. "God damn it!" he exploded. "I just can't *believe* this! You've handed over Grandpa's house to—to the man we both dislike so much? To that phony, that hypocrite, whose mousy little daughter can't even find herself a husband in spite of his millions?" He covered his face with his hands and uttered a cry of anger and despair. "You gave away the only thing of value in both our lives!" he whispered. "You couldn't have held out one afternoon longer. . . . A single afternoon . . ."

Yvonne's face was bathed in tears, and she shook her head. "You sold our patrimony like Esau's birthright," Charles muttered with disgust. "For a mess of potage!"

Then he stood up, and picked up a bottle of the champagne he had brought. With unexpected violence, he threw it headlong at one of the French windows, shattering the glass, which splintered it into thousands of glimmering shards. Yvonne's lips parted, and her eyes filled with awe and horror.

"Let Alfred replace this windowpane!" Charles said, tossing the words out with complete contempt. "Let *him* have to bother with the contractor! After all, this is *his* house now, isn't it, Mother?"

But Yvonne simply stared at him, incapable of words, as he stormed out of the gallery.

CHAPTER V

Amelia shook the snow from her high, two-toned boots and set her umbrella down on the side of the stairs. Her wide-brimmed black felt hat was soggy, its feathers drooping, and she flung it impatiently to the floor. Her hair was pinned up in a chignon from which rebellious wisps escaped, curling naughtily onto the shoulders of her three-quarter-length coat. Several inches of red wool skirt protruded above her boots. The war had shortened hems and made clothing more practical; and now, this winter of 1919, Amelia could move around as rapidly as she liked, without having to worry about tripping over floor-length gowns.

She was late, as usual, and so, without glancing up, she began to run up the wide stone staircase of the Ministry of Finance. On the second landing, she paused to catch her breath. Ornate carved moldings adorned the doorways of the offices facing her, and she thought, How overdone. No wonder the city was dying, struggling to retain its identity after a disastrous war and a crippling famine. We are living in a baroque environment during modern times; we aren't keeping up. That was why the Hapsburgs had been exiled, and the great Austro-Hungarian extravaganza had been reduced to this tiny republic, now dominated by the socialists.

"*Gräfin* von Guttman."

Amelia started. Outside one of the ministry offices, briefcase in hand, stood Peter Habig, the haberdasher.

Amelia stared at him in surprise, her heart pounding inexplicably. He was wearing a dark gray suit, and his swarthy face, with the long nose and the deep, dark eyes, gave him the appearance of an Italian prince from the seventeenth century—quite fitting in the lavish ministry.

"Herr Habig. What are you doing here?"

"I could ask the same of you," he replied. "One wouldn't expect to run into the flower of Vienna in the dreary corridors of the Ministry of Finance."

She remembered how he had taunted her at the von Stecher hunt, belittling her nursing activities, and then adding insult to injury by bluntly implying she'd been too young to interest him. How long ago had that been? Two years? Two and a half? And what about now? she asked herself. Am I still too young?

Unexpectedly, the memory still stung. And so, with some asperity, she tossed back, "I help out in the office that allocates the Entente relief credit." To help ease the general postwar famine in Vienna, the United States was reaching out a helping hand across the ocean, lending funds to the beleaguered Austrian government.

"You haven't changed, then," he murmured. "Still noble and selfless . . ." She could see sparks of humor in his dark eyes, ringed so handsomely with curling black lashes.

"And what about *you,* Herr Habig?" she countered. "How noble and selfless are you?"

He smiled broadly, and set down his briefcase. "Nobility would be out of character for me. Don't forget, dear *Gräfin,* that I'm only a merchant, not an aristocrat!"

He was still trying to make her look like nothing but a foolish child—she could see this clearly. Well, she wasn't a child, not any longer. "Why is it you can't consider me a serious person, with concerns for the welfare of others?" she demanded.

He leaned back against the balustrade of the staircase, and she couldn't help but admire the grace of his taut, well-proportioned body, sleek as a panther's. "You're very pretty," he told her frankly, his eyes moving from her face down her lovely body and resting for a few telltale seconds over the area of her chest. "And you're accustomed to parting the seas with a toss of your very pretty head. It's not that I doubt your seriousness, it's more that I doubt how long it will last. Working in the Ministry of Finance can be an amusing experience . . . for a few months. The aristocracy isn't dancing much these days, so why *not* throw your energies into the Entente?"

So . . . He hadn't changed at all. His stance was still the same as that morning at the von Stechers'. Amelia gauged the irony in his voice, and replied, icily, "Why *not,* indeed? *Children* ride to the hounds, don't they, Herr Habig? But only adults work at the ministry. You must grant me that this has become *the* place for meeting interesting members of the opposite sex. And guess what?

These young men, even the envoys from the United States, stand a far better chance of staying around than those I used to nurse at the hospital two years ago."

With the beginning of her discourse, he'd started out laughing, baring his large white teeth. But the harsh image of death she had brought to mind immediately dispelled his good humor. Still angry, she thought: *Good!* But then her curiosity took over, and she wondered about his briefcase. "*You* had some *real* business here, I presume, Herr Habig?" she asked. "Something of world import? Or was this merely research for your business? 'Let's see what the office clerks are wearing today,' or something like that. . . ."

His eyes sparkled anew with merriment. "Clerking in an office isn't a sport," he teased her. "And I'm afraid my specialty is still limited to sportswear. No, if you must know, I've been talking to the minister about organizing relief groups to go into the country to bring staples back to Vienna. My own small contribution to resolve the famine," he added softly, his eyes fastening on her and measuring her up.

He wants to know who I really am, she thought. As *I* want to find out what lies beneath his cool veneer. Silence had fallen over them, and she felt him change, from a taunting, inaccessible businessman to a simple man who shared her commitment to their city in its moment of crisis. She wanted to say: Talk to me, Peter Habig. I am a grown woman, ready to listen. Not just an empty-headed debutante, impatient to waltz off into the outstretched arms of a powdered admirer. *Talk to me.*

"Your family has done more than its share to help out," he finally said, his voice so different now, gentle and compassionate. "Your brother's generous donations of coal from your mines are being used right now to fuel the trains that will transport my people as they travel into the country. Frankly, I was surprised by Count Richard's gesture. Most of the aristocracy hasn't cared, and I've wondered how they could stay so blind, now that the empire has crumbled into a tiny republic, with the Social Democrats in power, leaning to the left like a lopsided Tower of Pisa!"

Amelia sighed. "Sometimes I grow scared. We're Jews, you know. When things begin to go wrong in a country, the extreme right wing inevitably blames the Jews. So you see, Herr Habig, the Social Democrats are less frightening to the von Guttmans than the Christian Socialists. We'd rather share our wealth than risk our lives."

Having spoken so openly, Amelia looked down, embarrassed. It was the first time she had ever voiced her fears, and they were still so vague, so unformed. . . . "I really don't understand politics," she said. "My brother and I are close, but he has his friends to talk to about such matters, rather than me. You'll have to forgive my ignorance."

"You're far from ignorant," he countered gravely. Then, changing his tone, he asked, amused, "Do you still have a line of suitors queuing up along the Ringstrasse, waiting to catch a glimpse of their favorite face?"

"They were so numerous, Herr Habig, that I stopped trying to recognize each one of them," she replied, smiling. Then, tilting her head coyly, she demanded, "But may I presume that you were among the crowd?"

"I don't like crowds," he declared. "One on one is much more satisfying."

Amelia could hardly contain her excitement. His eyes were on her, and this time there was no mistaking his recognition of her womanhood, her sensuality. His own excitement was visible on his face, in the intensity of his eyes, and in his coiled muscles. And then, all at once, he consulted his watch and shook his head. When he looked at her once more the tension was gone, and in his eyes she could read only the polite, aloof concern of a virtual stranger about to take his leave.

"I've detained you sufficiently, *Gräfin* Amelia," he declared, taking her hand and clicking his heels as he made an elegant bow. "You're late now, and so am I. I hope I haven't caused you any inconvenience. Be sure to give your mother and brother my best regards," he added formally.

And all at once he was gone, and Amelia was standing all alone on the landing. He'd said nothing about seeing her again, and she felt a moment of complete dejection. He was so infuriatingly sure of himself! *How I'd enjoy giving him a good run for his money,* she thought, wondering whether he was still a free man or if his heart was already pledged to another woman.

* * *

Spring was threatening to burst into full blossom in Paris; Anne could sense it, the same way one felt an oncoming storm when the sky grew overcast and pewter-colored. She could smell the fragrance of fresh buds on the tall horse chestnut trees, and feel the gentle fingertip caress of a newborn sunshine when she went walking through the streets.

She thought of this as she passed through the huge carriage entrance into the dark building on the Boulevard Malesherbes; even when the sun shone everywhere else in the city, on this large, tree-lined boulevard gray shadows prevailed. Why did her cousin Yvonne live there? she wondered. Wasn't natural light the most important element for an artist?

Anne climbed the narrow staircase, pausing at each landing and cursing her overweight body at every step. Her large breasts heaved, and beneath the frail linen of her day dress, her stomach withstood and bore its punishing assaults of her corset stays, like lances through the soft folds of flesh. Her father said she wasn't fat —just a large woman, with big bones. But whatever the euphemism, Anne felt cumbersome: she was five foot seven and weighed one hundred forty-eight pounds, much of it settled around her hips and breasts.

Finally she reached the fifth floor, and, wiping her brow with one gloved hand, she pressed on the doorbell. A minute passed; then the door opened and, instead of confronting Yvonne, Anne found herself staring into Charles's blue eyes. He was wearing a maroon velvet bathrobe and seemed pale and sleepy.

"Well, Anne!" he began. "I guess I wasn't expecting anyone. Did you and Mama have a date together this afternoon? Because she's not here. . . ."

Anne could feel herself turning red in spite of her will to control the sudden flow of blood to her face. Charles had such magnificent eyes, like glistening gems caught in an ivory mask, perfectly chiseled. "I came without calling," she replied, embarrassed. "I had to go to the doctor, on the Place de l'Etoile, and I really wanted to speak to Cousin Yvonne about something. So I just came." She shuffled her feet awkwardly, then scrutinized Charles and murmured, "You're ill, aren't you?"

He smiled. "Just a head cold. But we're ahead of schedule on the project I'm designing, so I thought a day in bed wouldn't hurt. But look here—come in! I have a kettle of hot water on the stove. We can have a cup of tea together, all right?"

Anne followed him into the small apartment. Her head was suddenly swimming, making her dizzy. She could smell Charles: a masculine smell, musklike and pleasant, not that of some flowery cologne, like her father's. She felt herself overpowered by his presence, and pulses were echoing throughout her body, sending warnings. Warnings, or good tidings? She didn't know how to interpret them because she'd never experienced this sensation before.

The living room where Charles escorted her was almost threadbare. The carpet needed mending and the mustard-yellow sofa needed to be cleaned, but marvelous, glowing watercolors and gouaches adorned the walls. Anne sat down on the sofa and folded her hands on her lap, waiting as Charles had instructed her to do while he went to the kitchen. She felt a pang of pity, thinking: A man like that shouldn't be fetching his visitor tea. Has the situation gotten no better for them? Can't they afford even a peasant girl to help out with the housework?

Presently he returned, carrying a silver platter with the familiar *R* monogram, on which stood a beautiful bulbous teapot, a water pitcher, a cream dispenser, and a sugar bowl—all antique and beautifully fashioned in solid silver that was badly tarnished. He set the tray down, and she saw that the two cups he had precariously placed on the edge of the tray were about to topple over. "Let me pour," she offered shyly.

Charles inclined his head, his eyes twinkling. "Be my guest!" Even in this shabby decor, debilitated by his fever, he had a self-assured grace. Still standing, he looked at her with amusement, touched by her sudden confusion. She looked down and began to pour the tea.

"You're an adept hostess," he commented, finally sitting down beside her. "To the manner born . . ." His tone was somewhat ironic.

"In Russia, we're brought up on tea," she murmured, handing him his cup. As he leaned toward her to take it, his thigh accidentally brushed against hers. Anne started, blushing, thrills like hot flashes spreading through her. He smiled, and for a moment their eyes locked: hers, horrified, electrified—and his, amused. A man sensing his own sexual power and unable to resist flexing this precious muscle.

" 'Anne, ma soeur Anne, ne vois-tu rien venir?' . . ." he quoted in a singsong voice, his smile teasing her. " 'And her sister Anne replied: "I see nothing but the sun which makes a dust, and the grass looking green. . . ." ' "

"That's from a fairy tale," she said, her voice trembling. She took a sip of tea and closed her eyes against his physical beauty, which was causing such havoc to her senses.

"That's right, little Sister Anne. So, in Russia, you were brought up on tea *and* the tales of Charles Perrault. . . ."

She was mortified. Was he making fun of her? She'd never known what to do when people teased her, and had never been able to come up with clever retorts. Now she felt more confused than ever.

"Why don't you tell me what you came to see Mother about," he said conversationally, as if reading her mind.

She cleared her throat. "It's just that I . . . Well . . . I'm not sure really how to say this. Charles . . . Papa wants to have a housewarming party at La Folie. We've done some . . . redecorating, you see, and he wants to invite a lot of people over to see it. I—"

She set down her teacup, because her hand was shaking. His face looked all at once withdrawn, remote . . . so very cold. *She'd said the wrong thing!* "Charles," she stammered. "I didn't mean to . . . I mean . . . Look, I came to ask Cousin Yvonne to please attend. I know how you both must feel. . . . . But you see, Papa's written to Aunt Barbara, in Vienna, and invited her to come with Richard and Amelia. Aunt Barbara grew up with your mother. I know she'd like to see her . . . and you, too."

Anne's heart was pounding, and her throat felt parched. She licked her lips and ventured a glance at her cousin. His expression now seemed tormented and moody. Even his eyes appeared darker, clouded with anger.

"Look," he told her, not unkindly. "I can't blame *you* for what your father did to my mother and me." And then, his voice growing impassioned, he continued, "But all I ever had, besides the love of my mother, was La Folie! It was *ours*! Your grandfather gave it to mine to protect my mother and me! What Alfred did was not only cruel, it was totally immoral! I can't forgive him, and I never will. He went against his own father's wish, when he might have purchased any of a number of houses ten times more luxurious than *my mother's house*!"

Anne shook her head, beside herself. "Oh, Charles, what can I say? I didn't mean to stir up this business. I—"

He took a deep breath, then let it out in a huge sigh. "Anne, I know my mother. She will want to come, to see your Aunt Barbara. Mama's no fighter. But, God damn it, *I am*! Alfred isn't going to humiliate *me* in front of all of Paris!" he cried. Then, more calmly, he added, "No, Anne, you have your party, and enjoy yourself. You're a sweet girl. I'll give Mama your message and she'll make up her mind as she sees fit. All right?"

She nodded quickly, suddenly eager to be away from all this mess, away from Charles's obvious, naked pain, which she had brought him through her tactlessness—away, too, from this apartment, so different from La Folie, which her own father had torn away from them, his own cousin and her son.

"I've got to go," she stammered, rising.

At the door, he touched her arm. "I appreciate your coming out of your way. Good-bye, 'Sister Anne' . . ."

My God! she thought, going down the staircase, her cheeks inflamed. *Charles touched my arm!* I've never wanted to be touched the way I've just been touched. I wanted him to make it last, to touch me again . . . on my face. *I wanted him to kiss me!*

Consumed by her mounting embarrassment, Anne bit fiercely into her lip and thought about the trip home, and her father. She had to concentrate on other things than her cousin Charles. Charles is never going to kiss you, a little voice inside her head was telling her. Charles is ten times as good-looking as you, plain, pudgy Anne! He has other fish to fry, other women to chase . . . other loves to pursue. A man like that . . .

She was surprised to discover tears on her cheeks.

CHAPTER VI

Amelia von Guttman had never been inside a house that affected her so deeply as La Folie. As she moved through the rooms, alone, it occurred to her that the exquisite beauty of every tiny bibelot made her feel ashamed.

Vienna was supposed to be the city of charm and music, culture and elegance. But already Amelia was convinced that Parisians outshone the Viennese the same way majestic, colorful peacocks outshone the noisy cuckoos too busy with their own histrionics to preen their wings. She came from a land where superfluous adornment implied good taste and opulence. Even the aristocracy had middle-class sensibilities. Here, on the other hand, simplicity underscored balance and harmony, and she could recognize true beauty—the taste of the well-rounded elite.

Strange, that a girl like her cousin Anne, retiring and a bit awkward, could have put together a work of art such as the interior of this marvelous mansion! Anne reminded Amelia a bit of her own mother, Barbara. One could sense the same shyness in them both, the same fear of rejection. Anne's, of course, was more obvious, due to her youth; but Amelia had always surmised that her mother's extreme heaviness had its own protective coloring. Fat girls didn't have to deal with the complexities of the courtship game.

How very odd, then, for Anne to possess such an extraordinarily refined eye for the balance and harmony of furniture and art, of light and space. Barbara had never bothered with aesthetics in their own house, dressing the interior as haphazardly as she dressed her own person; and Amelia had observed that Anne, too, didn't know how to combine textures, colors, and lines when it came to her clothing. She likes the house more than herself, Amelia ventured to guess. It's as though she was sure of the house, but unsure of her own value. . . .

Amelia wondered how she herself would fare in Paris; would she still be as sought after, as appreciated for her wit and presence as she seemed to be in her own city? She felt strangely out of place and unsure of herself for the first time in a long, long while.

And yet, although it underscored the gaps in her own upbringing, this beautiful house also made her want to stay. She felt that somehow she and La Folie belonged together. But how bizarre this all seemed, for it was as though the house were enveloping her, absorbing her aura and her emotions into its walls, adding them, like an artist mixing colors, to the many auras and personalities of those who had lived there before. *I am a de Rochefleur,* she thought, suddenly awakened to the idea: and this house was the very soul of that disparate family, its very heart and imperishable reflection.

Amelia was enchanted by the quiet little town of Saint-Germain. Her first day there, Anne took her for a long walk, and they had strolled through the castle grounds and crossed over for a look at the French and English gardens across the street. Then, arm in arm, they had wended their way back to the house.

La Folie stood a mere thirty yards from the French garden. Its façade was of red brick, though its windows were framed in white sandstone. The majestic ground floor stood raised above street level, and the second-floor balconies were protected by carved stone railings. The third floor had been lined with gray slate, and square turrets overlooked both corners of the façade.

Behind the house the garden stretched out, and far in back sat a low building where the horses were kept. All of this was closed off by a high wall from the intrusive eyes of passersby.

The main entrance to the house was on the rue Lemierre: it was a sculptured door with a hammer that had been turned into an elegant knob. But on the other side, giving onto the Avenue Gambetta, stood a carriage entrance that led through the house to the garden at the back. The entryway, with Napoleon's proud initial surrounded by a crown of laurels, divided the mansion into two separate wings of unequal proportions. Alfred de Rochefleur, his daughter, Anne, and their four servants resided in the larger area; the smaller was reserved for guests, and Amelia's room was there.

The main residence began with the ground floor, where Alfred had set up the reception rooms. Anne had refurnished the dining room in the delicate style of King Louis XVI, and had hung the walls with light blue silk. Opposite stood the huge living room, its intimidating proportions softened by its warm color scheme, which combined spring green, peach, and mimosa yellow in a pattern of field flowers that was repeated from the drapes to the slipcovers on the twin sofas.

The furniture was all eighteenth-century French, showing off the inlaid woodwork of Boulle and Stumpff. Already, after a week, Amelia knew each piece in this room by heart: she had memorized the way the sunlight fell over the brass and copper marquetry, bringing to life the contrast of metal and wood; and the way the chandelier turned each tabletop and cabinet panel into a haunting playground of light and color.

Next to this majestic living room and giving right onto the back garden, was a large gallery enclosed in glass. It was there that the de Rochefleurs spent most of their leisure time. In front of one of the large French doors, Anne had placed a flat-topped desk designed by Boulle, with a tooled leather top and ormolu mounts. Comfortable armchairs were disposed on either side.

Beyond the gallery lay a windowless corridor, then, on the garden side, a bathroom and a powder room, and, on the street side, three large rooms. Of these, Anne's boudoir was the most spectacular: the red and white silk that dressed her massive four-poster had been especially hand-painted for her in Lyon, center of the silk industry of France. The suite was gracefully completed by a small sitting room and an all-purpose library.

The second story was laid out in similar fashion, and Alfred had given it completely over to his daughter. The delicately molded ceilings were high, and Anne's bedroom reflected her predilection for Louis XIV: her bureaus and armchairs were of expensive woods inlaid with solid silver trim and gold leaf. Her bed, with its high canopy and small fringe marquee, was covered and trimmed with the most exquisite ivory-and-gold velvet, handwoven from silk. While her boudoir on the ground floor was cheered up by the more recent Impressionist painters, here Anne had favored the old Dutch masters Vermeer and Hals.

In the days of Baron Charles and of Guy, the third floor had been unadorned and functional. More than half had been occupied by an oversize laundry room with a brick floor, under the attic where the wet clothes had been hung to dry. The rest of the space was still taken up with the more cramped servants' quarters and the servants' kitchen, as well as two storage rooms. On the front, a small staircase hidden behind a door led toward the slanted attic and several empty rooms on both sides, which occupied the two turrets adorning the façade.

Alfred de Rochefleur had completely converted the laundry room into a bedroom for himself. He had covered the brick floor with thick Persian rugs and had chosen the simpler, more masculine style of Louis XIII for his furnishings. The bedroom backed off the staircase. Adjacent to his room, Alfred had converted a small area into a bathroom equipped with a tub. The sole, be it minor, inconvenience was that when he needed to work, he had to go down to the library on the main floor, near Anne's boudoir. All his books and files had been put there, and his daughter had turned the space into a kind of family den, warm with furnishings from eighteenth-century England, carved in soft woods with rounded edges and highly polished surfaces.

The other rooms on the third floor were occupied by the servants, a family of four who ran the household like clockwork: the butler, Goujon, who also doubled as gardener; his wife, Marie, the cook; and their two daughters, Brigitte and Marthe, who served as chambermaids. Finally, taking up most of the basement, lay the vast kitchen and the pantry, a cellar for the heater, and four excellently stocked wine cellars. Alfred had spent a fortune lining the kitchen walls with cork to ward off the dampness.

Amelia wondered what the Goujon family thought about her uncle. She had witnessed a scene that had left her shaken. At dinner one night, Goujon had served a wonderful cold crême of cucumber soup. Her uncle Alfred had regarded the tureen and raised his eyebrows; then he had shifted his stare to the butler, his eyes cold and piercing. "Mademoiselle Anne ordered a light broth for tonight," he had said, his voice almost honeyed, mild, questioning.

"It was very warm today, Monsieur le Baron," Goujon had demurred. "Mademoiselle was out this afternoon, and Marie was unable to consult with her. She thought—"

"It's not her place to *think,*" Alfred had declared, spitting the words out. "Only to execute! The cook follows orders: she is paid to stir the pot, and *that is all*! Do you understand, Goujon? You are here to open doors, to dust windowsills, and to walk around us like the shadows you are . . . and don't ever forget this!"

Then, abruptly, he had waved away the tureen of soup and risen from the table, the corners of his mouth disdainfully turned down. Alfred had not returned, and the evening had been spoiled, everyone too embarrassed to continue the previous, light-hearted conversation.

And that was why Amelia wondered about the cork-lined kitchen.

The second wing of the house gave onto the rue Thiers, and was, of course, connected to the main wing by the carriage entrance. It was there, close to the small stable where Anne and Alfred kept their stallions, that Amelia, Richard, and their mother had been set up in style for their visit.

The layout was simple but elegant: a five-room suite hung with peach silk, furnished in the new Art Deco style, which, with its emphasis on oval panels and carvings of flower baskets, recalled an epoch a century old.

Outside, in the back of the house, the garden had been sectioned off into two unequal parts. Behind the main residence, old chestnut trees lined the partition wall and shaded a portion of the elegant lawn, through which two tortuous graveled paths wended their way. On both sides of the lawn, artfully landscaped flower beds cried out with color, as an arrangement of begonias, tulips, petunias, marigolds, and daisies of various hues brightened the formal garden and gave it life. A series of natural hedges nearly eclipsing the tall stone wall set off the delicate trellised arbors that bordered it.

Amelia stood pressing her nose against a glass pane in the gallery, and looked out at the white gazebo that was the crowning centerpiece of the garden. Someday, Amelia thought fervently, *I shall be mistress of a house like this; but who will be its master . . . ?*

Suddenly a tremendous depression settled over her. Every eligible bachelor in Vienna wanted to kiss her, would have given half his inheritance for the honor of marrying the Lady Amelia von Guttman; only one didn't care. Peter Habig, the haberdasher, could exist very well without her, letting weeks slip into months without making the least effort to gain access to her presence. He was seen about town escorting this widow and that divorcée, quite the social butterfly in spite of his socialistic pronouncements. *Perhaps I'm just a fool,* Amelia thought bitterly. *He probably doesn't even think of me unless coincidence throws us together. I'd be a greater fool to fall in love with him!*

But I'm *already* in love with him! she realized, closing her eyes to the unexpected heartache. I'm in love with a man who doesn't know I've left Vienna, and who wouldn't miss me even if he did. . . .

*   *   *

Charles felt his frilled silk shirt as a second skin, glued to his body. He wished he'd never agreed to attend the housewarming at La Folie. Now, whether he liked it or not, he was there, in the house that should have been *his.*

His mother had insisted that they come for the formal ball. Yet no sooner had Yvonne walked in, arm in arm with her son, than a gigantic middle-aged woman had descended on them and swooped his mother into a massive embrace. Stunned, he had watched them move away, their arms about each other's waists, and he'd surmised that this was the Viennese cousin, Countess Barbara von Guttman, his mother's childhood companion. He'd been left standing by himself, completely ignored and forgotten in the excitement of the two cousins meeting again.

He looked about for Anne, hoping to catch her eye and have somebody to talk to; he didn't know anyone, no one at all. He and his mother hadn't had the means to "enter society," and so this was his first sally into the world of the upper crust.

Apart from feeling slightly uncomfortable in his new tuxedo, he knew that he looked good. His tall stature, his good bone structure, his blue eyes and blond hair, and his small, lightly waxed mustache, all combined to give him an air of elegance money could not buy. Part of him was excited to be mingling with the powerful and wealthy, with Alfred and Anne's cohorts; and it further excited him to have the opportunity to watch beautiful women parading right in front of his eyes, close enough to touch.

He wasn't sure whether he liked the new fashion: girls with short, bobbed hair, their bodies excessively thin in their tube-shaped dresses. He was standing by himself in the gallery, looking out toward the garden, when suddenly a soft voice murmured: "It's a dream landscape, isn't it? Hundreds of tiny colored lights, strung through the leaves and flowers like the Christmas decorations in *The Nutcracker.*"

Turning slightly, he was taken aback by the young woman who had spoken to him. She was unusual . . . extraordinary. He thought that he had never seen such a lovely face, like fine Dresden china: blue-white skin, the tiniest upturned nose, soft pink lips, high, pronounced cheekbones, and eyes that captured the soul. Eyes of the deepest cobalt blue, and almond-shaped. Blinking, he let his eyes travel over her and found himself staring rudely at the woman's figure, encased in a tubelike dress, but curvaceous, with full breasts and hips below a small, teasing waist. A turquoise-blue gown to match her perfect eyes. Who *was* she?

She'd spoken to him with a slight accent. An almost imperceptible German accent, he thought, freezing. His own father had been German, predisposing him to dislike all Saxons, Jews and Gentiles alike. And after this war in which a million and a half young Frenchmen had perished, he wondered how a German girl could have the nerve to come to Paris—even a girl as beautiful as this one, with her lustrous black hair piled on top of her head in what was no longer the fashion but, annoyingly, became her nonetheless.

"You like the ballet, mademoiselle?" Charles asked, somewhat dryly.

She had moved next to him, and he could smell the rich scent of her perfume. She turned to look at him, tilting her head to the side: "I like all fairy tales," she remarked softly.

"And why is *that?* Is your own life monotonous, perhaps? Or is reality too dull for you, in general?"

His blue eyes were piercing into her, and he wondered why he was being so hard. She was so enchantingly beautiful, he almost needed to break the spell and reduce her to a flesh-and-blood girl, like the others around her. She sighed, then replied, "Why must it be one or the other? We've just emerged from a terrible war, monsieur. I think romance should be put back into our lives, to regenerate our spirits. In my city of Vienna, girls are brought up on romance. Is this so bad?"

She was blushing now, for she had caught him staring at her as she was speaking. Embarrassed, she introduced herself. "I'm Amelia von Guttman. Anne de Rochefleur's Austrian cousin."

Of course! An absurd desire to laugh came over him, and he surrendered to it helplessly. She frowned at him, more confused than ever. Abruptly, he stopped laughing, aware that he had been shamefully impolite in more ways than one.

"I'm sorry," he said. "It's just that, you see, you and I are cousins too—second cousins. And here I'd taken you for a brazen German fräulein, a foreign invader! I'm Charles Lévy, Yvonne's son; you must be Barbara's daughter."

Amelia smiled. Her smile made her even lovelier to him because it softened her eyes, lighting up her features. She put her small hand on his forearm and impulsively reached up to kiss him on the cheek. He felt embarrassed and entranced, as though in the presence of someone not quite human . . . a nymph, or one of the three Graces.

"How wonderful to finally meet," she declared warmly. "I, too, took you for a stranger. And I'm so glad we turned out to be relatives!"

"You're staying here at La Folie?"

She nodded. "It's so beautiful! Have you seen everything? Or should I take you through all the rooms?"

"Thanks, but no. This used to be my mother's house, so I know it well. It looks as if Alfred's remodeled quite a bit, however, from what I've glimpsed of the reception rooms."

"It was Anne, actually. Isn't she amazing?"

Charles felt himself beginning to relax. "Anne *is* a surprise, I must say. One wouldn't have expected anything quite so grand from her."

"Anne is two people in one. There's the quiet girl on the outside, who no one really knows; and then, there is somebody deep and pensive on the inside, who feels profoundly. But that's the private side of Anne, and we rarely get to see it."

"You're quite a philosopher, Amelia," he teased.

Again she blushed. "Oh, no. Richard's the brain. I'm just . . . well . . ."

"The beauty in the family?"

She very nearly turned away, totally embarrassed. "I don't want to be known for that," she murmured, her eyes suddenly moist and passionate. "What I look like has absolutely *nothing* to do with *me*, with who I really am! I mean, I don't control that, don't you see? And most people care only about that, and never bother to search below the surface."

"The way you did with Anne."

Amelia didn't reply. Instead, her eyes took on a faraway look: and Charles wondered, Who is she thinking of? He could feel himself growing edgy, and realized with a start that he was *jealous* of whoever Amelia had been thinking of, her face entranced. "Shall we take a stroll through the garden, Charles?" she asked at last.

"Of course. Whatever you'd like."

He offered her his arm, and she took it, leaning just enough against him so that her breast brushed against him. As they passed through the open doorway into the alley beyond, she turned to him

and asked mischievously, "Well? Do you still take me for the foreign invader?"

Before he could stop himself, he was answering her. "You've
simply invaded my heart," he told her, and they both had to look
away, flushing deeply. But it was all right. Charles knew he hadn't
offended her, that he could trust this girl. She had made this whole
wretched party all right, and his presence at La Folie meaningful
instead of simply painful. He wished he could go on, tell her other
things . . . but already his mother was approaching them, and
Amelia was letting go of his arm, her attention on the newcomer.

* * *

Why had her father pressed this overwhelming person on her?
Anne wondered. Was money *that* important? ". . . And then, my
dear, he simply took the curling iron and pressed a lock of my hair
through it, and I knew, absolutely, that he would be my slave
forever!" Arabella Fayard was telling her a story with overtones
that Anne understood and that acutely embarrassed her—a story
about her hairdresser, of all people.

"Who does *your* hair?" Arabella suddenly demanded.

"Marthe does . . . my chambermaid," Anne stammered.

"It shows, darling. Come with me, and I'll take you to Antoine.
It's *the* place these days. Nobody who is *anybody* goes to dull old
Dondel anymore, and for heaven's sake, *nobody* stays at home and
lets her maid do it! What does a *maid* know, anyway? Hair design
is an art, not a household chore."

Anne tried to smile, but tears were pushing their way into her
eyes, and she could feel every hair on her head weighing her down,
making her heavier and more sluggish. Marthe had done elaborate
things up there, interweaving strands of pearls through the curls,
and now Anne thought: It's true. Everybody else here has bobbed
hair—everyone but the old ladies and Amelia, that is; and Amelia
is so beautiful, she could get away with being bald!

The party was proceeding well; her father was pleased. But
Anne's feet were hurting from going up and down the stairs at least
twenty times, taking guests up to view the upper floors. Women
she'd never met before were continually walking up to her and
whispering, "I hear you've done wonders in the private quarters.
Now, I realize that no one should be bold enough to intrude there,
but given our long-standing friendship . . ." People were hypo-
crites, she thought bitterly; they differed only in the extent of their
particular hypocrisy.

Arabella Fayard was small and voluptuous, her blond hair trimmed in a chin-length bob, her green eyes slanted and catlike. Her ivory gown had a low, round neckline that proudly displayed two plump breasts pushed up by a tight brassiere . . . two creamy fruits, Anne thought meanly, intended to draw the attention of every male in the room.

Arabella was twenty-seven or -eight, and her husband was almost thirty years her senior. She was British: everybody knew this. But beyond that, nobody had been able to collect the slightest tidbit about her background—only that she was the steel magnate's second wife, and that he had brought her back from one of his trips, the way he might have brought home a famous work of art: proudly, smugly, and still somewhat awed by his prowess at having captured such a *rara avis*. She was attractive, stylish, and sensual; but she *wasn't a lady,* Anne thought, and no amount of money would ever be able to mask this deficiency.

All at once, among the sea of faces gathered around the richly laden hors d'oeuvre table, Anne spotted Charles Lévy. For a moment she was struck numb. How handsome and impressive he looked in his trim tuxedo. He was easily the most attractive man at this soirée. How broad were his shoulders, and how narrow his hips! She felt goose bumps spreading over her, and embarrassment. Hadn't he told her that he wouldn't come? She hadn't expected to see him, and now all her feelings of desire were cropping up again, as well as the yearning to be near him, to listen to his voice, to smell his scent, to—

"Who are you looking at so intensely?" Arabella's mocking voice broke in.

Anne shook the shameful thoughts from her head, and replied softly: "Just my cousin Charles. I didn't think he'd be able to come here tonight."

"Which one is he?"

"The tall young man with the blue eyes and blond hair. Over there."

Arabella's eyes fastened on Charles, and Anne watched her staring at him. The woman was cold and shrewd, her face inscrutable. For a minute she looked at the young man, then turned back to Anne and declared: "So little Anne has a mysterious cousin. What a good-looking man he is . . . *my word*! Like a proud peacock, standing among plucked chickens! I'd be most interested in meeting him, darling. But not right now. I feel a sudden urge to pay a visit to the powder room and run a comb through my hair!"

Anne watched her retreat, slim hips undulating beneath the tight silk of her ivory skirt. Something about the woman made Anne suddenly apprehensive. She looked at Charles, and saw him laughing with his mother and their cousin Amelia. No, Madame Fayard, Anne thought defensively. You aren't going to meet Charles. I don't like you, and he wouldn't either. You're cheap and common, and he doesn't need to be placed in contact with the likes of *you*.

* * *

Too many things were happening at once. Charles could feel his heart hammering inside his chest, and it was almost painful. Why had Amelia affected him this way? He was grateful for the momentary lull in the conversation, which had allowed him to excuse himself to repair to an upstairs bathroom, where he was hoping to sort out his feelings in private.

The hallway stretched out was in semidarkness, pierced by carefully arranged electric candles ensconced in recessed niches along the wall. Lost as he was in his own thoughts, he didn't see the woman in the hall. "My goodness!" she murmured, and he realized he had nearly bumped right into her.

"I'm dreadfully sorry! I wasn't looking."

"Yes, I can see that!" She was an attractive woman, and his eyes couldn't help but be drawn to that bosom, so exposed, so tender, so peaches-and-cream. "Really, monsieur," she was saying. "The very least you could do after giving me such a scare, is to bring me a glass of Dom Pérignon!"

She was a little older than he . . . maybe five years. She looked so self-assured, tawny and resilient like a jungle puma. Charles had had very little experience with society women, and suddenly the young man felt confused, inept by comparison.

Now, ashamed of his social clumsiness, he blushed and stammered, "Of course. I'd be glad to." He turned back to the staircase, in search of Goujon, the maître d'hôtel, who was gliding from room to room on the main floor, bearing a tray of champagne glasses. Halfway down the stairs, Charles realized he had never introduced himself to the sultry blonde.

When he returned to the upstairs corridor, she was standing in the very spot where he had left her. She plucked the coupe from his hand and dipped her lips into it, then threw her head back and downed the entire glass. When she was finished, she smiled at him, pleased, and wiped the wetness from her lips with the back of her hand, like a naughty child. It made him break into laughter.

"Aren't you curious to learn who I am?" she asked him, her green eyes narrowing as they examined him. But she gave him no time to answer. "I know who *you* are. You're Baron Alfred's cousin, Charles Lévy."

"Indeed I am. But—"

"I'm Arabella Fayard."

"Oh!" he murmured, impressed. Everyone knew about Armand Fayard, the tough, brainy manipulator at the head of France's steel industry. "Are you . . . his daughter?"

The blonde laughed, a deep, sensual laugh. "How very sweet you are," she declared, reaching up to touch his cheek for the most fleeting instant. "I'm his wife."

He felt himself color with embarrassment. Arabella Fayard shook her head, amused. "Don't worry. I took it as a welcome compliment. Haven't you learned yet that flattery will get you *anywhere* with a woman . . . ?"

And then she turned on her heel and glided away. He stood in the semidarkness, more confused than ever. What a strong woman this was . . . so magnetic and primitive beneath her sophisticated attire. A different kind of woman altogether from his Viennese nymph, so softly romantic and gentle.

Amelia, he thought, almost guiltily. I must return downstairs, to find her. Charles was surprised to discover that feelings that had lain dormant all his life all at once emerged, with the appearance of Amelia von Guttman, onto the stage of his existence. Quickly he dismissed the voluptuous Arabella from his thoughts, eagerly rushing down to look for his image of perfection, his vision of loveliness, his Amelia.

* * *

Charles swallowed a mouthful of Scotch and felt the smooth liquor warming its way to his stomach. The den, with its fine Gainsborough hunting scene, its engravings and polished oak paneling, was too hot; Alfred had started a small fire in the enormous hearth, although it was springtime and this was just for show.

With his back directly to the fireplace, Charles could almost feel the flames reaching out threatening to scorch him. But he couldn't change his position: he was the youngest man present, and had it not been for Anne, he would not even have been included. It was she who had taken his arm and brought him to her father and his friends, announcing: "Papa dear, surely you didn't mean to leave Charles all alone with the ladies!"

But the omission had been intentional, Charles was certain. Alfred had acknowledged him with a brief smile that hadn't reached his impenetrable eyes, and a dry introduction: "Gentlemen, our cousin, Charles Lévy . . ." And Charles had looked around the den and recognized the faces, all well known, most of them, like Alfred himself, members of the all-powerful Bank of France, which managed the French government's finances.

He'd sought Anne's eyes and found them smiling at him, encouraging him to stay and not to be intimidated by the company into which she had thrown him. She *wants* me here, he thought. But *why*? And then it had come to him that she truly was his friend, and that she believed in him. That he belonged with these powerful men because he, too, was meant to become powerful; that a destiny of greatness was calling to him, in the form of this gathering in the de Rochefleur den.

Charles had endured three hours of festivities over various samplings of hors d'oeuvre, the tiny French quiches and brioches stuffed with cheese and vegetable pastes making way for real Russian *zakouski,* Anne's tribute to her mother's heritage. Now a formal dinner was about to be staged, and the gentlemen were fortifying themselves with various spirits before confronting Alfred's extravaganza. Charles touched his black bow tie and gave his attention to the man who was his supreme boss, but whom he'd never before met in person.

Albert Meyer spoke in staccato sentences, and already Charles imagined himself parodying his pronouncements to amuse his mother, Amelia, and Anne. The Old Man of the French railroad industry—thin, shoulders drooping, long nose, sagging cheeks—resembled the gnarled limb of an aging tree. "The League of Nations wants only to rob us of our hard-earned victory!" he expostulated for the third time that evening. "Wilson is a dreamer!"

"Better a Wilson than a Lenin," Alfred countered. "You're speaking to one who's experienced the revolution!"

"Nonsense! I don't like *any* foreigner telling us how to run our affairs! When we allowed Clemenceau to resign, we were allowing softness and sloth to take over our courageous nation! It was the Tiger who brought us to victory, not those mealymouthed Americans jumping in at the last minute!" Meyer had turned red in the face and was sputtering with excitement.

"Come now, Albert," a strong, thickset man next to him interposed. "Calm yourself. Let's face the facts, shall we? The Tiger has grown senile, and our country is still wounded. Up north and in the east, where we're revamping the old German ironworks, the devastation is so pathetic, we shall need all the help the government can give us. As a premier, Millerand will be all right; I know he was once a socialist, but there's no one more ardent than a convert. He's a good leader for our newly elected parliament. No, I believe we're headed for an era of prosperity; the French people are waking up, and that's why they elected so many returning veterans to the Assembly. It's *they* who'll keep Lenin and his damn Red Plague outside our gates, once and for all! They've fought a war, and they don't want another!"

Charles was impressed. He'd recognized this man at once, from descriptions and caricatures in *Le Figaro* and *Le Temps,* whose business sections he eagerly devoured each day. *Fayard.* Armand Fayard, head of the Fayard Steel Industries; who wouldn't have known him? Charles couldn't help recalling the small, shapely blonde in the ivory gown, and wondering about her with the steel magnate—an unusual couple, to be sure. Pretending to examine the Scotch in his glass, he observed Fayard surreptitiously from beneath lowered lashes.

This was a proud man, a pioneer, an entrepreneur. He was younger than Meyer, perhaps fifty-four or -five. Not as tall as the Old Man, but stockier: a man reputed to work out with lifts and weights in a suite in his twenty-room mansion in Versailles. He looked like a bulldog, with heavy jowls that were blue-black with five-o'clock shadow. His thick hair, more pepper than salt, had been clipped into an American crewcut, and his virility was evident.

This is the kind of man *I'd* like to become, Charles thought. Brought up by a woman, with only his grandfather, Guy, to emulate, Charles suddenly felt the familiar yearning for a father at this point in his life. Fayard had unexpectedly turned and was now addressing him, his voice raspy and his tone direct.

"You're a young man, Lévy. And our new Chamber is a young one too. Do *you* believe we have any realistic reason for fearing Gospodin Lenin?"

Charles swallowed. Armand Fayard was watching him intently. He felt caught short, and weighed the risks of daring to disagree with the man who controlled his fate. The small group of businessmen were all looking at him expectantly. He caught Alfred's dark eye, telling him to tread softly, not to alienate any of his important cohorts . . . and it was this patronizing warning that finally impelled him to speak.

"I think you're right, monsieur," he replied, directing his reply to the steelman. "What the French nation must concentrate on right now is not politics so much as economics. We need to rebuild, and we need to put to good use those raw materials yielded to us by the postwar acquisition of Alsace and Lorraine. If we spend too much time worrying about Lenin and Trotsky, I'm afraid we'll be spinning our wheels. Russia is like a wounded hippopotamus; it needs to heal before it can be strong enough to start attacking its smaller neighbors. And as for the Americans, they're too far away, and they're tired of meddling in our affairs. Wilson's dream of uniting with Europe has made him look ridiculous among other statesmen: his own Senate refused to ratify the League! My guess is, it won't accomplish anything noteworthy."

Alfred's smile had frozen as Charles spoke, but now it turned yet more ingratiating as he placed a hand on Old Man Meyer's shoulder. "You gentlemen may not know that our young cousin is a Swiss national. His observations, you understand—"

"I understand only that he makes sense, my dear Alfred," Fayard cut in. And in this instant of recognition, man to man, Charles's anxiety was suddenly released, like air being let out of a balloon, and he understood as well how Arabella might have fallen for this much older but strong and virile human being. The small blond woman drinking champagne, triumph in her eye . . . Was she pleased and proud to be his wife? Yes, she had spoken her name as one flashes a brand new diamond, to dazzle her audience as well as herself. The Fayards made a vital, vibrant pair, strangely well matched in spite of the age difference between them. . . .

And all at once, Charles's mind wandered, and to his horror he found himself imagining nights of passionate sex between Armand Fayard and the pretty blonde. And from an image of them together, his thoughts jumped absurdly (or *was* it so absurd?) to himself and Arabella. He hadn't had such sexual hunger since his teens, and had to admit that the reason was that he was starved. When was the last time he had really made love to a woman, wanting to drown in the waves of her passion, explore every curve of her body?

But that's not who I really want, he thought, miserable and

ashamed of his lustful fantasies. I want a woman who will be more
than a bedmate, more than a mistress. I want a soulmate, someone
I can alternately talk to and worship: I want Amelia, the most
unattainable woman in the world, because she is an ideal. . . . Yet
I want to make her real, my own reality. *I want her to become
aware that I am special—I want her to fall in love with me and want
me too. . . .*

I must become *someone,* he thought, desperate. *Someone powerful and undaunted, like Armand Fayard.* Right now, Charles was a
nobody without a coin in his purse, and Amelia, a wealthy heiress
accustomed to the finest luxuries. Yet she was the woman for
whom he'd plodded through twenty-two years of pitiful existence
. . . the one who would make every last effort worthwhile after
all.

Money bought love, didn't it? Fayard's riches had obviously
helped, or he would never have obtained such a young, exciting
wife as Arabella. No, to win Amelia, Charles would need extra
leverage . . . something through which to attain fame and fortune. Till then, he'd simply have to bide his time and hold his
enthusiasm in check. If she'd waited until her twenty-first year,
Amelia couldn't be at all desperate to marry. She'd wait . . .
while he built his own empire, and made his own way.

CHAPTER VII

"Countess von Guttman is on the line, for *you*," Froncenet announced in his punctilious tone of voice.

Charles felt a rush of excitement, followed by an abysmal letdown: it had to be Barbara, not Amelia! Calling him *here*, at work? He stared back at his superior, annoyed at the man's condescension, then walked out of the drafting room to the receptionists' cubicle.

A pretty girl handed him a telephone receiver, and, his heart in his throat, he said: "Hello . . . it's Charles."

Merry laughter rang in his ear. "Charlie! It's me, Amelia! Tell me, was it really bad form to ring you up over *there*?"

"No, no, of course not! It's . . . I mean, I'm always pleased to hear from you. Nothing's wrong, is it?"

What a silly thing to say! Nobody called up laughing when something was wrong. But she was plunging ahead, her voice tripping like a lilting brook rushing over rocks and pebbles. "I saw an advertisement in *Le Figaro*," she announced. "It was for a *thé dansant* at the Select. Uncle Alfred was appalled! He said the editor at *Le Temps* calls the new dance craze more dangerous than the Spanish influenza! Shall we throw caution to the winds and go? You, Richard, me, and Anne!"

An absurd delight made Charles feel light-headed, as though he'd consumed an excess of champagne. "When?" he asked.

"Today! Look, Richard and I are leaving on Thursday. We still *waltz* in Vienna. I want to be able to show my friends how young people dance in Paris! The tango, especially—I adore the tango! Will you come?"

He shook his head helplessly. "I can't. I'm at work. But perhaps, if you could wait, I could go with you this evening. There's a dance place that's quite nice on the Avenue Montaigne—"

"Oh, all *right!*" she cried, pretending to be peeved at him for being such a stick-in-the-mud. He'd never experienced this before: a beautiful girl teasing him, taunting him, flirting so obviously. Was she a flirt, or was it that she actually *liked* him? Or perhaps this was simply the way young women behaved in Vienna.

"Monsieur Lévy," the operator said, "we need the receiver back."

In a daze, he handed it back to her. Dancing. He'd test her feelings tonight . . . what she *really* thought of him. What better place than a dance hall?

* * *

"For Anne's birthday in September, Uncle Alfred's going to give her a black Bentley, upholstered in bottle-green leather," Amelia said, sensually reclining in her chair. Her fox-trimmed evening jacket had slipped off her bare shoulders, and Charles couldn't take his eyes from their appealing alabaster curves. He wanted to reach out and touch them, first the left, then the right, letting his fingers dwell on her soft, fragrant skin.

"That's very nice of him," he replied stupidly. On the dance floor, elegant Richard von Guttman was doing the one-step with Anne, who was red in the face from exertion.

"I think it's a silly present, frankly," Amelia stated. "Anne doesn't know how to drive. She'll have to hire a chauffeur just to use her own car. She's afraid to learn."

"While you, on the other hand, would love nothing better than to learn how to parachute down from the skies," he teased. "Do *you* drive in Vienna?"

"Sometimes. My friend Nanni von Stecher—"

Charles didn't want to hear about people he didn't know, in faraway places. He wanted Amelia to stay in Paris, never to leave again. Thursday was just three days off, and then she'd be gone, and she'd forget him so easily among all her cheerful acquaintances. Her "smart set." He *had* to tell her, then, didn't he?

"Would you like to dance this one?" he asked. It was a long, lingering tango. He'd be touching her and brushing against her. Amelia was already on her feet, casting off the offending jacket with a quick shrug of her shoulders. What would it cost him but his pride, if she rejected him . . . ?

* * *

It was a good thing she'd kept in shape, Amelia thought, dipping back precariously, her fluid body held in check only by Charles's hand on the small of her back. She hadn't had such a good time in centuries . . . in *eons*! The orchestra was wonderful, the Negro saxophonist *such* an exotic character. And Charles really was a *good* dancer, better than most of the men she knew in Vienna. Better than that infuriating Peter . . .

Charles likes me, she thought, smiling at him. When he smiled back, he smiled with his entire face. His eyes softened, as if he held her, like a small swallow, in the palm of his hand. He made her feel . . . vulnerable.

He was a much better-looking man than that good-for-nothing Peter Habig, who hadn't even sent her roses for her birthday. The entire house on the Ringstrasse had been decorated with roses: three hundred long-stemmed roses of different varieties, sent by dozens of lovesick young men. But not even a single red rose from Peter. She'd waited all day . . . for nothing. And *everyone* knew that Amelia von Guttman celebrated her twentieth birthday on the twenty-eighth of April.

He didn't send anything *just to hurt my feelings,* she thought, the wound reopening at the memory. He loved to slight her, make her feel insignificant. And here she'd been waiting, like a fool, for him to finally come forward . . . for him to claim her, ask her to marry him. . . .

Stop dreaming, Amelia! she chided, tears blurring her eyes. What had actually taken place between them? Meetings at other people's receptions, waltzes at other people's balls. And once, an early morning chance encounter in the park, both of them on horseback. Afterward, he had invited her to the Sacher for Viennese coffee, spiced and hot, and some sweet breakfast cakes. Across the table, his dark, velvet eyes had stroked her face, making her feel all warm inside, as though mercury were coursing through her veins. Accidentally, his booted foot had touched hers, and he had smiled, knowingly. An intimate kind of smile—as between, yes, *lovers.* She'd felt swept up in an eddy of embarrassment, as though instead of their toes touching, she had accidentally brushed against . . . against . . . As he helped her back onto Mufti's saddle, his hand had pressed hers. He had bent his head to . . . kiss her? She'd hesitated, one toe already poised in the stirrup, but he had straightened up almost at once. Everything between us has been an *almost,* Amelia thought, disgusted.

It wouldn't do for Charles to see her cry. They'd come here to have a good time, and that horrible Peter wasn't going to spoil it for her, as he had spoiled so many other evenings by ignoring her or pretending to be interested in other women, none half so attractive as she was. . . .

Anne was nowhere in sight; she'd probably excused herself to go to the ladies' room, because Richard was sitting down alone at their table, ordering more champagne from the waiter. The music died away and suddenly Amelia was drooping exhaustedly on Charles's arm and he was asking, "Would you mind if we went for a small walk, just you and I?"

Tremendously depressed, but refusing to give in, she looked up at Charles's chiseled face, right into the deep blue of his beautiful eyes, ringed with perfect black lashes. He was *so* much more classically perfect than Peter . . . so much nicer, too. "I'd love it," she replied, forcing her mouth into an exaggerated smile of pleasure.

The Champs-Elysées loomed wider than the Ringstrasse, Amelia thought, hugging her fox jacket. A thin breeze was blowing scents of horse chestnut flowers and smoke, women's perfume and the smell of exhaust fumes.

An inky sky was dotted with the full panorama of the Milky Way, each constellation clearly delineated above the two young people and the rooftops of Paris. Charles took her hand and she never even thought to withdraw it. Instead, she smiled at him.

They were walking toward the Arc de Triomphe, lit up this midnight into eerie majesty. A full moon added to the lights of the streetlamps, and Amelia thought: *I don't want to go home.*

"Oh, Charlie," she whispered. "I wish there was a way I could stay here, in the most beautiful city in the world, with you, and Anne! Vienna breaks my heart. It's never recovered from defeat. Now when I walk around there, I smell decay. People have lost hope."

She stopped, and he gazed down at her in the yellow reflection of a gaslight. His face seemed older, the lines from his nose to his strong, well-defined mouth more pronounced. He had the face of a man of responsibility, of someone who was thoughtful, careful . . . and sad. She raised her hand and touched his face. "Dear Charles," she murmured. "How good you've been to me during this visit . . . and you didn't even know me!"

"I know you now." He took her hand from his cheek and enveloped it between both of his hands, ever so gently massaging her chilled fingers. They stood there silently, not even smiling, and then, simultaneously, they resumed their strolling pace toward the Arc.

"I would have thought you'd be dying to go home," he remarked to her. "All your suitors will be waiting for you at the train depot."

She laughed once, shortly. "What do *you* know of my suitors, Monsieur Levy? Has my brother been giving you an earful?"

"*Should* he have been?"

She blinked, and regarded him a little quizzically. "What do you mean?"

"Are there a lot of suitors?"

"Oh," she answered, shrugging vaguely. "*You* know. They come and they go, like rainstorms in springtime—"

"And there's no one special?"

This time she stopped, beneath a wonderful old tree by the roadside. "Why?"

"Why aren't you married, Amelia?"

"Why aren't *you,* Charles?"

He swallowed and looked away, unable to sustain the searching stare of her cobalt eyes. Unrelenting eyes. She wasn't going to yield an inch to help him along. And so he said, "There are two reasons why I'm not. The first should be obvious: I've only been at Meyer Frères for a year, and I don't have any money. No girl worth her while would take me under those conditions."

"And the second?"

"I had to wait for the Viennese Diana to come on her white horse, and call in her hounds. The most enticing huntress in the world has cornered my hart—or shall I say, my *heart?*"

Amelia started. Then, overcome with embarrassment, she half turned away, biting her lower lip. "No," she stammered. "You don't really mean that."

"I *don't*? Somehow I was certain that I did. Amelia . . . I don't want you to leave, you must realize that! I care for you a great deal more than simply as a cousin."

Distress tightened her features, and she laced her fingers nervously together. "Oh, Charles . . ."

"You have somebody else? Tell me, Amelia!"

Quickly she conjured up a vision of Peter. Tall, lean, smart, his dark eyes seeing so much more than he chose to talk about. Or was *she* the one who had always seen too much? Ruthless now with herself, she thought: Peter Habig owes me nothing! I'm the one who wanted more—he never promised me a thing! And now, here is the most handsome Apollo I've set eyes on in Paris, and instead of enjoying myself, I'm continuing this absurd charade of a romance *that will never be*! Wake up, Amelia! Charles is attractive. Maybe if he kissed me just once, I could see if I could bear it? And . . . *I might just have a good time*!

Carefully, she turned back to him. "No," she replied softly. "There's no one."

The only way to force Peter Habig out of her heart was by bringing back reality, by having fun, by being young and carefree and enjoying this beautiful vacation. Charles was looking at her gravely. "I love you, Amelia. I wish there was some way I could marry you right now and keep you beside me."

Dismayed, Amelia shook her head. "No!" she cried. "Don't, Charles! No, don't even mention this! I don't even want to *think* of marriage!"

"Why not?" he questioned, his voice caressing her like a warm breeze.

She attempted to laugh, shrugging a little abruptly. "It's so—so *serious*, Charlie! Hardly appropriate for an evening of frenzied dancing and carefree laughter and jokes. I want to pretend I'm a child again, and you, too, and that we've been let loose inside a gigantic playground called Paris. Let's play, and to hell with problems—ours, and the world's! All right?"

Instead of replying, he bent down, put his hand beneath her chin, and kissed her. She gave in to the kiss, parting her lips and feeling the petaled softness of his lips, tiny pillows of warmth that covered her mouth. He placed both arms around her and drew her tightly against him, and with a soft moan she allowed his body to press her against the tree. There was a male hardness beneath his belt that she could feel, and, oddly, it excited her.

She let Charles kiss her, kissing him back, and for a moment the pain of Peter seemed to dissipate. Perhaps this is exactly what I need to remind myself of who I am! she thought. I cannot allow any man to swallow me up and do with me what he will.

"I love you, Amelia, and I shall always love you," Charles was murmuring, loosening his embrace. He appeared overcome with emotion. Somewhat dazed, Amelia stood catching her breath, pulling her little jacket back over her shoulders and touching her disheveled hair. Then she looked up, and blinked.

"Charles," she said, mortified. But he was still gazing at her with adoration, unaware of anyone but the two of them beneath the sky of jet hammered with pavé diamonds.

Anne and Richard were standing not two feet away, staring at them. And Anne's face mirrored horror, repugnance, and disbelief.

"Anne," Amelia said tonelessly. "Richard. You both surprised us . . ."

But Anne had turned abruptly and started to run down the Champs-Elysées, toward the Place de la Concorde. Amelia turned to Charles, whose mouth had fallen open, and to her brother, who simply shook his head in bewilderment.

"Don't ask *me*," Richard declared. "*I*'m just the spectator who walked in late."

* * *

Anne's world was like a calm sea suddenly struck by a tidal wave. Tears blurred the light from the streetlamps as she ran down the Champs-Elysées, but all she wanted was to put as great a distance between her and *them* as she possibly could.

Anguish gripped her; she could feel the pain tearing through her like a malignant poison. Her complicated headdress had come tumbling down, and she angrily brushed some wayward strands off her forehead. Finally she paused, tears streaming down her face, and fell onto a roadside bench, low, muffled moans escaping from her uncontrollably.

She couldn't think; she couldn't reason. Around her, everything appeared black and evil, cruel and hopeless. It felt to her as though her life had abruptly come to an end, and that she'd entered a no-man's-land that was neither death nor life but simply a palpable, crushing ache.

How could they have done this? How was it possible she hadn't seen this coming? Amelia, so bright and beautiful—and Charles, her beloved Charles, the easiest man in the world to adore, to fall in love with! *I am nothing, I am no one,* Anne thought, hating herself. This was her fault, as her own mother had so often predicted: she was a woman no man would want, except for her dowry, and a man like Charles, an honorable, hardworking man, would be unimpressed by her father's money.

Amelia had money too. Amelia had everything. The unfairness of the situation hit Anne like a blow on the head, and she doubled over, suddenly nauseated. She had not felt so alone, so torn apart, so bereaved, in her entire life. *She had lost a dream.*

It was already past midnight, and traffic had been reduced to a few stray revelers driving by with the hoods of their jalopies down, their laughter catching her ear: *people acting normally, as if her own pain was of no importance.* I am such a small fleck of dust on this miserable earth, Anne thought with agonizing self-pity. And then she heard a car's brakes screeching, and a man cursing aloud. She raised her tear-filled eyes and saw a Rolls-Royce stopping right in front of her; a stocky man was emerging from the driver's seat.

Instinctively, she straightened and pressed her back rigidly against the wooden bench. She felt a surge of panic. The man in the dark shadows looked vaguely familiar. *All I need now is to run into an acquaintance,* she thought desperately.

The man had reached her now, and stood right in front of her; she noted his tall opera hat, his black coat with its thick seal collar, and knew that she knew him. A raspy voice, like an aging pugilist's, said urgently: "Mademoiselle Anne, whatever reason you have for being out here without an escort, it isn't safe. You must let me take you home."

With a start, Anne recognized Armand Fayard, the industrialist. A wave of embarrassment overpowered her, and she stammered: "Really, monsieur, it's all right . . . I'm all right! I don't want to go home."

Armand Fayard was a strong man, compact and imposing. When he bent down to her, she could smell cigar breath and a light cologne. "Come, you need a drink," he was telling her assertively. "A cognac perhaps. Evidently, young lady, you're very upset."

And he was pulling her up, urging her toward his car. It wasn't until he had shut the door on his own side, and revved up the engine, that she looked at him and asked timidly: "Where are we going?"

"Somewhere quiet where we can talk. And where the gossipmongers won't be able to see us. I have a small pied-à-terre not far from here, for the nights when I'm working late, or when Arabella and I have planned a night on the town. Driving back and forth to Versailles can be a damn nuisance!"

Anne felt her eyes well up with tears, and thought, violently: *Who gives a damn?* He and his Arabella can both go to hell, for all I care! She cared only about Charles, and about his feelings for Amelia. But Fayard continued speaking. "Your father and I are very different men, but I've always liked him, though we've never exactly been friends. We met years ago, in engineering school. We were miles apart at the time. In those days I was poor, with only

my ambition to guide me; he was the son of one of the richest
bankers in Europe. But somehow I always knew that my luck
would change. And, oddly enough, it was on his recommendation
that your grandfather, Baron Henri, arranged my first loan so I
could buy an ironworks mill in the Terrenoire district. That was
one of the last times I saw Alfred; only a few weeks later, I learned
through the grapevine that he had gone to Saint Petersburg to
marry a Russian heiress . . . your mother!"

Twin tears spilled over onto Anne's cheeks, and she brushed
them away with her fingers. "That's very nice," she replied tonelessly.

He turned to look at her and smiled. His small, dark eyes were
gleaming with sympathy. "But you couldn't care less, am I right? I
was just telling you this so that you'd understand why I couldn't
possibly have left you sitting there alone. The de Rochefleurs have
been in and out of my life for too many years! And so we're going
to ignore protocol, and you're going to come upstairs with a crusty
old married man who's going to light a fire in the hearth and listen
to your confessions."

He pulled up in front of a venerable granite house fronted by an
imposing oak door. Anne didn't know which street they had
turned down, but recognized the general area: it was near the Ritz
Hotel, close to her father's office. She allowed Armand Fayard to
help her down onto the pavement, feeling as though she were walking through a dream.

There was an unreal quality to this chance meeting, coupled
with the unspoken pressure not to displease or contradict this man
because of his long-standing association with her father. She felt
oddly trapped, as when Alfred had told her to escort Arabella
Fayard through their house. All her life she'd done as her parents
had instructed, and she could almost hear her father's echo admonishing her to follow this man, because he was a heavy depositor at the Crédit Industriel.

His flat was on the first floor, and when he unlocked the door,
Anne was surprised. Finely lacquered Oriental furniture had been
disposed all around a beautiful square living room, and a Japanese
ink drawing, hundreds of years old, adorned the area above the
fireplace. This was indeed a charming room. "Arabella has fine
taste," she said, to fill the empty silence.

He turned to her, irony painting an amused smile over his features. "In here it's *my* taste," he informed her. "Arabella has her own fun with Versailles."

"I see." Anne sat down on a silk print sofa and folded her hands primly in her lap. Fayard teased the logs in the fireplace, his back to her. This man was comfortable with his own physical power: he moved with the ease of a ballet dancer, though he was built like a sumo wrestler and wasn't young. He was the most masculine man she had ever observed, a man without any shadow of a woman's soul. Whereas Charles had the grace of a polished matinée idol, with a gentler sophistication, and her father had a physical cowardice most often attributed to women. Fayard turned around, went to a cabinet inlaid with red and green designs, and took out a crystal decanter and two brandy snifters. After he had poured out two generous servings, he came to Anne and sat down beside her, handing her a glass. "Cheers," he declared, downing a third of his brandy.

What am I doing here? Anne wondered, swallowing the warming cognac and feeling strangely lightened of her burden. "Tell me, Mademoiselle Anne, about young women today," Fayard was asking. "Whatever caused you to be so unhappy? I was under the impression that all you young ladies of the world lived only to have fun!"

"I . . ." All at once, before she could suppress them, the tears came back. She tried to swallow them, but found a sob breaking loose from her throat. Helplessly embarrassed, she covered her face with her hands and burst into tears.

"My dear Anne!" Fayard put a warm hand on the back of her neck, which only served to make her sob more hysterically. "Come now." He began to rub her neck gently. This time she turned away, and pressed her face against the pillows of the sofa to hide her grief.

"No one should be this unhappy," Fayard stated. "Who did this to you? What happened?"

Anne shook her head hopelessly. "I'm so alone . . . so miserable! My cousin Charles is in love with Amelia, and . . . and . . . I've wanted him for over a year! Ever since he came back from Switzerland, I've been hoping he'd notice me, that he'd fall in love with me . . ."

Armand Fayard raised his brows, appraising her, his hand still on her back. "You're too young for love to be treating you so cruelly. Come now, a sweet girl like you ought to have many other beaux than an impoverished cousin."

She jerked up, startled. "You know about Charles?"

Fayard looked away uncomfortably. "Alfred mentioned his situation in passing. And you yourself introduced us, if you'll remember, at La Folie. A very smart young man."

"Do you think . . . Papa doesn't know . . . ?"

"About your feelings? No, not at all. But he certainly wouldn't approve were you to pursue this young man with marriage on your mind. Marriage is serious business, Anne. Your father's an important man. That makes *you* an important woman."

All at once, Anne was galvanized into heated debate. "Isn't a man's *character* the most important thing, Monsieur Fayard?" she cried. "Look at your own story! You weren't born to wealth, like Papa! And yet you're perhaps the more important personality of the two!"

He smiled. "In my own fashion. And, of course, you're right. Charles Lévy impressed me when I met him. He reminded me a little of myself at his age. Ambitious, measured, and sharp. But you could find the same qualities in a man of your own position. It's just as easy to fall in love with a rich man as it is with a poor one: or didn't my wife explain that to you?" His eyes were twinkling now, with faint irony.

Anne stared at him, perplexed. Who *was* this man? she wondered. A powerful industrialist who ruled over a growing empire; a man whose ambitions had been fulfilled, whose friends presided over the French economy; a man who had married a beautiful woman young enough to be his own daughter: yet somehow . . . not truly a happy man. A certain wistfulness sometimes appeared in his eyes, as though he were regretting a lost opportunity, or mourning a lost adventure. Here was a vigorous, healthy man who seemed to be in absolute control of his own existence, and yet he gave the impression of being as alone as Anne herself. So it wasn't just a matter of power. . . .

He sighed. "Love is a strange condition. There's blind love, which can kill us. And then there's the gentle love that's based on mutual understanding, and that can give us life. If Charles loves this Amelia, then it would appear that he doesn't understand *you* at all. You have much to offer. A young man should see through the tangle of curls you've created on that pretty head of yours, and appreciate the mind that ticks inside. A good mind is worth ten good figures, and a kind heart is worth one hundred. You, my dear, possess both."

Anne bit her lower lip, embarrassed. "Charles doesn't know I exist," she whispered. "How could he know I love him?"

"Tell him. I believe in being direct. That's how you'll compete with Amelia. Who *is* she, anyway?"

"My cousin. We're all cousins."

Fayard chuckled. Then, unexpectedly, he put a strong arm around Anne's shoulders and drew her to him in a warm, paternal embrace. At first she stiffened against it; then, relaxing, she laid her head on his chest and closed her eyes. An odd sort of peace was settling over her. Maybe Fayard was right: she'd speak to Charles and compete head-on with her Austrian rival, Amelia.

"You've been so kind to me, Monsieur Fayard," she said, picking up her brandy snifter and finishing off the cognac. The room seemed like a haven: warm, friendly, safe. "Kinder to me than Papa ever was, in all my life. He never took the time to speak to me about anything I thought was important."

Fayard tilted her chin up with his finger and peered at her. "That's a shame. You're very special. You make me think back to my youth, when I met my first wife. You're very much like her: solid, compassionate, gentle but strong. I like you, Anne de Rochefleur. . . . I like you a great deal."

The cognac had made her a little tipsy. Had Charles really kissed Amelia on the Champs-Elysées? Had any of this happened, or had she simply experienced a terrible nightmare? Which was reality and which was the dream? She looked around her, at the polished Oriental furniture, the beautiful silk screens, and the ink drawing over the fireplace. What was she doing here? She felt confused, but singularly comforted. Perhaps there was some hope, after all.

"Monsieur Fayard—"

She found herself speaking at the same time as he, and they both laughed, she awkwardly, he with warm amusement. "I simply wanted to thank you," she said modestly.

"And I wanted to thank *you*. You made me realize that there still exists purity of feeling among mankind, that interest, and greed, rule only some of us."

This virtual stranger had made her feel better. He'd listened as if he cared. Timidly, she placed her hand over his, and smiled.

An expression Anne couldn't understand passed over his blunt, masculine features. He turned away. Then, abruptly, he faced her, reaching over to take her by the shoulders with both hands. She knit her brow, puzzled. "We are each of us an island, stretching out with all our might to make a connection," he said.

"What about Arabella?" she couldn't help asking.

He sighed. "Arabella . . . Arabella is *herself*. I understand her drives and her subterfuges, and I think she's smart enough to have surmised this. Beyond that . . ." His voice trailed off, and he caressed her cheek. "My dear, sweet Anne . . ."

She didn't move. It felt so good, so comforting, to be caressed by this rough man. He liked her. Nobody had ever liked her before. She'd hoped that Charles might like her, and had believed Amelia did. Only now, what did any of this matter?

His fingers lingered on her smooth, flushed cheek. He fascinated her: the coal-black eyes, the thick nose and lips, his crewcut . . . Then, abruptly, he swept her into his arms and was kissing her, pressing his lips over hers, parting them and thrusting his tongue into her mouth. The breath was knocked out of her, and she let him do it, the room tilting to one side from the brandy and the emotions of the evening.

Anne tried to cry out, but he was kissing her and she had never been kissed by anyone before. She had to push him away, had to do something! Why was he kissing her? And then, as she was pushing him away, he bent down and kissed her throat, and her cry died inside. His lips felt good on her skin, it was exciting, just as the novels she had read on the sly had promised! It felt good, and he liked her, and best of all, she wasn't alone.

It did no good to try to sort things out. The cognac was taking effect, and she felt lethargic, incapable of fighting back. And then, before she knew what was happening, he was touching her, exploring her face with his strong fingers, touching her throat, her collarbone, the tops of her breasts. Anne could feel her nipples hardening, and colored deeply with embarrassment. Yet he didn't notice a thing, his face closed and intense, looking hard at her and yet not seeing *her*, Anne. . . .

Was this how men wanted to possess a woman? she asked herself, unable to prevent her own hands from reaching out and touching his face, feeling the hard bristles of his beard. In this strange, exotic room, everything seemed permitted . . . any conversation, any revelation, any behavior. *Any intimacy.* She closed her eyes, pretending she wasn't here, that instead she was some-

where alone with Charles, on a warm, moonlit night in the tropics.
She wanted him to hold her, kiss her . . . do with her whatever
he pleased, whatever his male nature demanded of her, his
woman . . .

She'd drunk the cognac too quickly. The room was spinning and
spinning around, and she knew, without understanding or wanting
to understand, that her evening gown was being peeled off her
shoulders. The flames from the fire were reaching out, making her
too hot, causing her heart to beat erratically, too quickly . . .

"Anne, Anne!" Fayard was calling, his words muffled. Now he
was lying right on top of her and she thought, *No! Not this!* But he
was much stronger than she, and she didn't have the will to fight
him off. With a cry she attempted to prevent him from pulling her
skirt off, but there was no skirt, he'd already gotten rid of it: she
was lying completely naked on the Oriental sofa . . .

Afterward, when everything was over, she cried out in pain and
humiliation, grabbing her gown off the floor to cover herself. The
effects of the cognac had worn off; stark reality was settling in. She
was here with a stranger, to whom she had told everything, about
Charles, about Amelia. And he had done *this* to her . . .

Armand Fayard was nowhere to be seen. She raised herself on
an elbow, peering around the room. And then he appeared, completely dressed, immaculate, and she shivered with shame, unable
to look at him. He walked over to the sofa and handed her a large
towel. "I'm sorry," he was saying to her, his voice quiet but
strangely guiltless. "I really had no idea that it was your first time.
Most girls your age . . . in this world we live in . . ."

Tears spilled down her cheeks. "No," she whispered. "It was my
own fault. I should never have come up here with you, Monsieur
Fayard." And then, her chin trembling, she managed to look at
him. "Please, where can I get changed?"

Later, when they were driving back toward Saint-Germain-en-
Laye, she looked out at the starry sky and thought: *Something
happened that should never have happened.* But mixed into her
shame there was also a new awareness of her own strength, of her
own presence as a woman. Something had happened, but not entirely against her will. She looked at Armand Fayard, grateful for
the silence he made no effort to break, and felt a strange bond
between them.

Something had happened that had not been meant to happen; it
had simply occurred, like any other accident of fate. It would never

happen again, of this they were both certain. Yet, Anne was not as sorry as she had expected to be. What Fayard had done to her, in some small manner had helped to ease the terrible rejection she'd been handed by Charles and Amelia.

As she stood fumbling for her key at the carriage entrance to La Folie, she felt his hand on her shoulder. "Good night, Anne," he whispered. Then she heard his steps on the pavement, and the door of the Rolls-Royce opening. *I'll never be the same again,* she thought, stepping into the silent house. But then . . . who *shall* I be . . . ?

CHAPTER VIII

"This package arrived for you, from Paris," Richard announced, handing his sister a box wrapped in brown paper. Amelia put aside her book and looked up in surprise. Through the leaded-glass French windows of the comfortable library of their home on the Ringstrasse, the June sunshine was dancing off the uneven planes, highlighting her dark hair.

"Open it, silly," her brother urged, perching on the arm of her chaise longue. "It's from Charles, isn't it?"

Amelia peered at the return address, and smiled. "It seems to be." Her quick fingers prodded an opening in the wrapping, and she tore it off. A small square velvet box and a thick vellum envelope came tumbling out.

"Open the box first," her brother directed.

Her expression puzzled, Amelia worked the tiny gold catch, and the top popped open. "My God!" Richard cried out, flabbergasted. But Amelia simply stared, openmouthed, breathless.

Propped up on a bed of white satin, a gold band supported four tall prongs displaying a brilliant-cut diamond solitaire, its many facets gleaming green, red, blue, and rose.

"Its color is immaculate," her brother declared. "Small, but perfect, I can tell! Think how much this must have set him back, poor fellow."

"I—I—" Amelia stammered, handing the box to her brother and standing up, upset. She ran her fingers through her long hair. "Richard . . ."

"Read his letter."

Amelia picked it up and clumsily pried open the envelope to extract a single piece of paper. "I can't believe any of this," she whispered. *"Listen:*

My beloved, You must have guessed in Paris that, with you departed, my own life would become a sea of meaningless emptiness. I love you more than I have ever loved a single human being . . . more than I love myself. Please accept this token of the strength and purity of my feelings as an engagement gift, and I shall make arrangements to come to Vienna and petition Aunt Barbara properly for your hand, as soon as you let me know when would be convenient. Until I hear from you, I shall remain, now and forever,

Your devoted admirer—Charles Lévy–de Rochefleur."

"Seems clear to *me,*" Richard commented wryly. "And I could have foreseen it that night on the Champs-Elysées!" He set the box down carefully on a side table.

Tossing the letter next to it, Amelia turned to face her brother. "Oh, come on, Richard! From an innocent little kiss to *this*—a marriage proposal!"

"He never hinted?"

Amelia blushed, suddenly remembering. "Well, now that you mention it, *yes.* He told me a lot of sentimental nonsense, but you know, no different from anything I'd heard before. Richard, men tend to *say things* when they get carried away by the moonlight or the color of a girl's eyes! And so I didn't take him seriously. I even teased him and told him I didn't want to hear anything deep and ponderous, that I just wanted to have a good time, an enjoyable vacation with friends!"

"You should take care who you kiss in the moonlight, Amelia," her brother admonished her.

"Haven't *you* ever kissed someone just for the fun of the moment?" she challenged.

"Maybe." Richard looked away, a little deflated. Then, reviving, he confronted her again. "But if a girl looked as if she might be getting serious thoughts, I made sure to cut everything off as quickly as possible, so there wouldn't be room for any misunderstandings later on! With *you,* Amelia, men lose their heads. You're a tease, and look at the mess you've caused now, 'wanting to have a good time'!"

"Well, Count von Prim-and-Proper, it's *my* mess, and *I'*ll handle it myself!" she cried, defensive, ashamed, and furious all at the same time. Lifting her head proudly, she turned her back on Rich-

ard and hastened out of the room, grabbing the small velvet box off
the table as she went.

She nearly ran into the butler in the hallway. "I was just coming
in to tell my lady that her summer jodhpurs had arrived," he stated
pompously. Amelia thought it amusing how he always addressed
each member of the family in the third person, as in the old days.
But today she was annoyed, after Richard's reprimand.

"That's nice, Weldheim. And did they walk here by themselves,
or did they come on horseback?"

Embarrassed, the old majordomo coughed. "The gentleman delivered them himself. In fact, *Gräfin* Amelia, he's in the hallway,
where I told him to wait."

"Which gentleman?"

"Well, my lady, the owner. Herr Habig."

Amelia felt the color draining from her face. "Why didn't you
tell him to come in?" she demanded sharply. "He's not an er-
randboy!"

The old majordomo began to answer, but she impatiently cut
him off. "I'll bring him in myself."

Why did he come? she wondered, preparing her demeanor. Off
came the frown, on came a glistening smile, a bright-eyed expression, and the tilt of her head that always intrigued men. She
straightened her posture; then, catching her reflection in a baroque
full-length mirror, she did a double-take. Hesitating for just a few
seconds, she gazed at the small black velvet box in her right hand.
Then, with a toss of her head, she slipped the diamond ring on the
third finger of her left hand. It fit perfectly. Almost defiantly she
strode into the foyer, holding out both her hands in cordial greeting: "Peter! How nice to see you!"

"Dear lady." He took her hands, raised them in half-mocking
tribute to his lips, then dropped them just as casually. If he had
noticed the ring in the dim light of the entryway, he made no sign
of this now. Instead, he bowed slightly, and she thought: He looks
at me the way no other man does: right into my very being. He
looks, and forgives none of what he sees. . . .

He'd never been inside their house before, she remembered.
"Won't you come in?" she inquired graciously.

"I'm only the delivery boy today. Perhaps I should have come
through the back entrance?"

She wasn't amused. Primly, she showed him how little his sarcasm could affect her, by shrugging and leading the way into the drawing room.

Without being asked, Peter Habig sat down beside her on the plush red sofa. "You look very well," he declared, appraising her. "How have you been since your return from the City of Light?"

"Strange you should ask," she answered coyly. Her heart was aching, and she wished she could confront him with her pain at his casual lack of interest. But it was best for a woman to take the upper hand, to reject the man before he had the chance to reject *her*. I'll show him how little I need him, even if it *kills* me, she resolved.

"My cousin Charles has asked me to marry him," she told Peter matter-of-factly. "And look what he sent me." She held out her left hand so that the sunlight could play over the crystalline facets of the solitaire.

He picked her small hand up and touched the diamond ring. "It's a pretty ring. But that's not what you want."

"Oh?" she challenged him, her heart beating quickly. "And what *do* I want, in your venerable opinion, Herr Habig?"

"You don't know what you want. One day you like being the flower of Vienna; the next, you dream of settling down in an old farmhouse and having fourteen children. You're a confused young woman, captivated by your own ability to charm people, especially men; but also, nice enough to feel a bit disturbed by all the havoc you've been wreaking through your charm."

Shocked, Amelia shook her head. "How wrong you are!" she cried. "For the past three years I've wanted only one thing, only one man! I can't bear to think how terribly false your judgment is. Why—"

"Only one man? Do you mean the French cousin? Or is he just a convenient decoy?"

Tears were rising to her eyes, and she turned away. She could feel him next to her, his thigh pressed close to hers. In a minute she would break into tears, if he didn't go away of his own volition. Instead, he touched her on the shoulder. "Tell me, Amelia," he urged her gently. "I need to hear it from you."

Flabbergasted, she turned back to face him. "Peter . . . but why . . . ?"

This time he seemed impatient. "I've had enough of all this coy pretense. I'm a haberdasher, remember? Not a count, to the manner born and bred! I'd simply like to be told, to my face, once and for all, how it is you feel, and for whom. Don't try to put me off by telling me it's none of my business: it *is* my business, Amelia. Because time is too precious to continue to be wasted. You're only twenty, but I'm ten years older. I'd like to marry soon and have a family, and if it turns out I've been mistaken all this time, then I shall take a bow and depart, and turn my attentions to someone more open to receiving them!"

"I . . . I'm not sure I understand . . ."

He stood up, suddenly nervous. "I thought my feelings were rather obvious. I've cared for you since the very beginning, when we met at the von Stechers'. But at that time, you were too young. Then later you started to toy with me the same way you were toying with all the other men who were crazy about you. I wasn't about to play *that* game!"

"And so instead, you allowed me to feel your scorn! You danced with every pretty woman but me, you rode next to every debutante except me, and now suddenly you want me to believe you care! What about that morning at Sacher's? I wasn't toying with you then, was I? You never even kissed me!"

He was standing right over her, glowering at her. She stood up too, enraged. "You call this a 'waste of time'? Do you think I ever loved poor Charles? I wasn't going to marry him, but I said it to get rid of you once and for all! Just so I wouldn't have to be reminded, week after week, that I had fallen in love with a dark, sinister man who thought I was too young, too spoiled, and . . . and . . . a Jew, to boot!"

He burst into laughter. "I'll buy the first two," he finally said. "But not the last. Honestly . . . I'm not that sort of man. Religion, in any case, makes no difference in my life. My family's been Catholic for centuries, but if yours insisted on a Jewish wedding, I wouldn't hesitate for a moment. You're spoiled and young, yes . . . but I am not an anti-Semite."

She asked, her voice soft and hesitant, "A Jewish *wedding*? Are you saying that you *meant it*, about wanting . . ."

Peter sighed. He was very tall, over six feet, and now he placed his hands on her shoulders and looked right into her upturned face. "That's what I said. Will you marry me, *Gräfin* Amelia, instead of continuing to make both our lives miserable?"

"Oh, my God," she whispered, tears falling onto her cheeks. Peter lifted one hand from her shoulder, touched the tear, then bent down to kiss it. She moved her face and found his lips, and wound her arms around his neck. For the first time, her life seemed to possess a center: the two of them together were that center.

Richard, reappearing on the threshold, simply sighed and shook his head.

* * *

The apartment was dreadfully hot, although Yvonne had tried to create cross ventilation by opening most of the windows. Now she stood outside Charles's door, wringing her clammy hands. Something terrible was happening: she felt certain of it, and had felt it since this morning when the small package had arrived through the mail, from Vienna.

Why was Amelia sending Charles a package? Yvonne had asked him that when he came home from work. And his face had blanched. Then he'd taken the package and the letter with him into his room, closing the door almost in Yvonne's face.

She didn't like to pry. Charles was twenty-two. A lot had happened that he hadn't shared with her, and now she was expecting the worst: the unexpected.

She knew there had been something between him and Amelia. How could anyone not love Amelia? She was the brightest, prettiest girl Yvonne had seen in a long, long time. Of course Charles would have fantasized about capturing her attentions. But then, after she'd returned to Vienna, he'd seemed particularly preoccupied, hoarding his money and not telling Yvonne what he was planning. Had he really hoped to marry Amelia?

I'd like him to find someone and be happy, Yvonne thought; but not Amelia von Guttman. Amelia was too sophisticated, too charming, too beautiful. The kind of girl who took Shakespeare's words seriously, believing that "all the world's a stage." Charles needed someone more steady, someone to adore *him* the way, years ago, she herself had adored his father.

The memory of Willy still hurt, after twenty years. Yvonne pushed it to the back of her mind and gently turned the doorknob. Charles's room lay in the penumbra of twilight, and he was stretched out on his bed, motionless, his eyes shut. *Like a dead man,* she thought, panicking.

Yvonne tiptoed into the room and touched Charles's forehead. It was cold and moist. "Go away, Mama," he murmured. Her heart turned over, and she looked around. On the small desk sat the opened package: a velvet box, its lid up, revealing a solitaire diamond ring. In a single moment Yvonne understood.

She sank down on her knees, wanting to speak and yet afraid to disturb his privacy. She ached so terribly for her son that she didn't know what to do. She'd nursed him through a plethora of childhood diseases, had mediated arguments with his friends at school, and had sat back and listened to his tales of ambition. But she had never before seen him so distressed. He was lying there as if struck numb by Amelia's gesture—as if the girl had annihilated his manhood in one single motion.

Suddenly he sat up, and she started. He held his hand out to her, and she saw that he was holding a piece of crumpled paper. His eyes were gleaming, even in the dusk. "Tell me . . . how is it possible for a woman to lead a man on without feeling too ashamed to face herself in the mirror the next morning?"

Yvonne looked at him closely. "Why?"

"Amelia told me there was nobody. That meant that I had a chance! And now . . . she writes me a stupid note, informing me that she's getting married next month to some *haberdasher* she's been in love with for three years! *Three years!* How could she have kissed me, then? How could she have looked me in the eye and assured me that *there was no one else*?"

"Perhaps she was a coward," Yvonne said softly. "Or perhaps she wasn't sure. Wasn't sure of loving him, or wasn't sure of *his* intentions. . . . I don't know."

He looked at the crumpled letter and shook his head with amazement. "Do you know, Mother, that I'd never loved a woman until her? That Amelia was the first woman I ever fell in love with?"

Yvonne sighed. "I suspected as much."

"And did you suspect *this,* too?"

"How could I have? I barely knew Amelia. I'd only just met her myself. But I did feel that she was too experienced . . . not in terms of any physical involvement, but rather in her dealings with men and the art of being courted. And believe me, there *is* such an art, and it requires time, effort, and practice. She had the practice and you didn't. You fell in love, and she went through a simple flirtation: a new country, a new setting, a new man. Once she returned to her own home, she was able to put the whole thing in perspective . . . which is what I wish *you* had done, my son."

"But then she's nothing but a tease!" he cried. "Carrying on with me the way she did, kissing me with such abandon, when in fact she was kissing me no differently than she had kissed dozens of other men!"

Yvonne put her palm over Charles's forehead and kept it there, lightly. "Darling, don't let this turn you into a bitter man, as your father turned me into a bitter woman. And don't allow Amelia to dwell in your thoughts, or she'll grow into an obsession, the way *you*'ve become poor *Anne*'s obsession. What I'm trying to say is, live your life, don't fret over it and worry it to death. Nothing could be worse for a human being. . . ."

* * *

Anne . . . Why was it that for the third time that day he'd brought her memory up from the catacombs of his mind, allowing her to intrude upon his sketch of a train engine? Annoyed; then intrigued, Charles set his pen down on the graph paper and pressed his fingers onto his temples.

His mother had said to him, in passing, . . . *as you have become poor Anne's obsession* . . . He hadn't ever thought of it that way: in fact, he'd never much bothered thinking about Anne at all! She *was* "poor Anne," a shadowy creature associated with Alfred, the man Charles hated second only to his own father.

Yet in point of fact he liked Anne. Nice, plain Anne, steady as a background tapestry. In actuality, she wasn't all that bad. Overweight, perhaps, and lacking the personal dash that drew him to women who attracted him either sexually or romantically. But she'd been a good friend to him, hadn't she? She'd been his *only* friend, discounting his mother.

Yes, naturally he'd been embarrassed by the ardent look he'd caught on her face, once or twice. *In the beginning.* Because now when he looked at Anne, he'd come to *expect* that look of slavish adoration: it had become a part of her expression.

His mother had been trying to tell him something, that his chasing Amelia had reminded her, in its impossible outcome, of Anne's chasing *him*. The pain of Amelia seared him so badly that he had to cover his eyes, letting the sharp ache pass through his body with renewed outrage. Amelia had devastated him by turning him down. *I'll never be the same,* he thought, wanting to push her image away, yet unable to follow through. He loved her; but she was marrying another man, and he simply *had* to face reality, and go on with his life.

I'm not going to let her destroy me, he decided, anger replacing the pain. I'll show her that she made a mistake. What is it that I've

always wanted, that was always lacking in my life? *Power!* I shall
become a powerful man, and then she'll have cause to regret her
foolish impulse to marry that Viennese social climber!

I'm never going to let a woman gain control over me again, he
resolved. I'm never going to let my heart make the decisions for my
brain. I'm going to do what's most expedient for a change, what's
best for *me.*

I want power; I want money; I want to be the proprietor of La
Folie again, he summed up. And that meant recognizing that right
now he was powerless, without funds, and a "poor relation" of
little consequence as far as Alfred was concerned. Yet there was
one person who held the key to all three of his goals: and this
person was Anne, "poor Anne," who loved him as she'd always
loved him . . . with all her heart.

* * *

Charles felt uncomfortable in the grandiose living room, so
changed from when he and his mother had lived there on their
return from Switzerland after the war. The nubby silk cushions of
the eighteenth-century divan, with their delicate flowered patterns
of mimosa yellow and warm peach on a verdant green background,
appeared almost decadently appealing. Bracing himself for an interview with Alfred, Charles had chosen to sit on an upright armchair, with an inlaid scrollwork of silver and tortoiseshell on its
ebony frame.

Nervously, he tapped a cigarette out of his gold case and lit it. A
life-sized Degas dancer, on pointe in a lace tutu, drew his attention
away from his preoccupation, and for a moment he smoked in
peace, studying the canvas above the fireplace.

"Good evening, Charles," Alfred stated, breaking into his day-
dream by entering the room. The young man rose, self-consciously.
Impeccable in a black tuxedo and white silk ruffled shirt, Alfred
was clearly prepared for a formal occasion. His very appearance
indicated that he would be granting Charles some precious minutes
sandwiched between a busy day at the office and a social event
from which, obviously, Charles himself had been excluded by his
lack of standing among the Parisian upper crust.

Alfred made a majestic gesture indicating that they should sit
down. He reached for a briar pipe on a small table, and ceremoni-
ously tamped tobacco into its mouth. He struck a match and lit the
tobacco, and puffed. Meanwhile, Charles watched, mesmerized by

these nonchalant, familiar motions, his mouth dry with apprehension.

"What can I do for you?" Alfred finally demanded, studiously polite, not quite gracious. After all, he didn't *have* to be gracious to Yvonne's son.

"I've come to talk to you about Anne," the young man began, licking his upper lip. "About Anne and *me,* actually."

Alfred's right eyebrow went up quizzically. "What have you to do with her?" he asked, lightly amused.

Making sure to look Alfred directly in the eye, Charles plunged in. "I'd like to ask you, Cousin Alfred, for Anne's hand in marriage."

Alfred's lean face revealed nothing; it remained impassive, like a stone frieze, his perfect chiseled features in deep reflection. Then the dark eyes came alive, and riveted themselves to the young engineer's face.

"Charles, I'm always delighted when a bright young man expresses an interest in my daughter. Every father wishes for his only daughter as many proposals as possible: it's flattering, isn't it, to be courted? But naturally I must only consider for her those offers that match my own expectations."

"What you're trying to tell me, Alfred, is that my present situation doesn't meet those expectations."

"No, my boy, I'm not *trying:* I'm *telling* you. Anne is my only heir. She will marry a man of equal social prestige, and of equal financial worth, or she will not marry at all. Surely you can understand my concern. A girl like Anne—innocent, kind, open—is bound to attract a great many fortune hunters. It's not that I'm putting you in that category, Charles, but neither can I discount the possibility that your interest in my daughter may be vested in her enormous dowry, and in her eventual inheritance of total control over the de Rochefleur banking dynasty."

Charles's stomach suddenly grew queasy. His face felt drained of blood, yet a light perspiration was breaking over his forehead. "Alfred, it's precisely *because* of Anne's vulnerable position in regard to fortune hunters that I've been bold enough to come forward today. I may not be the son-in-law you hoped for, because of my current financial situation. But I am, nonetheless, a de Rochefleur. You always liked and trusted my mother. Compared to a man whose background might be clouded in unknowns, with me you have an open book."

"I might not feel inclined to read it," Alfred shot back dryly.

"I'm your own flesh and blood, for God's sake!" Charles cried, impassioned. He could feel La Folie at his fingertips, just barely—yet desperately—out of reach for him.

"Whatever you think of me," Charles pressed on, "*you*'re the head of this family, and you control us all. Were I to behave in any fashion unbefitting the son-in-law of Baron Alfred de Rochefleur, you would only have to raise an eyebrow to bring me back in line! Would it be so easy with a stranger? And let's face it, a rich man might be far more troublesome!"

"What makes you think I would choose a puppet for Anne's husband?"

Charles drew in a deep breath. How was he to answer this truthfully, yet without further alienating the girl's father? "It's not that I'm a puppet for anyone. It's just that Anne is almost twenty-one, and hasn't had much of a social life. She doesn't like large parties, and so she hasn't had much . . . exposure. Perhaps you're hoping for a Parisian version of our cousin Richard: handsome, immensely wealthy, and worldly-wise. But a man like that makes daily rounds of the latest debutante balls, and has a list an arm long of the most desirable, sophisticated heiresses in the city. Of all men, *you* should understand this, Alfred. In your own youth, *you,* like Richard, had your pick of the most elegant, witty young women in Europe."

What Charles had said was not half so important as what he *hadn't* said. His spoken words passed through Alfred's mind like a quick spring shower, while his unspoken ones remained in the air like a dark, ominous cloud, presaging certain storm. The Richards and the younger versions of Alfred chose their mates among the Continent's Amelias, not its Annes.

To back up his own résumé, Charles brought up yet another trump card. "I may not have money now, but I am going to rise within my company. You can ask your own friend, Monsieur Meyer. I'm going to be promoted soon—my superior informed me of this just a few weeks ago."

Alfred clamped the pipe between his teeth, and kept it there as he spoke, rising. "Charles," he declared. "You haven't managed to convince me. You're Yvonne's son. That is the unique point you made that struck a respondent chord. Anne's very shy, but I intend to hire a companion for her, and then she'll have someone with whom to travel throughout Europe and Great Britain, as she'd have done long ago had her mother been alive. Time's been lost, but my daughter is still young enough to 'make the rounds,' as you say, and be introduced to appropriate suitors." He removed the pipe, examined it, then sighed. "I'm sorry, but we're going to have to cut this short. I'm expected at the Baron de Gunzbourg's in twenty minutes. Thank you for your visit."

"But . . ." Charles rose too, totally deflated. La Folie was retreating from him, fading away before his very eyes. He couldn't let this happen—not when Anne, and Anne alone, seemed to be holding out a hand to pull him out of obscurity. "Can't you at least speak to Anne? I know *she* wants us to get married. She's in love with me! Don't her feelings count in any way?"

Alfred smiled, but his eyes remained a cold, impenetrable black. "Anne is a woman," he declared softly. "A silly, sentimental woman. And I'm a businessman. Go back to work, Charles, and concentrate on your career. But don't count on a promotion too soon: for each engineer's spot, there are seven applicants."

An uncontrollable rage swept through Charles. "You can't treat me this way!" he exploded.

But the older man cut him off. "I've treated you far better than you deserved. You owe me the mere fact of your career, you arrogant young fool. So get out now, before you really make me angry and I say what we'll both end up regretting."

"I wish you *would* say it," Charles challenged, his voice trembling with barely contained hatred and impotence.

From the doorway, Anne's father's eyes stripped away the final vestiges of his dignity. "As you wish, then . . . *Albert Meyer gave you a job because I asked him to.*" He sounded both weary and impatient. "Don't make me sorry that I did!"

Charles's mouth was still open, aghast, long after Alfred had exited from the room.

* * *

Anne sat at the breakfast table, her head pounding brutally. *I'm going to be sick,* she thought as the blue silk walls appeared to close in on her, then unexpectedly tilted to the side. The soft-boiled egg in front of her stared up, gobs of yellow goo dribbling down the eggshell. How could any human being eat such a disgusting meal? The egg smelled of sulfur, and suddenly Anne could wait no longer. She stood up and bolted from the room, clutching her mouth to keep from vomiting.

As she crouched in front of the toilet, retching, she heard her father tapping at the door to the powder room, calling her name.

Green bile spurted out of her mouth, and then the burning indigestion subsided. Slowly, the objects in the room began to fit back into their settings. She stood up and washed out her mouth, splashed water over her perspiring face, and emerged from the powder room.

"You look terrible, Anne," her father said. "You've gained weight, yet you've been eating like a bird." His voice was filled with concern. "Perhaps I should send you to that spa in the Bavarian hills where they make overweight young women walk several miles a day, and exercise, and watch their diets. How much do you weigh now, Anne?"

She felt miserable. Her stomach had puffed out below her breasts, which seemed swollen and painful. He was right, of course: she'd noticed all of this herself. "One hundred sixty pounds," she stammered.

"I'm going to call Letellier. He'll come and give you a checkup later today. Your skin's broken out, and your eyes are bloodshot."

"I don't want a doctor!" The words came rushing out before she could stop them. Now she put her hand to her mouth, aghast. *I know why I don't want Dr. Letellier . . .* I don't need him to tell me what's wrong. *I know! And I've known all along,* even though I've tried to pretend that night never took place.

"Why?" Alfred was insisting. "It could be something serious."

"It's nothing, Papa. Just tension, I guess. I'm not digesting my food properly, and I'm retaining water. That's all it is. I wouldn't want to disturb Dr. Letellier for such an unimportant reason."

But suddenly her father's face contorted into a furious expression, turning his complexion to a bright crimson. "That's absurd!" he cried out. "There's only one reason a young woman would refuse to be examined by her family doctor! I couldn't bear to confront the facts as they've been staring at me, Anne, for *weeks* now: I simply couldn't—wouldn't—believe it of my own daughter. *You're expecting a child!* I know what a woman goes through in the early months. I know all about *morning sickness,* and bloating, and sudden dizzy spells and hot flashes. Tell me I'm wrong, Anne! For God's sake, and your mother's, *tell me I couldn't possibly be right,* that you've done nothing as disgraceful as what I've suspected."

Anne stared at him, her eyes enormous. "Papa—"

"Tell me, Anne, that no man has touched you!"

It didn't matter anymore, did it? She knew now that Charles would never love her, even in spite of Amelia's decision to marry

Peter Habig. What greater catastrophe could possibly top that shattered dream? Yet it looked as though *this* was turning into an even worse nightmare. Her father was right: She'd committed a disgraceful act, and all she could think of was her mother, and how relieved she was that Sonia had died and was not present to witness this scene. Sonia would have sent Anne away forever, would have banned her from the house, disinherited her for this unspeakable dishonor.

I am going to have *that man*'s child. I can no longer talk myself out of facing this. I'm going to have to go away somewhere, like those girls with bad reputations who had to be sent to the Crimea because they'd "kissed" too many boys in Petersburg . . . only everyone knew they'd done more than that! And what will happen to the baby?

She began to cry. "It's Charles, isn't it?" her father accused. His face was suffused with blood. She had never witnessed him like this, almost apoplectic.

"No!" The irony of Alfred's supposition might have made her laugh bitterly, except that she was caught in the worst crisis of her life. *How she wished that she had never run into Charles kissing Amelia, that night two months before.* Then none of this would have taken place. Armand Fayard was a heavy depositor at the Crédit Industriel, a respected member of the Paris elite . . . and, on top of that, a married man with no intention of divorcing his young wife. The whole thing had been a dreadful mistake. *He and I mean absolutely nothing to each other,* Anne thought. But yet we've somehow managed to conceive a baby. . . .

"If not Charles, *who? Tell me,* Anne!"

Panic-stricken, she searched for a solution, for a name that she might throw at him. Someone unimportant, someone who would not be held accountable, who *didn't live in Paris.* Or someone already dead. But . . . who?

"I'm not sure," she murmured, imploring him with her eyes. "It was . . . it was the night of the formal dinner. I'd had too much champagne . . . *I don't remember who it was*! I swear it, Papa! I went upstairs to lie down, and suddenly someone else was in the room . . . and he forced me—"

Tears fell from her lower lashes to her cheeks, and she wrung her hands in despair. Her father's face, so horribly pained, so full of anger and outrage a moment ago, appeared to relax, and the purplish color, to drain from his cheeks. She had, almost unwittingly, hit on the magic formula. By saying that she had been forced, she'd taken away some of the blame, some of the shame, from her own shoulders, and therefore from his as well. By making herself a victim, she had removed the onus of guilt. *Any*one could be forced; *any* woman, no matter how virtuous, might have been raped by a drunk or a madman.

"Very well, Anne," Alfred said, his voice low. But now she heard an uncharacteristic tremor in his speech. "This is a damn complicated situation. I'll have to think of some way to get around this problem. Go upstairs to rest. It will be all right."

Relief swept over her features, and she nodded. He hadn't hit her; he hadn't accused her. He hadn't sent her away . . . yet. But, as she reached the door a new wave of horror assailed her: Would Charles feel compelled to rescind their friendship now, once he learned what was happening to her? For even without his love, she'd been relying on the comfort of his presence and his encouraging words.

Anne felt caught between Scylla and Charybdis. Whichever way she turned for relief, a new danger threatened to engulf her.

* * *

"Charles should be home any minute," Yvonne said, pressing her perspiring palms on her skirt. She stood over her cousin Alfred, unable to guess what he had up his sleeve. Tonight he certainly appeared mild-mannered enough. . . .

Suddenly she cocked her head. The front door was being unlocked. Yvonne ran toward it and caught her son as he was tossing his raincoat over the costumer rack. "Alfred is here," she whispered, trying to prepare him.

Charles stiffened. "What does he want?"

He saw the tired lines around her eyes, tiny, fine lines like cobwebs designed around her lovely sapphire eyes. What new heartache had Alfred de Rochefleur come to bring them *this* time? He gently pushed his mother aside and marched into the living room, ready to confront the man who had thrown him out of La Folie and cast his pride into the mud beside him.

But Alfred was standing quietly by the bookcase. As always, his sartorial elegance struck Charles, who felt a quick pang of envy: with money, a man could be stately and imposing, his jackets tailored to perfection, his silk shirts hand-sewn, his shoes a shining moroccan leather that gleamed just enough to show the minute finish. But this evening Alfred looked singularly exhausted, and the gray in his hair seemed more evident than it had only a few days earlier at La Folie.

Before Charles could open his mouth, Alfred stayed him with a wave of his hand. Approaching his young cousin, he said in a voice as humble as he could muster: "Charles, please, I've come to apologize. Would you be gentleman enough to accept my apology?"

Charles took this statement as if it were a blow to his head: he felt stunned. But quickly he regained his composure. "What is it you've *really* come for, Alfred?"

"An apology is not reason enough?"

"Not where you're concerned." Charles loosened his tie, sat down, and reached for a cigarette from the silver box on the small side table. As he lit it he kept his eyes on his cousin, trying to figure out this sudden change in attitude. His first anger had ebbed away with the other man's amazing opening statement. Now a slow thrill was starting to build up in him: their roles appeared to be reversing themselves, inexplicably. What did Alfred want, badly enough to come all the way here?

"I've reconsidered. I think it would be a good idea for you to marry my daughter after all. You're right: I'd feel that Anne were more secure with a husband himself born into our family. I'd like to give you my blessing, Charles, and to tell you how sorry I am for the things I said to you. You're a good man, and I'm glad you love my daughter."

Charles caught his lower lip thoughtfully between his teeth. Finally he asked, "Where's the catch, Alfred? What's wrong with Anne, that you should suddenly beg me to marry her? I have no money, and little social standing. Why *me,* when before I was the worst prospect you could think of. And why *now*?"

Alfred coughed. "I told you, I jumped too quickly the other day. Fathers of only daughters tend to do that. We tend to be more protective than we should—"

"I don't believe you for one moment. You're a goddamned hypocrite, Alfred! You *need* me to marry Anne. I'd like to know *why.* It can't be financial gain: I know all of Mother's assets and liabilities, and there's no earthly benefit you could derive from us. So it must be something else. The question is: *What is it,* Alfred? What's happened to the high opinion you had last week of Anne's chances of alluring a *proper* husband?"

Alfred looked away. Charles knew then that he'd hit upon the truth, and his tension eased considerably. It was going to be all right. The cards were now in his favor. The rules of the game had changed.

Finally, Alfred spoke, not looking at Charles. His voice seemed muted with pain. "The truth is that Anne is pregnant. She was raped, Charles. But who in Paris is going to believe that? Only you and I, who know the kind of woman she is. You *must* marry her, Charles! You can come work for me, at the Crédit Industriel. . . ."

"There's no need for that," Charles replied. His tone was strong, but even. "For now, Meyer Frères isn't a bad place, even though I owe you my position. No, Alfred, what I want is to live at La Folie, and for you to leave it to Anne and me jointly in your will."

Alfred stared at him, speechless. "I want shares in the de Rochefleur banks," Charles continued calmly. "I come from the same stock as you, and was named after the man who founded the institution. I may have been born on the distaff side of the family, but it's time some of this injustice was rectified. I don't want to spend the rest of my existence as your poor relation, the man whom you rejected as unsuitable for your only daughter. And you agree, don't you, Alfred? Anne deserves to maintain her own position in society. Besides, Albert Meyer will surely look differently on his most junior engineer if the man happens to hold important shares in the bank he does business with."

Alfred's face was lined like white parchment. "You know how to hammer your point home," he said tightly.

"So what's your final word?"

Alfred rose, pulling on the lapels of his navy blue jacket. "I have no choice." He had the voice of a dying man, dull and weary. "I'll have my attorney draw up the papers tomorrow morning."

Charles smiled. "Then I'll come after dinner to speak to Anne."

Their eyes met, and Charles knew that finally the scales had tipped in his favor.

* * *

Goujon had illumined the garden, not with the thousands of tiny bulbs that had decorated it the night of Alfred's party, but with a soft, muted glow that emanated from below the ceiling of the gazebo. The two young people were walking slowly, Anne's hands instinctively resting on her stomach, which just barely protruded from below her waist.

She looked almost beautiful right now, Charles decided. Shadowlight became her rounded features. Tonight she resembled a

Raffaello madonna, all gentle curves, her hazel eyes ringed with long lashes that he'd somehow never bothered to notice. But she seemed distinctly unhappy, remote and turned inward on herself, hiding her shame.

I wonder if there really was a rape, Charles asked himself. But he also knew that he would never commit the indelicacy of asking her about the incident. He had promised himself never to open this Pandora's box.

"Dear, sweet Anne," he now murmured, taking her by the shoulders and halting their slow walk in the trellised bower. "Can you guess why I've come tonight?"

With her usual honesty, Anne shook her head. And prayed, anguish spreading through her: *Please, God, don't take his friendship away from me now, when I most need it.*

"I've come to ask you to marry me."

Anne frowned, uncomprehending. "Don't tease me," she reproached him, her voice unsteady.

"Come," he suggested, taking her by the hand. "Let's sit in the gazebo and plan our future. I want you to be my wife."

They stepped up onto the white planked floor, and suddenly Anne felt herself go weak at the knees: *Her father* . . . She was listening to an incongruous proposal from the only man she'd ever loved—but her father had bribed him! How else could she explain this unbelievable change of heart? Alfred had promised her a solution to her problem. And Charles, without money or prospects, would, to her father, have constituted the best prospect.

Charles was helping her sit down, the way a thoughtful man helps a pregnant woman. *He knew!* Turning her head from him to hide her violent shame, she thought, with sudden certainty: *He knows everything!*

From the gazebo, they could see the hedges and flower beds outlined in the golden haze of Goujon's recessed nightlamp. Gently, Charles caressed Anne's hand, which lay inert in his palm. "You aren't speaking," he murmured curiously.

Then she turned to regard him, and he saw that her face was bathed in tears. "Anne . . ."

"You made a deal with my father," she told him, her voice even but quivering. "That's what all this is about."

Surprise caught him unprepared. Embarrassed, suddenly ashamed, he bit his lip. "I care about you, Anne. And I'll be a good husband. You know that I'll always be considerate, that I'll treat you like the lady you are."

Humiliated beyond limit, Anne lowered her head into both her hands and wept. He touched her shoulder. "Don't," he begged. "I'm not going to ask you any questions. Not now—not ever. I'll raise your child as my own and give it my name. We'll be a family, Anne. You, me, and the baby."

She dropped her hands into her lap, and faced him. "But it's not what you think. You see, I love you, Charles—I've *always* loved you! And I used to dream of this for *years*! Only, in my own opera, the libretto followed a different line. You were going to marry me *because you loved me too.* . . ."

Charles wondered at that moment if he would ever be able to live down the shame he was feeling. Awkwardly, he put his arm around Anne's shoulders and drew her close to him. They sat together, looking out at the simple, lovely lines of La Folie, and a kind of peace fell upon both of them.

Then, all at once, Charles grew conscious of something else building up in him. It was the same excitement he had felt when Alfred came to the Boulevard Malesherbes to beg him to accept his apology. *La Folie was calling to him!* The homestead was alive, vibrant and compelling, drawing him to it like a woman, like a giant magnetic force. He glanced at Anne, to see whether she, too, was feeling the same pull. But her face reflected only pain, the pain of having won the game through dishonest means.

Well, *that makes two of us,* Charles Lévy thought, feeling the first chill of the evening.

BOOK TWO

Gambit

CHAPTER IX

"Alexis is asking for his good night kiss, monsieur et madame," the English nursemaid said in her Devonshire accent. She was standing in the dining room doorway, looking quite weary.

"Well, then, children, you must go," Alfred declared, smiling at his daughter and son-in-law. His eyes passed briefly over Anne, half indulgently, then fastened on Charles's face for less than a few telltale seconds. The stalwart English nanny, Miss Hastings, her starched linens only slightly less white than they had been in the morning, stood deferentially to the side, waiting.

"Yes, indeed, we *must*, Papa," Charles replied. He touched his waxed mustache and inclined his head respectfully toward his father-in-law, making sure to return his smile. Their eyes met, locked . . . then moved away, politely backing off.

Anne blushed. Gently, she placed her hand over her husband's arm, and pressed it. Charles took the hint and began to lead the march out of the dining room into the second wing of La Folie, where Anne had turned the guest installations into a nursery riotous with carousels and wicker, train mobiles and toys. Tons and tons of toys, bought at the Bon Marché and ordered clear over from New York City's F.A.O. Schwarz department store, home of the most fantastic toys and stuffed animals in the world.

Marriage had given Anne a certain soft glow that became her. Too full-figured for the fashionable bob hairstyle, which looked perfect on the flat-chested, matchstick flapper girls of her debutante group, she had nevertheless dropped the tight, old-fashioned headdress of a thousand rolls and curls. Instead she wore her brown hair down to her collarbone, where it gently flipped inward, giving a proper setting to her expressive hazel eyes and somewhat undistinguished nose and mouth. She had simplified herself and, in so doing, had become less awkward and more appealing. She had finally captured her own essence, in much the same way she had once learned how to capture the essence of a room's design.

Hesitantly, she stole a sideways glance at Charles. He looked so elegant in his maroon velvet at-home jacket. He really liked dressing for dinner and joining her father in the dining room, playing the role of country squire to the hilt. Anne was proud that she had afforded him this luxury, though sadly she had to remind herself that that was precisely why her handsome cousin had married her.

Her own life hadn't changed much since marrying Charles in the summer of 1920 and giving birth to Alexis in February of the following year. As she walked to the nursery on her husband's arm, this winter of 1922, she had a vivid recollection of her wedding day: yards and yards of handmade Belgian lace, trailing behind her; red carpeting beginning at the curb outside the majestic Temple de la Victoire, and leading all the way to the nuptial *huppah*, decorated with flowers flown in from Nice and Grasse: exotic lilies and orchids and baby rosebuds; hundreds of fashionable guests in evening attire, because her father had insisted on the pomp and circumstance of an evening wedding.

Anne remembered how cleverly the couturier had hidden the nascent signs of her pregnancy below the princess-waist sash of seed pearls and satin. Charles, dapper in his top hat, frock coat, and gray striped pants, had crushed the crystal glass beneath his gleaming black leather shoe, and they had partaken of the ceremonial wine from a silver goblet emblazoned *L/R*. Yvonne told her that the very same goblet had been used by herself and Charles's father at their own wedding twenty-three years previously. (A fine beginning, the bride had thought, a little unkindly. Given how *that* groom had ended up. . . .)

They had taken their honeymoon in Britain, starting out in London, and staying at Claridge's Hotel. They had visited art galleries and the British Museum and, at night, had reveled in the theater, not wishing to miss anything, from *King Lear* to Diaghilev's Ballets Russes performing *Pulcinella* at Covent Garden. It was in London that Charles had discovered that his bride was passionate, a fire that needed to be teased but that once started, blazed with warmth and vigor. He'd been surprised. But less so when she hadn't wanted him to see her nude and had insisted he keep the lights turned completely off.

From London they proceeded to Yorkshire, and visited the countryside. Anne had noticed that Charles, though solicitous and kind, seemed more restless than in London. *I am not enough to keep him from becoming bored,* she decided, plunging into gloom. *I am not enough.*

And, ashamed of her baseness of spirit, she added: *I am not Amelia. . . .* Amelia, who was engaged to marry a Viennese man she loved. *Amelia shouldn't be a threat anymore,* Anne reproached herself.

When they returned to Paris, Old Man Meyer had called Charles into his office, and, coughing to avoid having to look the junior engineer in the eye, had offhandedly announced that a new position had just been created to accommodate the complicating additions to the employee roster: assistant to the all-important personnel manager, Jean Laffitte. Did Charles want to fill this newly formed slot?

Charles had said to her that night: "It's very easy to ignore the existence of a lower-level employee called Lévy. But it's less easy to forget the fact that Baron Alfred de Rochefleur's son-in-law is lost somewhere within the confines of Meyer Frères."

Anne had demurred, fastening her beautiful green-gold eyes on her sarcastic young husband: "But if you weren't truly talented . . ."

Her words had drifted off. He'd looked at her, that was all. What he'd acquired had been a talented new addition to his *name,* for, being a Swiss citizen, he had decided to proceed according to solid Swiss tradition: He had appended his wife's family name to his own, becoming, officially, Charles Lévy–de Rochefleur. In a moment of unheeding candor, he had even remarked, "Eventually most of the people who know us will grow bored with this excessively long surname, and will only bother to remember the last part."

She had sighed, and understood. She had married a Lévy, to become, once again, a de Rochefleur. She had married a man; he had married a name.

La Folie remained the same. But Charles, imperceptibly, had altered its atmosphere. The cold, immutable loveliness of the rooms now glowed with a new warmth, while her father's frosty hauteur frightened her less because he was no longer the only figure of authority. Yet one setback had occurred, from an unlikely source: Charles' mother, Yvonne, had gently but firmly refused to move back, insisting that her old apartment on the Boulevard Malesherbes was exactly what she needed for her painting. Anne

had not known how to comfort Charles, who felt rebuffed. Yvonne
Lévy had a strange pride: having once lost her home, never again
would she conceive of residing within its walls.

Miss Hastings opened the door to the nursery, and politely
stepped aside to let the parents enter. Anne went first through the
door, rushing to the crib where little Alexis was standing. He
jumped up and down when he saw her, holding out his arms and
pleading: "Mama!"

She scooped him up and out of the crib, holding him tight. He
had been born long, but light, and still was tall and slender for his
age, without that chubbiness characteristic of so many babies. His
face was a pale oval, with large black eyes and curly black hair.
People told her he looked like her father; she wondered whether, in
fact, he resembled his own. What was assuredly certain was that he
didn't have any point in common with Charles, except perhaps a
familiar elegance rarely discerned in so young a child. Anne kissed
the top of his head, which smelled of talcum powder, and looked
over at Charles.

Her husband appeared to be standing at attention, all smiles, his
posture erect and proud, his eyes focusing on a faraway picture of a
little child on a white elephant. What was he thinking about? Was
he even here, in this room? *He'll never like my son,* Anne thought,
trying to bury the hurt and cover it up with hope. *I may be mis-
reading him.* For Charles always behaved impeccably toward
Alexis.

But Charles was thinking: If the child loved me, he'd call out to
me once in a while too. It's always 'Mama! *Mama!*' He doesn't love
me, and in fact he doesn't even like me around. He's another man's
son, and doesn't look like me or Anne. Sprung out of nowhere, a
changeling.

Yet Alexis Eugène Lévy–de Rochefleur wasn't full grown. He
wasn't even two years old. From his secure position in his mother's
arms, he was peering with serious dark eyes at his father . . . this
blond man with the waxed mustache who always came with Mama
to kiss him good night. A dry kiss, planted on Alexis's forehead,
every night. *Go away,* Alexis thought. Had he been capable of more
developed thinking, he might have added: Why do you come since
you don't like me?

And his father would have answered, smiling coldly and staring
him down with his blue, blue eyes: "Because your grandpa is
watching me. . . ."

* * *

When the weather permitted, Charles liked to take a brisk walk at lunchtime, if he didn't have to meet anyone; the expensive restaurants near his office, on a side street off the Avenue des Champs-Elysées, made him balk a little. He found it difficult to eat a heavy lunch and then to follow it up with one of Marie's elaborate four-course dinners. Besides, walking enabled him to sort through his day and resolve a number of problems.

He was twenty-four years old, and, on this unusually warm winter day, he wondered just how much he had accomplished so far. He could feel the impatience building up inside him, the gnawing restlessness that sometimes took hold of him, dragging him down into depression. Had he been right to jump so quickly at the personnel job? He'd seen it as a stepping stone to a position of greater control within the company, and, he had to admit, as work affording him the entertainment of working with people rather than blueprints. While most of the time he felt good about the choice he'd made, sometimes, like today, he worried about the future.

A café au lait and a fresh croissant would be nice right now, he told himself, stopping in front of an open-air café, its terrace fronting the Champs-Elysées with its graceful line of chestnut trees, their limbs now totally bare. These tall and stately trees always made him feel that the world *could* be controlled and trimmed into a harmonious picture in spite of the odds against it. He sat down at a small table and ordered, his sense of irritation beginning to seep away.

Out of the corner of his eye, he could see two women seated to the right of him in the café. He turned to look at them. One, a redhead, was a complete stranger, but the one with the wide-brimmed, flowered hat sparked an instant recognition: Arabella Fayard, the wife of the steel magnate. It had been more than two years since they had met at La Folie, years in which he had often recalled her gamine face, with its catlike green eyes and elfin smile. The way the tops of her breasts had pushed out of her décolleté, begging to be taken out and caressed. . . .

He could feel himself getting excited, and quelled the sensation. This was absurd. She had obviously let him slip from her mind, and besides, she was married. At that moment, she raised her arm to flag down the waiter, and her glance fell on him quite by accident. Her hand stayed in the air, stilled by an obvious instant of déjà vu. He smiled, inclining his head to indicate that yes, they had once met, though she had not as yet placed his familiar face.

I *have* to talk to her, he thought, suddenly impatient. The waiter was presenting her with the bill, and she opened her bag to take out some coins. Then she and her friend both stood, and Charles felt a sense of panic come over him. She wasn't even looking at him, and she and her companion were going to leave the premises. *I can't let her walk out like this!* he thought, abruptly standing up without knowing what to do. For he couldn't very well go after a virtual stranger, a chance acquaintance he had met only once and who, besides, was not alone now either. He hadn't even paid his bill. . . .

On the edge of the curb, opposite Charles's table, the redhead suddenly bent toward Arabella and kissed her cheek. She began to cross the wide avenue, leaving the Englishwoman alone on the pavement, no more than a few yards away from him. For a moment Arabella stood adjusting her hat, watching her friend cross the street. Then she shivered and pulled her fox coat tightly to her body. A chilling breeze had risen.

Impulsively, Charles emptied his pocket of all his spare change and dumped it out on the table: the waiter would find much more than what was owed when he returned to the terrace.

Arabella had started to walk down the avenue toward the Place de la Concorde. She wasn't far ahead of him yet. Charles caught sight of her immediately, and started to run. At the curb of the rue de Berri, waiting to cross the street, he caught up with her, and finally stood close enough to speak. But his mouth had gone dry, and so the moment passed, and they crossed the street together without her even being aware that he was there.

"Madame Fayard," he said at last when they had reached the other side.

She turned, blinking, her brow furrowed. "Yes? We've met, haven't we?" And then, before he could tell her when and where, she herself made the connection. A slow smile of recognition lit her face. "The innocent young cousin . . ." she murmured. Cocking her head at him, she raised her brows. "Little Anne didn't do badly, monsieur. Armand and I were in Italy when you got married. I was sorry to have missed the wedding."

He needed to steer her away from the subject of his wife. Taking a chance, he plunged in. "Would you have a cup of coffee with me, madame? Or are you in a hurry to get somewhere?"

She shrugged charmingly. "I was going to a fitting at Chanel. But I suppose that could wait. They'll take my husband's money *any*time, thank you, so it may as well be tomorrow as this afternoon."

Jean Lafitte would be wondering where Charles was, but then again, he hadn't done something for himself, something just for his own pleasure, in years! He'd call the office from the café, and invoke a vague physical malaise and the need to rest awhile on a friend's couch. Arabella's perfume, an exotic blend of flowers and musk, thrilled him almost as much as her presence beside him.

Charles offered her his arm, and she took it. A diminutive woman in an absurdly large hat, she reached his chest level and no higher. But every inch of her was feline allurement, every curve a tease, every bit of fur a tantalizing hint of what lay underneath. And, as if to encourage their chance encounter, the breeze subsided just as suddenly as it had materialized, and the sun peeked out from behind the clouds.

Charles's head was in a fog. They were walking silently, neither attempting to fill the silence, until, nearing the Place de la Concorde, Arabella murmured, "Where were you planning to stop for coffee?"

Dazed, Charles opened his mouth to reply, but she planted herself in his line of vision and raised a delicately painted crimson nail to his lips. "I waited for six months to hear from you. After that, I threw my hands up in the air and asked the gods to take it from there! But I knew that someday, somewhere, our paths would cross again. I'm surprised we didn't meet sooner . . . in Deauville, or in Biarritz, or right here in Paris, at the theater."

"I think you just made up this story. You hardly recognized me half an hour ago."

"Ah." She arched her brow. "The male ego . . . Let's get to the point, Charles. You may call me Arabella. We might as well dispense with the formalities, don't you think? As for a café *express* —I've never particularly been a coffee aficionado. I'd prefer a glass of Dom Pérignon, *brut*—well chilled in tall frosted flutes of Christofle crystal. Frankly, wouldn't *you*?"

He stared at her, mystified. "Come now, be a good boy," she told him. "Flag down the taxi coming down the street. . . ."

Charles had never known that the anticipation of sex could be so intoxicating. It wasn't the excellent champagne—it was Arabella, undressed down to her hand-embroidered lace pantalettes and brassiere, seated on the black silk coverlet of the enormous four-poster bed, her legs tucked beneath her.

He was still aghast at her self-confidence. As if the experience were perfectly routine, she had asked the driver to take them to "her little pied-à-terre" on the elegant rue de la Paix, close enough to Alfred's office to have given Charles a bad case of nerves. She had unlocked the front door and revealed a rather cold but spectacular Chinese living room, then taken him to the black and gold bedroom. The walls were a deep Florentine gold-leaf hue, hung with Chinese etchings engraved in black ink. She had left him there, instructing him to relax, and had presently returned with the champagne, grapes, exquisite beluga caviar and tiny pumpernickel squares . . . and herself, seminude.

He couldn't eat. She ate for both of them, voraciously. She sucked the drippings from her fingertips and he watched, fascinated. Everything about this woman was sensual. "You remind me of a puma," he told her.

"Stalking my prey?"

"Is that what I am? Your prey? Your choice for the month, or for the week? Another amusing snack?" He couldn't help the sarcasm, because suddenly he was jealous. Jealous of all the others who had undoubtedly come here before him, to be sucked dry and then tossed out like empty shells into the garbage. She was his first adventure . . . but what was *he* in her life?

She stiffened, visibly displeased. "Listen, you cocky, oversensitive young neophyte. I'm a married woman. Armand Fayard is one of the most powerful men in France. Do you think I'd jeopardize my marriage for just *anybody*? Besides, in more ways than one, I love my husband."

"So I'm not just one of many?"

"You are *you*," she snapped. "I like you. Isn't that enough between a man and a woman?"

To make her point, she swept the tray to the side and leaned over. Her golden head was now in his lap, and she lay staring up at him. He had loosened his tie, and now, her fingers adept, she unbuckled his belt and began to undo the buttons of his pants. The tantalizing pleasure of her fingers caressing him as she worked the buttons made him close his eyes.

He could wait no longer. Gently pushing her aside, he stood up and removed his clothing. She lay waiting on the bed, a tawny jungle cat, well fed and poised for action. It crossed Charles's mind that he'd forgotten to call his boss. He didn't even think of Anne. Like a starved man, he fell on Arabella with a moan, unsnapping her brassiere and immediately taking a hardened nipple into his mouth. It tasted of orange blossom.

She was slipping off her panties, and soon was pressing her firm stomach against his equally firm penis. *"Now,"* she ordered. And then she took hold of him and parted her legs, guiding him inside her without the slightest trace of shyness or shame. She lay back on the silk pillows and crossed her arms behind her head.

It was her smile, hedonistic and self-involved, which gave him license to do whatever he wanted with her voluptuous body. For as long as he could hold back, she would be his this afternoon. Charles Lévy raised her legs above his waist and stuffed a pillow beneath her buttocks. Then, forgetting everything but the pleasure of their bodies, he plunged his penis to the very center of her being until she cried out in ecstasy.

And still, he would not give in to his own release.

Hours later, as they strolled through the Luxembourg Gardens hand in hand, she told him that her husband's offices were no more than a few blocks away from Alfred's. "Aren't you afraid?" he asked her, revealing his own anxiety. "Anyone might see us."

"All right then, yes: I'm a little afraid," she said. "Armand is a proud man, and besides, you know very little about me. What you don't know, what I've made sure *no one* in Paris knew, is that I come from a very modest family in Brighton. I went to work in a hat shop in London when I was sixteen, and believe me, I never intend to be poor again."

She paused, looked into Charles's eyes, and squeezed his hand. "But I also have to admit that I'm enjoying this. There *is* a thrill in being just a little bit afraid, in tempting fate and indulging in forbidden games. It adds to the excitement, don't you think?"

"I think you're just a little bit crazy, Madame Fayard," he replied, stopping in his tracks and taking her face in his hands. "And I'm equally crazy for doing this. Your husband could see to it that I lose my job, and make trouble for me everywhere in town."

"But your wife would never disinherit you." She smiled. "Armand wouldn't hesitate to send me right back where he found me. So you see, I'm in far greater danger than you are."

Charles brought his face to hers and covered her lips with his own. When he felt her arms wrap around his neck, he crushed her to him with a vehemence that took her breath away.

* * *

Charles sat gazing out the window of his office, the swirling autumn leaves reminding him of the strange, swirling tides in his own life. For more than four years now, he had been assistant personnel manager at Meyer Frères—almost as long as he'd been married to Anne. But for the last two, Arabella Fayard had brought excitement into his humdrum existence. Arabella's vivifying lust, her sense of fun and adventure, had prevented Charles from sinking into the doldrums of a personal and professional life that repeated itself in a leitmotif he knew by heart, day in and day out.

Inside the office, the middle-aged draftsman scraped the toe of his shoe nervously on the thick pile of Charles's carpet. Charles looked at him and thought: What about *him*? Surely no enticing, outrageous Englishwoman was throwing him handfuls of golden confetti as she served him champagne on ice. Unexpectedly, the young man felt a stirring of compassion, and he felt himself oddly moved. Every human being must have the same moments of frustration that so frequently shadowed his own thoughts, moments of wondering where life's magic had disappeared, and if all that could be left was *this* . . . daily existence.

"You're not an engineer, Philippe," Charles said softly. "You have to understand that a degree commands a great deal more money. If you want to rise in the organization, why don't you go back to school? You're a good draftsman."

"I'm a forty-five-year-old man with a wife and three children. If I *did* return to university, where would I find the money to pay my rent and the food for my family?"

Charles laced his fingers together on his desk. "You could freelance for us here, in your spare time. Believe me, Philippe, I wouldn't be encouraging you if Monsieur Lafitte didn't think you showed promise."

"I came to you for a raise, Mr. Lévy, not for encouragement and a pipe dream. I've been with the company for fifteen years."

"But still, you're not an engineer. We can't promote you; the best that we can do, we've been doing: giving you increases from year to year, and a healthy bonus. Take my advice. Go home, speak to Catherine, and give me your answer tomorrow. You'll see that she'll agree with me, and will want you to go back to school to get your degree."

The draftsman took a deep breath, and let it slowly out. "I suppose you're right. It's just that . . . well . . ."

"You're a little scared. That's more than understandable. We're all behind you, one hundred percent. Go home. Think it over. Life is full of promise, Philippe. If you've allowed it to defeat you at your age, think how bitter you will be at sixty. You'll constantly look back and wonder what might have happened had you taken my advice, way back when."

Philippe looked up from the floor, and his eyes met Charles's. Suddenly he smiled. "I think you've just convinced me," he declared, extending his hand across the assistant personnel manager's huge oak desk.

Charles grabbed the hand in both of his, smiling back. Yes, he thought: life was a banquet, laid out enticingly—and it was up to each human being to reach out and take what was being offered. *My time will come soon,* he told himself. And I'll be ready for it.

* * *

Anne felt apprehensive about the arrival of Juliette Fildermann and Jeanne Netter, and sat fidgeting in the formal living room, adjusting a vase, checking to see if there was dust on top of a picture frame, tying and retying the sash on her dress. What did these women want from her?

Jeanne Netter, in particular, unnerved her. Anne had met her twice before, in passing. She was beautiful and warm, an impressive woman, a well-known attorney who was divorced, and who was a militant Zionist. Juliette Fildermann was not, like her companion, a professional woman; but she was the wife of a famous doctor, and her activities on behalf of Palestine were known around Paris. They were two of the founding members of the French WIZO, the Women's Jewish Zionist Organization, which spread its philanthropic branches throughout the world.

What do they want with me? Anne thought.

Goujon announced the ladies, and Anne rose. Jeanne Netter really *was* a beauty in her nubbed silk suit, and Juliette seemed quite sure of herself as they walked in. Goujon bowed and silently departed, returning a little while later with a tea tray. Exchanging meaningless pleasantries, the guests sat down and waited while their hostess busied herself pouring tea and handing out petits-fours on small dishes of signed Meissen porcelain.

"My dear Madame Lévy–de Rochefleur," Jeanne Netter began, and her deep, sonorous voice rang clear and confident in the large old room. "To put it bluntly, we've come to recruit you for our organization. You surely know that there are WIZOs all over the world, and each country has elected to sponsor a particular institution in Palestine."

"There are centers that care for the children of mothers who must work, nursing schools, children's hospitals," Juliette interposed. "France was the only important nation not to have had a WIZO. And so, two years ago, Yvonne and I, as well as the daughter-in-law of the Grand Rabbi of France, founded a French branch. We felt ashamed, as Jews, that our country wasn't represented, that we were the only ones not making a contribution."

They want money, Anne thought, relieved. She rose. "I'd be glad to write you a check, of course. What kind of institution is the French WIZO sponsoring?"

Jeanne Netter smiled. "Our Canadian friends were kind enough to let us take theirs. It's a small agricultural college for young girls; there are only twenty students, and it's called Nahalal."

"Then I'll give you a thousand francs," Anne said in a rush. She wanted them to leave because talking to strangers, especially women of the world, still made her acutely uncomfortable. She could handle them better when Charles was with her: his presence brought her confidence. Jeanne Netter probably found her awkward and inelegant, and Juliette looked right into her, appraising her coolly.

Madame Netter laughed lightly. "That's a lot of money. What we really came to ask is that you join our group. There are approximately seventy-five members right now, and we are canvassing Paris for prominent Jewish women who can lend us their time and good name. Would you consider it?"

Anne turned red. "But—why would you ask *me*? I've never been part of any group, and what have I ever accomplished to make you think I could add to your organization?"

Gently, the attorney said, "You are the Baroness Anne Lévy–de Rochefleur. If anyone should add to our prestige, it's you. And besides your name and family connection, you are young, energetic, and bright. We'd like you to join."

"Next month, in December, we're going to hold our annual sale to raise money for our philanthropies. We'd like you to take a booth and help us sell something. Some of the ladies have crocheted lace doilies; others are going to sell culinary delicacies; and then, of course, there is our special booth with trinkets and food-stuffs imported from Palestine."

"I . . . I'll have to give it some thought," Anne stammered, still standing. "Thank you for coming."

When the women had left, she sat down and tried to think. They wanted her because of her name. But that was all right: what else had she ever done besides being born to the right parents? No one had ever personally sought her out; everyone she knew in Paris, she had met through the debutantes she'd known six years ago, and who had barely tolerated her because of her lack of sophistication. Later they had continued to tolerate her because of her name, and because Charles was on his way to becoming a Somebody. But she had no real friends, except her husband. And she wanted to become involved in something meaningful.

She valued her religion. It was important to her. She had been reared a Jew, and felt a Jew. There are so few of us left in the world, she thought. One *has* to do something: one must stand up and be counted. I'll do it, she decided, suddenly feeling better and stronger than she ever had. She'd prove to the world that there was more to her than a flowery name.

* * *

Charles adjusted the folds of his blue silk dressing gown, and sat down in the comfortable lounge chair. Its soft leather cushions sank like butter under and around his body, and he could feel the tensions of the day beginning to recede, as if an invisible geisha girl had started to massage them away.

He liked his bedroom. He had always dreamed of a masculine den in which to compose himself and hide from the world. The new Bauhaus decorative style pleased him aesthetically as well as in its concept. He appreciated its simple, clean lines, the way the chairs and sofas espoused one's natural body contours. The retrospective decor of La Folie, though very beautiful, made him feel thrown back to other times, times when the hustle and hysteria of contemporary existence had not yet altered society. Yet he considered himself a man of the '20s, a pacesetter, a modernizer. Although he appreciated the lessons of the past, he would not have chosen any other epoch in which to live his own life. And he had expressed this never more clearly than in the bedroom he had chosen on Anne's floor, so close to her delicate antiques, which soothed her spirit in much the same fashion as his Bauhaus pieces calmed his own. The disparity in their selections underscored for Charles the essential differences between them.

He picked up a ledger and started to look through the entries he had made over the previous week. It was his work ledger and included expenses he had been forced to make on behalf of the company, and raises and advances he had authorized. It had been a good week, although the best thing that had happened was the Philippe Monet affair. It made him feel good that because of their conversation, the draftsman had decided to return to school. Charles felt, again, that he had made the right decision in exchanging the drawing board for the job in personnel four years before.

He heard a timid knock on the door, and started. "Come in," he said, sitting up.

Anne walked in, her hair loose over her shoulders, her peach dressing gown trimmed with Brussels lace emphasizing her heavy bustline, tucked in at the waist and hugging her rounded hips. Charles felt a moment of awkwardness. Since the beginning of his passionate affair with the seductive Arabella Fayard, two years before, he had found it difficult to be alone with Anne in situations of intimacy. Sex between them always took place in the dark, and was accomplished with a minimum of optional trimmings. He couldn't help feeling a little guilty. It was easier, therefore, to deal with her at a public concert, or even around her father or her child, than it was to be face-to-face. For then her honest gaze inevitably unnerved him and put him to shame—not for his adultery but for his virtual neglect.

Charles cleared his throat. "Hello, Anne."

Anne looked around for a place to sit, and finally chose a deep armchair by his bureau. It was their first moment alone since that morning, without Alfred and Alexis. "Did you have a good day at the office?" she asked tentatively.

"Very good, thank you." He smiled at her. "I helped someone, I think, a good man who just needed some encouragement. What about you?"

"I had a good day too. I . . . had some visitors. Two prominent members of the Women's Jewish Zionist Organization, the WIZO. They came," she added shyly, "to recruit me."

Charles's brow furrowed. "You're not going to join, are you?"

"Actually, I'd just about decided to do it. It's a really worthwhile group, Charles, and my life . . . well, besides you and Alexis, I haven't been accomplishing much of anything. It's like your job—today you helped someone, and it made you feel good. I'd like to work toward something, to do something for more than just myself and my family! Can you understand? Or do you object?"

He swallowed, and laced his fingers together. He felt a strange sense of discomfort. He wanted to answer: Yes, I *do* object—and yet, looking at her, and hearing her plea for an identity more meaningful than simply as his appendage, he felt it would be cruel to stand in her way. Perhaps he owed this to her.

"You *do* mind," she observed, lowering her eyes.

"Well, Anne, it's not the work that I object to. I know it hasn't been fun for you, living here in the suburbs, seeing so few people, just playing with the boy and waiting for me to come home from the city. I'd been hoping . . ." Their eyes met, and she blushed, knowing the sentence that hung in midair. He'd hoped that by now, almost three years after the birth of Alexis, they would have had a child of their own. But that hadn't happened. Anne felt flooded with guilt, and looked away.

"Be that as it may," Charles stated, closing the painful subject. "It's something else. I somehow feel estranged from the Jewish religion, from religion in general. Mama was very lax when I was growing up, and I didn't formalize my Jewish education. Anne . . . I don't *feel* like a Jew. I'd like to feel like a Frenchman, but even there I've been thwarted. I'm a Swiss citizen on alien soil, and frankly, ugly as it may sound, being a *Jewish* foreigner makes my situation even harder. There may come a time, professionally, when a really choice position will have to be given to another man, less capable than I, by simple virtue of his being French, and a Christian. That's the world we live in, pure and simple."

"That doesn't justify indifference," she countered softly. "By being afraid of xenophobic rejection, you're *encouraging* anti-Semitism. The Jews have been wanderers throughout history. Isn't it time we, the privileged few, stood up for our beliefs and acted on them to help the less fortunate? The WIZO supports institutions in Palestine. I'd like to help."

Charles was astounded. He had never expected such strength of purpose from her, such powerful convictions. She was making him feel ashamed of his own uncertain beliefs. Still . . . "I just don't feel comfortable about it," he declared. "The Catholic French don't make a point of wearing *their* religion on their sleeves; neither do the Protestants. Why do the Jews need to band together in

Palestine instead of attempting to work out their problems in the individual countries of their birth? I am not, primarily, *a Jew.* I am a man, a businessman, a husband, a Swiss citizen. The fact that my forefathers practiced a religion that I've never really adopted doesn't mean that I must live out my own life branded with this identity! Quite frankly, Anne, I don't believe in *any* religion. I stopped believing in God when my grandparents were killed in such a stupid, ghastly accident."

"But darling, the WIZO is a *women's* organization. I wouldn't expect you to become involved in it. It would be *my* group, *my* project, *my* commitment."

"And you are *my* wife. Whatever you do, Anne, will be credited to *me.* If you are going to become a Jewish leader, then people here will assume that I share your ideals."

"This would be bad?"

He sighed, exasperated. "No, no, not *bad.* That's too harsh a word. I just meant . . . Oh, hell, Anne, I don't really know what I meant! Do as you please."

"Thank you, Charles." Her face appeared to relax, to radiate a sudden warm glow. Then, gratefully, she came over to him and sat down on the arm of the chaise longue, very close to him. He could smell her perfume.

She was sitting above him, and he had to look up to see her face. Full lips, and the beautiful eyes. Nice, shining hair. The lace collar came down to just above her cleavage, and her breasts were just at his eye level. A woman. He tended to forget this, that Anne, too, was a woman, like Arabella. Charles had simply allowed Anne to seep into the wallpaper and blend in with the house. He hadn't really *looked* at her for a long time . . . if ever.

Anne was sitting there, quietly. Her hand was lying in her lap, and he suddenly took it, surprising them both. It was a nice, warm hand, strong and firm. He felt overcome with tenderness, and embarrassment. This was his wife, and he barely noticed her.

Anne bent down and, very gently, reached out and touched his face. He caught her other hand, and sat up straight, so that they were sitting almost level now. She wasn't beautiful, but she did possess a certain handsomeness. Besides, marriage represented a fortification against the unpredictable enemy—loneliness—that threatened to attack him at any moment. With Arabella there were feasts of lust, but little tenderness, little compassion; they inhabited different worlds, and came together only for sex. Anne was his friend: she cared about him as no one ever had except his mother.

Charles pulled Anne toward him, and when their faces were very close together, he took. her in his arms and kissed her, with gentleness that was very close to pity. Pity for both of them, each so alone in his and her own right. Normally he never kissed her, and so she was surprised and touched. And then she began to respond, and he could feel the strength of her bosom pressing against his chest.

Holding her familiar back with fingers that were just a little shy, he decided that, tonight, he didn't want to sleep alone. Tears of gratitude were pearling Anne's lashes, but he pretended not to notice as he led her toward his bed.

CHAPTER X

On the morning of her second WIZO benefit sale, Anne walked into the large rented hall holding Alexis by the hand. The twenty-five-year-old woman and her little boy stamped their boots to shake off the December snow, and to restore their circulation. The huge conference room was still being set up for the sale, workmen assembling booths. These were composed of two tables of unequal size, a small one in front of a large one, the whole arrangement covered with green dropcloths that fell to the floor. Next to the booths were small cashier's tables for the WIZO ladies in charge, with chairs behind them.

"Come," Anne said to her son. "Help Mama to set everything out on the two tables."

Alexis would soon celebrate his fifth birthday. For his age he was tall and thin, with dark curly hair and enormous black eyes. Now, obediently, he began to take things out of his mother's large cardboard box: embroidered baby clothes, lace pillows, little girls' dresses. This was the most wonderful place he had ever been. Better than the circus or the Small World Theater, which put on children's plays. And the best part was that he would spend a whole day with his mother. This almost never happened. The little boy set out the pretty things on the two tables, trying to make them look even prettier for all the nice ladies who were running around from booth to booth.

Anne was sitting behind her cashier's table, beginning to feel stage fright. Alexis looked at her and understood. Mama was afraid of people . . . unlike his father, who got along with everybody and knew just what to say to make them laugh. Alexis felt sorry for his mother, and so he tried to make her feel good whenever he saw her being afraid, to make her understand that he loved her and that she had nothing to be frightened of.

His mother was deep in conversation with a beautiful lady with blond hair, who was taking out her checkbook and writing something down. Alexis looked around and decided that she wasn't going to miss him if he wandered over to look at the other booths.

What beautiful things the ladies were selling! There was a stand with nothing but books on it, and one with food in jars that he had noticed before in the delicatessen. Then there was a wonderful stand with oranges, honey, dates, Carmel wine, interesting embroidery in gold and silver threads that he had never seen anywhere before. And brooches and necklaces and bracelets, all of silver filigree, delicate as a butterfly's wings. This stand had a cardboard sign propped at the front, which read PALESTINE.

An old lady was bending down to ask him his name and to whom he belonged, and then Alex had a splendid idea that would make all of his mother's fear and nervousness disappear. She'd reward him the way she always did whenever he was particularly good or particularly clever: holding him tight and kissing him. She smelled of lilies and talcum, and her bosom was ample and soft, like a fresh down cushion.

He said to the lady: "My mother is really nice and she's selling lots of pretty things. Why don't you come over and buy something from her?"

"Very well, young man," the lady replied, smiling brightly at him. "Just lead the way!"

He was going to make his mother very happy. He would go around the large hall and ask all the ladies to come over and buy from his mother. Alexis sighed, extraordinarily pleased with himself.

At the end of the long and exciting day, the good-looking lady with the gold chignon and the pearl-colored suit, whose name was Madame Netter, came over to speak to his mother. "Anne," Madame Netter told her, touching his mama's shoulder very gently. "You and Alex brought in more customers than any other booth in the hall. I want to congratulate you on behalf of our whole group."

"It wasn't really my doing," his mother demurred. But her eyes were shining and she was blushing. "It was Alex's salesmanship. I didn't do so well last year, do you remember, Jeanne?"

"It was your first sale. Now you're an old hand at this, dear."

The two women stood smiling at each other, and Alex felt good. His mama looked as though Madame Netter had given her the most beautiful basket of roses, just like that, for no specific reason.

She seemed embarrassed and unsure whether she should accept the compliment. And yet very, very pleased.

Finally she said: "Thank you, Jeanne. I'm glad I helped our cause." And then she let Madame Netter plant a kiss on her cheek.

Alex squeezed her hand proudly.

* * *

Anne couldn't believe what was occurring. The Sarah Bernhardt Theatre, across the street from the Châtelet, had suddenly come alive in a most unexpected fashion. She had convinced Charles to take her to the premiere of the new spring season of Diaghilev's Ballets Russes. He didn't much care for the ballet, but having been born in Russia, Anne adored it and seldom missed an opening. The innovator of European dance never failed to surprise his audience —and for Anne, whose life was stitched in tradition to the last millimeter of petit point, it was exhilarating to experience such outrageous displays of creative energy.

Anne could feel pinpricks of excitement rising over her bare skin. An ermine stole lay draped over her shoulders, just right for a springtime evening, but it was hot in the large theater, and she shrugged it off. She leaned forward, peering through her opera glasses at the stage, from which the curtain had barely risen to gasps from the audience. This was clearly not going to be a classical rendition of *Romeo and Juliet*. The painter Joan Miró's avant-garde curtain already told her that, as well as the spectacle of the dancers practicing at the barre in simple, everyday attire. Diaghilev's new Russian import, Balanchine, was listed as the choreographer of this piece.

"What *is* this?" Charles was demanding just as whistles and catcalls rose from the stalls and aisles.

Anne looked from the stage to the audience, and gasped. The neat velvet stalls, with their expensively dressed patrons, had been broken into by a group of hooligans. A lady behind her was saying, "It's the Surrealists! They're outraged that Diaghilev was able to woo two of their 'purists,' Miró and Max Ernst, to work on the decor! Look upstairs!"

Pamphlets were raining down from the gallery. Suddenly Charles rose and extended his hand to his wife. "Let's get out of here before all hell breaks loose," he told her tersely. "I've had enough."

Anne hesitated. It looked as though the spectacle on this side of the stage might have developed into quite an evening's entertainment. But it would have been wrong to oppose her husband. Charles detested scandal of any kind. He hated crowds and always feared what he called "mob insanity." And so, swiftly, she grabbed her fur and hastened after Charles.

Armed policemen were already making their way into the theater. Anne scurried after Charles, who was striding out, making room for her to pass behind him with sharp jabs of his elbows.

They pushed their way past hundreds of people into a crowded lobby, and thence to the fresh air outside. Anne clutched her tiny headdress of egret feathers, to make sure it was still all there. Her heart was beating rapidly. "Thank God we're out of there," Charles was saying, catching his breath.

"I thought it was rather fun," Anne timidly counterposed.

"And *I* thought it was the best part of the ballet!" came a clear, energetic voice from behind her. Anne whirled around, surprised, and found herself staring at Arabella Fayard and . . . Armand. Anne's lips parted, the color draining from her face.

Arabella was laughing. "Fancy meeting you two here!" the Englishwoman declared. "Dear Anne, we so seldom run into each other these days. And *what a night*!"

Anne knew she had to say something, to cover her embarrassment. She hadn't been face-to-face with Armand Fayard in six years, since that time when he had seduced her. Although her father socialized with the steel magnate, Charles tended to stay away from the important businessmen who made his own beginner's status cry out by comparison. "We'll mix with them when the time is right," he would tell her, his tone half bitter, half dreamy. "When I'm a success in my own right, *le tout Paris* will beg to include us at their tables!"

Anne stood speechless now, aware that three people were looking at her expectantly. If she didn't say something, Charles would wonder why. And Arabella, with her appraising eyes, would suspect something. . . .

Charles was being perfectly charming, as usual. He was taking Arabella's hand, raising it to his lips, remarking, "Why, how very nice to run into you both. Madame Fayard, monsieur, it's a pleasure to renew our acquaintance."

"Well, an old man like me gets tired of these left-wing demonstrations," Armand Fayard explained, chuckling. "Arabella wanted to stay, of course, but it was getting to be a regular riot in there, and hardly funny."

"The woman behind us thought the demonstrators were part of the show!" Arabella said, laughing. "Oh, well, trust Diaghilev! I've always enjoyed his productions. Do *you* like him?"

"I think he's brilliant," Anne replied sincerely.

"When I married a Russian, I didn't realize I'd also married the whole Russian ballet," Charles quipped.

The four of them fell silent. Arabella played with the diamond clasp that closed her white-and-gray mink cape at her throat. Armand Fayard seemed not to mind the silence, but Anne found it excruciating. Arabella was kicking the heel of one shoe with the toe of the other, distracted, a little bored. And Charles . . . Anne turned to look at him and saw a closed expression—his stone wall, as she called it. He was appraising the Fayards while politely waiting for one of them to speak.

"I hear you've become active in the WIZO, Anne," Arabella said. "It must be very time-consuming."

"It's rewarding," Anne replied. "And I don't really have that much to do. . . ." She'd wanted to say: I have a lot of free time, because we have only one child. Embarrassed by what she had nearly stated, Anne bit her lip.

Arabella appeared to read her mind, and jumped right in. "And your baby? It's a little girl, isn't it, Anne?"

"No, it's a boy. Alexis. He isn't a baby anymore—he's five." She was blushing. "He doesn't need me fussing round him every minute."

"Do *you* have children, madame?" Charles was asking politely.

Arabella laughed. "Of course not! I'm not the motherly type. And frankly, I hardly think Armand would appreciate a brood of little ones."

"One wouldn't be bad," the industrialist stated, his eyes on Anne. He wasn't smiling, but his eyes were kind, steady, encouraging. *Does he know?* Anne wondered, panicking.

"We wouldn't mind a second," she stammered. "Would we, Charles?"

"Well," her husband said smoothly, "it doesn't matter one way or the other. A good marriage stands on its own merits, not on the number of offspring it happens to produce. At least," he demurred, smiling, "that's my own humble opinion."

He was trying to tell her that he wasn't angry about her miscarriage last month. He *had* minded, though, she realized. He'd wanted his own son. But Dr. Letellier had warned her to be careful, not to get pregnant again right away. How kind of Charles to have found this way to reassure her.

She was still ashamed, deeply ashamed, that she had given in to Armand Fayard so many years ago. She'd never forgiven herself for having behaved in such an amoral fashion. It wasn't that she hated Fayard. She hated *herself* for what had happened. Armand Fayard was asking Charles, pleasantly, "I've been told you climbed to assistant personnel director at Meyer, Lévy. A wise move. It's always good to vary your experience, and to come into personal contact with the people who keep a company rolling. Are you enjoying the work?"

"Very much, sir. I'm very grateful to Monsieur Meyer for having had so much faith in my abilities so early on."

"Is Charles more married to his job than he is to you, Anne?" Arabella joked. "There are *days* when Armand simply disappears."

"Oh, Charles doesn't do that. He's the best husband a woman could hope for. If he's being detained, he always telephones."

Arabella was staring at her strangely. Had Anne said something wrong? But Charles was stroking her arm, and she could feel warm approval through his fingertips. It was going to be all right.

"I'm delighted that your marriage has brought you both such joy," Arabella Fayard declared, her green eyes like two emeralds, shining and cold. "And it was certainly amusing, running into you like that in the middle of a riot. It added a spark to the evening, didn't it, Armand?"

"Oh, definitely, definitely," the steelman concurred. He was smiling at both Anne and Charles. "My dear Anne, be sure to tell your little boy about the more colorful aspects of tonight's performance—and I don't mean Miró and Ernst's decor! Children do love the unexpected, don't they? Sabers and soldiers and that sort of thing."

And then, very quickly, it was over. In a flurry of courtesy, hands were kissed, good-byes were proffered, and Arabella had taken Fayard's arm to go in search of their driver. "I'll get our car," Charles told her. "You'll be all right, waiting by yourself?"

Alone, Anne leaned against a wrought-iron lamppost, idly listening to some other couples who had left the theater. Almost everyone had stayed inside, and the performance had resumed. She saw, out of the corner of her eye, a number of policemen gathered around the entrance. But she was thinking of Fayard, and of how, out of the blue, he had brought up Alexis before taking his leave.

There was absolutely no reason for Armand to suspect. Some men, particularly the older, childless ones, were drawn to wistful thoughts about other people's young children—that was all, nothing more. Anne breathed a sigh of relief.

Arabella was an odd woman, though, she thought, remembering the ball at La Folie, when the catlike Englishwoman had practically devoured Charles with her green eyes. With a sudden flare of jealousy, Anne thought: I could never be friends with such a predatory woman.

Charles was driving up, and Anne picked up her skirt to hurry forward to meet him.

* * *

Charles stared at the simple vellum card adorned only with an equally simple *F,* and felt his stomach contract and his heart beat faster. *He knows,* he thought. Somehow, the other night, though Arabella and I both thought we'd carried it off, our performance wasn't good enough for Fayard. . . . He didn't dare look down and read the message, and for a moment he put the oversize card on his desk and held his forehead in his hands.

I have to face this. Grow up, Charlie. It will be worse for her, much worse. He picked up the card again and looked at it.

Armand Fayard's handwriting was big and bold, like the man himself. *Read it,* Charlie. And so he read:

"My dear Charles:

I would like to meet with you this week, for lunch. May I suggest a small restaurant on the rue Geoffroy-Marie, near the Folies-Bergère? It's called Chez Boilaive, it's unpretentious, and they serve the best pot-au-feu in the city. If the time is convenient for you, I shall meet you there at 1 P.M. on Thursday. Please make sure to confirm through my secretary. With my best regards to your charming wife—"

Fayard had simply scrawled his initials on the bottom.

Why else would he want to meet me, and in such an unlikely place? Charles wondered. Men like Fayard lunched at Lapérouse, Prunier, Le Grand Véfour, or Fouquet's, so accessible to successful businessmen with centrally located offices. The answer was obvious: *He doesn't want to be seen by anyone he knows.*

He knows about me and Arabella, Charles decided. And he doesn't want to risk anyone else's finding out by seeing us together.

There was no choice. As a man, Charles had to face his accuser. *But what would he say . . . ?* Fayard held all the cards, Charles thought wryly, frustration choking him—*or did he . . . ?*

* * *

Charles was beginning to enjoy himself. Even a murderer is allowed one last meal, he told himself, trying to joke aside his apprehension. And I'm only an adulterer! The waiter, Louis, picturesque in his shirt sleeves and black vest, was ladling more delicious pot-au-feu into their soup plates.

Across the checkered tabletop, Armand Fayard sat buttering a roll. At first Charles had felt uneasy coming here. The street lay on the outskirts of the Jewish district, and the young man wondered whether the industrialist had been making a point—a humiliating one—by selecting a restaurant in this area.

But then Charles had been forced to let down his guard. The food was wonderful, tasty and plentiful, and the cheerful voices of the patrons rounded out the invigorating atmosphere of Chez Boilaive. And then there was Fayard himself. Charles had to admit that he thoroughly liked this man, even if, later on, the ax would fall and he would pronounce Charles's days on this earth numbered.

Perhaps this was Fayard's way with his enemies: make them feel good first, so that when disaster hit it would take them completely by surprise. In the meantime, Charles observed his lunch companion, and drew a quick conclusion. Fayard was not a snob. He was self-confident and without any illusions about his identity; he was self-made, and proud of what he had accomplished. He was sensual and down-to-earth, yet highly sophisticated when it was necessary. He dressed as well as Charles's father-in-law, but without any of the added frills that Alfred affected. Armand Fayard was canny, he was wise, and he was well read in those areas he himself considered important.

I wonder why Arabella still wants me, after four years, when she has such a virile man at home, Charles wondered. By comparison, although he still delighted in her sexually, he found her singularly less interesting than her husband. Fayard was a genius, yet a simple man. Arabella was street-smart but most often obvious.

The two men had begun by discussing French politics, and

Fayard had told Charles that only Poincaré's return would be able to save the nation's economy.

"You aren't thinking of running for office yourself, monsieur?" Charles questioned.

Fayard smiled and chewed on his stewed beef. "The politicians don't control the nation," he said softly. "Businessmen do. I see the future in steel rods, not behind the walls of the Elysée Palace. And what about *you*, Lévy? Where do you see your career taking you?"

Charles colored. The question had risen out of nowhere, it seemed. Yet, knowing Fayard, it had been carefully preplanned. But why? "I'm not sure," he replied, surprising himself with his honesty.

"You obviously have made up your mind not to remain with Meyer."

"Well . . ." Charles hesitated, then plunged in. "Jean Laffitte, the personnel manager, isn't going to be retiring for a while. And when he does, he won't be pushing my candidacy: I'm not one of 'his boys.' Meyer imposed me on him, and I know why. Let's face it, my father-in-law had a lot to do with my promotion. And I'd rather be somewhere where I'll be operating on my own merits, and where my performance alone will determine my future. But, for the moment, I'm learning about how a company runs, and I am not unhappy."

Fayard wiped his mouth with a neat white napkin, drank down some hearty Châteauneuf-du-Pape, and riveted his small black eyes to the young man facing him. "Charles, do you have any idea why I picked this place to meet you?"

Now the ax is being lifted, Charles thought. But he did not betray his emotions. Leveling his own gaze back at Fayard, he answered, "Frankly, no. I wondered about that myself."

"It's very simple, my boy." Now Fayard was lacing his fingers together on the table. "It's my staff's job to keep up with the brightest young men being fostered in the industry. I've been following your career since I met you at the ball Alfred gave before your marriage to his daughter. And by the way, that's a nice girl you've got, sincere and smart. You must be very proud of her, and of your son."

Why has he veered off the subject? Charles wondered, a little annoyed. "Anne's a very good wife."

"And the boy? What's he like?"

"He's quick, he's bright. He isn't noisy or troublesome, the way some children are. He's a good child, Monsieur Fayard. Thank you for your interest."

"I like to find out how a man considers his family," Fayard stated, taking a deep breath. "It rounds out the facts and numbers that my staff puts together. I don't hire paper soldiers or stick figures: they make for very poor executives. What I look for are men with gumption, who don't mind taking risks . . . calculated risks . . . and who have hearts beating underneath their hand-made Oxford shirts. Do you understand me, Charles?"

The young man was finding it hard to think at all. Somewhere in this neat speech, the steelman had delivered a totally unexpected piece of information, and now Charles sat stunned. At length he shook himself back into composure, and murmured, "I'm not sure."

"I'm offering you a job," Fayard announced. "As Paris director of personnel. Oh, certainly, my man in Nancy who supervises the mines and the shops holds greater power than you will. But it's a step toward bigger and better things within a fast-growing industry, one that will soon be more essential to man's development than any other.

"I'd like you to go home, Charles, and discuss this with Anne. Perhaps also with Alfred. Your job would involve a lot of paper work and a lot of coordination, keeping track of what's going on in the Lorraine and my other factory sites. Let my offer sit for a week. And, by the way, don't worry about salary. I'll match what you're making at Meyer Frères, and add a twenty percent increase to sweeten the deal."

Charles sat back, flabbergasted. "I wanted to avoid the possibility of our being seen together prematurely. The business world is rife with old wives carrying tales into their backyards," Fayard concluded, summoning Louis to order their coffee. "But I like you, young man. I think that if you threw your lot in with Fayard Industries, you wouldn't live to regret your decision."

Smiling, he added, "And neither would I."

* * *

A pewter-gray sky lay draped over the industrial complex. The advent of autumn 1931 had brought a humid chill to France's eastern region. Charles Lévy–de Rochefleur and Armand Fayard walked at a steady pace inspecting the site of the extensive company works in Lorraine, from the iron ore mines to the steel and blast furnaces, to the foundries and the finishing mills, moving from intense heat to the cold outdoors without pausing for a moment's respite.

After the Great War, when the eastern province of Lorraine had been won back from a defeated Germany, Armand Fayard had bought back important German works near Nancy and modernized them. The Lorraine area was rich in phosphoric "pig iron," crude iron directly handed over from the blast furnaces after being smelted down. To turn it into steel, the iron had to be alloyed to small quantities of carbon and other metals, in order to prevent rusting.

Throughout the Fayard "empire," which included, besides Lorraine, steelworks in the center of France as well as in Belgium and Luxembourg, Armand Fayard had evicted the old-time foremen and installed in their stead scientifically educated men who were more open to novelties in the process of steel manufacturing. The finishing mills, where the steel ingots would be rolled into salable products, needed to be run more efficiently. Charles had been sent "on location" a number of times, for Fayard had wished to test his acumen as an engineer.

Charles had watched, his brow dripping sweat, as "blooms" and "slabs" were prepared in a first finishing mill, then taken to a second where the blooms were rolled into "billets" or sheet bars, and finally into rods, smaller sections, or sheets. He had inspected tons of semiproducts, the rolled steel that would be sold as is, for the purchaser's own plant to finish rolling.

But it was Fayard's habit to remain personally in charge, overlooking nothing. Every morning in his Paris sanctuary, he would spend three hours checking out reports from his mines and factories, coordinating facts and figures. He sat like a spider at the center of an intricate web, aware of every thread and realizing that each one was linked back to him.

Armand Fayard, though in his mid-sixties, was still an active, physical man—his barrel chest bulging with muscles—who liked to visit his work sites. Charles, more delicate of temperament, had at first felt less than enthusiastic about visiting the Lorraine area, where the leaden, overcast sky induced monumental migraines. He had frankly preferred his plush office on the rue Cambon, with its fine Persian carpet of interwoven reds and blues, its stately mahogany furniture, and the Picasso etching he had had placed beside his bookcase.

But then, with successive visits, he had begun to grow excited. And the breadth of his expertise had increased with his responsibilities. He had mediated in negotiations with angry eastern Europeans who had felt cheated by being paid less than the more sophisticated French and German workers. Now an eight-hour day had been established throughout the Fayard Industries, and he himself had been compelled to implement a three-shift system at the plants to compensate for the shorter hours.

Charles had been forced to learn the characteristics of the various kinds of steel, of each of the plants, and of the methods of transportation peculiar to each area of production. Since 1926, Charles had learned a great deal about the complex mechanism of the steel industry. From simply looking after Fayard's personnel files from the Paris headquarters, he had moved into the tributary branches of the industry. He had learned to "speak the language" of the steelworkers and to be trusted by them. But Fayard had also trained him to sit down in boardrooms and haggle over railroad prices with the railway owners and the French government.

Charles's respect for his boss had grown enormously as he had learned to know him, and his habits, better. Armand Fayard was vice-president of the all-powerful Comité des Forges, which controlled ninety-seven percent of the iron and ninety-three percent of the country's steel production. After the war, he had assumed the mission of coordinating the armaments industry, and had begun to stretch his empire into foreign domains. And now Alfred de Rochefleur's bank, the Crédit Industriel, was in the process of setting up an international holding company to manage the Fayard assets.

Armand Fayard liked to pay "ambush visits" to his managers, dropping in on them unexpectedly. It was his method for keeping them on their toes at all times. Now, as he hunched his huge shoulders against the insidious cold, he turned to Charles and said, "We're being hit hard by the slump, my boy. The whole French economy is suffering."

"Maybe the Germans will finally pay their wartime reparations?"

Fayard laughed. "Not a chance. You know, those Hitlerists over there are spreading out like an inkblot. There are millions of them now. And the Austrians are planning to form a customs union with Germany. But they're still broke. Even if they *wanted* to pay us back, they wouldn't have the funds to do it."

The two men had reached one of the foundries. Fayard leaned against its wall and faced his young companion. "Do you want to know what I think the *real* problem is? We had Poincaré and Aristide Briand. But they're both old and sick. A country cannot live for long on the lifeblood of its grand old men. It needs new blood. And who do we have? Tardieu, fallen from grace through scandal, and Laval, who wants to *lend money to the Germans,* for hell's sake, in return for a promise not to rearm! What kind of deal is *that,* Charlie? To trust our enemy?" He sighed. "France needs the brilliance of young minds, young leaders. A nation is no different from a business. It needs heirs."

Charles sucked his lower lip in silence. The theme of heirs cropped up now and then in his conversations with Fayard. The old man was sixty-five, and Arabella was now thirty-seven, no longer of such perfect childbearing age.

He was growing bored with Arabella, after nine years. They slept together three times a week, often in the rue de la Paix apartment, when Charles could be certain that Fayard was definitely somewhere else. But even their sex had become ritual. Not that it wasn't still erotic. Arabella was sensuous, vigorous, and adventuresome. But she was also tough, brassy, basically uneducated. They belonged to two different worlds, and where her youth had tamped out the boundary line at the beginning, her rapidly approaching middle age now underscored it.

Fayard was a self-made man, but a wise one. He had bought himself a flamboyant showpiece for a wife, from whom he hadn't expected more than her capabilities could provide. But he was disappointed to be leaving no one behind him. Charles thought: This man is desperate for a son. He's been grooming me for the position for the last five years. Does that mean . . . ?

The young man could feel the juices of ambition speeding up inside his veins. To be *Fayard's surrogate son* . . . All the great families of France had produced heirs. Even the de Rochefleurs, with Alexis. *To step into Armand Fayard's shoes and run the Fayard Industries* . . .

Charles looked down pensively at his shoes. Arabella lay between them like a wicked Circe from whom he couldn't easily escape. *She'd never let me go,* he thought. *I'm her toy, her possession.* And, frankly, who else was there in his life to indulge his sexual fantasies?

There was something else too. Arabella, shared by the two men, represented an invisible link between them, a bond. Fayard didn't know it, but for Charles an additional excitement existed because she was *his wife*. For there was no one in the world that Charles more admired, or hoped more to emulate, than his supreme boss, his mentor, his patron.

I've already started following in your footsteps, Charles thought. I've been sleeping with your wife for the past nine years.

"You're a lucky man," Fayard was saying, his voice a little raspier than usual. "You have the boy. You have that new blood I was talking about . . . that heir."

"But an heir to *what*, Armand?" Charles countered softly.

The older man looked at him, magnetizing him with his sharp black eyes. "I need someone to look after the holding company. Someone who can make a bridge between me and the Crédit Industriel . . . between me and the de Rochefleurs."

Charles opened his mouth, then found that he had no words with which to formulate a coherent answer. Finally he asked, "Why *me*, Armand? I'm no financier."

Fayard rubbed his gloved hands together. "You're a businessman. I've let you learn all facets of my affairs. Why not this too? And besides, I trust you. I've had five years to watch you up close, and you haven't disappointed me yet."

Once again the specter of Arabella slipped between the two men, laughing at Charles, warning him. A gust of wind came up, and abruptly Fayard turned his back on him and pushed open the door to the foundry. A blast of heat hit Charles in the face, and he plunged inside after his boss, overcome.

* * *

Amelia had chosen warm, vibrant greens, yellows, and peach tones for her upholstery, and vividly colored Aubusson carpets for the parquet floors. Everywhere in this house so full of lights and shadows, she had placed vases and bowls with fresh-cut flowers, and green plants that stretched out like creeping vines. The servants were amused because their mistress liked to supervise the housekeeping, although she was far from punctilious and always merry and soft-spoken. But she took pleasure in her home, and each tiny bibelot reminded her of its history or of how it had happened into her life, and for this reason bore special significance to her.

Amelia felt her heart swell, and wondered, as she sometimes did, what she had done in previous lifetimes to deserve such perfect joy, such enchanted harmony. The theory of reincarnation made absurd sense to her and helped explain what she believed to be her magical bliss today. She considered herself basically selfish, and often chided herself for this bad quality. Peter was anything but selfish: he was always helping people, ordering casseroles of food to be delivered to a sick employee, or paying for a cashier's mother to go to the hospital. *She* might not even have remembered that a cashier was on the payroll, she thought, ashamed.

Peter was leaning against the grand piano. His image always thrilled her, sending wonderful sensations from her heart to her stomach, and down into that secret part of her body. He was a passionate man who loved to touch her, to stroke every part of her when she lay naked in his arms, to kiss and fondle and gently nibble her erect nipples and the soft, sensitive flesh of her inner thighs, teasing her until she cried out for him to stop and penetrate her.

After the lovemaking she almost never returned to her own room. Sated and sleepy, he would pull her to him as he lay on his side, his lean, well-muscled legs and stomach fitting perfectly into the curve of her slender backside. And she would float off to sleep, wanting to burst with gratitude because of the gift of his love, because he had chosen *her*—self-centered, scatterbrained, unintellectual Amelia von Guttman—to share his life. And they had their child to prove it: creamy-skinned Christina, her cheeks the color of ripe peaches, her eyes cobalt blue like her mother's, her hair jet-black like both her parents'. Another gift that he had brought to her, seven years ago.

Peter was tall, dark, sensually handsome, his profile strong but finely chiseled. This summer evening, the last day of July 1932, he stood informally attired for a dinner at home with a few close friends. His tan bush jacket, of hip length, had padded shoulders, a tailored collar, and two sets of pockets, and he had casually belted it over matching pants. He resembled an African hunter, and had in fact helped to popularize the safari fashion among their "smart set." Amelia glanced at her brother, deep in conversation with Peter. Though Richard was always elegantly clothed, his traditional silk jacket cut a less spectacular effect than her husband's outfit.

Next to Richard the opera singer Lotte Lehmann stood delicately balanced, one hand on Richard's arm, absently twirling a champagne coupe through her fingers. After dinner, Peter would ask her to sing an aria or two for their guests, out of the kindness of her heart. Following in the footsteps of his father, Richard appeared to have developed a predilection for glamorous divas. Completing the picture, the Count and Countess von Stecher—Karl stiff and Prussian-blond and Nanni vivacious and pert in a sleeveless green gown—stood sandwiched between Lehmann and Peter.

All at once Amelia's mother sailed in, her huge puffed sleeves like the silk wings of a monarch butterfly. Her perturbed face, like her dress, glowed crimson. Immediately Amelia felt an alien sense of alarm, and hastened in her wake toward the small group by the piano.

Pausing dramatically in front of them, Barbara von Guttman stopped Nanni von Stecher in midsentence, and drew bewildered stares. Amelia walked up, and instinctively Peter placed his arm around her bare shoulders. "What is it, Mother?" Richard asked.

"I just heard the German election results on the radio," Countess von Guttman declared. "And that man Hitler's Nazi Party won two hundred thirty seats in the Reichstag! The announcer said this makes them the largest, though not the majority, party in parliament!"

Von Stecher raised his brows and allowed himself a rather disdainful half smile. "He's just a posturing comedian," he stated. "Surely, Gräfin, you don't take him seriously?"

Peter's jaw tightened. "Have you read *Mein Kampf*? He may be posturing, Karl, but he's hardly a comedian. His first step, if he accedes to power, will be to annex Austria." Then, tightening his arm around Amelia, he added more softly, "And to eliminate any race or culture he imagines would threaten his beloved Aryan purity."

"You mean the Jews," Richard filled in.

An uncomfortable pause followed his statement. Lotte Lehmann held her champagne coupe to the light of the chandelier and examined the effect. Nanni von Stecher scratched a tiny mole on her left forearm. Karl's smile remained sketched on his lips, but his china-blue eyes slid imperceptibly from Peter to Richard as he stood waiting.

"Hitler asked President Hindenburg to give him the chancellery of the government, but so far the old man is stalling," Barbara announced.

Amelia shivered and looked into Peter's eyes, seeking reassurance. She saw only cold, white anger. "Hitler is the greatest men-

ace ever to loom over Europe," he said. "He's a megalomaniac and
a bigot. Worse: He means what he writes. And the German people
are like sheep. They'll follow any shepherd promising to lead the
country out of economic disaster. No matter how inhumane his
means."

"You're overrating the man's power," Karl von Stecher insisted.

"I don't think so. He's appealing to the men of the right, who
will accept his notion that Jews and socialists are part and parcel of
the same baggage. Nobody wants to lose their money, and everyone's afraid that Stalin's system might infiltrate western Europe.
Hitler's been playing on this fear and using the Jews as scapegoats.
He's suggesting that they're responsible for skimming the profits in
Germany."

"We don't think so over here, and that's all that matters," von
Stecher asserted.

"Nevertheless, Karl, the Christian Social Party in Austria stands
both for conservatism and anti-Semitism. I'm sorry, I certainly
don't mean to offend you. I know that you belong to this party and
it's done nothing actively against the Jews in this country. But the
reality is clear: A Jew can't be a member of your party, and your
greatest enemies are the socialists."

"The Reds in Moscow frighten everybody," the blond count
stated. "And that has nothing whatsoever to do with the Jews."

"Karl has never been an anti-Semite," Nanni von Stecher spoke
up. "God knows, Amelia—you and Richard were our friends for
many years, long before you ever married Peter! To want to fight
communist and socialist influences within these borders has no
connection whatsoever with Herr Hitler in the Reichstag. We
wouldn't hold you so dear to our hearts if we believed in 'Aryan
purity'!"

"It's all right, Nanni," Amelia murmured. "Peter didn't
mean—"

"I meant nothing against Karl and Nanni, any more than they
mean ill against us, or Richard, or your mother," her husband
broke in. "But I feel the stink of apocalypse beginning to blow
toward us from Germany, like a gust of warning wind. I wasn't
born or reared a Jew, but what my wife is, I am. Therefore, spiritu-
ally I have become a Jew, not in religion but in heart and soul. And
I'm afraid for our beautiful country, and for its Jews, if Hitler
seizes power across the border."

Hauser, the Habigs' frail and elderly butler, chose this inopportune moment to cough from the doorway. Peter looked at him, annoyed. "I beg your pardon, sir, but dinner is served," the old man explained, apologetic for his interruption.

Lotte Lehmann smiled, and slipped her hand through Richard's arm. "I hear your cook is absolutely the best in Vienna," she crooned to Amelia. "Count von Guttman has described so many splendid meals. . . ."

Amelia glanced at Peter. He still seemed angry and worried. But Richard had set his drink down and was gazing longingly at the beautiful opera singer he had just recently begun to court. Barbara was sighing audibly and shaking her head, but already she had taken a few steps forward, leading the way to the dining room like a dowager queen. And the von Stechers had, with evident relief, decided to sweep their host's unwelcome implications from their minds.

What had just occurred? Amelia wondered, her stomach still knotted. Peter had come dangerously close to insulting their good friends, the very people at whose estate they had first been introduced. Amelia's qualms would not abate. Glancing at her husband, she shuddered slightly. Was their existence so fragile that a small, pompous man a country away could threaten their crystalline security?

Surely, no one could touch us, she assured herself, looking toward the priceless treasures in her beloved living room. No one could break into the world we have so carefully created. . . .

* * *

Amelia felt Peter moving beside her, and she reached out to throw an arm over his waist. She knew that if she didn't open her eyes, this sweet semisleep would continue to hold them together for a few more minutes. At forty-three, this February of 1934, Peter was still as muscular and lean as he had been thirteen years before, when they had married; and thirty-three-year-old Amelia liked to snuggle up to him in bed, to fit her slim form to his, to feel the warmth of his body giving her warmth. It helped to start the day this way, she thought, trying to pretend she was still asleep.

Amelia's hand moved to her husband's taut stomach and felt the rippled muscles with light, tentative fingers, and then, to make sure he would not rise and leave her just yet, she let her hand move down to the tufted hair below his belly. Peter moaned, and Amelia continued, savoring each sensation as her fingers closed about his penis and he slid back down into the bed. It was difficult to keep her own eyes closed, but it was also better this way, more exciting.

Peter moved onto his side, and she felt his strong, hard body pressing against her. He was lifting her lace nightgown and kissing her, while his hands cupped her breasts and rubbed the nipples. I wonder how much longer it will be this magical, she thought, opening her legs so that he might enter her. And then he was inside her, and she stopped thinking altogether.

Afterward, she propped herself on the pillows and watched him lying beside her. A few white strands were now threaded into his black hair, and this added to his distinction. He was handsome, virile, but vulnerable here next to her, his nudity offered up to her with neither shame nor pretension. Perhaps this was the right moment to tell him, she decided, admiring the line of his neck as it flowed into his shoulder. She still felt thrilled by the way he looked, although she'd known him half her life.

All at once the trilling noise of the telephone burst through the shell of their intimacy. Amelia jumped back, and Peter sat up. "What time is it?" she asked in consternation.

"A few minutes to seven." He reached over to grab the receiver on his side table. Close to him, Amelia felt a tangle of emotions: alarm, anger, loss. Their island had been invaded.

But Peter had shaken off all signs of sleepiness and eroticism, and was listening, alert. She listened, too, to what he was saying. "It's all right, Liesel. I'll be over as soon as I can. Try not to panic."

"Who's *Liesel*?" Amelia asked him when he had set the receiver back into its cradle.

"Young Hoffmeier's wife. The men down at their housing complex have been getting excited, and she's worried they may try to start something."

"That doesn't make any sense," Amelia retorted as he struggled into his clothes with hardly a look in her direction. She felt violated, as though this strange woman had thrust her own problems between Peter and her . . . just as she'd been about to tell him the news.

"Hans Hoffmeier's become involved in the local Schutzbund," he told her. Hoffmeier was one of the junior bookkeepers at the Maison Habig, where his father, Kurt, had for many years been Peter's chief accountant. The Schutzbund was an army formed by the Social Democrat Party in the 1920s to combat the growing

power of the right-wing militia, the Heimwehr, a Fascist organization Peter had lobbied against. Its leader, Major Fey, practically
controlled the Austrian chancellor, Engelbert Dollfuss.

Amelia was confused by the political situation in their country.
Peter had been furious when "Millimetternich," the tiny Dollfuss,
had declared an end to parliamentary democracy and instituted an
authoritarian corporate state. Peter had refused to wear the red-
white-red ribbon of Dollfuss's Fatherland Front, in principle, to
display his opposition to the chancellor's actions.

And yet "Millimetternich" had outlawed the Nazi Party in Austria. He had taken a stand against Hitler. "A lot of good *that*
gesture will have," Peter had scornfully declared. "Major Fey does
whatever he pleases with his little army, and as far as I can see
there's little difference between his views and those of our mus-
tachioed house painter in Berlin."

Peter wasn't an advocate of the Schutzbund, either. He was,
Amelia knew, a man of intense ethical convictions, who believed
that nothing good ever came out of blind, brutal force. Yet the
Heimwehr frightened him more than the workers' army, for it was,
he felt, built on hatred of the poor and the powerless . . . not
unlike Adolf Hitler's brownshirts in Germany.

Peter felt that something bad was taking place throughout Europe, that the Fascists were taking over everywhere. A year ago
there had been much bloodshed connected with Hitler's being
named chancellor by President Hindenburg, and this had been
only the beginning.

Just last week in Paris, a tremendous riot had been instigated by
the veterans and other right-wing groups, and the Mobile and Republican Guards had had to be called in to restore order. Amelia
had cabled Anne at La Folie, suddenly worried about her cousins.
But Anne had cabled back that no one in the family had been hurt,
that although Charles had witnessed some of the fighting from a
balcony of the Fayard offices, he hadn't been personally involved.

Amelia felt a little dizzy, imagining French veterans and the
Republican Guard clubbing each other while crowds pressed forward, caught in the frenzy. Hitler's "blood purge," and now the
rioting in Paris, meant that Peter's worries were not exaggerated.
A mounting hysteria appeared to have been unleashed all about
them, closing in on their small country.

Yet Peter wasn't sure in which direction Austria was now
headed. And without a parliament, political activity didn't have

the same effect. Men dabbled in it like angry little boys intent on stirring up controversy, but no real progress could be made in the realm of social equality. Peter wanted to wait before involving himself again in a political movement. He wanted his voice and his vote really to mean something.

"Why are you getting mixed up in this?" Amelia now asked, a shade resentfully, about Hans Hoffmeier. "What can you possibly tell this young man that will make him listen to you?"

"I'm not sure." Peter regarded her with a curious expression of confusion and pain. He shrugged. "I'll listen, first of all. I owe it to the old man, for all his years of devoted service. Hans and his wife and children live in that large municipal complex in the Margareten district, so I'd better leave as soon as possible before anything happens."

"*Peter! Wait!*" He turned at the door, staring questioningly at her. She had to tell him now, although she didn't know why it suddenly seemed so urgent.

"What is it, darling?"

"I—" But all at once it didn't seem right, telling him this way. "Peter . . ."

He came back, sat down on the bed, looking into her face with probing, anxious eyes. "What's wrong?"

And so she put her hands on his shoulders, and buried her face in his neck. "Nothing's wrong. I just wanted you to know that I'd been to Dr. Kuntz yesterday. We're going to have another child, next September. It's been such a long time, hasn't it? Christina will be nearly ten when this baby's born."

He pulled away and took her face in both his hands. He was smiling, and kissing her face all over. Yes, it was good that she'd decided to tell him now.

* * *

"What's *he* doing here?" the tall, florid leader demanded.

Embarrassed, the junior accountant ran his fingers through his thick mop of red hair and murmured, "It's my boss. Liesel called him."

"I imposed myself," Peter Habig declared, placing himself neatly between the two men. "And now that the Inner City's been cordoned off, there seems no way for me to return home or go on to my office. What the *hell*'s going on here?"

"What right have you to mix in our business?" the leader retorted angrily. He was about Peter's height, but with a bulging set of muscles that appeared hewn in iron. Now he plumped out his chest and glared at the other man, challenging him.

Politely, Peter held his hand out. "My name's Habig—Peter Habig. And Hans told you, his wife asked me to come, to prevent bloodshed. But it never occurred to me that something *this important* was about to take place."

He looked around. They were standing in the middle of a dance hall, modestly decorated with last week's wreaths and paper flowers. When Peter had arrived in Hans Hoffmeier's housing complex, Liesel Hoffmeier had immediately directed him to this place, where the workers and their wives usually gathered on Sundays to listen to a band and dance. He had entered, wondering at the incongruity of selecting a recreation room for a meeting of the local Schutzbund . . . and had stumbled right into the middle of a revolution.

All around them young workers were dragging in arms, revolvers, and guns, piling them up against the back wall. They were quickly converting the dance hall of the municipal block into a veritable arsenal. Appalled, Peter had found his junior accountant and demanded to be told what was going on. The young man, alternately impassioned and awkward, had blurted out the entire story.

Early that morning the police had broken into the Social Democratic headquarters at the Hotel Schiff in Linz, a city in Upper Austria. They had been searching for Schutzbund arms, and shots had been fired. "Who fired first?" Peter inquired, his sense of alarm rapidly increasing.

"We're not sure." The young man had looked down. Then, leveling his clear blue eyes at his boss, he had continued: "The Social Democrats in Vienna have just declared a general strike as a collective sign of solidarity."

"Major Fey's been waiting for a provocation like this to strike back," Peter had announced disgustedly. "Your naive gesture of support's going to be read as a declaration of civil war."

Now the tall, muscular leader said to Peter, "We don't need you to stop any bloodshed. If the Heimwehr attacks, we'll fight back, that's all. We're prepared."

Peter couldn't help following his gaze around the room. Stacks of weapons and rifles were now piled ceiling-high, and at least fifty men stood milling around the dance-hall floor. He shuddered.

"Nobody needs you, rich man," the leader taunted. "You can still leave, you know."

But Hans Hoffmeier said, tentatively, "My father told me you were always on our side, that when you were young, you belonged to our party and voted Social Democrat."

Peter smiled. "That was another era. The days when we had just become a republic, and Otto Bauer was the idealistic figurehead of this organization. Things have changed, Hans."

"Things seldom change, Herr Habig. I don't agree with Jens here: we *do* need you. We need you to fight against the clericofascists, this Fey and his Heimwehr. Just *think:* everyone knows you're married to Countess von Guttman. She's *Jewish!* What do you think will happen to our Austrian Jews if Fey has his way?"

"Fey will never have his way."

"We don't think you're right. That's who we're fighting against, Herr Habig—the Adolf Hitlers of the Austrian nation! And we need good men on our side."

"We're workers, Hans," Jens, the florid muscleman, interposed with disdain. "This isn't a parlor argument we're talking about."

"And my boss isn't a parlor politician. My father knows him very well, and I've been around him all my life. Herr Habig had the courage to marry a Jew. And he has the conscience to think of his employees, and to give us decent wages and benefits. Things are going to get very hot in here, and I'd like Herr Habig to stay."

Peter flushed, embarrassed. "Thanks. But it's not my fight, and I promised your wife—"

"Wives have no place in such affairs. No woman, no matter how smart, can understand why a man has to stand up for his beliefs. We must back up our integrity, but they don't care about this principle because it wasn't *meant* for them to care! They're *women,* for God's sake—they care about making babies, and cooking meals, and sewing and mending. They care about love. But what's love, Herr Habig, if we don't have a country? Or if our country has been taken over by Catholic fanatics like Major Fey, who's nothing short of a Fascist?"

Peter, acutely uncomfortable, stood rubbing his hands over his upper arms, deep in thought. He wanted to get out of that dance hall, and quickly. He visualized Amelia, and felt the deep pride of knowing she was pregnant. He considered his little daughter, Christina, the portrait of her mother and his own delight. Next time, perhaps they'd have a boy. . . . *What the hell was he still doing with these workers?*

But Hans, at twenty-two, had managed to unearth half-forgotten sentiments that had animated Peter when he'd been that age. Pride. Self-pride and pride of country. The need to believe in something greater than himself, more global even than patriotism . . . something called humanity. Every man and woman deserved his dignity, and it was each man's duty to fight for his own dignity as well as that of his fellow human being.

"You've just lost your chance," Jens called out to him sarcastically. "We've bolted the doors and are about to barricade ourselves in. You can't leave now, Habig, even if you want to."

Peter found himself looking right into Hans Hoffmeier's eyes, which revealed a naked bond, a pride of brotherhood, and a staunch bravado. He was *daring* his boss to force his way out, to leave all the workers behind him now.

For a moment, Peter defied him with his own intense eyes, holding him at bay. Thinking of Amelia, Christina, and his unborn child. Hungrily wanting to be home with them, in his beautiful old manor house. Missing them acutely in his heart and with every fiber of his being.

If Major Fey and his Heimwehr were ever to gain control of the Austrian government, Peter's little family would no longer be safe, in spite of his gentile name and all their combined wealth.

Peter felt a sudden surge of vigor, of anger, of eagerness. He hadn't chosen to become involved, but now he *was,* and it felt right to him.

By evening, Peter realized that the situation was far more drastic than he had previously envisioned, and he felt a swelling of anxiety. Through an open transom, the women of the housing complex of the Margareten district had passed sandwiches to their men, and they were eating: tense, without speaking, most of them perspiring from apprehension and expectation, as before a battle.

Peter had counted sixty-eight men barricaded inside the dance hall of the Reumann Hof. After a full day with them, listening to their complaints and to their hopes and dreams, he felt disconnected from his own reality. Now, sitting down on a lopsided wooden chair, he tried to think about his wife, about his home. But Amelia's lovely face, with her diamond earrings and her delicately rouged lips, suddenly seemed unreal to him—or rather, a part of another, distant reality. He wondered what was happening to him

—a rich man, a member of the elite, a capitalist, among blue-collar and lower-level white-collar workers. For he felt more closely attuned to *their* fate than to his own wife's. . . .

He looked around him, and, from a foot away, Jens Thiessen smiled at him. After his initial hostility, the flush-faced muscular leader seemed to have mellowed toward Peter. His smile displayed two rotten teeth, bringing home the disparity between their two worlds. Life was so bleak and dismal for most of the people here in these simple apartments . . . so totally unlike his own existence in the Old City.

"I was just thinking about my family," Peter said. "My wife has no idea where I am. And there's no way to telephone her at all."

"With the Inner City cordoned off, and the blackout, she'll figure you were held up somewhere. Don't worry, Habig. Women know how to take care of themselves."

"Amelia doesn't," he answered automatically. "She's never had to."

They fell silent. Hans Hoffmeier came up and crouched next to Peter, munching on the last of his sandwich. "Fey's been around," he muttered in a low voice. Jens approached, and Hans elaborated. "I have bad news. Liesel just passed us a note through the transom. There's been shooting all over the place. The police and the Heimwehr even blew up some of the other housing complexes, and women and children were killed. Mass murder."

Peter felt the blood freeze inside his veins. "If he comes around here, I'd like a chance to speak with him. I'm an impartial observer —I might be able to help. There's no need for shooting—"

"You're a few hours too late, Habig," Jens Thiessen commented ironically. "Impartial observers remained in their own homes, taking no risks. From the moment that Liesel Hoffmeier brought you in here, and you chose to remain, you became one of us, whether you like it or not!"

I've made a mistake, Peter thought, intensely pained. I gave in to an impulse, when my better judgment should have sent me home hours ago.

But I had no choice, he argued. They'd barricaded this place and closed off all exits!

I could still have gotten out. Where there's a will, there's always a way. *I'm here because I wanted to be,* because I hate Major Fey, and because I've spent the last sixteen years running a luxury establishment for the wealthy, like a country squire in his ivory tower, out of touch with human concerns and the people that keep Austria going.

Suddenly a rude noise made them all jump, and a man cried out, *"The Heimwehr!* Listen!" A series of explosive sounds reverberated through the dance hall: shooting in the distance. Immediately, Jens called out, "Every man to his position!"

A mad scramble ensued. The men frantically raced for their guns, and flung themselves behind the crude barricade of upturned chairs and tables piled near the windows. Peter felt a surge of excitement, and fear. He remained immobilized, goose bumps spreading over his flesh.

"Here, Herr Habig," Hoffmeier whispered, handing him a rifle. "Come on!"

"Maybe I can still do something to stop this," Peter countered.

"You'd better duck," the young man replied tersely, his hand on Peter's elbow.

Outside, a flare-up of lights emblazoned the windows. Peter could see the outlines of many men in the dark uniforms of the police, and the more muted colors of the Heimwehr. They were holding lights and guns. He heard a disembodied voice, then saw a man with a huge paper funneled into a loudspeaker standing on a makeshift podium, outside the dance hall. The voice blared out: *"Come out with your hands up! Give yourselves up now! In the name of the Republic of Austria!"*

Right before Peter's eyes, one of the older workers jumped on top of the long table by the window, and broke through the glass pane with the butt of his rifle. He shouted back: *"Never, you Fascist pigs! We'll fight to the death!"* This drew other yells, other impassioned voices raised against the Heimwehr. It was panic. And the tension of waiting to see who would fire first.

Peter heard himself say something, and realized that he was reciting a Hail Mary. At the same time, he was automatically checking his rifle. Beads of sweat fell from his brow onto his hands as he worked, making space for himself behind some chair legs. This was crazy. It made no sense at all. He was caught in a conundrum, thinking of Amelia at home, wondering and wringing her hands. And his mother, who hadn't heard from him all day, and who had probably been told he'd never even telephoned his office.

And then it happened. Peter saw the Heimwehr officer throw something, and he heard the glass shattering into a million shards as a grenade hurtled through the window pane. Outside, the flare of lights glowed an unreal yellow in the darkened sky. The men beside him jumped back, and he felt himself being thrown from his spot onto the floor. Hans Hoffmeier's arm was protecting his torso.

"God almighty!" Peter muttered, sitting up and looking around at the carnage all around . . . bodies bloodied and dismembered right next to him. He felt a wave of nausea and fury. How *dared* Fey do this!

A tremendous crash broke into his thoughts, and he saw the hole in the front door, blasted by the second grenade. Rifle butts appeared on the other side. Peter fumbled with his own gun, shouldered it, aimed . . . and tried to pull the trigger.

Instead, he felt the most incredible pain he had ever experienced slicing through his right hand. Nauseated, he doubled over and dropped the gun. He looked at his hand, amazed to see a large red gash dripping streaks of blood, and his forefinger hanging loosely by a thin skein of flesh, dismembered.

Mustering all his self-control, Peter glanced toward the hole in the door. He saw rifle barrels pointing at him. In an instant, he managed to duck down behind another body, registering in the back of his mind that it was Hans Hoffmeier, and that the young bookkeeper had been killed.

And then the grenade blasted through the wall, and Peter had no time to think any further. In a single split second a flying grenade hit him full in the head, and what had been Peter Habig exploded into thousands of particles of flesh, and bone, and blood.

Later, when they came to count the casualties, Peter's headless body was identified by Jens Thiessen just before the latter was carted off to jail with the rest of the survivors of the Reumann Hof massacre. The tall, blond Heimwehr officer who heard Jens's pronouncement displayed a horrified face to his superior, Major Fey. "Peter *Habig*? The sports couturier? What on earth was *he* doing with *them*?"

Major Fey frowned. "What was *he* to you, this Habig?"

The other man hid his face in both hands. "He was my friend," Karl von Stecher replied, his voice breaking. And then, abruptly, he turned on his heel and left the dance hall, retching.

CHAPTER XI

The voices were ominous because everything else was wadded cotton, muted and soft, as Amelia felt herself drift back into consciousness. Soft white pillows, a soft eiderdown cover, gray light forced out by drawn curtains. No one was paying attention to her, and she looked around to find the owners of the voices.

Her brother was there, and her mother. And Peter's mother, all dressed in black. What was she doing here? Amelia wondered. Next to her stood old Dr. Schleicher, with his stethoscope and some linen towels. "Is she going to be all right?" Richard was asking.

"Well, yes and no. She'll be in shock for a few days. The tincture of valerian should help if she becomes hysterical again."

Why were they all speaking about her? Why were their tones so ominous? Amelia cautiously sat up, then placed her bare feet on the carpet. She stood up, a little dizzy.

She could see the open door, and the sunlight playing on the landing beyond. Dr. Schleicher was going out. Amelia stepped up, hiding behind the door to hear what else they had to say. Was she ill?

"It was a terrible mistake," Richard was telling the doctor. "We should never have told her. I blame myself, really. She loved him so much. . . ."

"The mistake was Fey's. The entire tragedy could have been avoided," Schleicher retorted. "I wish to God that Peter had never gone to that young man's apartment. Everyone who knew Peter had to appreciate him."

Amelia felt something hitting her in the stomach. All at once, everything was coming back to her in vivid detail. *Peter was dead,* murdered by the Heimwehr. *Peter wasn't coming home anymore . . . he was dead.*

It wasn't possible. Peter, her husband, her love, her life, was lying dead in a funeral parlor, awaiting burial. She hadn't said good-bye. He'd died alone, without a chance to hold her or to be told how very much she loved him. . . .

But I can't live without him! she silently screamed. Amelia flung the door open wide and rushed out onto the landing. Dr. Schleicher, followed by Richard and the two mothers, was already halfway down the second set of stairs, and she began to hurtle down after them, wanting them to do something, wanting them to negate everything and tell her that he wasn't really dead. "Richard! Richard!" she cried, and everyone turned to look back at her. Her mother even took a few steps toward her, holding out her hand.

"Amelia! Get back in bed!" Barbara called. But it was too late. She was already running down to them, in her bare feet and white piqué nightgown. She felt her right foot turning, felt the excruciating pain in her ankle, tried to catch on to the banister . . . and fell forward, rolling over her feet and somersaulting down to the next landing.

Her last conscious thought, as they all rushed up to her, was that it would be all right to die, now that Peter was dead. . . .

When Amelia came to, she was once again propped up on white pillows in her own room. But there was a searing ache between her legs, and in her lower abdomen. Gingerly, she placed a hand over her stomach, instinctively protecting the baby she'd been carrying for two months. Her right ankle, too, hurt terribly.

Dr. Schleicher's kind face was bending over her. "You're going to be fine, Amelia," he whispered. "Just fine."

"But it hurts down there, Doctor."

He looked aside. "Amelia, you've lost a lot of blood. That was a nasty fall."

Her fingers flew to his arm, tightening around it. "Blood?"

And then he sighed. "You've lost the baby," he said, taking her by the shoulders. "But the good thing is, you're all right, Amelia. You're all right."

* * *

When the German Reich finally annexed Austria in March of 1938, Amelia Habig was thirty-seven years old and had been widowed for four years. The year of her husband's death had witnessed yet another murder: that of the diminutive Chancellor Dollfuss, at the hands of some of the Nazis whose party he had outlawed in Austria. "Millimetternich" had been replaced by Kurt von Schuschnigg, a man equally reactionary.

Amelia had followed these events with a strange detachment. After Peter's funeral and her recuperation from her miscarriage, she had not cared to resume her previous existence. Without the husband she had passionately loved, she had floated around like the spirit of her former self, a spectator rather than a willing participant in all aspects of her life.

Mostly she led a quiet existence in her Renaissance mansion, with her daughter, Christina. Good friends visited them, and she saw her mother and Richard at least three times a week. Richard had never chosen to marry; at forty-three he was still considered among the city's most eligible bachelors, and preferred to be open in his polygamy. Unlike his father, he had been careful not to leave illegitimate offspring strewn throughout Vienna. He managed the extensive and lucrative von Guttman dynasty with a hand that was both dominant and gentle: his coal miners loved him for his fairness, and feared him for the same reason.

On March 11, 1938, the Germans asked Chancellor von Schuschnigg for his resignation, and installed a cabinet of their own choice, headed by Seyss-Inquart. On Sunday, March 13, President Miklas officially passed the reins to his successor. Seyss-Inquart was instructed to begin implementing the laws of the German Reich in Austria, while officially waiting for a plebiscite that was to take place on April 10 to determine whether the Austrians would accept this amalgamation into their sister empire. But everyone knew that this was a mere formality—the Austrian Anschluss was already a fait accompli.

The patriotic opposition—of which the Jews as a single body were a part—settled into this new state of affairs with stunned resignation. Now Nazi parades, accompanied by loud martial music, proudly unfurled their banners in the open streets, and Christina and her governess were instructed no longer to take afternoon walks in the park. And then one afternoon, Richard came to explain his business to Amelia: he had sold some of the mines and moved the family's liquid assets to Coire, Switzerland.

"Soon," he told her, "we may all have to move. Especially you. You've got two strikes against you, little sister. You're a Jew, and Peter was a known anti-Nazi. I want you and Christina to go to a priest I know, Father Stadler."

"I've heard of him," Amelia replied quietly. "His nickname's

'John the Baptist.' Where are you afraid the Nazis would send me? To a prison? Do you think I care? My life has so little meaning now that Peter's dead—''

"That's nonsense, Amelia. You have a daughter! Stadler will write you a false certificate of Aryan descent."

"And who will believe him? We're the most important and best-known Jewish family in Vienna. We'd fool no one."

Richard sighed. "You and Tina might. Your last name is different. Not everybody knows you were Countess von Guttman."

She looked at him levelly. In her clear blue eyes he read the futility of everything he was proposing. "Perhaps things will normalize, Richard. Maybe the plebiscite will make us lucky."

But her words rang hollow to both their ears.

On the afternoon of April 1, Christina and her governess went for a drive to visit Countess von Guttman on the Ringstrasse. When they came home, the thirteen-year-old girl burst into her mother's sewing room and cried, her face flushed with excitement, "We saw some *Jews* scraping graffiti off the walls on the Schwindgasse! And there were some men with brown shirts and that funny sign, like a crooked cross, who were kicking them and forcing them to grovel on their hands and knees!"

Amelia stared at her daughter, dumbfounded. Slowly, she removed her spectacles and set them down on the sewing table. "What do you mean, *Jews?* Who told you who they were?"

"Our chauffeur, Stefan. He said to Fräulein: 'The Nazis are using the Jews to cleanse the town of anti-Nazi propaganda!' He sounded really angry about it. And then he asked her if she was pro-Nazi, or pro-Austria. She answered that she hadn't realized patriotism meant 'anti-Nazi,' and he asked: 'Do you want our country to be free and safe?' And she asked: 'For whom?' ''

Amelia licked her dry lips. " 'For whom?' What a strange reply."

"Then he looked at her and they both looked at *me*, and Fräulein took my hand and petted it and said, 'I wouldn't want anything to happen to hurt my sweet girl,' and Stefan said sarcastically, 'The Nazis aren't about to pick out the good ones. She'll go, and so will Frau Habig, and the Count and Countess von Guttman.' And Fräulein shuddered, and asked me not to tell you about their conversation. She said I was too young to understand political discussions."

Christina made a space for herself among the patterns her

mother had set out on the second chair, and sat down. Her pretty heart-shaped face, milk-white with her mother's sapphire eyes, looked vulnerable and young in the evening light. "If the von Guttmans are so important," she ventured, "then why should it matter that we're Jews? Papa wasn't even Jewish! And Uncle Richard is seeing that ballerina, who isn't Jewish either. What difference does religion make, Mama, as long as we all believe in God? Why should the Nazis care about who worships what, or how?"

"I don't see the sense of that either," her mother replied. But she stood up, restless and disquieted, and began to pace the floor of the small room. Anger was filling up her heart. "Tina," she finally said, "there's always been prejudice, in every country, in every age. And the Jews happen to be good businesspeople. It's easy to be jealous of their success, or their money. But the Jews are a proud people, darling, and have always walked the path of honesty and courage. Cowards—and the Nazis are the worst possible cowards —are often afraid of us because we've been smart, and because we've been honest. If we'd lied and cheated to achieve success, we'd look more like *them,* and seem less peculiar!"

The young girl nodded, still somewhat puzzled. "Fräulein gave me a gold cross to wear on my chain, instead of my mezuzah. She said it would be better, 'given the circumstances we were now living under.' " And she fumbled with a long gold chain and displayed the cross.

Unable to speak, Amelia took the cross from her daughter, and shivered.

The next day, around teatime, the majordomo, Hauser, announced the Countess Anna von Stecher. And right on his heels, Nanni scurried in, reaching out toward Amelia.

"What a lovely surprise!" Amelia stated, smiling her welcome. "Hauser, bring us a tea tray in the living room."

"Oh, my darling, I don't plan to stay long," Nanni protested. She fussed with the jabot on the front of her silk blouse. "I just slipped in to tell you something, that's all."

"Surely nothing's wrong between you and Karl?" Amelia queried.

"No, it's not that." Nanni looked around the room anxiously. "But you know I love you. And so I thought I should come and warn you, before it's too late. . . ."

"Before *what*'s too late? I don't understand."

"Karl thinks you and Christina should leave Vienna," Nanni

breathed out, not looking at her friend. "The plebiscite will change many things. Austria will have to adopt the laws of the Reich, and in Germany the Jews have been treated as second-class citizens since 1933. Everyone is leaving, Amelia. You should too."

"Karl is pro-German, I take it."

Nanni nodded. "It's come down to that, yes. He feels the National Socialists have turned their country around since the Great War, and that our economy needs them. But none of this matters. If the Nazis take over officially on April 10, you and your family will have to wear the yellow Star of David, and give up this house . . . and God knows what else!"

Amelia stood up abruptly. "I've always lived here. I've never been one to spend much time abroad. Where would we go? And what about Mama, and Richard? Our assets—"

"The Nazis aren't going to leave you many assets," Nanni countered. "If I were you, I'd pack my bags this very night and go to France or Switzerland, while the borders are still open. You're a rich woman. You and your brother have more 'assets' than most families dream of for a lifetime of luxury, even if you end up losing some of the coal mines. Believe me, Amelia, pack your suitcase *now*!"

Horrified, Amelia collapsed into Nanni's arms, bursting into sobs.

* * *

In the middle of the night, Amelia was rudely awakened by the sound of splintering glass and sudden shouting. Her heart hammering, she grabbed her robe and ran to the staircase.

From the landing, she could see what was taking place in the foyer, several stories below. Hauser, in his tattered bathrobe, was pleading with some strange hoodlums in uniforms of the Nazi SS. She could recognize the insignia, for since the beginning of the Anschluss they had been thronging the streets of Vienna. Two of the men grabbed the old butler by the lapels, and were shaking him, threatening him with the butts of their revolvers.

Terrified, Amelia couldn't move, couldn't utter a sound. Part of her feared that they were now about to be killed, that there was no recourse. Another part knew that she had to help her servant. Still another told her that Christina was her first priority. And so she rushed to her daughter's room, flung open the door, turned on the lights . . . and found herself staring at the huddled forms of Christina and her governess.

"They're going to kill us," Fräulein whispered. "We have no-where to hide!"

Amelia turned the lights off and went to the bed to join them. Christina was weeping silently. *That's how they murdered Peter,* she thought. And waited, trying to think of means of escape, and finding her brain a sudden dull hollow.

Now she could hear the rest of the servants, and more breaking glass. Sounds of drunken men, laughing. She couldn't make out Hauser's frail voice anymore, and wondered, Have they already killed him? Her cook was screeching something in a hysterical tone. . . .

But now there were two voices coming from the stairs. They were singing a song, one of the martial songs the Nazis loved. She could make out the slurred words, and her blood curdled: "When Jewish blood spurts from our knife, then life goes twice as well!"

"We don't stand a chance, Mama," Christina murmured. Her hand in Amelia's lay frozen, and her voice was muffled with terror.

Then the door was kicked in by a boot. The three women held on to one another, paralyzed. The lights were flicked on. An SS man, tipsily waving a canvas bag from which Amelia could see a silver candelabrum protruding, appeared on the threshold. "Where's the woman?" he called out, his words uneven but loud and strong.

Nobody answered. Behind him, Amelia could now discern two other men, with guns. *They're going to kill my baby,* she thought, and stood up, all at once resolute and proud. They'd kill her no matter what, but she'd be damned if they'd touch Tina! "Which woman do you want?" she demanded.

"The rich Jewish bitch! We all want her!" The three men laughed, their faces red and demented in the yellow light.

"I am Amelia Habig," she declared softly, and walked up to them, erect and dignified. "What are you doing in my home?"

The first man reached out and grabbed her by the shoulder. He smelled of malt liquor, and his eyes were bloodshot. His fingers were digging into the gentle flesh beneath Amelia's robe and night-gown, and she wanted to scream out in terror and pain. But she knew that to survive this incident, she was going to have to put up a front—to show her courage and face them. Hadn't she told Christina that the Nazis were cowards, but the Jews brave and true?

The second SS man pushed forward and shoved himself against

her, cornering her against the door. He sang, right in her face:
" 'When Jewish blood spurts from our knife—' "

"You're not going to kill me," she told him levelly. "You've
come for other reasons." She motioned at the canvas bag. "What
do you *really* want? The keys to my safe?"

"We already found them!" the third man said derisively. "Your
butler submitted them. What we want, little woman, is a piece of
your Jewish whore's ass. Just a little piece . . . but tasty!"

From the bed, Christina started to sob convulsively, and the
governess rocked her in her arms. Amelia glanced toward her,
anxiously. "Let's go into the hallway," she said.

"Not on your life! What we do, *they*'ll watch. I want them to
remember what gets done to arrogant Jewish bitches whose families have titles that don't rightfully belong to them!" And the man
grabbed Amelia's nightgown, and began to tear it off. The crinkled
percale made a horrid ripping noise. The other two SS backed off
to give him more space, laughing and cheering him on.

Amelia stood quaking inside. But she controlled her mounting
panic by thinking of Christina. She tried to keep her face from
registering her fear, and held her chin high. The man had torn the
nightgown in half, and her robe had fallen down her back.
Seminude, she stared at her assailant, daring him to continue. He
was drunk, she was cold sober; he was crazed, she was in full
possession of her faculties. Surely, *surely* heaven was on her side,
and she'd be able to stave off these men. . . .

But they were three, and she was one; and they had guns, and
she had nothing but her clean spirit and her determination.

What good would it do them to murder us? she thought as her
eyes closed to block off the vision of the SS man unbuttoning his
fly. She felt him press against her. Amelia had not felt a man's
penis in four years, and the only man she had ever been with was
her loving, gentle husband. Revulsion pumped through her like a
spasm of nausea; a spurt of bile shot into her mouth, and she firmly
swallowed it down. Tears pressed against the back of her eyeballs
and, with equal resoluteness, she squeezed them back. There was
tomorrow to look forward to . . . and Tina's joyful chatter and
the safety . . . the safety of her brother's arms, of her mother's
bosom. . . . *This* was not the reality on which to concentrate. She
had to somehow block it out.

Her back was clamped hard against the door, and the man had
flattened her breasts with his body, glued to hers. Because she was

completely dry, he had to shove his penis inside her with even greater brutality than either had anticipated. Amelia couldn't help screaming, and the tears sprang out from the sudden, ripping agony. The rapist laughed again, enjoying her expression, as he rammed his hardened organ against the gentle wall of her cervix. She felt as though her center were being punctured, and felt a warm stream of blood sliding down her thighs.

In the early dawn, Christina's whimpers were the only sounds that broke the silence in the girl's bedroom. Finally emerging from shock, Amelia stood up, and sponged herself off with a remnant of her nightgown. Without looking back, she walked on wobbly legs onto the landing outside, and peered down. The foyer appeared ransacked, and her chambermaid sat hugging herself, weeping, collapsed by the grandfather clock. Amelia's insides were still searing, and her breasts and lips were bruised. But God had been on her side: she and Christina were, miraculously, still alive.

Only then did a boiling, crimson rage surge through her body; and, without stopping to check on Tina and her staff, she went to her bathroom and ran herself a tub of scalding water.

* * *

"Amelia! What on earth's happened to you?" Karl von Stecher exclaimed, rushing toward his unexpected visitor. He had been working on his account books in the study, when his butler informed him that Frau Habig had arrived, insisting on an immediate interview. His face now registered shock, for hers was puffed and purplish from the abuse she had received during the night. He blinked, his usually cold, impassive features melting into an expression of concern.

Amelia's eyes were burning with a strange light. She strode up to him, her chin jutting forward truculently. "Amelia," he murmured, instinctively stepping back. *"What's wrong?"*

And then she spoke, her voice low and quivering with passion. "You goddamned bastard! You knew about it before it happened, didn't you? Did you send them yourself, Herr Graf, or did you just learn of their intention and do nothing about it? Tell me the truth, you slimy Prussian coward!"

"Amelia, are you mad?" he retorted, alarm registering on his features.

"I'm perfectly sane! But you knew they were going to come and vandalize my home! The windows are shattered, the paintings are slashed, all my jewelry and our valuables have been stolen. And my butler, Hauser, has been shot through the arm! Why did you do this to us, Karl? To your old friend's widow?"

"Take it easy, Amelia," Karl von Stecher soothed, his voice beginning to tremble. "I don't know what you're talking about—"

"Really? Did you know that Nanni came to warn me? *She knew!* She knew something was going to happen *last night!* What's become of you, Karl? What have the Nazis done to turn a decent human being into a living monster? What did they offer you to turn you against us like this?"

"Amelia—"

She stopped him with a motion of her hand. "Enough, Karl. I've had quite enough! Tina and I will leave before the week is up. Richard is sending us to Paris. You and your friends will have a new mansion to play around in, and you may even steal our coal mines to fuel all Vienna. Richard's expecting this, although he's a fool and isn't ready to leave everything behind. But it doesn't matter—you haven't won yet. I have news for you: The Jews are not going to melt off the face of the earth and be forgotten! We're a race of survivors!"

His dead-white face remained frozen in shock as she turned her back on him and walked out the door, her high heels clicking on his marble floor.

CHAPTER XII

Charles hadn't seen Amelia in eighteen years; could it be possible that he had kissed her on the Champs-Elysées almost half a lifetime ago? Lost in his memories, he sat in the backseat of his new maroon 1938 Phantom III Rolls-Royce; at the wheel his chauffeur, Daniel, neatly uniformed in severe navy with silver buttons and braid, wound his way home through the streets of Saint-Germain-en-Laye.

She had arrived from Vienna the night before, exhausted, and he had found a pretext to come home very late so he wouldn't have to face her right away, unprepared. But tonight he had run out of excuses. She'd be there with Anne, waiting for him. The thought of her stirred up memories of youthful hope and longing, an unassuaged longing that the years had found no way to fulfill, in spite of all his success and his long affair with Arabella Fayard.

But his "feelings" were not real feelings, Charles chided himself. They were based on a dim recollection rather than a real person. He was remembering a willowy girl of twenty, and this was sheer absurdity—she would turn thirty-eight this month, and had a thirteen-year-old daughter. Surely she was no longer the "old Amelia" he had pined away for and proposed to in 1920.

The car stopped in front of La Folie, and Daniel jumped out. As soon as Fayard had officially named him his vice-president two years before. Charles had hired a chauffeur and given up the pleasure of driving his own car. He missed the driving, the sense of personal power over the machine, the sense of freedom and privacy. But "success," to Charles, had for so long been represented by Alfred de Rochefleur, that he had sacrificed his simple pleasure for an image: Alfred, elegant and aloof, being driven everywhere by a liveried servant.

Perhaps, he reflected ruefully as Daniel helped him out of his seat, we don't outgrow our early years. Perhaps the fragile memory of loving Amelia, like the bitter memory of having envied Alfred's luxury, held more real meaning in his life today than a three-hour tryst with Arabella or a statement of his financial assets from his accounting firm.

When things had begun to spoil in Austria, he had for the first time in many years thought about Amelia. Until then he'd kept his memories under close wraps, pushing them back into the far recesses of his consciousness. It was as though Amelia von Guttman had never existed, as if, his whole life through, he had never really been in love. Even when Peter Habig had died such a horrible death, he'd made a point to steel his heart against the young widow, shutting out Anne's compassion by appearing stone-faced and aloof until, in sheer frustration, his wife had stopped talking about the Habigs. Had Anne been relieved by his apparent lack of concern? Had she remembered that, at one time, Amelia had been his first choice for a wife?

But then Hitler had marched on Austria, and Richard had sent an urgent letter to the Lévy–de Rochefleurs. He'd explained how Amelia and her daughter had suffered an unspeakable trauma, and that he was forced to send them at once out of the country. That he himself was choosing to remain and weather the storm, with his mother—he because of his desire to keep a hold on the coal mines, and because he had fallen in love with his young gentile ballerina, and Barbara because at her age she had no desire to uproot herself and readjust to a different way of life. "Perhaps we are both fools," he had written. "But I am hoping our family name will wield enough clout to shield us from direct harm. With Amelia, there was the additional blemish of Peter's final stand against injustice. . . ."

An intense discomfort had crept over Charles. Part of him suddenly wanted Amelia here, to test his feelings anew; the other part wanted to keep her as far away as possible. She was dangerous, both because he had loved her and because she had rejected him. His love might be revived, destroying the delicate fabric of equanimity he had woven as a framework for his life these past eighteen years; and if she were to reject him again . . .

It would have to be Anne's decision to let Amelia stay; after all, Anne had to feel the same ambivalence toward her cousin—a mixture of compassion and fear, fear of a past rival revived from the yellowed pictures of an old family album. And so Charles had read

Richard's letter aloud at breakfast, and watched Anne closely. Sure enough, Anne had opened the door. She had done so with a strange reticence, however, looking down at her hands and hiding her eyes. "We must have Amelia come to us," she had said hesitantly. "We should at least make the offer, Charles."

"What a generous notion," he replied, observing her.

"It's the only human thing to do," Anne added, her voice a little hoarse. "She's our cousin, after all."

She still remembers, Charles thought. And she worries, too, just as I do, about the specters of the past. . . .

Maybe Amelia will have gotten stout, and loud, like some Austrian women, he cheered himself on. And then nothing in any of our lives will be affected.

But was that what he really wanted . . . ?

As soon as Charles had handed Goujon his coat, he saw her. He was still in the foyer, and so he could not see him, for she was crossing the corridor into the living room. She was walking with that same wonderful grace, like a ballerina: small steps, erect back. Her figure hadn't changed: only now the fashions allowed a good deal of leg to be visible, and he was delighted by her gently molded calves, her small, slender feet. She still wore her dark hair long, and had pinned it up with fresh flowers. *She hadn't changed.*

Goujon had slipped away, and now Charles moved toward the hallway to catch a final glimpse as she entered the living room. And then, inexplicably, she turned and saw him. She looked at him, her lips parting slightly . . . not smiling, but receptive, a little surprised. For a moment they remained gazing at each other, almost without expression—he in awe of her beauty, her amazing eyes like dark turquoises.

And then she broke the spell and smiled. "Hello, Charles." And she held out her hands to him in welcome.

He felt a jagged sorrow pierce to the core of his being. The right woman was welcoming him home, only she wasn't his, and had never been more than a dream flickering before him like an elusive candle flame.

* * *

It was amazing, Amelia thought, how much Anne changed once the WIZO women arrived. Her lovely nature seemed to come out, like a flower that opened only to the light, and she took on a glow that turned her plain face almost beautiful. These, Amelia realized, were *Anne's people.*

There were some thirty-five women here for tea, which Goujon had elaborately served. Anne waved him away impatiently so that she could close the door and find herself cocooned among her cohorts. Tactfully, Amelia stayed on the sidelines, encouraging Anne not to worry about her until everyone was settled in for the program.

"You're going to help me host this month's meeting," her cousin had told her before the arrival of her guests, her voice quivering a little from anticipation. "You're so confident around people, Amelia—not like me."

But Anne looked confident enough, Amelia now observed. Going up to this one and that, taking someone's hand between both of hers to add warmth to a greeting . . . Anne was full of surprises, as she had been as a young woman, when she had amazed all of Paris by so superbly furnishing La Folie. She was one of those burning hearts that suddenly rose out of nowhere to lead a nation . . . an ignored leader who had long ignored herself, and who, most of the time, forgot this aspect of her nature.

Charles hadn't been too pleased by Anne's volunteering their homestead for the meeting. Amelia had seen little of him since her arrival in Paris; he worked excessively long hours, and often took dinner in town. Whenever they were together, he avoided speaking to her directly, and she did the same. They both tended to address Anne, Alfred, or Christina—Alexis being away at boarding school —or else spoke to each other while appearing to be looking above the other's head. Their kiss on the Champs-Elysées, his subsequent proposal, and her rejection still stood between them, an awkwardness neither of them could circumvent. And so, subtly, they avoided each other.

That day at breakfast, Alfred did not come down, complaining of an attack of the gout; Christina was sleeping late; hesitantly, Anne told Charles that she would be hosting the WIZO meeting at La Folie that day. He raised his head and looked at her, creasing his brow. "Can't you at least pretend to be doing this behind my back?" he said, annoyed and ironic.

Anne blushed, and started to play with the linen napkin on her lap. "Darling, it's my turn. You know we don't have an office or an official meeting place. Jeanne Netter has had us over for the last three months. . . ."

"Madame Netter is divorced, if I recall correctly. She doesn't have a husband who objects to such extreme displays of Zionism."

At that point, Amelia felt an unexpected flare-up of irritation. She looked Charles right in the eye and demanded, her tone cool but direct, "Why should Zionism be such an embarrassment to you, Charles? We live in troubled times; surely this would be the right moment to back Anne up, rather than make things more difficult for her. Zionism is necessary; the way things are going, we Jews are definitely going to find ourselves in need of our own country."

"Come now, Amelia. Palestine is a British protectorate, not a Jewish state. And Anne has always been fully conscious of why I oppose organizations like the WIZO. We need to learn to adjust to our own country. We need to acquire the power with which to dictate policy. That's the only way the Jews will ever survive as better than second-class citizens! Look at the Rothschilds—look at your brother! Look at my father-in-law! They don't stand afraid, and they aren't looking for a Jewish homeland. Even if one existed, they would opt for remaining in their own countries, among their own associates, mingling with people of all sorts of backgrounds . . . not merely Jews."

Anne wasn't saying anything, but it was clear to Amelia that Charles's words were causing her pain. Her eyes looked suddenly bloodshot, and she was pressing her hands together in distress. Amelia was furious. Looking at Anne, she smiled, and reached out to touch her hand. Then she said to Charles: "You are an insensitive human being. I'm sorry—I'm in your home, appreciating your hospitality, but this is no excuse to keep quiet when injustice prevails. My brother, since you mention him, happens to be *terrified* of Hitler! He's staying on in Vienna because my mother is sixty-seven years old, ailing from arthritis, and set in her ways . . . and because he's hit middle age, and like a lovesick adolescent, is pining for a stupid dancer without a brain in her head who, if the need arose, would wash her hands of him in a minute! And Anne's father? Hitler hasn't walked into France yet, unless there's news I hadn't heard; were he to do so, Uncle Alfred would take the first boat to Palestine, I'm sure of it!"

"I didn't know you were such a Jew at heart, Amelia," Charles commented dryly. For the first time he looked levelly at her, his stare dark blue and unpleasant.

She flushed and shot back, impassioned: "I wasn't! I married a gentile, and half our friends weren't Jewish! Our religion never mattered to me until I saw what sorts of people the Nazis were!"

Wetting her lips, she paused, then plunged back in: "They *raped* me! Do you have any idea what that means to a woman? They raped me right in front of Tina! And so I'm sorry, but I understand Anne very well. . . . It's time we all stood up proudly and proclaimed our heritage, before it's snapped away from us and torn to bloody shreds!"

Anne's face, bloodless, stared at her, dumbfounded. Amelia looked at Charles and saw that he, as well, seemed too shocked to speak. Finally Anne whispered: "Oh, my God . . . I had no idea. . . ."

"It's not breakfast conversation," Amelia said, her voice still vibrant with pain. "But Charles, you forced me to tell you this. Do you get my point?"

But he couldn't answer. His face reflected horror, then anger, and finally frustration. He stood up abruptly and threw his napkin down on the table. The two women watched him quickly leave the room, his footsteps clip-clopping unevenly on the parquet floor. "It's too awful for him to digest," Anne stammered, hushed.

"Maybe. But if he can't face the truth now, then he never will. There's nothing either of us can say to him, then—he's shut himself off from understanding."

And, sighing, Amelia sat back and closed her eyes, suddenly exhausted from the strain of her argument.

* * *

The WIZO women were no different, Amelia thought, from the society women of Vienna with whom she had done volunteer work all her adult life. Polite, pleasant, attractive. Anne seemed flustered with the responsibility of making each of her guests feel at home, and yet, she thought, her cousin appeared far prouder and more sure of herself than when, years ago, Anne had had the burden of being hostess for her father's housewarming festivities. . . .

Now a plump but elegant woman in a trim, nubby linen suit was approaching Amelia, and Anne scurried up to make the introductions. "Juliette, this is my dear cousin I've been telling everyone about—Amelia Habig. Juliette Fildermann, our vice-president. . . ."

Amelia offered her hand and a smile. "I'm pleased to meet you, madame."

The other said, her voice warm with compassion: "Anne told us about what happened to you. How the Nazis burst into your home and ransacked it in the middle of the night. I fear that this may sound crude of me, my dear, but . . . would you tell all of us, in a few words, your first hand impression of the Nazi terror?"

Amelia stood dumbfounded, and raised her shoulders helplessly. "It . . . it's not a pleasant teatime topic," she demurred. "I—"

"It's an *essential* topic, Madame Habig. We all need to hear what it's really like." Juliette hesitated, then dove in: "It's new, and it's terribly painful to you . . . I'm sure of that. We've all listened to our German refugees, God knows. But Anne has told us you might join our group; we need you! And we need a heightened awareness of what's going on, so close to our own borders."

Amelia shut her mind to a sudden, intrusive vision of the SS man plunging his penis into her clean, perfumed body . . . of shutting her mind against Christina's hysteria. *Anne, Anne, how could you make me go through it again?* she pleaded silently, trying to compose herself. And then, taking a deep breath, she gave in. "All right. If there's time in your busy agenda—"

"We'll do it right now," Anne said, giving her a hug. "Thank you, Amelia."

But did any of these well-coiffed, scented ladies even remotely comprehend that she was going to *have to relive this*? Amelia walked to the center of the room, Anne's arm linked through hers, and her cousin clapped for attention. Immediately, silence fell over the living room at La Folie.

Anne's voice, clear and sonorous, resounded to her assembled guests. "My dear friends, this afternoon we haven't planned a program. In fact, Jeanne, Juliette, and I went so far as to cancel our scheduled speaker, Dr. Robert Stern, the celebrated Zionist leader, because . . . well, because we had another very special speaker in mind. An unexpected one, to be sure.

"Just two weeks ago my cousin, Madame Peter Habig, had to flee from Vienna and take refuge with us here. While I have always loved Amelia, her reasons for coming here with her young daughter were anything but happy. . . ."

I can't be hearing this, Amelia thought, stunned. Looking out over the thirty-five women, all comfortably seated now, she thought: *Anne planned this all along!* She planned this, and told me nothing. *She didn't even ask me if I'd be willing!* A cold fury shook her, and for a minute she seriously considered walking out. She had been placed in such a difficult spot—If she walked out, she would look ridiculous in front of the most influential Jewish women of Paris; and if she spoke, all the pain, still so raw, would explode anew inside her soul.

At that moment Amelia bitterly hated Anne Lévy–de Rochefleur. Yet curiously, the waiting faces, open and hungry for her ugly, brutal knowledge, gave her new resolution. Perhaps Juliette Fildermann had struck the right chord: She *had* to speak out. Because if she didn't, her entire diatribe against Charles, that very morning, would have been nothing but bluster.

"Thank you for inviting me to join you, and for giving me the opportunity to bring you a special message," Amelia began, her voice trembling. Her magnetic cobalt eyes roved around the room, fastening on a face here and there among the women. She passed her tongue over parchment lips and cleared her throat. "I . . . I didn't want to speak. To tell you the truth . . . I didn't want to come to this meeting in the first place. I didn't want to come to Paris. You see, once upon a time, in an era that is now a closed book of fairy tales, I was a fairy princess in a land of castles constructed of spun sugar. It was called 'Vienna.' My brother and I lived perfect lives; he was the darling of all the eligible damsels of the city, and I . . . well, I married my Prince Charming." She paused and looked around, her eyes burning deeply into her audience. She could see that her words had begun to move them, and so she proceeded, slowly, because it was difficult to speak about the things that had hurt her.

"Let me tell you about my family. My mother was the daughter of Baron Henri de Rochefleur, and my father was the sole heir to Count Helmut von Guttman. And while both my grandfathers honored the Mosaic faith, not one member of the younger generations gave it the slightest thought. Oh, here and there we celebrated a holy day, here and there we honored a tradition. Ours was a chaotic household; my mother was as lax in our upbringing as she was in her own religious convictions. The religion I grew up believing in was position, status, might . . . call it what you will, it spelled out 'unique.' My brother and I were brought up with a deep consciousness of our uniqueness, of our own worth. We were *God's chosen people,* not because we were Jews but because we were the von Guttmans of Vienna."

All eyes were riveted to her face. Amelia breathed in, then slowly exhaled, for a tremendous anxiety had built up inside her. Tears rose to her eyes, and she allowed them to fall heedlessly onto her cheekbones. "On April second, my beautiful world came crashing down in ruins at my feet. Three men from the Nazi SS marched into my lovely Renaissance mansion, wounded my houseman, terrified my maids, and stormed upstairs into my daughter's bedroom. They raped me in front of her. And then they looted my valuables and left me on the floor, bleeding, and broke every window in the house before making their exit. That is why I'm here. The Vienna I knew no longer exists. It has turned into mayhem, and violence is now as rampant and accepted as prostitution is in every major European city. Thousands of Jews have fled their apartments, while others are rotting in Gestapo prisons, awaiting their fate. I have seen truckloads of terrified Semitic faces staring blindly into their neighbors' eyes, driving by on the streets—and behind the wheel, the smiling, frozen Aryan faces of their Nazi captors. God only knows what will happen to my brother, and to my mother now. . . ."

Amelia suddenly broke down, letting her face fall into her hands. And then she continued, in a hushed voice. "I am what they call a *Hitlerjude*. I was one of those who had to be convinced by external events before I realized how dear and important my faith was to me. As I stand here I am one of you, in heart and in spirit. I espouse your cause, and I am glad you welcomed me." Her eyes sought Anne's, and she saw that her cousin's face was bathed in tears. She reached a hand toward her, and said, "Thank you, Anne, for forcing me to face this . . . for forcing me to *face myself*. . . ."

For a moment nobody moved, nobody breathed. In the stately living room, all eyes remained glued to Amelia's face. A strange, electric sensation passed through her, and she felt something she had never experienced before: it was as though, in their hearts and minds, these women had reached out to touch one another. Amelia gazed out at these total strangers and felt them all reach out to her, felt their invisible hands reaching for her hand.

"My story is your story," she concluded, her voice catching as she moved to embrace Anne, who had come up beside her. "And nothing that has touched you will not touch me. For in this room we have all become sisters."

* * *

"Monsieur de Rochefleur, the president would like to see you in his office, as soon as possible."

Charles raised his head from a sheaf of receipts, and nodded at the secretary. He motioned for his young employee to exit noise-

lessly. Charles capped his fountain pen and stacked the papers
evenly together, thinking, with enormous satisfaction, that his prediction had at last come true: Associates in the business and social
worlds were beginning to drop the cumbersome "Lévy" name, retaining only the appendage of his mother's maiden name. (Charles
didn't want to think of "de Rochefleur" as *Anne*'s name. He possessed as much right to it as she did, he reasoned: if her father had
given it to *her*, his mother had the same right to pass it on to *him*.)

Charles de Rochefleur. He turned the name over lovingly in his
head. If only he could think of a way to seize the title that went
with it. . . . Perhaps, once Armand stepped down and handed
him the presidency of Fayard Industries (for who else was there to
take over the business?). Perhaps then he would subtly start to add
Baron to his signature; and, like docile sheep, his acquaintances
would begin to forget he had ever been born simple Charles Lévy.

But this was only wishful thinking. Still, Charles sat back for a
moment and contemplated the tangible signs of his success. Besides
his fine Persian carpet and his mahogany furniture, there was the
original Picasso etching that he had placed near his bookcase, to
offer him inspiration every time he went to look up a legal case or a
new statute in one of the hardbound leather volumes lining the
shelves. His eye rested with pleasure on the ornate Fabergé clock
that Armand had given him for his last birthday, his thirty-ninth.

On that occasion, last August, Arabella had given him diamond
cuff links. It made Charles uncomfortable to wear them to board
meetings; Armand had commented on their beauty, and he had
found himself blushing like a schoolboy. Later, he'd felt annoyed at
his own weakness. After all, he wasn't taking anything away from
Fayard's relationship with his wife, any more than he was from
Anne. Had he not been Arabella's lover, some other younger man
would have been lying in her rue de la Paix bed.

But it's *Armand's* bed, too, the guilty thought intruded. Charles
pushed it far back in his mind with considerable irritation.

He was supposed to meet Arabella at five this afternoon; but
now, inexplicably, the notion bothered him. She was forty-three
and fine lines creased the corners of her lips and eyes; her coiffeur
was using a tint to cover occasional strands of gray that had
wended their way into her brittle blond hair. Charles was growing
increasingly disillusioned with her; after all, their affair was now
sixteen years old. Routine was bound to have eaten insidiously
away at the excitement and energy of their sexual adventure. All

the more so because it was that alone. Sex, without an overlay of emotional attachment, tended to succumb more readily to the rusting effects of time.

Now, as Charles rose and adjusted the lapels of his suit jacket, a split-second image of Amelia Habig flashed through his brain: Amelia, with her cobalt eyes and her slim, graceful figure. His heart suddenly swelled with longing and wistfulness, and he had to pause, struck by the emotional emptiness of his existence. Then he remembered her at breakfast that morning, arrogant and hostile, and his anger flared.

He had every reason to hate Amelia Habig. She had thwarted his happiness as a youth, and now she was siding with Anne against him in this ridiculously overblown matter of the Jews.

Women have no place in decisions of state, he thought bitterly. They should remain out of politics and decorate their lives with nothing of greater consequence than the opera guild or the patronage of a new musician. A woman should be muted, like a delicate background landscape, not harsh and powerful like the women today . . . like Arabella and Amelia, and, he was discovering with dismay, even Anne.

Upstairs, the presidential suite of offices made Charles's resemble a goldfish pond contrasted with the Mediterranean. The gray-templed assistant who ushered him in was as smooth as a British member of parliament and as unobtrusive as a British manservant. Fayard's enormous office faced the rue Cambon, its huge beveled-glass windows adding a touch of ageless beauty to the formidable interior, all in the Weimar Bauhaus style. A steelman himself, Fayard liked his chairs of tubular steel, his taste running to purity of line and simplicity of fabric rather than the ornate. His walls were starkly white, with paintings by Matisse to break up the harshness, and with large pots of glazed ceramics to add light and grace with their profusion of white blooming flowers.

Fayard's hair was still close-cropped and thick, but now it was uniformly white. He had developed jowls and begun to display other signs of age. But his presence still filled a room, even one as gigantic and impressive as this. Now, from behind his desk of steel, unpainted hardwood, and leather, he raised a hand in greeting and smiled as his protégé approached. "Charles."

"I came at once," the younger man said respectfully. When Fayard motioned him into the chair facing him, Charles sat down.

"We're letting ourselves get knee-deep in horse manure," the old man declared disgustedly. He leaned forward, his eyes sparkling with animation. "And it's a good time for our country to start minding its own business. Alienating the Germans isn't the way. They still have raw materials we need, and vice versa. We need their trade."

"But if the Germans get their way in the Czech Sudetenland, where will they stop?" Charles asked.

Armand Fayard sat back and considered his protégé with a disillusioned expression. "I myself dislike Hitler, and consider him a madman. But if we pacify him with Czechoslovakia, maybe some of his hunger will be assuaged and he won't move any farther . . . like a sated lion with no need to continue his hunt for fresh meat. At least we wouldn't have two enemies against whom to prepare: Adolf *and* Joseph!"

"That's a little dishonorable," Charles interposed politely. "We gave the Czechs our guarantee in the Locarno agreements of 1925."

Armand Fayard stood up and paced the floor behind his desk. Suddenly he wheeled about and confronted Charles. "Dishonorable, maybe. But we're not dealing here with boys upholding their school's honor. We're a continent struggling for survival . . . each nation for itself. And in the meantime a tremendous upheaval is taking place in every major country. Centrist politics have all but disappeared, and the Right and Left are fighting each other to the finish. I wouldn't want two more years of Monsieur Blum!"

Charles could feel pinpricks of apprehension, a definite discomfort agitating him. Something was bothering the old plutocrat, and that something, Charles was starting to intuit, was Charles himself. And so, hesitantly, the younger man asked, "What's the real problem, Armand?"

The small black eyes fastened on his face, and Fayard declared: "I've never paid the slightest attention to a man's religion, Charlie. You know that. I don't even give a damn about my own! But the climate in Europe has turned nasty. Look at what happened to your own cousin! *This is the wrong moment to cling to a religion I damn well know you couldn't care less about.* You're my right-hand man. I need you. I'm going to need you to go into Germany during the summer, to reconnoiter—to see what they are doing over there about rearmament. Hitler *is* an enormous worry, and we can't trust anything about him. There are those who foresee an unavoidable confrontation, and for this, we, the leaders of the French steel industry, must take precautionary measures."

A quick excitement seized Charles. "You want me to scout around unobtrusively, using my Swiss passport and proof of my German birth to gain easier access to our brethren in Deutschland, and to bring home the facts."

Fayard smiled ruefully. "That's the idea. But, Charles, you know there's a definite impediment to my sending you there this very minute . . . and that's your being a Jew." He paused, then gave the younger man his honest, direct stare. "Surely you, a nonreligious individual, must have given the matter of conversion a thought. You have a seventeen-year-old son. If there's a war, he'll have to fight, won't he? Imagine what would happen if he were sent to a Nazi prisoner-of-war camp? Or worse yet: Consider the possibility that right here in France, the extreme Right should take over. They might lean toward Hitler, and *let him in*! Not ordinary conservatives like you or me, capitalists out to protect free enterprise, but crazed, incensed men such as Pierre Taittinger or the other Pierre, Laval! Think of Alex, and think of your wife! *Convert, my boy, before it gets too late.* Arabella and I would sponsor you in an official ceremony."

Charles couldn't speak. Fayard's direct approach had taken him by surprise, caught him unawares. . . . Only *just how unawares*? This morning he had expressed grave discomfort at Anne's WIZO activities, yet had been unable to explain to either his wife or Amelia why her Zionism embarrassed him. But now he possessed the key to the problem: He was an essential part of Fayard's organization, and it was becoming a business inconvenience—a hindrance to his boss and to the smooth running of their operations—to have him remain a Jew.

"I'm afraid Anne would never agree to this," Charles replied, his own blue eyes as candid as Armand's. "And I'm not sure of Alexis either. Anne has him more or less brainwashed about our 'heritage.' "

" 'Heritage'? Does any man really know the ins and outs of his so-called heritage? For God's sake, Charles, Anne's own mother might have been fooling around with a Russian prince, and then *she wouldn't even be Jewish according to Jewish law*! None of us knows for certain! Your son is a child, Charles, a very young man. You can't allow him to digest in toto the kind of romantic hogwash Anne's been feeding him."

Charles stared at his boss, more than a little shaken. Fayard had taken such a deep interest in his family affairs that it was almost too much, too intense, to deal with. *Yet I've always cried out for a father figure,* Charles thought; and here was the man who had volunteered . . . the man whom, three times a week, Charles had been cuckolding for sixteen years.

"I'll give it serious thought, Armand," he replied, accepting the other man's handshake and feeling a sharp pang of self-hatred. "And I'll definitely speak to Anne."

But even as he walked out of the presidential suite, absorbed in thought, his head bent low, Charles knew he was never going to let Anne know what Fayard had told him. He would have to find another means to accomplish the mission in Germany, for Anne would never understand.

In the elevator, he again found himself thinking of Amelia. With an enormous sense of sadness, he realized that she, more than Anne, would find him repugnant for even sitting through this conversation with Fayard. She would not comprehend how his boss could have spoken strictly as a pragmatist and a businessman, not as a Fascist or an extremist. Her concepts of right and wrong, morality and immorality, were as far removed from the world he inhabited most of the day as Anne's were.

I wish I could explain it all to her, he thought, the longing returning with a renewed sense of loneliness. For Charles de Rochefleur had no one to share his thoughts with, no one in whom to confide. Amelia judged him to be cowardly and thoughtless, superficial and crass. And once, so long ago, he had placed all his hopes on her, and wanted to devote his life to making her proud. . . .

Why was he thinking of *her,* when, like a comet, she was no more than a flashing illumination on his horizon? Right now she was a guest in his house. But tomorrow she might decide to move to Switzerland, or even to another part of France. And then he would have lost even the vaguest aura of her brightness, and his sky, as before, would be dark and threatening, an engulfing infinitude of aloneness.

I need Arabella to drown my fear of life, he thought, assaulting his despair with savage determination. I need her tawny legs around my waist and her beautiful breasts in which to bury my face. *That, and only that,* is what I need.

CHAPTER XIII

Alexis de Rochefleur had grown into a handsome youth of seventeen. As he sat in the reception room outside President Fayard's office, he examined his surroundings. Tall green plants stood in every corner, and on the walls, huge canvases by Joan Miró, vivid splashes of color very simply framed. The furniture was upholstered in comfortable, silky-soft leather and suede.

Then, keeping his eyelids discreetly lowered, he turned his attention to his father. Charles was sitting opposite him, his long, graceful legs crossed as he perused a magazine. Alexis felt a vague discomfort, watching Charles; his father's meticulous good looks, his blond perfection, reminded the young man that a universe separated them, and always had. Something inexplicable and yet definite. Was it the cool Prussian blondness that contrasted so deeply with Alexis's own dark eyes and curly dark hair, or was it the aloofness that Charles's manicured appearance always seemed to convey?

I am nothing like him, Alexis thought. He knew exactly how to appraise himself: He was a man now, tall, thin, with a long face and rather delicate features, his long nose preventing him from ever being called a "pretty boy". Oddly enough, it was that noble Roman nose, above a thin, yet strong mouth, which also gave him his distinction. His father was a Greek god; he himself was not handsome, but what the girls in Rolle, at the tea parties, had described to his friends as "interesting," "intriguing." Still, Alexis decided ruefully, I'd rather have my father's beauty than my own particular brand of appeal to the opposite sex, if indeed I have one. . . .

Charles abruptly set his magazine aside and said to his son, "You won't be nervous with Fayard now, will you? Remember what I told you in the car: One day, not too far hence, this com-

pany will belong to *me*. You speak to him humbly, politely, but
with the thought in mind that soon your father will be sitting
exactly where Fayard is sitting right *now!*"

"I'm really not nervous, Father," Alexis replied, smiling.

Why was everyone making so much out of this meeting? His
mother had appeared flustered, at first opposing Charles's bringing
him into the city to see his boss. "But I'd like to meet Monsieur
Fayard, Mama," he had explained to her gently. "He's one of the
big powers in France, and I think it would be fascinating."

"You're going to be a lawyer, Alex," his mother had countered.
"You decided that yourself. You have no need to crowd your short
spring holiday with this excursion that can lead you nowhere."

His father had cut her off, furiously. "Anne, it's a stupid whim
on the old man's part, all right? I myself think it absurd that
Fayard should bother with a young whippersnapper like Alex! But
if Fayard wants to meet my son in person, then, by God, *he shall
meet my son in person!* And if he wants my son to jump through
hoops for his personal amusement, then Alex will smile until his
jaws hurt and *jump through hoops!* We're speaking about *Armand
Fayard,* the man who controls my destiny—and you're throwing
childish objections at us that don't make the slightest sense!"

"Alex doesn't need Armand Fayard," his mother had replied,
raising her chin slightly. Very quietly, she had added, "He's going
to inherit my shares of the Crédit Industriel, and I'll be the major
stockholder when Papa dies."

Alexis could not believe his ears. His parents almost never argued, and his mother never, but *never,* opposed his father and
confronted him. He'd often wondered why handsome, charming
Charles had deigned to marry his mother, whom Alexis adored but
who, he realized, was anything but a glamorous, worldly woman.
He had his own idea of the scenario, and it caused him pain to
think of it. It made him feel hostility toward his father, and Alexis
already was sorry for the distance that existed between them . . .
a distance that, being only seventeen, he had no idea how to bridge.

The door to the inner office swung open, and a woman stepped
out. She was beautiful, short but extremely voluptuous, with a tiny
waist and a plump, round breast beneath her creamy silk shirtwaist
dress. Her platinum-blond hair was bobbed at chin length, and a
flowered hat adorned her head. Her eyes, a spring green, were
tilted upward like a cat's, and she had the sprightly gait of a young
girl. But she wasn't a young girl, Alexis realized. She was his moth-

er's age, or older . . . and in the instant that he noticed this, her eyes landed on him and caught his stare. Amused, she smiled. Alexis blushed with embarrassment, rising to his feet just as his father walked over to her.

With a small gesture, Charles indicated the young man and said, "Hello, Arabella. This is my son, Alexis. Madame Fayard."

"Alexis, how do you do?" She gave him her small hand to kiss, and as he brought it to his lips, he inhaled her rich perfume, feeling overwhelmed. She was exactly the sort of woman he and his friends fantasized about, the kind of older woman they all dreamed of seducing in a country inn, showing off the savoir faire they wished they possessed. . . .

Arabella Fayard was adjusting her hat, her head tilted sideways. "Well, Charles, how nice to have seen you," she said to his father. Her tone sounded strangely arch, almost playful. Like a whiff of sea breeze, piquant and vivifying. Alexis watched her walk briskly to the elevator, her hips swaying slightly.

And then he looked at Charles. His father was running his hands through his hair, his eyes on the back of Arabella's legs. *Charles and the Fayard woman liked each other!* This much was evident, both in her tone of voice and in Charles's face, which somehow seemed more *alive* than usual.

Charles knew how to handle women of the world, Alexis thought, suddenly envious. He possessed an inborn ease around them that the young man feared he himself would never have. One could learn manners, but charm?

They heard the elevator door open and close, and the motor purr into action. "You should have spoken to her," Charles reproached him, his voice hard and cold.

Alexis opened his mouth to reply, then shut it again on the memory of Arabella's smile as she had caught him staring. She'd been flattered! She'd *liked* his looking—and now his father was resenting him for it!

It was going to be a good day, after all.

Armand Fayard's eyes were sharp, all-encompassing, shrewd and clear. Alexis felt himself the object of such close scrutiny that it made him self-conscious, until he remembered that he was here to meet an interesting man, and that was all. He'd always been curious about his father's boss and mentor. But *Fayard is only a man, and so am I,* Alexis reasoned. And so he returned his gaze in as honest and forthright a manner as he could muster.

"Tell me about your boarding school, young man," Fayard demanded. He smiled at Alex and urged him on with his intense eyes.

"Well, sir, it's called Le Rosey. It's in Rolle, Switzerland, on Lac Leman. It's a beautiful place. We live and study in an old manor house surrounded by a park; in the winter we move to Gstaad, where we ski and skate. There are two scholastic programs, one according to the Swiss system, and one geared for the French students who will have to pass their baccalaureate exams over here. That's the one I've been following since my father signed me up when I was twelve."

"He knows how to answer a question," Fayard commented to Charles. "To the point, but fully developed. A fine quality, my boy. And after this final year, what do you plan to study?"

Very briefly the young man's eyes went to his father; but quickly he looked back at Fayard. "I've always wanted to be an attorney, sir. I'm going to come back here and attend the Faculty of Law."

Fayard raised his brows. "I see. You've never thought of banking, like your grandfather?"

Alexis wet his lips. "Frankly, no. I'm interested in human relationships, and in government. It seems to me that law is the only field that comprises both those elements."

Fayard nodded. "Interesting. What about a chance to follow in your father's footsteps? Anything tempting you in *that* direction?"

Charles cleared his throat, and interposed: "Well, that's been a secret hope of my own, Armand. But you know how young people are—they never want to listen to their parents' advice. Probably Alex believes the steel business is boring."

Alex smiled at his father, and shook his head, very pleasantly. "Not boring at all. The legal process fascinates me, that's all. I'd like to give it a try, at least. Who knows? I may not even pass my bac, and then all this would be a moot question, wouldn't it? Or I could flunk out of law school, and that would be the end of *that* endeavor!"

"Your father tells me you've been at the top of your class at Le Rosey since you were a child. That hardly presages a dismal failure, Alexis." Armand Fayard smiled. "Let me tell you why I wanted so very much to make your acquaintance. It isn't just out of friendship for your father—it's for my own selfish reasons. My tax accountants have advised me to start a new program, hiring university students, or those who've completed their lycée degree and are about to enter university, to clerk for our various depart-ments during the summer. But naturally we have to make plans a year ahead. I'd like to have you work in our legal office next year. The job wouldn't be much: you'd be at the beck and call of each of my attorneys, and you'd be researching cases for them and running about town getting documentation they'd need for their most complex ones. But it would teach you a lot about the law, besides getting your foot in the door right here, at Fayard Industries. Who knows? You might even enjoy working for a large corporation when you finish your legal studies, and then we'd simply hire you back full-time."

Alexis was shocked. At first he found it impossible to speak. Charles was getting ready to interject something, and to judge by his expression, he didn't seem too pleased by the big man's offer. And so Alexis jumped right into the fray and declared: "I'd like nothing better, Monsieur Fayard. It would give me added incentive to pass my *bac* . . . something to look forward to when I graduate. And I'll make sure not to disappoint your faith in me—I'm a hard worker: you can count on that."

Fayard turned to regard Charles triumphantly. "And *you* were so sure he was going to refuse! Young men have more sense than we often give them credit for, my boy. You should be proud as hell of that son of yours—*I* would be, if he were my *own*. . . ."

"My whole family is overwhelmed by your generosity, Armand," Charles declared. But his voice was somewhat reserved, aloof. He turned to Alex and stated curtly: "Perhaps you don't yet fully understand the opportunity that is being handed to you on a platter. I would have dreamed of such an opening, when I was your age!"

Alexis replied softly, "But I *do* comprehend, Father. And I shan't let either of you down."

Fayard reached over his desk to take the young man's hand, and surprised him with the warmth of his handshake. But, from the side, Alexis perceived a stiffening in his father, a certain withdrawal. Finally Charles rose and announced, "It's time you took the train back to Saint-Germain, Alexis. Monsieur Fayard has an industry to run. . . ."

* * *

Christina parted the curtains in the sitting room and drew a quick intake of breath, seeing *him* strolling by himself on the other side of the ivy-covered stone partition that separated the main garden and *their* side. Her mother had cautioned her from the beginning not to abuse Cousin Anne's hospitality and to stay as much as possible in their own quarters, in the smaller wing of La Folie.

Soon she would begin to attend the local Lycée de Jeunes Filles, and this would occupy her time. She missed Vienna terribly. When her mother was around, things weren't so dull . . . but lately Cousin Anne had been taking her places, and leaving Christina at home with her books and the servants.

And then *he* had come home for the spring break from his boarding school—Alexis. Christina made sure that he couldn't see her, should he look up when he turned the corner and walked back the other way, toward the house. She pulled the silk curtain and hid behind it, observing him.

He was the first young man that age whom she'd had the chance to watch from close up. He was seventeen . . . almost a university student! And so tall, and composed, and self-assured. She liked his quiet jokes at dinner, how he made his mother and her mother laugh. She liked his smile. He wasn't beautiful, not like her cousin Charles. But he reminded her of her father: the same dark looks, the same long face and long nose.

Christina wondered what boys like that thought of when they walked by themselves. Probably he was dreaming of a matinée idol. She was sure he went to dances at his school and was introduced to very pretty girls who laughed at his jokes, too. She remembered her mother's stories about "coming out," and about all the young men during the war who had wanted to marry her.

With her free hand, Christina lightly touched her hip, the rounded thigh. She caressed her waist and slowly, tentatively, touched her own growing breasts. She was proud of them. She was beginning to look more and more like her mother—like a woman. And sometimes, when she was left alone, she went into her mother's closet and pulled out hats with veils, silk underclothes, lipstick, rouge. . . .

A tremendous loneliness settled over the young girl. She watched Alexis from her seat behind the curtain, curious and also saddened, because they might have been friends. He looked as alone as she. Perhaps, if she went out too, he'd think she hadn't known he was out there; she would act surprised, and then, being polite, he would have to make conversation. Alexis didn't look like the kind of fellow who'd refuse to talk to her because she was only thirteen.

Now she was excited. She checked the mirror and patted her

high cheekbones. It was important that he like her, that he be her friend. Soon he would be returning to Switzerland, and then, if this opportunity was missed, they'd always remain strangers. Cousins could be like brothers, couldn't they?

But Cousin Anne had married Charles. They'd been cousins themselves. Cousins could be lots of things, not just make-believe siblings . . .

Christina scampered down the stairs, through the main wing and out into the main garden. She pushed her long hair off her shoulders and walked resolutely onto one of the gravel pathways. She knew that any moment, he would have to see her.

But he was absorbed in thought, his head bent low. So close, so far . . . She advanced, crunching the gravel beneath her patent-leather toes to draw his attention—and then he started, and saw her. "Christina," he called, smiling. "It's such a pretty day!"

She caught up with him. He was so much taller that her head only reached his shoulder. Kindly, he put an arm around her. "Lonely?"

She was startled by his perceptivity. "I miss my old life," she confided, her voice small and miserable. "Mama loved Paris when she was a young girl, but now . . . ."

"Of course. I miss my own school friends when I'm home for holidays."

"What kind of friends do you have, Alexis?" she asked, consumed with curiosity.

"All sorts. Some to play tennis with, others to talk to about girls." He blushed, realizing he had spoken too quickly. "Some to go over our schoolwork."

"Do you go out much? With girls, I mean?"

He laughed. "We have cotillions at the neighboring girls' school. We practice our manners with them, then go outside and smoke cigarettes in the bushes, behind the masters' backs. I don't know which is more fun, really!"

She walked silently next to him, thinking how vastly different his life was from hers. How different boys were from girls. She didn't have the remotest desire to smoke. The strange thing about Alexis was that he spoke so openly of fun and frolic with his friends, yet he seemed, to her, to be such an independent sort. "I imagined you by yourself, reading poetry books," she remarked shyly.

He laughed, but the laughter was hesitant. "I like people *sometimes*. Other times, I do like to think, alone."

"My father was like that," Christina told him. "My father was the most wonderful, warm, dear man in the world," she said, her voice trembling and breaking. "He loved us so much! He loved Mama, and me. There was going to be another baby, you know, when he was killed. We lost so much, Alexis! You can't understand it, can you? All the terrible things that happened to Mama. Don't you ever wonder why she's so sad all the time?"

Very gently, Alexis led her to the gazebo and made her sit down next to him on the bench. "She's sad, sweetheart, but it's going to get easier as time washes away her pain. And of yours, too. You'll see—you'll make friends at the school, and soon they'll be taking you to parties, and you'll forget everything that happened at the end, in Vienna."

"I'll never forget my father," she whispered fervently.

"I wish there was something I could say. . . ." He looked at her, and she was touched by his sincere sympathy. Then he sighed and looked out into the distance. "I don't know anything about that sort of love. My father has never liked me, Tina. We get along. He drones at me about his business, and what he expects of me, but it's my mother who loves me."

"Do they love each other, your parents? Mama thought she was going to die when Papa was killed."

Alexis's face reddened with suppressed anger. Quietly, but with resolution, he pounded one fist into the palm of his other hand. "*She* loves *him*. *He* doesn't love anybody, least of all her and me. He puts up with us because of Grandpa."

"What do you mean? What has Uncle Alfred to do with this?"

He stared at her, his dark eyes burning ardently. "I was born in February; they were married the previous July! Doesn't that tell you anything, Tina? You're a big girl—you know about men and women, don't you? *He made her pregnant!* She was a young girl, only a few years older than I am now, and she'd have done anything at all to gain his goodwill. *She always loved him!*"

Christina was embarrassed. She asked in a low voice, avoiding looking at him: "Why couldn't he just have proposed, and married her before . . . ?"

"Because he had no money, and she did! If she hadn't been expecting *me,* I'm sure Grandpa would have turned him down flat. So you see, he *had* to take advantage of her—it was the only way to engineer the marriage! And we've been paying for it ever since, she and I: he can't stand us, especially me. But he can't really let on how he feels, or Grandpa would force my mother to get a divorce!"

Christina was shocked. "In Vienna, lots of people I knew got divorces. But it was always hard on their children."

"It wouldn't have been hard on *me*," Alexis spat out, and she was amazed, and repelled, by the strength of his emotion. How could anybody hate his own father to that extent?

And then he rose, taking in a deep breath of crisp spring air. He turned to her, and she saw that his mood had lifted and he was smiling. "Come on, let's forget about my father, okay? He's not so bad. And let's forget about Vienna and what happened. Let's you and I go out for a horseback ride to the park and exercise the poor beasts, shall we, Tina?"

She smiled back at him, suddenly happy. He hadn't chased her away. Instead, he'd opened his heart to her and shared his own painful childhood. He was a very nice boy . . . the nicest.

"I'd love to go riding," she replied, and slipped her small hand inside the larger one he held out to bring her to her feet.

* * *

Charles paced up and down in the library, deep in thought. *There was nothing wrong with Alex.* The boy was growing up into a conscientious, pleasant, well-mannered young man, and if he was independent, part of the reason was that Charles had paid him very little attention as he'd been growing up. Independence wasn't so bad, but sometimes Charles felt a hidden hostility in Alexis.

It's only the hostility *I've* always felt, reflected back at me, he decided. He simply couldn't make the connection with Alexis that a father normally made with his son. *Alex wasn't his son.*

And yet, Alex was the only child he had, a strange paradox driven home by Fayard's strong interest in the boy. Fayard had never had a child, and believed that Charles had to do right by Alex. And, because Fayard had grown quite close to Charles, he was now extending the same paternal arm toward Charles's son, with more genuine enthusiasm than Charles himself could muster.

A light tap on the door startled Charles out of his reverie. Alexis was standing in the doorway, waiting to be told why his father had sent for him. Charles made a motion for him to sit down, and Alexis chose an armchair opposite his father's: All the better to watch me, Charles thought bitterly. He's always observing, judging, adding up bits and pieces of information like a goddamned accountant.

"I'm going to be taking a trip in July," he said, trying to look at Alexis with friendly interest. "Your mother and Amelia want to go to Nice for the summer. While they are there, at the Hotel Negresco, I shall be touring the Rhine country in Germany."

The young man said nothing, but his dark eyes showed surprise. "Monsieur Fayard wants to learn what the *Boches* are up to. Want to come along?" Charles tapped a cigarette out of his gold monogrammed case, and then, as a careful afterthought, extended the case toward Alexis.

The boy hesitated only for a second. He took a cigarette and accepted a light from his father. Charles could see that he had pleased Alexis by treating him as an adult. They puffed silently, then Charles demanded, "Well?"

Alexis frowned thoughtfully. "You're going to scout the territory, Father? But won't that be dangerous, as a Jew?"

Charles had expected this. With some discomfort he stood up and concentrated on picking a piece of lint from his pant leg. Then he turned his back on his son and began to pace the floor once more. "Armand had a false passport made up for me," he said at last. *"Charles Médard.* No 'Lévy,' no 'de Rochefleur.' And I don't 'look Jewish,' so no one will cause me any trouble. I'll just be another French tourist enjoying the scenery."

"It's unethical to go over there for any reason whatsoever," Alexis countered. "Monsieur Fayard could send someone else— not a Jew."

"There's no one else he really trusts."

"Then you should refuse, Father. Let him go himself. He's not Jewish! *He* doesn't care what they've done there to innocent citizens. But the Jews are one people, without borders to contain them. It's up to us to boycott the Germans and not to spend one deutsche mark on their soil!"

"That's ridiculous. I hate the Germans as much as you do! But I've always loved France. I've always considered myself French, even though I was never able to obtain legal citizenship. Now, because of our religion, my boss has had to make up false papers to get me into the very country where I was born! It would have made this venture so much easier to travel under my own name, with a Swiss passport, because the Swiss have kept up a tradition of neutrality for so long, the Germans don't give them a second look anymore. And they would have been more open to me because I was born in Munich and my father was a German."

Flustered by the young man's dark, probing eyes, Charles exploded: "But Fayard can't pull strings with the Swiss! He could only obtain false French papers. This means that I'll be double-checked everywhere I go, and no one will be too frank with me. If, indeed, Hitler decides to go on the rampage, France may be the next country to be 'annexed'! And you, who *are* a Frenchman by birth, would stand by your goddamned principles as a Jew and ignore our responsibility as contributors to the French armaments industry, which may have to prepare for a cataclysmic war!"

"Maybe so," Alexis said softly. "I'd volunteer immediately to fight for my country. But right now we're not at war. And I wouldn't go to Germany under any circumstances, unless my government demanded it of me."

"That's what I should tell Fayard about his offer to send you across the border with me?"

Alexis was taken aback. "It was *Fayard* who suggested this?" For an instant he looked hurt. "I thought the notion came from *you,* Father."

Annoyed, Charles shrugged. "Of course it was mine. But Armand agreed and encouraged me to take you along. He's taken quite a liking to you. And you'd throw it all away for an *idea* of justice?"

Alexis rose, and faced his father. "I'm sorry you feel that way. And I'm sorry that I can't go with you. I would have liked the opportunity to travel with you, alone. But—"

"But your mother and her WIZO have prevailed upon your intelligence. Very well, Alex. I shan't force you. But I may never again ask you to accompany me anywhere."

A wistful expression crossed the boy's face. For a moment he hesitated. Then he nodded, and walked toward the door. "Good night, Father," he said softly. "And good luck."

Charles sank into his armchair, overcome with frustration. He could feel his blood pressure rising, his anger building. He was vaguely aware that someone had entered the library, but he didn't at first raise his head from his hands to see who it was.

"I heard the discussion," Amelia said.

Charles dropped his hands and looked at her. It was perhaps the first time they had been alone since her arrival at La Folie. Her presence right now was disconcerting: he wasn't ready to face her —not after what had happened between him and Alexis.

"I came in to look for a book, and when I heard Alexis talking, I almost went back to my room. But then I couldn't help overhearing what the conversation was about."

She was wearing a red velvet robe and black marabou slippers. Her hair had already been let loose over her shoulders, ready for bed, and he couldn't take his eyes off her. She wasn't wearing makeup, and looked eighteen. Yet she had just turned thirty-eight. She was an unbelievably beautiful woman, as simple in her grace and style as Arabella Fayard was studied and contrived. And all at once Charles felt a little frightened of her. She had heard the discussion, and would judge him harshly. And all he could think of was that scented spring night eighteen years before, when he had kissed her.

"You were wrong, Charles," Amelia told him, sitting down in the armchair Alexis had just vacated. "You've changed, you know, and it bothers me."

"Why should you care?" he demanded.

"Because we're family. Because we share a name and a background. Because once you were pure and beyond corruption, on fire with your ideals . . . like your son."

Her eyes were mesmerizing. They were so frank, so honest. They shamed him and yet infuriated him. "How dare you come in here and attack me?" he snapped. "Do you think your own life has been a straight-and-narrow road of purity and goodness?"

She blushed. "No. Has anyone's?"

Charles stood up and approached her. He looked down into that oval face, a face overpowered by those eyes he had never quite put out of his mind. "Yes," he murmured. "Once, I was an idealist. But I didn't believe in nonsense like religion. I believed in other ideals —in love, in intimacy, in honesty of mind and emotion! Do you remember those days, Amelia?"

Embarrassed, she passed a nervous hand through her hair. "Alex is a wonderful boy. He reminds me of Peter. And also of you, when we were young. Only Peter died for a cause he believed in, and you've rejected each and every cause, and care only about your career. Alex is your son! Don't you even know how to love him, Charles? You spoke to him like a stranger!"

Charles's throat was so tightly knotted, he could barely speak. Finally he said: "He *is* a stranger, Amelia. And I stopped knowing how to love anybody when you failed me. You were the last human being I loved . . . and the only woman who's ever meant anything to me."

Amelia's lips parted. She stared at him, her face white. "But that was *years* ago! And what about Anne?"

Charles sighed, and shook his head. "Anne's been a good wife. Of course I care for her. But I've never loved her. I loved only you, Amelia, and you dare to speak to me of honor and principles? Where were yours when you kissed me so ardently in the middle of the street, all the while loving another man?"

"That was the past. What possible good will it do to revive these old memories?"

"Because to me, Amelia, they are more real than reality. More real than the present. When you returned here, with Tina, I understood why I had never been able to feel love toward any other woman for eighteen years."

She looked at him, her face suddenly pained and anxious. "Don't," she pleaded.

"You can't escape from what I have to say. I still love you, Amelia Habig! I love you, and I also hate you for the waste my life has been, married to the wrong woman all these years because you preferred Peter! I'm still angry that you led me on, feeding your debutante's ego on my heart! That's the way things are with me, Amelia, if you want to speak about honesty and truth, and right and wrong!"

For a moment their eyes met. He couldn't figure out what exactly was going through her mind. She appeared upset, perturbed. Then she stood, a graceful woodland nymph clothed in red velvet. "You don't love *me,* Charles. What you love is a faded memory of when we were young, free, and happy. We all made choices along the way, and have had to pay the price. I never meant to hurt you —surely you must know that. As I never meant for my presence at La Folie to bring out anything but friendship in your heart."

Gently, she touched his arm. "I'm sorry, Charles. I think I've been intruding long enough in Anne's and your house. It's time Tina and I moved into a place of our own."

* * *

Charles loosened his necktie and undid the first two buttons of his oxford shirt. The July sun beat down on his head, but a light breeze was wafting toward him from the blue-gray Rhine River undulating below the walkway where he had gone for a stroll. Looking up, he saw the magnificent Gothic cathedral, its twin spires praying upward to a god in whom Charles had stopped believing ages ago. . . .

The city of Cologne was picturesque and charming, although heavily industrialized. He had come here to spend a few "quiet" weeks of "vacation": actually, of observation. He had checked into a peaceful inn on the outskirts of town and rented an old Mercedes. Off and on, he had toured the countryside to see what Hitler had begun to set in motion. He had made dozens of notes to bring back to Fayard: The Germans were setting up a line of forts to match the Maginot Line on the opposite side of the border. And, speaking perfect German, he had mingled in the taverns and conversed with the workers from the steel mills. The word was, Hitler was building tanks and airplanes en masse.

Charles felt particularly frustrated because Fayard was ill. He had suffered a stroke and was this minute lying in the American Hospital in Neuilly, recuperating, his entire left side paralyzed and slack. It hurt Charles even to think about it. *I really care about that old man,* he thought, surprised at his ability to feel such a fervent emotion.

Charles thought about Amelia, who had moved into a small, elegant suite at the Plaza-Athénée Hotel. He wished she could be here to share this view with him: the slow waters of the Rhine, and the old cathedral. Cologne, built in the days of the Roman Empire, had a romantic appeal that would have touched her. Charles stopped and breathed the warm air. I want to be near her, he thought. I don't care if she doesn't love me, if she doesn't want to be my mistress. I simply *need to be around her,* to smell her scent and hear her voice. To watch the graceful flow of her body.

He never missed Anne. Nor did he think about Alexis, either.

But lately, in Saint-Germain, when the Habigs had been with them, Charles had begun to feel a growing affection for Christina. Tina reminded him so much of Amelia, though younger and more vulnerably small. She was the daughter that he should have had, with the woman he had loved and still, to his amazement, continued to love. *I feel a greater pull toward Tina than I ever felt toward Alex,* he admitted. Because Amelia meant more to him than anyone, including Anne.

It was Amelia and Christina he missed. Not his own wife, or the boy he'd called his son.

A long, black Horch sports car was drawing up alongside him. Charles stopped, and looked inside the car, intrigued. Who knew him here? A chauffeur was driving, and in the backseat a woman entirely clothed in purple reclined, her head wrapped in a purple turban adorned with a single purple feather. Charles walked over, beginning to smile: a mysterious woman might be exactly what he needed to dispel the gloom of his mood—his dark thoughts about his mother, Fayard, Amelia, and an impending war.

The lady was turning down her window. As Charles approached she stuck her face out and waved. And, with horrified amazement, he recognized Arabella.

"What are you doing here?" he demanded, infuriated and appalled. "Where is Armand?"

She smiled, and her cat eyes crinkled. "In the hospital—where else? He's under constant surveillance, don't worry. And under constant sedation as well." Her gloved hand grasped his arm, and he pulled back instinctively. But her fingers remained tight around him.

"Say a nice hello to your wife, Monsieur Médard," she cajoled him with saccharine sweetness. Her eyes stayed riveted to him, piercing, ardent . . . and determined. "Aren't you pleased that Madame Médard just happened to arrange to join you on holiday?" She held out a small French passport. "I have my own connections, you see."

"How did you know exactly where to find me?" he confronted her.

"My dear, I *always* know exactly where and with whom to find you. And it wasn't hard, once I learned the make and license plate of your rented car."

With a sinking heart, Charles opened the door of the Horch, and slid into the backseat next to Arabella. It was at that moment that he truly began to hate her.

*   *   *

She was waiting for him on the bed, in a black silk negligée, her diamond necklace still sparkling on her collarbone. Charles hugged his white terry-cloth robe around him. His skin was tingling from the shower, and normally this made him feel sensual and healthy. But tonight, looking at her, he could only feel disgust—almost revulsion.

The memory of all the years he'd continued with her, afraid that if he dropped the relationship, she would cause a scandal and upset the delicate framework of his life, threatened to wash over him like a tidal wave of bilge water. All the anger, all the "civility" he'd used to conceal his true sentiments. . . . He'd long stopped feeling anything for her but animalistic lust, and had she been any less self-centered, she'd have realized that he used her body without the slightest regard for the person inside. But she'd seen only what she wanted to see.

"I've taken the liberty of ordering dinner from room service," she now said, her voice rich and husky. "Champagne, caviar, foie gras, pheasant under glass with wild rice and mushrooms, a salad of Belgian endive and hearts of palm, and, for dessert, a soufflé flavored with Grand Marnier. I was sure you'd approve of the selection!"

His dam suddenly, unexpectedly, burst. "You were *sure!* You were *sure* I'd want dinner here, you were *sure* I'd want pheasant, you were *goddamned* sure I'd want *you!* Where do you find the nerve, Arabella, to make my life your pet project, storming into it whenever you choose, without ever consulting me?"

Bewildered, she stared at him with wide eyes. "What's wrong, Charles?"

"Wrong? You ask me what's wrong? I'm going to tell you, madame, once and for all! *I've had enough!* Don't you understand, Bella, that sixteen years have played out our fun and games, and *nothing is left*? I have no feelings for you anymore, no real desire! Your presence here is less welcome than my loneliness. Can you hear me speaking?"

His heart was knocking wildly, exhilarating him more than any sex had over the past few years. He was finally breathing, letting go, *being himself!* Ever since Amelia had come to Paris he'd been desperately wanting out of his relationship with Arabella. But before, he'd been a coward, afraid of the possible consequences of such a breakup. Now he thought: To hell with consequences. I'll face them when and if they come to pass. Like a *man.*

Slowly, Arabella was rising, her face very white. "You mean . . . you're not serious . . ."

"I'm very serious," he answered, all at once terribly calm. "I want you to go home, Bella, tonight. Not tomorrow. *Now.* From now on I'm going to see whomever *I* please, whenever *I* so choose. I'm finished with being bossed around by a woman who isn't even my own wife!"

"I see," she said, her voice like a cutting blade. She grabbed the robe of her negligée and struggled into it, almost savagely. Then she looked at him, her eyes like two cold emeralds.

"I can suspect what this is all about," she stated. "Amelia Habig, the nightingale of Vienna! Everyone knows she's beautiful, everyone knows she's a widow, everyone knows that widows demand knights in shining armor to save them from their pitiful state! You're getting rid of me to replace me with your cousin . . . your wife's cousin! Because you'd rather be a knight than a simple man making love to a married woman!"

He simply gazed at her, speechless. "It's not the end, you know," she declared. "Things won't always be so easy for you, Charles. Tonight you're throwing me out like a used razor blade— but think on it, darling. Even old razor blades can draw blood . . . so don't underestimate me!"

And, furiously, she marched into the adjoining bedroom, slamming the connecting door so hard that the crystal chandelier began to tinkle as it shook.

Charles went to the bed and sat down, his legs wobbly. All his excitement had been drained away by Arabella's mention of Amelia. And yet, he reassured himself, she actually knew nothing, because, unfortunately, *there was nothing to know*! She'd grabbed at the first straw she thought she'd found . . . and that was all.

Arabella can't hurt me, he thought. Because if she does, she'll also be implicating herself. And she can't touch Amelia, even if she'd like to. No, I did the right thing. Because even though Amelia won't have me, I couldn't stand being Arabella's puppet for another moment.

Sighing, he slipped beneath the sheets, suddenly exhausted.

CHAPTER XIV

———— •❦• ————

Had his time in Cologne been only several weeks before? Somehow, those days seemed far removed, as if the whole experience had happened months ago or, better yet, to someone else. Now Charles looked out over the turquoise Mediterranean and the multicolored sailboats that animated its surface, and felt an enormous depression settling over his shoulders. Why had he come here to Nice, like a bloody fool, joining Anne and the others? Why had he imposed this "family vacation" on himself, knowing that it would only heighten his sense of frustration and impotence?

Anne was taking a nap in their hotel suite; the children—though Alex was hardly a child, and Christina, in her bathing suit, hardly looked like one—had gone on an excursion to Monaco with some new acquaintances. Charles had no idea where Amelia was, though she was probably napping in her own room, as was his mother, Yvonne. He was feeling restless, and the idea of settling in next to Anne on their bed filled him with a mixture of annoyance, boredom, and resentment. He hadn't touched her the whole time he'd been here, since his return from Cologne.

The single good thing that had happened recently had been his breakup with Arabella. That had been long overdue. She was an opportunistic, selfish, coldhearted bitch, and besides, he had gone to Cologne for business, not to fool around with his mistress.

Of course, he'd have to watch out. Charles didn't like fights, and he knew his opponent very well indeed. Rejecting her had opened the door to possible blackmail, a Pandora's box of female tricks that she wouldn't hesitate to bring out if the right moment ever presented itself. It would be up to him to forestall any such eventuality.

I really don't need her anymore, Charles thought, taking off his trousers and donning a pair of shorts and espadrilles. He needed to go out for some air, away from the oppressive nearness of his wife.

Outside, he stuck a sailor's cap on his head to block the hot noon sun. The beach stretched out invitingly, and he wandered among the umbrellas toward the family parasol, where he had spent many an hour looking out to sea, admiring the lovely women in their bathing suits, admiring Amelia . . .

Someone was lying on one of the beach chairs beneath their umbrella. He knew it was she, even before he saw the wonderful curve of her calves, exposed to the sun. He had memorized each part of her body that her bathing attire had allowed him to glimpse. And this, of course, had made the situation worse.

But he could not turn back. He felt a need to be close to her, speak with her. She had been cool toward him since his arrival: whether because of his mission in Germany or because of his declaration of love, which had impelled her to leave La Folie, he did not know. All he knew was that it hurt him.

She was wearing a wide straw hat under which she had tucked all her hair, and dark glasses, and she was reading. When he sat down beside her on the neighboring lounge chair, she turned to him and set the novel down: *Chéri*, by Colette. She smiled, but it was a smile of courtesy, nothing more. "Hello, Charles."

It was always awkward, being face-to-face like this. "I didn't know I'd find you here . . . honestly, Amelia."

"It's all right. I was just about getting ready to go back to the hotel for a short siesta."

A quick panic seized him. "Please, don't go. I'd like to tell you something."

She frowned. Immediately he explained: "No, nothing about *us*. Really, Amelia."

"There *is* no 'us,' Charles," she stated, her voice low but firm. "We're cousins, that's all."

Any humiliation was better than letting her go. They had so few moments alone, and in between he relived each one, even when her words had been cold or distant. "I need a friend to talk to," he stammered, suddenly pathetic, like a small boy. "Please listen to me, Amelia. There's no one else."

She sighed, and settled back into her chair, folding her hands over her stomach. "What is it?"

"It's Fayard. You know, I love that old man, but his stroke has impaired his thinking. He hardly reacted when I told him that

Hitler was rearming Germany. Now it's August, and from what
I've learned, France has constructed a sum total of zero airplanes
this summer! I hear Daladier's great plan is to start reinforcing the
Maginot Line in the fall, and that would be like putting a gauze
dressing over a cancer tumor."

"Why can't *you* order some plane construction?" she asked him,
as though he'd overlooked this obvious solution to one of France's
most pressing dilemmas.

"Armand is the member of the Comité des Forges, whose job it's
been to coordinate the armaments industry," he explained, smiling
in spite of himself at her touching naiveté. "I'm not even a member
of the committee. I'm only his vice-president at Fayard Industries."

Amelia took off her sunglasses and looked at him. "You've chosen the wrong person to discuss this with. I know so little about
armaments, and strategy. I'm just a woman, who, like most
women, hates wars, and violence, and death."

"Yet you are a staunch opponent of Hitler, aren't you? And
Hitler will crush the French unless we, the steel manufacturers,
turn our full attention to the efficient production of armaments."

Amelia's dark eyes bored into him. "Perhaps you're right. But
all I seem to hear from you is a businessman's complaint. *What
about your son,* Charles? Do you never consider *his* problem? By
reason of his birth, Alexis was reared French! He's going to be
eighteen next February, and if Germany declares war on France,
he'll be among the first to be recruited for the armed forces! Anne's
worried. I'm worried. What about you?"

Charles looked away, his heart pounding erratically. How could
he ever admit the truth to her—that Alexis was a burden, and that,
try as he might, he could muster no feelings of paternity toward
him? Yet she expected an answer, and, receiving none, she pressed
her hand over his arm and said, her voice impassioned, "The boy
needs you, Charles! He needs you to care, to show some warmth!
He's old enough to be drafted, like a man—but he's still vulnerable, like a child."

He met her stare, and she dropped her hand. "Amelia, what is it
I'm supposed to do? What do you want from me? What does Anne
want from me? I've done the best I could, haven't I, with Alex?"

She stood up, sighing. "It's not up to me to teach you how to be
a father. But, if I were in your shoes, I'd be bursting with pride to

have a son like him. And I'd be concerned about *his* welfare, instead of about Fayard Industries and the shortage of planes."

As she turned to leave him, he could feel his heart constricting. He was disappointing her again—this time because he couldn't get himself to love Anne's son. Yet, was this his fault?

Amelia didn't know. She simply didn't know the truth, that Alex was not his real child. But had she known this, would she have forgiven him his coldness toward the boy? A painful lump in his throat, he thought in anguish, *She would still condemn me.*

Inexplicably, this made him feel like weeping, as the thought of Alexis's being drafted had not been able to do. Suddenly angry with her, Charles clenched his fists to his thighs. *Grown men didn't cry.* And he never would, not even for her.

* * *

On November 7, 1938, Amelia Habig was putting on her makeup and listening to a Brahms concerto on the radio when the announcer broke through with the shattering news that a young German Jew, Herschel Grynszpan, had just shot Ernst von Rath, first secretary at the German Embassy in Paris. She ran to the telephone and asked the hotel operator to connect her with the offices of Attorney Jeanne Netter, president of the WIZO.

"We can expect the worst," Netter told her. "Grynszpan went crazy with fear. He's only seventeen, and was going to be expelled from France and sent back to Germany. To him, *anything* was better than having to return to the Reich."

Yes, Amelia thought: A Jew in the German Reich today was like a slave. And the only reason her brother and mother had been able to hold on to their comfortable life was because they had been paying dearly for this unheard-of privilege.

She sent Richard a wire, begging him to leave Vienna at once, before it was too late. And then she sat anxiously by the radio, waiting to learn whether von Rath would pull through or die. On November 9, it was announced that the first secretary had passed away. Amelia Habig sank to her knees and wept.

On the night of Wednesday, November 9, in the vast living room of the von Guttman mansion on Vienna's Ringstrasse, Count Richard von Guttman, forty-three, was applauding his beloved. Mitzi (Maria) Klinger, prima ballerina, was showing him on pointe how she would be dancing *Thamar* on Saturday night. At the piano, Countess Barbara von Guttman, sixty-seven, was accompanying the twenty-four-year-old danseuse.

All at once they were frozen into shock by the sound of breaking glass. At first none of them understood—but as the sound swelled in a mounting crescendo, Richard realized that every window in the house was being attacked. "It's the Grynszpan shooting," he cried. "Let's get out through the servants' quarters!"

In the hallway, the noise was deafening. "They're *inside*," he whispered, an arm tight around each of the terrified women. And they flattened themselves against the wall, their hearts beating in their throats, their legs numbed by fear.

When the mob burst in on them, carrying torches, Richard saw that they were setting the entire house on fire. It was a vendetta against all the Jews in the Reich, a way of making them pay for the murder of von Rath in Paris. There's still a chance of making a run for the servants' entrance, he thought, pushing Mitzi and his mother frantically ahead of him. And then Barbara tripped, and an enormous, red-faced Nazi hurled his lighted torch at her and caught her on the head. Barbara's bloodcurdling yell resounded through the house like the wail of a wild animal wounded to the death.

In the seconds that followed, Richard von Guttman threw himself headlong upon his mother's body, incandescent with flames. The smell was putrid, burning flesh and singed hair. He did not know that Barbara had died almost instantly of pain trauma, because she continued to burn and his own clothes caught on fire from her body.

And then the agony began, and he realized he was being burned alive, right there in the hallway of the mansion where he'd been born. Mitzi was running hysterically into the arms of a tall, handsome blond man armed with a long hunting rifle. She was screaming: "I am not a Jew! I am not a Jew! *Don't you remember who I am?*"

The last living image of Count Richard von Guttman was of his beloved and Karl von Stecher, the man who had once been his friend, making a sudden exit. Von Stecher had thrown his rifle down and was running with Mitzi through the blaze that had so recently been the sheltering fortress of the aristocratic von Guttman clan.

When news of the first nationwide pogrom in the German Reich —called *Kristallnacht,* or the Night of Broken Crystal, for the millions of Jewish homes whose windows had been shattered by incensed mobs of bloodthirsty Nazis—reached the French press,

Anne Lévy–de Rochefleur came unannounced into her cousin's suite at the Plaza-Athénée.

She walked into Amelia's room and declared, very quietly: "Charles is doing his best to find out about Richard and Aunt Barbara. But, in the meantime, we insist you and Tina come to La Folie for a few days."

Amelia parted her lips to protest, but Anne pulled a small suitcase out of the closet and began taking lingerie and nightwear out of the bureau drawers. "There are moments when the only thing that makes sense is staying together as a family," she told her cousin. "So do me a favor—no false pride now."

Amelia bowed her head and began to rock back and forth in the sorrow of mourning.

* * *

Amelia had been sitting by the window, stupefied by the intensity of her fear and grief. How long had it been since she'd had the strength to get up and brush her matted hair? It was the *waiting*, the terrible, dreadful waiting for news that could only be bad. The only question remaining was: *how* bad?

The door was swinging open, and she turned and saw Charles. Why hadn't he knocked? She looked at him, bewildered, and he came over to her, his face showing lines she had never noticed before. His dark blue eyes were so grave, so disquieting, that she felt her heart fluttering in her throat.

"Amelia," he said, kneeling by her chair and holding her arms, as if to steady her. "Please forgive me for having to bring you this news. It's about Barbara and Richard."

Amelia felt herself coming apart. She cried out, "They *can't* be dead! They *can't* be, Charles! I've already lost my husband and the baby I was carrying. Don't take away my mother and my brother too. . . ."

She dissolved into tears, unable to see Charles's face anymore. She heard herself crying out, but the words were amorphous, garbled sounds. Charles was thrusting something into her hand, closing her numb, cold fingers over a brandy snifter. He was forcing her to swallow, and she coughed, spilling brandy on her bedjacket. And then he was putting his arms around her and holding her, and she was sobbing on his shoulder like a little girl, her heart breaking.

How long was she sobbing like that in Charles's arms? The next thing she knew, he was applying a cologne-scented washcloth to her forehead, pressing down at her temples. "Meli, Meli," he was saying, using the nickname of her youth. "Meli, I'm here. I'm here, and I'm not going to let anything happen to you again. . . ."

Her eyes were swollen and her head was throbbing. Charles bent over her, wiping her brow. She had never noticed how gentle his face could be, how beautiful, like a young Apollo's. She hadn't had a man fuss over her with such care and concern since Peter's death, when Richard had had to care for her as if she were a baby. And now both of them were dead: Peter and Richard, the two men she had loved in her life. But Charles was here, stroking her hair and speaking softly to her, to ease the pain.

"Things will be all right from now on," he was saying. "I promise you."

"*How?*" she demanded accusingly. "*How* can you promise such a thing? I have nothing left but my Christina! No husband, no parents, no brother, no home, no lands! Only Tina, and I'm afraid now, Charles. Afraid that something could happen to *her* too! Maybe it's my destiny to lose everything that's ever been precious to me. . . ."

He knelt down again, and kissed her hair. "I can promise because now you are here with me," he murmured. "And because I love you far too much to *let* anything happen to you or Tina."

Suddenly Amelia blinked. Beyond Charles's prostrate form partially blocking the view, she saw Anne in the open doorway, silently watching. And then, abruptly, Anne was gone. There was only the empty hallway where her cousin had been standing.

Charles was still whispering something, but now she pushed him away, her grief splintering into shards of hysteria. "Please," she sobbed, "go away now, Charles, and leave me alone!"

And when he had left, closing the door gently behind him, Amelia decided that she had only imagined Anne looking down on her with hazel eyes that had judged her and condemned. What had Charles been saying to her . . . ?

What did any of this mean anyway? She had lost her mother and brother in a single horrible night. And nothing else mattered now.

* * *

Springtime was making a timid entrance on the Paris scene this year, 1939. The sun, like a shy maiden, peeked through white clouds, yet it could not warm the icy winds that penetrated one's bones. Charles was grateful for the welcome warmth of the Hotel

Plaza-Athénée, and wondered, somewhat apprehensively, whether Amelia would be quite as welcoming when she saw him.

He had told the desk clerk that Madame Habig was expecting him, and not to ring upstairs to her suite. It had to be a surprise visit, or she would steel herself against him as usual. He questioned her motives: Was Anne the reason for her cool distance, or could it be that she harbored no tender feelings for him whatsoever?

He rapped on the door. From inside the suite he heard a tinkle of laughter, and girlish footsteps. Then the door swung open and he stood staring into the animated face of Christina. "Cousin Charlie!" she cried, gracefully stepping aside to allow him access. And then she flung herself into his arms.

"Mama!" she announced brightly. "Look who's come!"

Christina led him eagerly into the living room, which was filled with flowers. How quickly people learn to love her, Charles thought, a little jealously. Were any of these roses and blooming orchids from male admirers? He'd heard that an elderly philanthropist, Emile Deutsch de la Meurthe, had sent Amelia a pair of handmade riding boots from Hellstern. Anne had reported this tidbit to him with a certain uncustomary smugness, as if wanting to underscore that Amelia Habig was being courted.

Amelia was dressed in a simple white linen dress, and her hair had been swept into a topknot adorned with a fresh coral miniature rosebud. She rose from her armchair and smiled. "I wasn't expecting you. Would you like some lunch? Tina and I just ordered from room service."

"I thought I might take you both somewhere special," he countered, taking her hands and lightly brushing his lips over her fingers. "It's your birthday, after all. Wouldn't you and Tina like to come with me to the Tour d'Argent?"

She shook her head. "We were already invited to lunch by Lucy de Gunzbourg, but we're being lazy. Besides, we've been sitting near our radio, waiting to hear what Hitler's reply to President Roosevelt will be. So far, no broadcast of his intentions. But if he wants war—"

"It's your day, not the Führer's," Charles cut in. "Let's concentrate on pleasant things, shall we? Look—I've brought you a present."

For a moment he read annoyance on Amelia's face, a delicate frown appearing. "Papa used to decorate the house with chocolate truffles and exotic flowers on April twenty-eighth," Christina said. "Remember, Mama? It was like a national holiday!"

Now Amelia's eyes clouded over with memories. Charles took advantage of this to touch her sympathetically on the shoulder. For a moment nobody spoke. Then Amelia remembered her manners and motioned for Charles to sit down beside her on the sofa. Christina drew up an ottoman and perched on it opposite them. "What's the present, Cousin Charlie?" she asked.

Charles smiled. From the inside pocket of his jacket, he withdrew a small package very simply wrapped in colored tissue paper. "I'm no good at wrapping presents," he apologized.

"You and Anne have already spoiled me today," Amelia stated. She gestured toward a chiseled figurine standing on the coffee table. "The music box is absolutely perfect. With Strauss's waltz . . ."

He wanted to break in angrily and tell her that Anne had acted thoughtlessly, bringing to mind Amelia's past. But when Amelia picked up the tiny ballerina, her face seemed so alive and exuberant that his words stopped in his throat. "It's a genuine Meissen porcelain," Amelia said softly. "My mother used to have one just like it on her mantelpiece."

"Let's see what *you*'ve brought," Christina urged.

He caught Amelia's smile of indulgence toward her daughter, and capitalized on it. "Let me explain before you open it," he said. "I came across this some time ago, when I was going through an old chest in our attic. I don't believe it's terribly valuable, but it belonged to our great-grandmother, Sarah, the wife of my namesake, who first purchased La Folie. And since you no longer have access to any of your family heirlooms, on either your mother's or your father's side, I thought that you're the one who should be wearing our ancestor's brooch."

Amelia's lips parted. But Christina had already begun to tear the tissue off. A plain, rather worn blue velvet box appeared. "Open it, Mama," the girl ordered.

Amelia sprang the catch. Inside lay an antique filigreed platinum butterfly, dotted with the tiniest of rubies, diamonds, emeralds, and sapphires. The entire effect was breathtaking, an object shimmering with delicate life, like a real butterfly. "It's magnificent," Amelia whispered. She lifted it from its box and held it to the sunlight.

"All I did was to have it cleaned," he demurred. "I'm glad you like it."

But a shadow of doubt had crept over Amelia's features. She handed him the brooch. "Shouldn't Anne be the one to own it? After all, you found it at La Folie. . . ."

"Anne already owns all of her grandmother's jewelry," Charles declared. "Alfred's mother left her de Rochefleur necklaces, de Rochefleur rings, de Rochefleur bracelets to fill three entire display windows at Cartier. But you," he added softly, "have almost nothing to remind you of who you are."

Amelia's eyes were on him, and their expression was unexpectedly gentle. "In that case, I'll gladly wear this beautiful butterfly. And I'll think of our great-grandmother every time I pin it on."

Christina jumped up and took the brooch from her mother's hand. Biting her lower lip in concentration, she fastened it to the bodice of Amelia's linen dress. Then she stood back, appraising her job.

"Perhaps you'll also think of the humble messenger who brought it to you," Charles said tentatively. He stood up. "And I think I'll skip that lunch you offered me. I'm swamped with work these days."

Amelia rose, too, and held out her hands. "Of course I'll think of you, Charles," she told him, smiling. And for the first time since she had come from Austria, her eyes held his unflinchingly, a wistful tenderness on her face. "I'm touched and overwhelmed by your consideration."

"It's a mere token of everything I feel," he said to her. But already she was looking away, and moving toward the door.

On Sunday, May 7, Anne came by to take Christina and her mother to see the film La Vie en Rose. Afterward they stopped at Rebattet for a sumptuous tea. Looking up from the bill, Anne's eye was caught by a shining object on the lapel of Amelia's suit jacket.

"What a beautiful pin," she remarked. "Is it something new?"

To her surprise, Amelia blushed. "Actually it's quite an old piece. It belonged to our great-grandmother, Sarah de Rochefleur."

"But I've never seen you wear it."

Christina was leaning forward, about to say something, when Amelia shrugged and declared, "I'd forgotten I had it. You know how that is. I came across it at the bottom of a suitcase . . ."

Afterward, Christina asked her why she had lied to Cousin Anne. Amelia turned aside, ashamed. "I can't help feeling that *she* should be wearing it," she answered. But the fact was, the pin kept troubling her. She'd lied to Anne, right in front of Tina. And the truth was, she wasn't at all sure why she had felt the urge to lie. For Sarah was her own ancestor as much as Anne's.

It wasn't until her father asked her to go through the library files in the den to look up an invoice, that Anne had occasion to think of the pin. Alfred had telephoned from his office, and Anne had immediately gone to the study and unlocked her father's drawer. When she turned the key and pulled out the drawer, she realized she had made a mistake: she had opened Charles's instead, and found herself staring at his unanswered correspondence.

Long ago, in the early years of their marriage, Charles had made it clear to her that he valued his privacy. She only used the small desk key if he himself asked that she do it, for a specific reason. And so Anne had started to close the drawer, when a sheet of paper caught on the bottom of the drawer above. She pulled it out, annoyed because it had partially torn and Charles would wonder how that had occurred.

Instinctively, Anne glanced down at the offending onionskin. It was the copy of a receipt, she noted, from the jeweller Van Cleef & Arpels. She did a double take. She couldn't remember having received any jewelry from Charles within the past six months.

Put it away, she told herself. But the worm of jealousy had crept into her mind. If not for her, then for whom had her husband been purchasing jewelry? And *when*?

The date of the invoice said April 28, 1939. And a description of the purchased item followed: "One butterfly brooch, platinum, set with twelve rubies, seven emeralds . . ."

Anne's hand trembled so much that she had to set the paper down on the desk. *So that was it, then.* Charles and Amelia had been seeing each other, behind her back. A vision of the two of them kissing in the moonlight, young and impassioned, exploded in her mind's eye. And then a newer one of Charles, on his knees before Amelia, promising her that nothing bad would ever happen to her or Christina. . . .

Sobbing with anguish, Anne thrust the invoice back into Charles's drawer, locked it, and ran from the study without bothering to remember why she had come in the first place. But rage had entered her heart. *If she thinks she can do this,* Anne thought, *then at least she won't get the satisfaction of breaking me down.* I'm never going to tell her that I know . . . and I'll never tell *him*, either!

But for the first time in years, she gave in to the luxury of hating her cousin. Because Amelia had lost everything dear to her, she had believed it would be all right to take what belonged to Anne. How could she, Anne thought venomously. *I trusted her like my own sister. . . .*

* * *

Alexis had never spent August in Paris. And it was a strange August, to be sure, heavy with the threat of storm, and the threat of war. He was working for Fayard Industries, in its legal department, while awaiting news of whether he had passed his baccalaureate examination. His cousin Amelia had given him the keys to her suite at the nearby Plaza-Athénée, so that he wouldn't have to take the train back and forth from Saint-Germain each day.

Nobody was there to bother him. His family had gone to Nice again, with Amelia and Tina. In June, when he'd come home after his graduation from boarding school, he had found his mother oddly withdrawn. But he had attributed this to his father's preoccupation with business. For, as of the end of April Paul Reynaud, the finance minister, had announced that raw materials would be allocated to the state, with priorities toward the manufacture of armaments. And this had meant a surplus of work for the Fayard employees, a slew of new contracts for steel parts that would be assembled into tanks, guns, and planes.

Charles had been in Paris the months of June and July. Now that Armand Fayard had partially recuperated from his stroke, he had resumed his control over the business; but he was still operating only at half his ability from his mansion in Versailles. Charles had commuted back and forth there in June and July, bearing sheaves of papers for Fayard to read through and sign.

During those two months, Alexis had lived at La Folie with his father. His mother had gone ahead to Nice, and his grandfather Alfred had taken his ailing bones to Switzerland, and so the two men had the entire run of the house to themselves, with only the silent shadows of the Goujons between them. It had struck the young man with unmitigated clarity that his father didn't like him at all, that he preferred to read his newspaper or listen to the radio than to chat with him, even about politics. And Alexis had felt lonelier then than he did now, with no one around.

It was true he had never learned so much, not in twelve years of formal education. It wasn't his actual job that was teaching him: mostly he was just the errand boy for the department, and when he wasn't, he spent his afternoons in the stacks of the legal library cataloging cases and looking up references. But, running back and forth, keeping his ears wide open, he couldn't help but hear bits of information that later, alone in Amelia's cool boudoir, he pieced together into a more or less comprehensible whole. And he felt more and more uncomfortable with what he heard.

He'd made a friend—François Durand, a young law clerk at Fayard Industries, waiting to find out whether he'd passed his bar examination. Durand, at twenty-three, had completed his military service two years before. He was a Socialist, and an ardent admirer of Léon Blum, the first, and only Jewish, Socialist premier of France. Durand was just enough Alexis's senior to have become an inspiration to the younger man: he had briefly fought against Franco in Spain, and that alone had turned him into a kind of hero to Alexis.

They discussed whether a war was avoidable, and whether that was good. "Traditionally, the Left has been pacifist," Durand declared, over a dinner of grilled steak and *pommes frites* on the Left Bank. "But now we have no choice: Hitler is worse than Franco. Fascism must be wiped out."

"Which branch of the military would you enlist in?" Alexis asked.

"I trained as an infantryman. But against the *Boches,* I'd want to fly. There's something exciting about air warfare . . . if warfare must exist."

Alexis felt his blood coursing faster. "But that's the area where we're least able to meet Hitler head-on. The Luftwaffe could beat us in an instant." He chewed silently, wondering whether to come out with his facts. "Listen, François," he finally said, looking his friend in the eye. "It seems to me that old man Fayard *wants* there to be a war. He's signed exclusive contracts with the government, and has set up a ball bearings plant in Lorraine for the exclusive use of the military. Reynaud called for the allocation of raw materials, and Fayard jumped right in, offering his 'help.' And the one getting the most help is Monsieur Fayard. . . ."

Durand nodded, taking a pack of Gauloises out of his breast pocket and offering one to Alexis. "I don't want this to sound like I'm trying to hurt you," he said. "But your father had a lot to do with this. They say that because he's Swiss, he's all for other people's wars. They say he's ashamed of being a Jew, and wasn't above trading with Hitler while it was still profitable to import German coal for our steelworks."

Alexis looked pained and concentrated on lighting his cigarette. "I've heard all these rumors. Don't worry, François—*he*'s the one who caused me hurt, not you. Sometimes the truth hurts! They call my father 'the weathervane' . . . he who turns whichever way the wind is blowing. But I'm not like him. I'm going to enlist and fight for our country—for *my* country—and then I'm going to set up a law firm to help the little people, the small businessmen that guys like Fayard and my father have been crushing in their mad scramble to take over the economy."

Durand, who came from a family of innkeepers in the province of Auvergne, and who lived in a maid's room in the district of Montparnasse, nodded, gulping down some *gros rouge* that tasted acrid and redolent of cork. "Count me in," he told his young friend, suddenly smiling.

But Alexis's summer wasn't only being spent with Durand, or in the stacks of the library. As soon as his father left for Nice on his month's vacation, word had come down from Versailles that Charles's son was to take up the relay and bring the old man his office correspondence. At first, Alexis had bristled: he hadn't liked being singled out over the other clerks, all of whom, like François Durand, were older than he and already enrolled in the Faculty of Law. Also, he had had mixed feelings about the man who had engineered to be granted such a large contract with the French government for the manufacture of armaments.

But he'd done his duty, and gone. And had found, once again, that Fayard's multifaceted personality transcended any category one tried to peg him in. Debilitated, half his body and face sagging from his stroke, Armand Fayard nevertheless breathed life and power into any room he occupied. And, for some strange reason, he liked Alexis and didn't hide it.

He likes me more than my own father does, the young man thought. Here was a man more powerful than Charles, older and more worldly than Charles, who bothered to ask Alex for his opinion. And when the young man, a little self-consciously, began to speak his views, the old man's sharp black eyes remained riveted to his face, drinking in every word. Sometimes he would smile. Sometimes he would frankly laugh. Other times he simply nodded, thoughtfully, from the pillowed fortress of his immense four-poster bed . . . a felled lion, still magnificent, though cut short in his ability to go on the hunt.

The poor man's hungry for human contact, Alexis decided, his awareness making him compassionate. That's why he talks to me as though I were an equal, one of his peers. He feeds on my strength and on my youth, and tries to use my legs to walk through his domain, and my eyes to peruse his dynasty.

"You seem to find it immoral to make money, Alex," Armand Fayard told him one afternoon as he handed the young man a stack of signed documents. "Yet where would *you* be if your ancestors had not made money their prime target?"

Alexis thought carefully about his answer. "It's not money that I'm against. In fact, I hope someday to make a great deal of it myself. What I oppose is coming by this money through dishonorable means. Dealing with Hitler, giving him our francs so that he can build up his Luftwaffe at our expense . . . that's immoral. And making huge profits out of rearming France is equally wrong."

"So you believe Fayard Industries ought to be giving away its expertise?"

Alexis sighed. "Probably we should sell it. But for a very small margin of profit. We're a rich enough company to be patriotic. Our government is so poor that it needs every sou to keep itself going." His voice rose, suddenly impassioned. "To increase rearmament, public works have had to be set aside, and state employees have had to be laid off by the thousands. Taxes have been levied, chiefly hurting the poorer classes. And meanwhile, what have you and my father been doing? You've been depositing huge checks into the company accounts, rubbing your hands together with pleasure!"

But then he felt ashamed, having been so outspoken and frank. This little speech was going to cost him his job, and be reported back to Charles. And then Alexis would never hear the end of it.

But instead, Fayard was cocking his head to the side, considering what he had heard. "Perhaps you have a point," he was saying. "Although that's only part of the story. We've also helped to create jobs by the thousands, well-paid jobs, to keep the mills going twenty-four hours a day, and the ball bearings plant full-time too. Think of that, Alex, before you judge us too harshly, your father and me."

And Armand's sharp black eyes settled on the young man with a strange, almost pleading insistence. Alexis blushed, suddenly confused. Fayard sighed, still gazing at him, then shrugged with re-signed frustration. "I wonder . . ." he murmured. "Sometimes, my dear boy, you make me wonder things better left unques-tioned."

"Sir?" Bewilderment was written on Alexis's face.

Fayard shook his head. "It's just that my own youth was so long ago," he replied. "And you remind me of myself, when I was young. . . ."

CHAPTER XV

Anne's hand was shaking as she salted her omelet, and she could feel her lower lip trembling as well. Her nerves were fraying. "You really don't look well," Amelia remarked, frowning with concern from across the breakfast table.

She dares to pretend concern, Anne thought furiously. But, as usual, she controlled the impulse to let loose at Amelia the torrent of anger she was feeling. Last night, at the casino in Cannes, where they had gone after dinner to meet some friends, Amelia had proudly displayed the butterfly on the bodice of her evening gown. *Adding insult to injury . . .*

But other preoccupations predominated over Anne's resentment toward her cousin. And so she voiced them. "It's Alex, Charles. I received another letter from him. He's certain that war will break out any day now—and he's determined to enlist and train as a pilot!"

"That's terribly romantic and brave," Christina piped up, her eyes shining.

Anne looked at her, annoyed. "It's also terribly foolish. I'm sure he thinks just like you, Tina . . . but he could lose his life!" Turning to her husband, she cried, "You've got to do something, Charles! We can't let Alex join the military. There has to be *some* way you can prevent it!"

Charles appeared as cool and composed as ever. "Look, Anne, I don't know what you think I can do. He's eighteen years old. If he gets called up, do you think *I,* a Swiss citizen, would be able to exempt him from serving his country? Frankly, my dear, I'm not opposed to Alex's doing his bit for France. It's every young man's duty, and it may turn him into a real man!"

Anne could hardly suppress the tears that threatened to spill from her eyes. "He's already quite enough of a man! I don't want him to turn into a *dead* man at the age of eighteen, while you sit here enjoying your breakfast . . . all of you, his own family! Doesn't anyone care besides me?"

"I do, Cousin Anne," Christina whispered.

Anne's features softened. "Thank you, sweetheart. But you wouldn't be able to stop him from enlisting."

"Darling," old Yvonne spoke up, placing a frail hand on Anne's arm. "Charles is right; it's no longer a matter of enlistment. If France goes to war with the Germans, every available man able to serve his country will be mobilized. So talking Alex out of enlisting isn't going to help at all. He'll be called up, and he won't be given a choice!"

Anne's heart was pounding so rapidly, the entire hotel terrace had begun to spin. She stood, and four worried faces stared up at her. But already they were a blur. Only her son mattered. "I'm going to take the first train back to Paris," she announced. "And *somehow,* I'm going to do what must be done!"

* * *

Anne nervously checked her image in the long mirror, causing the thin little maître d'hôtel to pause respectfully ahead of her. She saw a thirty-nine-year-old woman, with heavy hips and a pronounced bustline, encased in a knee-length brown dress of crisp cotton, and a simple, tailored linen coat of turquoise. Her freshly bobbed brown hair shone beneath the turquoise pillbox hat. Her legs were good, her eyes still her best feature. Yet Anne knew that compared to the elegance of Arabella, who knew how to shock and arrest the eye of every male who saw her, her own simple good taste was hardly unusual. She looked like what she was: a near-to-middle-aged matron, born to wealth and married to wealth. How would *he* respond to her?

All these years, she had pushed out of her mind the memory of that night in May 1920. She'd thought of Alexis as her son and Charles's. Whenever the truth had surreptitiously come back to haunt her, she had fretfully closed her eyes to the facts and plunged bravely on with her neatly arranged life. A life through which Armand Fayard had streaked with the rapidity of Halley's comet, quickly disappearing after his momentary flash of passion, but leaving the tangible proof of his passage behind him: her beloved Alexis. The only child she had brought into her marriage to Charles, she guiltily admitted. Yet, wasn't it better to have brought *this* wonderful, intelligent, sensitive boy to Charles, rather than the single miscarriage that their own coupling had provided in nineteen years?

"Is Madame ready?" the butler asked, hesitation marking his deferential tone. And she nodded, her heart hammering inside her chest.

He knocked on a massive door, opening it to a stentorian "Come in!" and announcing: "Madame Charles de Rochefleur, monsieur." He made a gesture for her to pass inside the hallowed enclave, and so she did. Now there could be no more retreating. The die was cast. . . .

The baroque room in which she was standing took her breath away. Its size alone was large enough to accommodate a hundred courtiers come to escort the Sun King to bed. A floor of black and white marble stretched out in an intricate pattern of tiles; and lacquered cabinets, along with solid silver pier tables, candlestands, and mirrors, proudly flanked the sculptured walls. Toward the back, a roomy alcove was set off by a scalloped canopy of silk velvet. Behind this canopy the enormous four-poster bed reigned supreme, with tall back stools placed in straight lines to its left and right against the wall.

Armand Fayard lay propped against a mountain of pillows in the bed, sporting a black silk pajama top. Strewn all around him were papers and envelopes embossed with the company logo: a crested eagle, his claws hooked onto the top of an imposing *F.I.*

"Golle," he called out to his manservant. "Pull up an armchair for Madame!"

Once she was seated, balancing her small crocodile bag awkwardly on her lap, the butler silently left the room. Anne found herself staring at the old man in the bed, his hawklike eyes detailing her with interest. His features appeared craggier than before, the lines mapped out more elaborately; the close-cropped hair had turned completely white. But what struck Anne as the most pronounced sign of age had come as a result of his stroke: the corners of his left eye and mouth drooped uncontrollably, and the folds of skin on that side sagged.

"Well, Anne," he boomed. "This visit is most unexpected . . . but an agreeable surprise, to be sure!" He was smiling, his eyes twinkling, and she suddenly remembered his charm. For all Charles's poise and grace, he lacked Fayard's sheer animal magnetism. And it was that very magnetism which, after all, had at least partially caused the event leading to this moment. . . .

"Monsieur Fayard," she said, bravely meeting his unyielding eye. "Alexis doesn't know I've come here. Neither does Charles."

"Rest easy—neither will find out from me," he reassured her. "But it's about the boy, isn't it, Anne?"

His eyes were so intense, so kind, so gentle, as he asked her this question. Yet Anne felt a flare-up of anger. This man had taken gross advantage of her when she'd been an innocent, heartbroken young girl. She hated the memory of that night, of her own silly, tipsy weakness—of her tremendous *need,* which he had captured and abused . . . the way all men abused women when the latter were openly, cravenly weak. She hated herself as she had been, and him for his rapacious lust, which had not known the bounds of common decency. And so she sat up a little straighter, and raised her chin. "You've always taken such an interest in our family," she declared, her voice oddly detached and even dignified. "And this matter requires the kind of power only a man of your stature possesses."

"Tell me."

A moment of silence ensued. "Monsieur Fayard—"

"Armand."

"Armand, there's going to be a war. You and I both know it. I—"

"Alexis wants to enlist immediately, in the air force. And you don't approve."

Anne grasped the clasp of her pocketbook and regarded Fayard with a look of intense emotion. "Armand, he's my only child! I don't want him involved in this war! And *you alone can help*!" Her voice dropped to an ardent whisper. "Please get Alex exempt from having to fight in what can only accelerate into a bloody conflict!"

Fayard's brows rose, and he considered her words, his face revealing nothing. Then he remarked, "Alex would be appalled if he knew what you were asking. You realize that, of course."

Looking down at her hands, she answered, "Yes," so low that he could hardly catch her reply. "But it was a risk I had to take."

He nodded gravely. "Anne, Alex is almost nineteen. He's a man. If he wants to enter the war, like all the youngsters his age, don't you think it's his right to do so? His right as a Frenchman?"

"Yes, but that doesn't change my request. I'm his mother! I can't bear the thought of anything happening to him!"

Fayard seemed lost in thought. Then he narrowed his eyes,

catching her unprepared. "You're his mother, and I'm his father. Isn't that why you came, Anne?"

She stared at him, all at once very pale. Then she nodded, her hazel eyes filled with the gravity of this admission. "You yourself knew this, didn't you? The way you've cared about him. . . . You *had* to have known!"

"I suspected as much. But the love I feel for him would still have existed otherwise. It's him I love—not simply a reflection of myself I've hoped to catch. We've done well, Anne. Our single mutual endeavor has turned out to be the greatest success in both our lives. Isn't that right?"

Once again she nodded. "Then . . . you'll help?"

"I'll do my best. This much I can promise."

Anne stood, overcome by a conflict of emotions. She wanted to dispel the intimacy that had to exist between them at this moment, by virtue of their common bond. She was grateful to Fayard, but still angry for what he had done to her. And, at the same time, she had revealed her secret for the first and only time since the conception of Alexis. She needed to be alone to sort through the tangle of her feelings.

"Thank you," she told him with a simple, proud nobility. "What must I do? What is it you'll need from me?"

"All his medical records," he replied briskly. "Have them here tomorrow morning. And don't worry—no one will ever learn about this little transaction. It will remain our secret . . . to make sure Alex stays alive."

Unable to bear any more, Anne nodded, grabbed her bag, and turned to leave the imposing bedroom. But on the threshold she nearly bumped into the chicly coiffed person of Arabella. Anne's lips parted and for a brief instant, neither woman spoke.

It was Armand who broke the spell, masterfully. "Anne came to bring me papers from Charles. With the current political situation, we can't afford to waste a single day."

Arabella smiled. "Well, my dear, how very loyal of you," she declared, her tapered fingers touching Anne's arm. "Charles, I assume, is still sunning himself on the Riviera?"

Anne nodded, patting her pillbox hat in place. "I had to come home. My son had been alone long enough. And God knows, poor Charles needs every day of rest."

"Poor Charles, indeed, has got himself a most devoted spouse." Arabella's fingers tightened sympathetically over Anne's bare skin, and her smile broadened. "Well now, it's my turn. I was just coming to bring Armand his noontime medicine. A wife's job never ends, does it, Anne?"

Mercifully, Anne was saved from answering by Armand Fayard, who erupted into an abrupt and loud fit of coughing. She took the opportunity to slip out, leaving Arabella running on delicate toes toward her husband.

* * *

Amelia turned on her side, throwing the light sheet off with an impatient foot. In her dream, she was standing by a swimming pool, looking into clear, fresh, cool water. She could see her own reflection, flushed and disheveled, on the smooth surface of the pool. And around her waist were two strong arms, pulling her away from the water, drawing her back. A face was nuzzling her neck, burying itself in her thick hair . . . hot, sensuous lips devouring her skin. . . . Who was this, kissing her from behind?

Amelia was hungry to unveil that face. Pleasure coursed through her nerve endings, which were on fire. A man kissing her, thrilling her. Peter? Peter was dead. She hadn't dreamed of him in years, because the dreams brought too much pain; and when she'd dreamed of him before, she'd seen his body in flames. . . .

The man was kissing her, his face hidden by her hair. Amelia felt something stirring within her, a memory of passion. She wanted the man to kiss her lips, to raise his hands to encompass the fullness of her breasts. *Turn around,* her real self told her dream self— but somehow her dream self couldn't move at all. She stood paralyzed, convulsed with longing and yet unable to turn around and surrender to her unseen lover.

Her dream self moved. She stepped forward, since she couldn't seem to step backward, and now stood teetering on the edge of the pool. The man made a frantic gesture to pull her back to him, and the surface of the water rippled. Amelia, from outside the dream, strained to detect something recognizable about the man. He had long fingers, with clean round nails, and a ring. A wedding band. On his other hand he wore a signet ring. From the bed, Amelia suddenly began to tremble. The signet ring! *She knew someone with that selfsame ring!* Only, who was the man?

As suddenly as the dream had begun, Amelia snapped out of her sleep, sitting bolt upright. She sat shaking, hugging herself, looking out at the crescent-shaped moon framed by her open window. It broke into fragmented slivers over the waves of the Mediterranean, like so many scattered silver bangles. . . .

She hadn't felt so hot, or so bothered, in years. And all because of a silly, senseless dream!

Amelia rose and sauntered over to the window. A cool breeze sifted in, caressing her hair. That man . . . that ring. And that unfinished moment of passion . . .

It wasn't natural to have stayed so many years without a partner, Amelia thought. Peter wouldn't have wanted her to be alone, mourning and grieving for more than five years. But then, of course, there had been the rape, and after that she hadn't wanted to even think of sex with anyone.

I'm thirty-nine, and terribly lonely, she told herself dryly. That's why I'm dreaming absurd silent-picture sequences, as though I were Greta Garbo posing for the camera. And so she briskly pulled down the venetian blinds and climbed back into bed, reaching for the bottle of Valerian to calm her nerves and black out the unresolved puzzle of the faceless lover.

* * *

After the busboy had come to remove the remainder of their copious tea, Yvonne hadn't wanted to leave the shaded warmth of her terrace, and so Christina brought her book outside and was reading aloud to her. Amelia felt a sharp pang: young people needed the elderly, needed the balance of their years of wisdom to even the thrust of their own wild impulses, to cap their bursts of energy with the experienced indulgence of the older generation. Children longed for grandparents. Tina longed for Barbara, whom she had dearly loved.

Suddenly overcome, Amelia grabbed her canvas bag and straw hat and walked out of the old woman's suite. In the corridor, a man was coming toward her from the elevator, raising his hand in salutation. It was Charles, suntanned, flaxen-haired, smiling, tall and strong. He made a handsome image as he strode toward her in his white linen suit, and for a minute she paused, smiling in response, allowing his physical presence to dispel her mood and her memories. Forgetting this was Charles, and letting the simple impression of his physique please her dormant sensuality.

And then, annoyed, she jumped back to reality. Charles was calling out to her: "How about a walk?"

She thought: I don't really like him. Besides, I left Yvonne's suite to be by myself. No, a walk is definitely not what I need—not with Charles, in any case.

But he was smiling at her with such winsome, boyish charm that she shrugged, and grinned back. "All right," she said, giving in and taking the arm he offered her.

They strolled through the sienna streets, in the shadow of the tall, spindly palm trees, inhaling the dusty air of Nice in the late afternoon. It didn't seem important where their footsteps were leading. Arm in arm, they chatted about small, mundane matters, carefully avoiding the larger issues that threatened the world as well as the fragile peace between them. The fact that the Russians had just signed a commercial treaty with Hitler—while continuing to negotiate with France and Britain—was kept out of their small talk. They were prescient enough to keep the real world from crashing down on the temporary haven they had just erected.

But Amelia was conscious of Anne standing monumentally between them. And yet where was the harm in taking a short walk with her cousin Charles? There was none; except that they had never done so, and she had stayed away because he had declared a love she neither felt she could return, nor felt *he* should be feeling.

She had liked Charles as a young man of twenty-two. She might have liked him more had she not been so preoccupied with Peter that summer of 1920. However, she didn't like the man Charles had become. She loved Anne, and Alexis. Charles didn't. Amelia was angry with him for his cool indifference to both of them.

And yet, somehow, none of this seemed to matter right now. Amelia's hand, resting lightly on Charles's forearm, brought her a sense of comfort from the warm contact. "You're my only family now," she said to him. "All of you, I mean. And I'm very grateful to you, Charles."

He paused, looking at her. "You're something else for me. You represent the promise of my youth, my beginnings. If we had married, Amelia, I might have turned into a different kind of man . . . a better one, to be sure. You would have kept my idealism alive."

She opened her mouth to protest. But what he said touched her and brought tears to her eyes. "Why? I wasn't so idealistic myself, as a girl. Don't you remember? I thought only about parties, balls, teas, early morning hunts. . . ."

"But you worked in a hospital during the war. You lived every moment to the fullest. You believed in whatever you were doing, whether it was kissing me under the moonlight, waltzing with a

Viennese admirer, or helping to bandage a wounded soldier. It was
this freshness of experience I admired and craved, because I never
learned how to enjoy the moment. My head always interfered with
my senses, and with the passions of my heart. I'd always be wondering about the consequences of the slightest action, the most
insignificant desire."

She sighed. "That's only because I never once had to think about
money," she admitted ruefully.

His face turned sad. "You really can't understand what it's like.
. . ." She could sense Charles's frustration, his anger at having
been born dispossessed. Having never understood this, she had
judged him harshly. And now she felt ashamed for having had so
much while he had struggled with so little.

They paused near a simple wooden bench, and sat down. Looking into a hazy distance, he said, "You may not believe this, but
once, when I was a young man, I vibrated with idealism. Life has
transformed me, Amelia. Forgive me for what I've become. But in
order to survive, we sometimes have to make a pact with the devil,
like Faust."

"No, Charles. That's an easy excuse! It was the same excuse our
old friends the von Stechers made during the Anschluss. But it was
your ambition to conquer, your lust for power, that forced you to
compromise your values. You could have sacrificed some of that
power to remain decent, Charles. You didn't *have* to make a marriage of convenience. You didn't *have* to deal with the German coal
manufacturers last year. You didn't *have* to go to Cologne as
Fayard's advance man last summer. You did these things because
you wanted more, much more, than the average man. More than
simple success, which your wits, and your background, and your
university diploma would have afforded you at the very least."

"You're right. I wanted much more. I wanted to be the kind of
man whose name gets written down in history books. It was losing
you that made me want power. If you'd married me, Amelia, I
would have been content to be the kind of man you just spoke of,
the kind of man who can be satisfied with moderate success because his major success lies in his family life."

"Who can know?" she remarked softly. "Perhaps you weren't
meant to live a quiet life, and, in spite of me, you would have
striven for greater spheres of influence."

"But we would have been happy, in any case."

Their eyes met, and his hand hesitantly found hers, and covered it. And then she looked down and saw the ring: the gold signet ring, which he always wore, and which she'd never paid attention to before. It was the same ring she had dreamed about . . . on the hand of her faceless lover.

The man she'd dreamed about had been *Charles* . . . her cousin Charles! But then, hadn't she realized that, and hidden the truth from herself? He loved her! He had loved her when she'd been twenty, and still continued to love the woman she had become, at thirty-nine. She had been alone for five years, dreadfully alone, rejecting every semblance of male attention for fear of hurting Peter's memory or falling short of what she and Peter had built together during their thirteen marvelous years as husband and wife.

Gently, he was raising her chin and kissing her lips, brushing them with the tender velvet of his own. But it was wrong! Wrong to be sitting here with him, with Anne's husband, while Anne was in Paris. Wrong to have allowed him to guess just how lonely she had grown. *Wrong!*

"Please," she begged, pushing him away. "Don't kiss me again. I won't allow you to tempt me, Charles. We can never be lovers, and you know this. Don't make it more difficult for both of us!"

And she quickly rose, looking out toward the jeweled city that shone in the afternoon sunlight like a burnished sculpture of bronze, coral, and turquoise.

But his hands were on her shoulders, and his voice was quietly decisive. "You're coming back with me now, Amelia," he told her. "We've both been waiting long enough. . . ."

Rays of late afternoon sunlight brought soft pastel shadows into Charles's bedroom. Gently he pulled Amelia inside, then closed the door and locked it with the chain. She was trembling, and so he took her in his arms and held her, aware of her heartbeat against his own. The vulnerability of the woman struck him, moving him almost to tears. Never during his sixteen years of trysts with Arabella had she appeared vulnerable or fragile to him.

Amelia was warm against his chest. He could smell her subtly floral scent mixed with the musk of Nice heat on her skin. He had felt protective toward her, romantic more than sexual, until that very moment, when her femaleness assailed him with an unexpected strength. And so, not wanting to wait and risk her losing her courage, he whisked her into his arms toward the large, canopied bed, and eased her down upon the pillows.

She hadn't spoken yet, but her eyes were on him, dark and magnetic, like the witch-eyes of Calypso on her magic island. Charles felt young, as though this were 1920 again and both of them pure, unbranded by life and other marriages, and the compromises that could be read like maps on both their faces.

How he wanted her! But he had to be careful not to frighten her away. He could still hear her voice that awful morning when she had told him and Anne about the SS soldiers. What they had done to her. Since then, he was certain she hadn't had a man.

He could see her pulse beating in her throat. With silken fingers he pulled the straps of her summer dress off her shoulders, and was amazed when she shrugged it off by herself, revealing white breasts with ash-pink nipples like velvet pansies opened to the sun. She was so white—like marble, the blue veins showing through her translucent skin. "You're not a dream," he murmured to her softly. "You *are* mine, after all. . . ."

"Yes. I am."

And then she kissed him with a small moan, falling into his arms like a surrender, giving up all thoughts to the moment's sensuality. She was breathing him in, her head swimming with new sensations, with his warm breath, the feel of his hair against the tips of her fingers. Meanwhile, he was struggling out of his clothes, awkward lest his movements stop the excitement with which she was touching him and exploring his face, his throat, his chest.

When he was naked, she unhooked the buckle of her belt and squirmed out of her dress. Then, suddenly shy again, she waited. Charles fumbled with her lace panties and she closed her eyes as he pulled them off. Then he lay on top of her and she cried out, with pleasure, feeling his strength cover her body.

They lay this way for several minutes, kissing, holding each other, giving her time to get accustomed to his weight. At last he rolled off her and began the slow, exhilarating discovery of her own secret parts: suckling her nipples until she nearly screamed with desire, then teasing her underbelly and tangling his fingers in her downy hair. She closed her eyes for the room had started to spin. His fingers were probing the petals of her most private parts, opening up her secret areas, wanting her to be warm and moist before penetrating her.

When at last he had finished with his foreplay, he entered her without the slightest effort. They glided together over the ocean of their passion, stroke for stroke, in perfect harmony. She wanted it to last forever, and he made every effort not to disappoint her.

Afterward, as she was resting in the cradle of his shoulder, she pushed out the guilt, and the memories—hers, his, their past, their present. But the tears welled up in spite of herself, and when he felt them on his chest, he asked her why she was crying.

"If Anne didn't love you so much, it wouldn't be so bad," she told him.

"I never loved Anne. I always loved you."

She sighed, and snuggled closer. "I know. But this is far worse than simple adultery—it's something I never imagined I would ever do. I suppose . . ." She sat up, gazing down at him. "I loved you, didn't I? But I was also afraid. Afraid of the man you had become—this cold husband, cold father, calculating businessman who was so different from the only other man I'd ever loved: Peter."

"Do you feel any guilt about Peter? To have fallen in love with another man?"

She shook her head. "He would have wanted me to be happy," she said, and then her eyes filled with tears. "But Charlie, will you and I *ever* be happy? There's no future for us, only an uncertain present built on lies and cheating. . . ."

"Let's not think about it now," he told her, moving to straddle her again. His growing erection pushed against her stomach and she bit her lip, wondering why she was allowing this to happen, and why, when she had run away from him once, she had let him change her life now.

Because it was too late ever to turn back. *The die was cast.*

CHAPTER XVI

The exciting news that Alexis had not only passed his baccalaureate examination, but had earned himself the most distinguished label of *"très bien"* ("very good"), was almost drowned out by more dramatic events that would have monumental repercussions on the world at large. Shortly after the family returned to Paris at the end of August, Hitler invaded Poland. And on Sunday, September 3, Great Britain at 11:00 A.M. and France at 5:00 P.M. declared war on the German Reich.

Alexis met his friend François Durand on the Left Bank at the Café des Deux Magots. Nervous fingers playing with the ends of his sparse brown mustache, Durand told him that he was enlisting the following day. "Nobody wants to fight," he said with disgust. "The Right's accusing the Jews of having invented Danzig as a plot to force France into the war, and the Left is suddenly pacifist again, disgruntled and ashamed of its friends the Soviets for making a pact with Hitler. Doesn't anyone realize that the Nazis will plow through free Europe unless *we personally* give them a beating?"

Alexis swallowed his red wine and looked earnestly at his friend. "*I* realize it," he remarked, a slight tremor in his voice. "And so I, too, am going tomorrow to the recruitment office. You're not Jewish, François, but I am. That gives me added reason for wanting Hitler dead."

Durand broke into a grin, and raised his glass. "You're my kind of man."

Bright and early Monday morning, September 4, Alexis rose, washed, and shaved; then, sprucely dressed in his best blue serge suit, he went down to the dining room. It was barely seven-thirty; he hoped to have a quick breakfast and run out before his mother came downstairs, because he was afraid of having to confront and hurt her with his resolution.

A clear, pale blue sky, hazily shadowed by clouds of the purest, cleanest white, illumined the large and sumptuous room where he had sat down to so many meals during his eighteen and a half years. This morning the walls of blue silk seemed to shimmer with sunlight, which also made the crystal sparkle on the long table. Goujon stood at attention by the entrance, in his white jacket, a fresh ceremonial towel under his left arm. Alexis smiled and greeted him, laughing inwardly at this excess of tradition, which was as useless as it was outmoded.

Immediately, as he strode in, Alexis saw that the room's only other occupant, besides the butler, was Christina. "I didn't even realize you were at La Folie, Tina! I thought you would be at the Plaza-Athénée, with your mother."

She shook her head, a trifle nervously. "Last night I asked Mama to let me come here to spend the night. I wanted to be sure and see you this morning, Alex."

He sat down in the upright Louis XVI chair that Goujon had pulled out for him. Surprise made him stare at her curiously. He hadn't seen much of her this past year: first, he had been at his boarding school in Rolle, and then she had been in Nice when he was alone in Paris, working for Armand Fayard. Christina Habig had grown up; she was fourteen, almost fifteen, maybe. Tall and well proportioned like her elegant, graceful mother, but more hesitant and shy than Amelia. She showed the hurt she had suffered much more openly than her mother: her dark blue, almond-shaped eyes appeared bottomless, and so full of pain sometimes that they made him look away in embarrassment.

Christina Habig had become a young woman. The girl he'd taken riding through the town had matured, and beautifully so. But it was not this that amazed him; it was her words. "Why did you want to see me, Tina? I mean, I'm flattered, of course . . . but do you have a particular problem?"

She smiled. She had lovely features, a heart-shaped mouth. Her skin glistened with freshness, untouched by powder or rouge. She was still extremely young, he reminded himself, in spite of her tallness. At fourteen, girls didn't wear makeup. He'd grown accustomed to the older "women" François had introduced him to during the summer: twenty-year-olds, the secretaries and hairdressers that Durand had met for a bite of dinner, and whom the law student had prevailed upon to bring along an extra girlfriend. Those women were *women.*

I prefer Tina, he thought, touched by the girl's vulnerability as she looked frankly at him, a little intimidated. "No, Alex," she told him. "It's nothing to do with *me.* But when I heard the radio announcer about the war, I knew you'd be enlisting. And . . . I wanted to catch you and wish you good luck."

Goujon stood to his left, presenting him with a silver platter of shirred eggs. Alexis ignored him completely, his lips parting in wonder as he gazed at the girl with amazement. "Tina," he murmured. "I can't believe it. . . . How sweet and thoughtful of you."

"It's not," she contradicted him, moving her eggs around on her plate, trying to disguise the trembling of her fingers. "I was afraid I might not see you again for a long, long time. And I also thought . . . well, that Cousin Anne would want whatever time might be left for you to be with her and Cousin Charles, and with your grandfather and grandmother. I didn't know if there would be a spare minute for me to wish you well and Godspeed . . . and to tell you I'll be missing you."

Goujon cleared his throat, to indicate that breakfast was yet waiting to be served. Alexis stood up and, gently pushing the old man aside, walked over to his cousin and placed his hands on her shoulders. "Tina, you're wonderful! Has anyone told you this lately? I love you! You're a great girl and I'm proud to be part of your family."

She smiled, shy and pleased. "I love you too, Alex," she whispered back. Then, rising, she kissed him on the cheek. "Take care," she said breathlessly, and ran from the dining room like a frightened doe.

Goujon emitted the most delicate of coughs, and announced in a subdued voice, "Monsieur Alexis's eggs are getting cold. . . ."

"Then I'll eat Mademoiselle Christina's," the young man declared, and burst out laughing. "Come on, Goujon, set that damn tray down and drink a cup of coffee with me! I'm going into the army to fight for the freedom of our country!"

* * *

The recruitment officer removed his spectacles and stared at Alexis with a strange, bemused expression. "I'm sorry, young man, but it seems you have a serious heart problem, and we cannot consider you as a recruit."

Alexis blinked. "Heart problem? I've never had a chest pain in my life! And the doctor next door . . . he never said a thing to me while examining me!"

The middle-aged colonel shook his head. "I know how you must feel. At a time like this, all patriotic men, young and old, want to do their bit for France. Perhaps Dr. Châtel didn't want to upset you; perhaps he thought it would sound less cruel coming from a bureaucrat like me. But the facts are irrefutable. We have a full dossier on you from one of the most eminent heart specialists in the country, Dr. Marius Rebatel."

Flabbergasted, Alexis leaned over the colonel's desk and exclaimed, "But I've never consulted such a man! I've never even heard his name!"

The older man sighed. "Please, son. Lying about your health may appear to be noble, but in the long run it can only prove a detriment to the army. We need every able-bodied man available, but the ones who aren't strong enough would simply be a nuisance. You would do us no good. So do me a favor—go home, and take care of yourself. There will be enough men to take care of France without our needing to resort to those with severe heart murmurs."

Then, growing impatient, the colonel raised his arm and, looking beyond Alexis at the young man behind him waiting to enter the room, he called out: "Next!"

* * *

Alexis buried his face in his hands. "I just don't understand! Mama, call our family doctor, Letellier! He's known me since the day I was born! *He*'ll be able to clear this up. Nobody else seems to believe me!"

He lifted his eyes to seek hers in supplication. But Anne's hazel eyes were cold and hard . . . remote. Her chin was proudly raised, her back erect. He had expected her to be upset, even frantic, at his announcement that he had enlisted. But, since coming home and confronting her with this bewildering question of a specialist he'd never even heard of, she had seemed almost unnaturally distant. He'd thought she would at least appear as surprised as he was. And that she'd offer sympathy over his rejection, knowing that all young men were now about to join the military forces to combat the Nazis.

"Dr. Letellier retired this spring, Alexis," she informed him, her voice clipped and precise.

The seeds of a mysterious, yet half-credible doubt began to take root in the young man's mind. "Mama," he said, hesitantly. "You don't . . . I mean, you didn't know about this Dr. Rebatel, did you?"

Two bright spots appeared on her cheeks. "Everybody knows about Dr. Marius Rebatel," she replied, her voice just a little too rapid. "He's the most famous heart man in Paris."

"But . . . *you* never went to see him, did you?"

She frowned, suddenly imperious and cross. "Alexis, you're fresh and quarrelsome today, aren't you? I'm sorry you were humiliated by this recruitment officer. But that's all you're going to hear! I won't pretend to be glad you aren't going to die in the trenches of the Maginot Line!"

He stood up, the truth dawning on him. "Mother, *you did this!* Somehow, it was *you who went to Rebatel* . . . you who manipulated this behind my back!"

"Shut up!" She was screaming now. Alexis had never seen her lose her temper this way, abandoning complete control. "I never did a thing behind your back! You were too young to remember, Alex—that's all! You almost died when you were an infant, and I took you to Rebatel. I just never told you about it later, because—"

"Because *what,* Mother?"

"Because I didn't want you to be afraid to live a full and normal life! I hoped that being reared in a quiet, genteel atmosphere here and in Switzerland, and planning to go into the legal profession, you might never be bothered again by your heart murmur. And so I kept the whole problem quiet!"

Alexis could feel his anger rising like boiling water. His whole body shaking, he cried out: "I don't believe you! You've never lied to me before, Mother, but you're lying now! *I never had the slightest heart murmur, and you never took me to this Dr. Rebatel!"*

Anne's nostrils flared, and she stated, her tone indicating the full extent of her indignation, "Believe it or not, Alexis! I don't care! And if you don't believe me, I'd suggest you make an appointment with Rebatel himself and demand to see your charts. Because I've had quite as much as I'm going to take from you today!"

Then, proudly, she turned her back on him and sailed out of the room, leaving him with his mouth agape, witness to his consternation and bewilderment.

*   *   *

The onset of war had galvanized Armand Fayard into action. Charles found it difficult to believe but, leaning heavily on an ebony cane, the seventy-three-year-old man was once again presiding over the managerial offices on the rue Cambon. He was issuing orders as if they were imperial decrees. Each morning, no matter how skillfully Daniel, the de Rochefleur chauffeur, wended the Phantom's way through traffic bottlenecks, Charles would find on arrival in his own office a fresh stack of signed documents delivered from upstairs, ready for him to implement at once. Fayard would already have started the wheels rolling, and Charles never obtained the satisfaction of being the one to set them into motion.

Fayard looked good; although his face still sagged in lopsided fashion, his color had returned to its natural ruddy hue. And Charles had to admit that he liked having his boss back. For the younger man had never lived the illusion of running the show: Fayard had been imprisoned in his four poster bed in his baroque palace in Versailles, but it had always been *his* word, not Charles's, that had activated the multitentacled octopus of the organization.

One day this will change, Charles thought, setting his jaw with determination. This will be my show and I shall run it as I please. And in the meantime, he had the satisfaction of running the holding company almost without interference, and directing the efforts of an entire laboratory of skilled engineers, paid overtime to invent new alloys with which to outperform the German war machine.

Charles had been lucky in regard to Arabella; he had not run into her more than once, and then she had greeted him normally, if coolly, in the presence of her husband. But an unexpected thorn had been thrust into Charles's side. For reasons beyond his comprehension, Armand Fayard had declared that since "the boy"—Alexis—had been rejected by the army, he would personally give him a chance to help his country in another fashion. So now, each morning, Alexis took the train into the city, attended the Faculty of Law, and joined his father at the office in the afternoon, where he continued doing clerical work as well as coordinating various projects for the president himself.

"Why does Armand bother to concern himself with an eighteen-year-old boy?" Charles fumed to Amelia. "It makes no sense! Who knows how Alex tried to ingratiate himself into the old man's good graces this summer, when he was alone. . . ."

He had taken to meeting her for lunch several times a week. They enjoyed a civilized meal in her hotel, or somewhere else of his choosing, and then, when he brought her home, before Christina returned from school, they would make love in her bedroom, the

door bolted tightly and the heavy curtains drawn. If perhaps they
dreamed of sunshine to illumine their entangled bodies and illus-
trate their love, their common sense forbade them this luxury.
Their movements furtive, struggling against unexpected interrup-
tions and the pressures of his business day and her daughter's
homecoming, they learned to please each other quickly, the urgency enhancing their excitement.

Sometimes he took the afternoon off, and it would turn out that
Christina had begged to go to a friend's house after class. And then
the lovers would relax in each other's arms, and discuss each other's lives and the peculiar dilemmas each faced.

It was on one such occasion that Charles brought up the topic of
Alexis, and Fayard's unusual interest in the young man. Animated
by an uncontrolled anger, Charles vented his feelings to his mistress. Amelia leaned forward and said, "But Charles, I don't understand you! If Fayard thinks enough of the boy, at his young age,
to want him on board, you should be pleased and proud, rather
than suspect him of some kind of underhanded manipulation."

Her face was grave as her large eyes held his steadily. He heard
much more what she *wasn't* saying: *You*'re the manipulator in the
family—*not your son!* But instead she remarked softly, "You always expect the worst of him. And you're so quick to jump to a
conclusion that would incriminate him. He isn't your enemy—he's
your child!"

He's *Anne*'s child, not mine, Charles thought. And I only married Anne because *you* wouldn't have me.

He wondered if somehow it might not be too late to reverse
matters. If he divorced Anne and proposed to Amelia, now that he
knew she loved him. . . . But in his world, *their* world, divorce
was still frowned upon. Besides, Alfred at seventy-three was in far
worse physical shape than Armand Fayard; and after her father
died, Anne would be among the richest women in France. It would
not do for Alexis to control his mother's funds. So they were stuck
in this vicious circle: he and Anne, married for form (for there
existed very little else between them since his return to Paris, now
that Amelia was truly in his life) and, seemingly, married forever.

How could he admit to Amelia how . . . yes, *jealous* he had
grown of Alexis? For he was still afraid of her judgment and her
uncanny perception into his true feelings. But she was saying,
"Fighting Alexis is as silly as Don Quixote's fighting the windmills.
You're a businessman, Charles, a leader! You're Fayard's right-

hand man—and what is poor Alex? A distant protégé to that old man, nothing more!"

Perhaps she was right. But that afternoon in early November, when he went up to the presidential suite to discuss some projects with Fayard, he came upon a scene that at once made his blood pressure rise and his temper flare. What he saw was the old man on his side of the desk, Alexis on the other: and between them, Fayard's oversize chess set of ebony and ivory, hand-carved for him by a Florentine sculptor of some renown.

"Hey," Fayard called out. "Come and look at the clever move your son's just accomplished: he sacrificed his rook to put my king in jeopardy!"

Charles forced himself to smile, and walked over. Alexis rose politely. "Hello, Father." Then, when Charles had taken the other chair across from Fayard, the young man sat down again and concentrated on the board. His oval face turned up to regard the old man, and, quietly, with a respectful assurance that Charles was forced to grudgingly admire, he announced, "Checkmate."

Armand Fayard burst into laughter. "Bravo, bravo! Now, my boy, fold up this set and let's listen to what your father has to report. Perhaps, with some luck and your kind of wits, we'll be able to put Hitler into a situation of checkmate!"

Alexis took the compliment with visible pride. Charles wished he could rise above his own hostility toward the young man and feel the pride any father ought now to be sensing. But he simply couldn't get past the fact that Alex wasn't his own child; and having reared a stranger in his own house, it was doubly galling to watch this stranger gain a stronghold in that other, yet more important area, his place of business. His own seat of power.

"What's on the agenda?" Fayard was demanding.

Charles glanced at Alexis, but Fayard nodded him on, frowning with annoyance. And so Charles cleared his throat and plunged in. "We've got the steel mills rolling out bars, rods, tubes, piping. Our multi-ton rolls have been working full-time pressing out all sorts of different sheet metals. And in the lab—"

Fayard picked up his spectacles and put them on, his small eyes riveted to Charles as the latter proceeded. "We're working on the development of specialty metals. For this, the engineers are trying to combine special alloys and a certain kind of stainless steel, requiring more advanced technology. The Americans have gained advantage over Europe with the intricacy of their technology."

"Then lure a good Cleveland boy over here," Fayard tossed in, almost conversationally. Since the beginning of the war he had taken over the presidency of the Comité des Forges, and was now the single most important steel magnate of France. It was he who was spearheading the armament industry, and coordinating its various branches. He thrived on this, and Charles, at his side, felt the same delicious sense of power. Their eyes, bright and quick and brimming with excitement, revealed it all, ignoring the presence of Alexis in the room, who sat watching them, fascinated and silent.

"We need especially large castings to manufacture armor plates for tanks and other heavy weaponry," Charles went on.

"But the essential thing now is to produce a sheet metal alloyed differently to make it impervious to penetration by explosives," Fayard countered. "Our soldiers need to be protected by the proper armor as they activate their weapons."

Alexis, from the bookcase where he was putting away the chess set, looked at them thoughtfully. He glanced for a moment at the king in his hands, and at the board, neatly folded up. Suddenly Fayard's voice made him start. "You think this war is like a chess game, don't you, son?"

Charles sat scrutinizing him, pinpricks of discomfort rising on his skin. Couldn't Fayard for once forget the boy's presence? But Alexis replied in a careful voice, "It's an uneven game at best, sir. We're at a total disadvantage. We're one country, with an ally across the Channel—while Hitler's armaments industry is boosted by the supposedly neutral Swedish ball bearings colossus, which apportions very little to us and sixty percent of its worldwide production to the Reich's war machine. On top of that, the Swedes control aspects of the steel industries in every part of Europe, but their sympathies, and therefore their interests, lie with the Germans."

Charles's surprise showed clearly on his face, but as he opened his mouth to ask a question, Fayard cut him off. "You've been doing your research, Alex," he commented, pleased. "Now, dig a little farther. Tell me what percentage of stock my company owns in the Swedish Enskilda Bank, which channels funds into the ball bearings operation you've just enlightened us about!"

Charles leaned forward, tensely eager to catch Alexis's answer. The young man's face was serious and alert. "Not enough to make a difference in the outcome of this war," he replied.

Total silence fell upon the room. Fayard's face revealed nothing of his reaction, nor did Alexis display the least fear that his words might have offended his boss. But their underlying meaning came through clearly to Charles. And, infuriated, he stood up and challenged Alexis.

"Have you gone mad?" he exploded. "What's the significance of this accusation, however politely you may have veiled it?"

Alexis didn't blink. "We're engaged in a combat to the death, for the freedom of Europe and the survival of the Jewish people," he declared calmly. "And although Monsieur Fayard possesses only three and a half percent of the stocks in the Swedish SKF, whichever way the war proceeds, he will earn a substantial profit."

Charles could find no words to refute the young man he had recognized as his son, and could now only be sorry he had ever participated in his education. He thought: If we were alone, man to man, *I'd kill him.* He's right, of course. He's right, and all three of us in this room know that. But that's part of the game . . . to make a healthy profit from every aspect of the industry. If it takes a war to enrich us, why should we play holier-than-thou and snub our noses at this new opportunity to make money? Why should we be different from the armaments men in any other country? And why did Alexis, an eighteen-year-old boy, have to throw in his grain of truth and try to show Fayard the error of his ways?

"Who the hell do you think you are?" Charles cried out. "Who asked you to investigate this company's activities, and Monsieur Fayard's holdings in companies abroad?"

His hand had balled malevolently into a fist, although he was keeping his arm rigidly close to his body. And then, to his amazement, Armand Fayard's booming voice broke in, its joviality oddly out of keeping with the discussion at hand.

"I gave Alex a free hand," he informed Charles. "I wanted to test his acumen and perseverance. I told him that in addition to challenging him at chess, I'd throw in a second, more intricate challenge: let him learn all there is to know about what we do. If he could do it, I'd reward him with an extra push when he graduates from law school . . . as well as making him one of our company counsels."

Charles felt the blood draining from his face. Fayard smiled, a strangely sweet smile for such a tough individual. "What I didn't expect was for Alex to accomplish this so quickly in the game."

"It shows us that we need to protect our files far more effectively than we do at present," Charles said, angry beyond expression. He

stood trembling, furious over the permeability of Fayard Industries
to the scrutiny of strangers . . . and even angrier over the intelligence of Alexis de Rochefleur, this law student who, in every way,
was already treading on his, Charles's, coattails.

Alexis de Rochefleur was making life uncomfortable for Charles,
and suddenly the forty-one-year-old man was vividly reminded of
his father-in-law, Alfred—the man who, once his nemesis, had dissolved into a shadow of his former self, no longer a dreaded foe but
now simply an elderly banker on the edge of death. Only now, his
grandson, tall and dark like Alfred in his prime, had crept up and
taken his place. *It's him I have to dread now,* Charles realized,
goose bumps rising on his arms. *I have a new nemesis, and his
name is Alexis Lévy–de Rochefleur.*

Would he always have to fear an enemy in his own house . . . ?

BOOK THREE

Kings and Castles

CHAPTER XVII

Charles had given up on God long ago, during the Great War; he liked to tell people that his atheism stemmed from the brutal accidental death of his grandparents Jeannette and Guy, in 1917. In fact, it had probably been caused by a process of erosion that started as soon as he had learned about his father's suicide, understanding that Wilhelm Levy's actions had reduced him and his mother to their dire predicament.

Wilhelm Levy had touched Yvonne's life sufficiently long to rob her of her country, her dowry, and her status in society. Even today, in 1940, Charles wondered whether, had he possessed La Folie and the security his mother's name should have afforded him, he would have married Anne. Would Alfred have been capable of bribing and manipulating him into recognizing Alexis? The clear answer, of course, was negative on both counts.

And yet, was he sorry? Sorry Amelia had turned him down in 1920, certainly. But sorry about Anne? He hadn't made such a terrible match, given the disillusionment caused by Amelia's rejection. He would have been too devastated to have fallen in love a second time: he'd continued to love Amelia until now. So, if not Anne, whom would he have chosen to marry? Another Parisian debutante, prettier than Anne, but not, he thought wryly, a *de Rochefleur*. A name that was synonymous in Europe with power and prestige.

And now they'd come full circle. He and his nemesis, Alfred.

In the spring, old Alfred had passed away, like a dry, fragile leaf floating off on a sudden gust of wind. Who, truly, had mourned him? His daughter loved him, but he had kept her spirit down when she was young, and had been against the only match she'd dreamed of making. His grandson loved him, but in recent years old Armand Fayard, a total stranger, had shown far more concrete an interest in Alexis than Alfred ever had. Like a shadow, the once mighty banker had simply dissolved into thin air . . . and watching the two thousand assembled mourners who had come to the graveside to witness the disposition of Alfred de Rochefleur's earthly remains, Charles had wondered how many of them had called themselves friends.

Faces. Faces he had been seeing throughout the years. The faces of France's most prominent citizens; faces once young and lively, when they had come to attend Alfred's housewarming festivities in 1920, and later, Alfred's daughter's hastily put together wedding to the improbable cousin from Lausanne. His own face, in the front row of the bereaved, had, that May afternoon of 1940, become as well known as theirs, as sought-after at receptions and political luncheons. And sometimes even more so, though Alfred had done little to send Charles on his way.

The elegant Grand Rabbin of Paris, Julien Weill, had intoned the kaddish: *"Yiskadal veyi skadash, sh'mai rabah":* "Magnified and sanctified be the name of the Holy One." And Charles had listened to these foreign-sounding words and thought, *What* Holy One? Who cares now about old Alfred? And he had shivered, looking around him again at the blank, formal faces of the mourners.

After the anxious waiting of fall and winter, the vigilant soldiers of France, behind their strongly armed Maginot Line, had found themselves prepared in vain: the Nazis had made a surprise move, circumventing the Maginot and penetrating instead through the Sedan gap into northern France. Hitler's troops were on the rampage, plowing through the Low Countries and the Ardennes forest. What would happen once they entered Paris? Would Rabbi Weill be able to find himself an audience of two thousand, even to bury a de Rochefleur, once the Nazis stood breathing down his neck?

A few days after the funeral, Anne, Charles, and Alexis had gone to the family law firm for a reading of Alfred's will. With last-moment trepidation Charles heard that the old man had honored their agreement of 1920. La Folie was to be his and Anne's, jointly; at last, his home, the home of his childhood, belonged to him once more, legally! The majority of shares in the Crédit Industriel had gone to Anne, of course, with a provision that should she die, Alexis alone would inherit her part. Grimly, Charles thought: *So the old fox wanted me out of it, after all. . . .*

Still, it hardly mattered. Charles possessed sufficient shares in his own name, given to him as part of Anne's dowry, to keep him neatly cushioned in profit and interest for the rest of his life. But his wife, not yet forty, was now among the richest women in the world, and certainly in Europe. Armand Fayard had had this to say in warning to Charles: "The Nazis are not going to allow a Jew to hold on to her assets in this country. Anne automatically became Swiss, when you married her: transfer your family holdings to Switzerland, my boy, the quicker, the better!"

Charles hadn't wasted time. He collected Anne and legally closed down the Paris headquarters of the Crédit Industriel, over the frantic objections of other, gentile, shareholders. He obtained all necessary writs to have a branch opened in Geneva instead. Then he and his wife traveled to Switzerland and did everything according to the book, down to the selection of Swiss officers for a hastily assembled board of directors. But the money was safe now . . . away from German hands.

Charles thought about this as he sat staring blindly at the casebook in front of him. What difference could Napoleonic precedent really have today, November 1940? France was no longer *France,* and the French steel industry no longer functioned autonomously, for its own and its country's profit and gain.

Drained by the funeral and the trip to Switzerland, Anne had mustered the family together for an early vacation that year. She selected the picturesque resort of Deauville, in Normandy. And so it was there, in their hotel lobby, that the Lévy–de Rochefleurs had heard the shattering news on the radio, on June 17. His voice quivering, eighty-four-year-old Marshal Henri-Philippe Pétain, the newly appointed premier, had declared that France could no longer hold out after the losses at Dunkirk, and was capitulating to the Germans.

The family stayed on, wanting to avoid being detained for days in the flotsam and jetsam of human traffic bound in panic-stricken droves for the capital; but, as soon as possible, they came home to a Paris none of them recognized: their noble French city decked out like a German garrison town, with German signposts and posters advertising the coming entertainment in bold Teutonic slang, lasciviously beckoning to the new occupants.

How did he feel? Amelia asked. She asked him this as though he'd been a Frenchman, like Alexis and Anne, who had openly wept. But he had felt his throat strangling: this was the country that had rejected him because of the accident of his birth.

"I don't know," he answered, cutting her off abruptly. His son had a lot to say about the terms of the armistice, which would not only demobilize the French fleet and air force, but cut the country in two (the southern two-fifths, excluding the strategic Atlantic Coast, remaining a free zone, while the rest, in effect, became annexed German territory). Alexis had a lot to say, but what would have been his lot, had Anne not kept him out of the armed forces the summer before? For millions of French soldiers had been trapped by the sudden capitulation of their country, and now remained prisoners-of-war behind German barbed-wire fences, their fate still pending.

"You are henceforth Swiss," Charles announced, tossing some documents on the table in front of Alexis. "You and your mother both are to burn your French papers right now. Armand Fayard is right: through me, you are both Swiss, and that's the only nationality worth a sou these days, besides the German."

"I'm French," Alexis countered, raising his chin defiantly. (The boy always defied him, no matter the issue.)

"You should consider your luck, and count your blessings that your father is Swiss. The Germans won't be able to touch you as a Jew without impinging on Switzerland's neutrality."

The boy shut up. But still, Alex, for sure, *felt French,* and felt the enormity of France's shame. Now, almost five months later, Charles had to admit he still wasn't sure how he really felt. He wanted the Germans out of Paris: but did he have a firmer clue as to his own identity in this territorial mess?

As a Swiss citizen, he was further protected because his country's neutrality superseded the religion of his birth. Anne, Alexis—they would be shielded from harm, as would he. But what of Amelia, Christina . . . ? As he pondered the issue of the Jews in Europe, he wondered what would happen to them now.

The French government, safely entrenched at Vichy, in the free zone, since the beginning of July, was collaborating with the Germans. Strongly anti-British, it had now showed itself to be strongly anti-Semitic. Among its first edicts that summer, the Vichy state had closed off government-controlled jobs from those of its citizens born to foreign fathers; it had opened to review all naturalizations approved after 1927; and in Paris, all mention of Judaism were eradicated . . . all Jewish-sounding street names having been changed by the Nazis. *As a beginning gesture. . . .*

But since October, the Jews had been further set apart: even those with French fathers had been removed from public posts, and if one examined the heralds of the press and the captains of industry, some—the Jewish ones—were, not so oddly, missing. Charles wondered how long Armand Fayard would continue to defy the occupants and allow his right-hand assistant to hold on to his present position. Charles knew that "technically untouchable" Jews in conspicuous situations galled the Occupation authorities, who waited to incarcerate them at the first sign of a so-called legitimate offense.

But a lot would depend on what Armand Fayard would decide to do, now that the Germans had reannexed the province of Lorraine and seized most of France's raw materials for their own use. The fate of Charles Lévy–de Rochefleur depended on the fate of Fayard Industries . . . and as the firm went, so went the fate of an entire nation of Frenchmen, just barely subsisting under the vigilant eyes of their Nazi jailers.

* * *

Anne had never felt more lonely in her forty years. Suddenly, this December, she felt herself alienated from just about everyone she knew. A little voice inside her told her that it was her own fault —that she was *bad,* and that because of this, God had punished her and made her stand alone. It was her mother's voice, reminding her of Saint Petersburg, her miserable debut, and the ensuing shame she had caused Sonia, who had dreamed of turning her ugly duckling into a swan so graceful, no man would have dared to let her sit through a dance.

Anne couldn't help but glance at her reflection in the large gilt-edged mirror in the hallway, and think: But I've grown better with age, haven't I? The heavy-hipped young girl with masses of ungainly curls on top of her head had been replaced by a quiet, mature woman, certainly not slender but far from unpleasant in her plump figure. She had learned to dress so that clothes flattered her ample bustline and drew eyes away from her hips. Today, conscious of wartime thrift, she wore a simple sack dress of green wool, belted with a wide sash of deeper green, and her hair, bobbed chin length, showed off its auburn highlights. The dim afternoon sun sought out small gold speckles in her hazel eyes, completing an effect that was almost pleasant. What, then, was still missing from this picture?

Simplicity was now of the essence, because the war had caused drastic shortages in everything, including clothing material. The women she knew were ashamed to wear anything fancy, and she, whose closets were still bulging, had felt guiltier than ever. Anne sometimes thought she had been born guilty; but there were other times when she believed that her Russian mother had made a point to make guilt her second nature. Mama, her unhappy little-girl voice countered, Why can't I ever do anything the way you like it? It wasn't just *this* picture: it was *every* picture from which something either stuck ungracefully out of place or was sorely lacking.

Sonia hadn't been the only one to spot her every mistake. Now that her father was gone, Anne thought with guilty relief that one less person existed to show his displeasure at her behavior. And yet, God knew, she tried. *She never stopped trying.* Hadn't she tried with Charles? She'd loved and she'd loved and she'd loved, and done everything to please him! Yet it hadn't been sufficient, and he'd gone right back to Amelia—Amelia, who didn't have to try, who looked beautiful when she awakened disheveled in the morning, with face cream on!

Charles hadn't come to Anne's bedroom in over a year. Until the summer of 1939 he'd made attempts to be with her at least a few times a month. Not like in the beginning, when they'd been trying desperately to have a child together. Now Anne felt certain that what *she* wasn't receiving, her cousin *was.*

Anne knew that Charles was visiting Amelia in her hotel. She hated herself, but she couldn't help going through his pockets and finding the receipts of meals charged to him at Amelia's hotel, now that it was no longer safe for Jews to go out much in public.

And, of course, Anne received confirmation through other sources as well. With the Nazis ruling Paris, the WIZO had been forced to disband. Jews were afraid to gather together. Yet, a few weeks before, she had run into one of her old friends from the organization, Elizabeth Abelson. Anne had been exchanging books at a bookstore in Paris, and Elizabeth had seen her and come up to chat, surreptitiously looking around to make sure no one was taking note of their conversation. "I haven't seen you for so long," she said, squeezing Anne's arm. "But I did happen to run into your husband the other day, with your nice cousin, Madame Habig. I was taking my daughter's baby for a walk in the Tuileries—"

"Did you speak to them?" Anne asked, trying to keep the urgency out of her voice. But she had been breathless with anxiety. She *wanted* proof, and yet she'd desperately wanted to avoid confronting the truth.

Elizabeth had shaken her head. "They were too involved," she answered apologetically. "You know, when two people are so intent on their conversation that they aren't even aware of the outside world. . . . Evidently, poor Madame Habig has a great many problems. I think it's very sweet of a busy man like Charles to try to lend a helpful ear."

Anne had gone home, shattered. Charles and Amelia were *in love!* For what else would have accounted for such total absorption in each other, as Elizabeth had noted it? Amelia's visits to Anne had been growing scarce, and she would almost always bring Christina with her when she did come. Had this been to create a buffer, to avoid facing the hurt expression in Anne's eyes?

But a spirit of madness had taken hold of Anne, and a few days after her encounter with Elizabeth Abelson, she asked her driver to take her to Amelia's hotel. She went up to her cousin's suite and surprised her washing her stockings. "Amelia," Anne said, "I came as soon as I felt brave enough to face you. Once, we were very close, you and I. Sometimes I weep with longing for the days when we could confide in each other, like two sisters. But you've changed. You're not my friend anymore. You've been seeing my husband behind my back—" Her voice broke then, but she cleared her throat and pushed on, determined to speak her piece and be gone forever from Amelia's presence. "I still love Charles, and so I'm never going to let him know that I've spoken with you. I'd advise you to do the same. I just don't want to see you anymore, Amelia, unless social circumstances should put us face-to-face and dictate that we acknowledge each other politely. I came here to tell you this, to tell you that *I know,* because it's important you not take me for a bigger fool than I am."

Then, looking into Amelia's white face, as her cousin's hands started to tremble over the cold sink, Anne was afraid she might start to weep. But her will power won out, and her eyes stayed dry. She walked out, not waiting for her cousin to justify herself or offer any explanation. And what might Amelia have said, to excuse her behavior? She'd stolen Anne's husband . . . her own cousin's husband.

Yet, in a sense, Amelia's betrayal was but a reflection of a general corruption and immorality that shattered Anne. What was happening all around her? Jeanne Netter had suddenly shocked everybody and converted, very publicly, to Catholicism. "A pointless act," Charles had remarked, for, by the new law, a person born with a single Jewish grandparent was indelibly Jewish. All the more so Jeanne, born with four, and a notorious Zionist.

Yet Anne felt most cruelly misunderstood by her son. In her entire life she'd loved two people zealously: her husband and her son. She would readily have died for either one. The moment he was born, it had ceased to matter to her that Alexis had been conceived during a moment of abject despair, by the wrong man. She adored him.

Since his babyhood, theirs had been a conscious union. Alexis had always returned her love, and made her feel secure as Charles never had. Anne had protected the boy from the scathing scorn of Charles's judgment, and from the icy frost of his neglect. In turn, Alexis had covered her with tender regard.

Recently Alexis's friend François Durand had returned from ten long months behind the Maginot. Now he was egging Alexis to join de Gaulle's Free French movement, headquartered in London. Anne had cornered her son one evening after dinner and said in a low voice, "We're Swiss now, Alex. Go to Fayard—he'll give you work to do for France. Let *him* advise you, since you won't listen to *us* anymore."

And Alex, his grave black eyes intently on her, had replied with quiet irony, "We're a strange family, aren't we? Nobody listens to anybody else."

She felt a terrible sense of panic. Grabbing the boy's arm, she had confronted him. "What do you mean?"

"I spoke to you, Mother," he replied, his voice unusually hard and distant. She dropped her hand and looked at him, afraid. "You heard me with your ears, but not with your heart. Instead, you went to Dr. Rebatel and took away my manhood!"

She wanted to retort: I tried to save your *life*! But Alex *didn't want to hear her at all*! He looked down at her then and declared, almost sadly: "It's no use, Mama. You've spent a lifetime covering yourself with a blanket of lies, to avoid having to take charge of your own existence! I can't live like this—always afraid my veneer will be cracked by a chance accident or a careless acquaintance. I'm sorry, Mother, but we each have to live according to the rules we've set for ourselves. Please don't make this any harder for both of us. . . ."

So she had lost her son, and rejected her cousin. And now Anne felt dreadfully lonely, at such loose ends that she had gone into the library and taken Charles's copy of *Mein Kampf* down from the

shelf, planning to look through it. Armand Fayard had thrust it
into her husband's hands months ago, and it seemed an important
work to peruse. The plump little housepainter, gone mad, was intent on taking over the world, and ridding it of its Jews. *I'd like to
know why,* Anne wondered, revulsion coursing through her. She
would read it now, in the gallery, until Charles and Alex returned
home from the city for dinner.

* * *

Anne couldn't remember life without the four Goujons. Nobody
had ever paid the Goujon women particular attention: Marie was
an excellent cook, and the girls, Brigitte and Marthe, made the
beds, cleaned the windows, washed and ironed clothes, silent and
smiling in the background. Only they weren't girls anymore, Anne
thought, caught up short: and neither was she. Both Brigitte and
Marthe were about forty years old, her age. But whereas *she* had
married and borne a child, neither of them had.

"It would have created an inconvenience in the household,"
Alexis had once declared, joking, of course, when someone had
inquired whether either of the Goujon girls had ever had a husband. Yet beneath the humor in her son's voice, Anne had heard a
measure of shame. She had lived with the Goujons since her flight
from Russia; Alex had never lived *without* them, except the months
he'd spent away at school. But no one had given them any special
thought, and beyond making sure that Charles did not forget them
at Christmastime, Anne herself had never thought to inquire as to
what they did on their days off, or whether they ever went to the
movies. How had this been possible?

Today, at almost noon, old Marie had been standing by the large
white enamel stove, wrapped up in sweaters and her topcoat (a gift
from Anne last Christmas), her head swathed in a thick red scarf.
She'd started to talk, rubbing her hands together. "The girls and I,
we've been taking turns lining up for food at the marketplace," she
said, making a clucking sound with her tongue. "We've been getting up at four-thirty, to be poised and ready at the door by five.
That's when the *Boches* allow us out of doors. It's every minute
that counts, madame. And we're ten minutes away from the commercial center! Think of it—at five A.M., we have to grope our way
to the bread line, in pitch-blackness, and I'm older and clumsier
than Brigitte and Marthe! We're lucky if we get to be among the
first sixty people queuing in line. This morning, I was forty-second.

It gave me such pleasure to see Madame Bonnier's uppity chambermaid way at the end. The way she gossips . . ."

Anne pulled a wooden chair out and sat down, blinking. "You've been getting up before daylight—just to get us *bread*?"

Marie raised her hands in a gesture of "What else?" and removed her kerchief, revealing perfectly pin-curled white hair. "Bread, and everything else . . . Madame hasn't bothered to examine the ration cards, but it takes imagination to create meals out of what the Germans allot us. Those *Boches* are buying up all the eggs before they're laid, and all the good vegetables. . . . We're lucky if we're left with two carrots per family, and the vendors weigh them with the dirt still clinging to the leaves! And it takes good peasant resourcefulness to make two hundred grams of tea last a whole month in *this* house. . . ."

Anne felt herself redden with sudden shame. Not guilt, this time, but shame. That fall, when the Lévy–de Rochefleurs had returned home from Normandy and found the Nazis occupying Paris, Anne had done what she had always done . . . what her father had taught her to do, at seventeen. She had sent Goujon to the city hall to "see about those cards." And she had never thought to ask to see one. She had taken his word at face value, that the Germans were "eating up everything," and had accepted the very strange meals he had started serving, because everyone knew that food was being rationed and that worse shortages were still to come.

That noon Marie had proudly taken out the family's ration cards to show her: five marked *A* for "adult," for Anne herself, Charles, Daniel the chauffeur (who was related to no one else living at La Folie), and Brigitte and Marthe—those aged twenty to sixty. A single card was marked *J.3* (for *Jeunes,* "youths," of the third, or eldest, category, the twelve- to twenty-year-olds) for Alexis. And last but not least, the old cook had produced two *V* cards marked *Vieux* ("old") for senior citizens over sixty. "That's mine," she had declared, "and that one there is Aristide's."

And that was how Anne, after twenty-three years, finally learned her butler's first name.

It was then that Marie moved closer, conspiratorially. "Madame may not believe this," she whispered, her words hushed in the completely empty room. "But after we bought our milk, and our butter—which made the Bonnier maid green with envy because I was buying on eight ration cards and she only has two—she leaned over and told me that *Hitler was coming to Paris*!"

Anne nodded. "My husband heard it on the BBC, at the office," she had said gently, thinking she'd be disappointing the old woman by being already privy to her news. "For the reinterment of the remains of the Duke of Reichstadt. It seems our old Pétain may have some patriotism left, after all: he's refused to come and meet the Führer while he's here!"

But Marie persisted. "That's not the point! Madame must understand that, of course, the Bonnier girl's a well-known gossip . . . but she swears that Hitler's going to be staying *in Saint-Germain!* I guess it's our bad luck to have been a garrison town since the days of Napoleon. . . . They've already filled the old barracks with three regiments of *Boches,* and she says they've started requisitioning all the good houses!"

Anne moved closer to the stove, suddenly chilled in her green wool dress. "They *can't* be," she murmured. "They *won't* . . . will they, Marie?"

And the old cook planted herself in front of Anne. "No, madame," she staunchly reassured her. "They damn well *can't* and they damn well *won't!*" Then, standing back and straightening her posture, the plump little peasant woman had announced: "Those *Boches* are never going to take *our* house, and Madame is not to worry about it so long as the Goujons are alive and breathing!"

. . . *And I've only just learned his name is Aristide,* Anne now thought, quickly flicking the tears off her cheeks.

* * *

The persistent ringing of the doorbell roused Anne as she stood contemplating her own image in the full-length mirror in the hallway.

"I'll get the door, Goujon," she called, hearing the old butler hastening up behind her, a little out of breath. How did he always manage to hear when a doorbell was ringing, emerging from the catacombs of La Folie to welcome the friend and put off the stranger? Like a Grand Vizir from the *Arabian Nights,* he stayed behind his Scheherazade, watchful as she unlatched the door. When she stepped back, nonplussed, Anne nearly gouged Goujon's foot with one of her high heels. At the door stood two German officers in trim *feldgrau* uniforms, Nazi swastikas on their armbands. Anne drew in her breath and felt herself pale. But she swallowed and asked politely, "Yes? May I help you?"

The older officer clicked his heels, looking her up and down in her green dress and elegant jewelry of sculptured Florentine gold.

"Madame de Rochefleur? I understand that this is your house. We should like to go through it room by room. We have been asked to find lodgings for some of our officers, as the Führer has decided to make Saint-Germain his headquarters whenever he will be passing through Paris."

Goujon had surreptitiously moved up beside her. *"Madame* does not wish her home put out for others' use," he declared, his usual gracious tone marked by a slight disdain. "It has been in her family since the days of Napoleon the First."

The first officer seemed taken aback. "Yes, well . . . I understand. But the Führer—"

"We are citizens of Switzerland," Anne interposed. "And if you requisition this house, you will be requisitioning Swiss, not French, property."

The officer smiled obsequiously. "Not exactly, madame. *You* may be Swiss, but this house stands on French soil, and is neither an embassy nor a consulate. It is private property, purchased in France under French law. I would advise you to let us come in."

Anne squared her shoulders and moved back, making room for them. "Very well, gentlemen," she declared. But her voice quivered slightly, and she felt grateful for the reassuring presence of the old manservant.

It wasn't until they had reached the threshold of the dining room that the younger officer turned and exclaimed, in German, to his superior. The older man stopped and regarded Anne, frowning. His eye fell on the book that she had been clutching to her side, for dear life. "You have been reading the Führer's book?" he asked, suddenly smiling.

Anne shivered. *Is that what I'm holding?* she thought, panicked to remember. She had been on her way to the gallery to read . . . oh, yes, *Mein Kampf,* that horrible man's personal bible. To better understand the workings of his crooked mind.

They don't know we're Jewish, she realized, looking at the young Lieutenant and at the older blond colonel standing beside him. *How I wish Charles were here, with his own blond hair and perfect Aryan profile!* But she smiled back, swallowing her nervousness. "Yes, you caught me outlining his principles of action."

She felt Goujon's amazement, then his immediate recovery and poise. The two German soldiers witnessed no change. But the older one touched his cap in salute, and bowed from the waist, gallantly. Anne stood her ground in dignity and waited.

"My dear lady," the colonel pronounced. "If you can see the world from our point of view, then surely, we can be gentlemen enough to let you enjoy your superb home in peace." He coughed. "Hermann," he stated to his subaltern, "Madame de Rochefleur looks tired. It's time we went on to the Bonnier mansion up the road. . . ."

After the officers had departed, Goujon locked the front door behind them. Anne stood looking at the book she held. Red ink from the binder had come off on her dead-white fingers, coloring her sweat the color of blood. Suddenly nauseated, Anne flung the book onto the gleaming parquet floor and ran upstairs. But she knew that behind her, the old majordomo had bent down to retrieve it, thinking that blessings, indeed, sometimes came in strange bindings.

CHAPTER XVIII

By the spring of 1941, the Jews of Paris had become subject to a whole series of edicts issued by the Nazis, and Amelia Habig decided that it was most unsafe to remain in so conspicuous a dwelling as the luxurious Hotel Plaza-Athénée. Jews had to register at the city hall of their community, which, within Paris itself, meant the particular district where they lived. They were not allowed to leave this community, and had a curfew of 8:00 P.M., after which they were restricted within their homes until 5:00 A.M. the next day.

Although hotel employees lined up for food on behalf of the hotel's patrons, they still had to use the ration cards to which the latter were entitled. There were monthly bread cards, cut up into tiny squares for each day of the month; and other cards with forty small squares with which an individual could purchase less than a hundred grams of boneless meat—or one hundred twenty-five grams, with bone—per week; one liter a month of paraffin; thirty kilos of coal a month; and one or two eggs. The vegetables were rationed, not by cards but by the vendors themselves, who took advantage of their customers because they, in turn, were being starved by the Germans, who were purchasing food for themselves with French money, for the Occupation forces had been looting both the industry and the treasury.

France was suffering from lack of raw materials in every area of life. There were shortages of electricity, and of fuel for transportation. Extinct were taxis, buses, and cars (save for those who, like the Fayards or Charles, purchased gasoline on the black market); the greatest luxury was to own a bicycle, although theft was almost immediate. Most Parisians walked, several miles a day, thinking nothing anymore of walking an hour to visit a friend or reach a particular store. Christina, who was now sixteen, walked to and from the private school where she was in the eleventh form, with one year left before graduation. Whether it was cold or hot, Parisians used their feet to reach their destination. And no one complained. Everyone was in the same position as his or her neighbor.

Of course, the underground train system, the métro, still functioned, although on an irregular schedule and sometimes not at all. Three out of four stations had been closed down, so that hordes of people would press anxiously toward the entrance to the fourth, forming a human tidal wave that surged from the street, down the stairs, and onto a platform that would be black with people. Inside the train cars it was the same story: Men and women crushing one another like sardines in a can, so that at one's destination it was often impossible to push and elbow through on time to make it to the sliding doors. Taking the métro had to be a matter of last resort, only for traveling to the opposite end of the city.

The Germans had been unable to vanquish the British air force, and the inhabitants of occupied Paris suffered from repeated air-raid warnings each time British bombers flew over the city, threatening Nazi property. Yet, somehow, Paris was being spared, as it had been for the most part when the Germans had been the enemy and a free France the target.

Air-raid warnings occurred day and night. If a person was outside when an air raid took place, he would rush to the nearest doorway or carriage entrance, or stumble into the first métro opening he could spot. Huddled among other frightened strangers, people chatted to pass the time until the signal resounded that the skies were clear. It was simpler inside a building: there, everyone ran to the cellar or to the first floor for a measure of safety, and it was only at night, when mothers had to carry their sleeping children downstairs, that air raids caused a particular problem.

But in the underground métro, the passengers were not able to hear an air-raid signal blasting. They would understand what was going on because the train would stop wherever it was, sometimes for an entire hour; but it was worst when the lights went out and the terrified travelers, crushed against their neighbors, had to spend their time immobile in a blackout.

Thank God this didn't happen with each air-raid warning! But having been caught a number of times in this predicament, Amelia felt a wave of guilt for not having moved her daughter to the free zone, where, at least for the moment, the French collaborationist government of Marshal Pétain provided freedom and the ability to lead normal lives.

For the line of demarcation had closed down, and it was now illegal to travel between the two zones without the proper identification card or *Ausweis,* from the Nazi government in Paris. And so the Jews who had, like the Habigs, remained trapped in the capital, carried identity cards perforated with the initial *J* for *"Juif."*

Being a Jew in Paris was becoming increasingly dangerous. Yet, how could Amelia have considered leaving Paris? *Charles was there.* What would her life have meant, without him? Even if they could not openly live together, at least they had his visits . . . and their lovemaking. Amelia was a woman who needed to love a man. Having lost Peter, the center of her life, she had slowly rebuilt herself around Charles. He had become more important than life itself, more important than logic and reason. More important, even, than honor.

She thought about the morning Anne had burst in on her, accusing her of having taken Charles. Amelia still felt deep, searing pangs of shame whenever she recalled this. Yes, she had done something terrible . . . but Anne's visit had not stopped the affair. An honorable woman, a loving cousin, would have broken off all further contact with the man in question, realizing she had no right to love him. But sometimes one had to close one's eyes to the laws of the Bible, and accept those of nature, those of the heart.

Amelia pressed her hands against her temples, and shook her head. It was too late for recriminations, for guilt, for honor—and for thinking of leaving the city to protect her child.

I'll take a small apartment, she decided. And although an inner voice angrily chided her for not having taken action earlier, a second, more indulgent voice reassured her that a small apartment in a quiet Parisian side street would be safe after all.

Charles would help her to find such a place; and then, of course, he'd visit.

* * *

This morning in late June 1941, a dry sun was turning the beveled-glass windows of the president's office into slanted diamond panels, showing off all the colors of the rainbow. But Armand Fayard looked taciturn as he sat back, shifting a Lalique paperweight at random on his desk before him, seemingly oblivious to the refractions that caught the glass sculpture from the windows behind.

Facing him, side by side in rust-colored leather armchairs, Charles and Alexis listened attentively.

"Our plants have been working at top capacity," the old man announced, sticking a cigar in his mouth and chomping down on it. Alexis rose and deftly reached for the lump of rough pig iron that was Fayard's favorite lighter, and lit his boss's cigar. "The Germans have paid us good money for our products. The last receipts we had from the CPS show a marked profit for the past quarter."

The Comptoir Français des Produits Sidérurgiques was the central administration for the French steel industry; and while the state set the maximum price to be charged by individual producers, it was the CPS that composed the invoices, helped to coordinate orders, and acted as bill collector for the private firms.

After the Great War the most powerful steel manufacturers of France had turned to the question of rearmament; and Armand Fayard, then vice-president of the Comité des Forges, had become chief coordinator of this project. Later, as its president, he had listened to Charles and set up a ball bearings plant near his own steel mills in Lorraine, and when war with Germany had appeared unavoidable, he had also opened a full-fledged munitions factory on the premises.

At first the French military had been his only client. But after France's capitulation, the occupying German forces had all but monopolized his business. They paid for their arms just as they paid for the eggs they purchased from French farmers—with the moneys they had taken from the French treasury. But they had also set their men inside the Fayard plants, to make certain that they, along with their Vichy allies, retained a monopoly on war supplies.

"We've had no choice but to sell to the Nazis and to the Vichy forces," Fayard said, his voice suddenly bitter. "The entire steel industry of France has had to submit. It was either that, or be totally taken over by the *Boches*. But our men have been growing more and more disgruntled. What began last year as the resignation of defeat, has now been turning into a renewed desire for action against the intruders."

Alexis's lips parted, but he waited, saying nothing. Charles also remained silently attentive, his eyes fastened on the old man.

"The German invasion of the Soviet Union may be their first step toward global defeat. We're going to have one hell of a sum-

mer," Fayard proceeded grimly. "But that's good! Hitler is going
at Russia exactly as Napoleon did—and he'll be beaten back just as
viciously! Many smart Frenchmen are waking up to this fact and
deciding that de Gaulle makes more sense than the Vichy puppets
whose strings are being activated by Herr Adolf."

"No Frenchman worth his mettle wants to fight the Russians as
a member of the German military," Charles commented. "And the
young people don't want to be sent to Germany as 'volunteer
workers' to help with the Nazi war production. The French have
never willingly acted as *slaves.* Which is why the underground
Resistance movement has been growing more active every day."

Alexis opened his mouth, but Fayard put out a hand to prevent
him from speaking up. "I know, I know. *I'm* responsible for holding you back, Alex." He turned to Charles and smiled. "The boy's
been crying for action. First he wanted to go to London, then he
told me he was going to join the Maquis with our other young
hothead in the legal department, François Durand. But I asked
him to do me a personal favor, and wait for my own idea to take
concrete shape. And now I'm ready. I'm ready for both of you."

Charles eyed his son. So Alex had been talking to the old man,
behind his back . . . But politely, he said to Fayard, "Please tell
us what we can do to help."

Fayard's face turned belligerent for a moment, and he sat puffing
on his cigar. Evidently he was ruminating on a private anger he
was having trouble articulating. Finally he declared, "I've always
hated the Germans. I've worked with them for our mutual benefit,
between the wars; and the truth is that I have no choice but to
cooperate with them now. But they know I'm doing it half heart-
edly, and that if I were younger and stronger, I would never have
stood for their entering my country and using it like a suburb of
the German Reich!"

Alex nodded, his dark eyes incandescent. Fayard cleared his
throat, and addressed the young man directly. "You once accused
me of using this war as a pretext for increasing my profits," he
stated. "Well, I'm a businessman. I've invested in the Enskilda
Bank, and I've covered my ass. When you're as old as I am, son,
you'll understand this better. But you'll never fully understand, not
the way your father does. Because you see, Alex, your father and I
share something in common. We were born poor, with no one to
back our first efforts. *Whatever we accomplished, we accomplished*

on our own, for ourselves. And so we're loath to relinquish it without a fair fight. *We never want to be poor again!*"

"Yes, sir," Alexis answered, the fire in the old man's face moving him, making him ashamed he'd never known poverty himself.

"Nevertheless, I am a Frenchman. And I want a free France. I want de Gaulle to be victorious, to restore this nation to its position of pride. I want the British to bomb the hell out of the *Boches*! And so I've come up with a plan, and, with your help, we're going to sneak supplies intended for the Vichy troops to the Resistance people in the south."

Fayard looked from Charles to Alex, his face strangely smug. "The Vichy orders are quite large at the munitions plant," he explained. "So it won't be hard to smuggle out a small percentage of arms to our fellows in the mountains. We're talking about small arms, of course: a few crates per shipment, which won't be noticed. We'll move guns, machine guns, shells, and bullets. I have a few loyal people in the plants—men you know, Charles. It will be your job to organize them, and Alexis's to find young people to get the arms over to the Maquis men. In this way, in however small a measure, Fayard Industries will be playing a role to rid this country of the Nazis!"

Alexis's face was flushed and he was already standing. "Count me in, Monsieur Fayard," he stated. "And you can be sure that my friend François will help me with all his know-how."

"That's my boy!"

The old man turned to Charles. His eyes held a question that crackled in the air for a split second as Charles hesitated. Charles could feel his son's eyes on him, too, challenging him to dare defy Fayard's objective.

But Charles was saved from having to answer right away by a delicate knock on the door and the appearance of Fayard's secretary, bearing a message. As the president conferred with his assistant, Charles was granted the unexpected privilege of time to reflect. But it was a vision of Amelia which came into his mind. She admired heroism and often spoke glowingly of her husband, who had died "doing what he believed." But do I believe in anything anymore? Charles wondered. Or have I become so goddamned blasé that nothing touches me?

Despair filled his spirit, and he thought: France is like an old love that has betrayed me. . . . Why should I help her now?

He could find no reply to ease his disturbed mind, and he

thought, I'll do it for *Amelia.* I'll do it to make her love and respect me, the way she loved and respected Peter.

The smooth, gray-haired secretary was unobtrusively sliding out of the room. "Well, Charles?" Fayard asked.

"Of course, you can count on me," Charles replied, reaching over to grasp the hand the old man was already extending.

* * *

Amelia's fingers trembled as they held the telephone, and she spoke hesitantly. "Madame Alatini? My name is Amelia Habig. My cousin, Charles de Rochefleur, told me to call you."

A high, pleasant voice came over the wire. "Of *course!* I've been wanting to meet you for such a long time. I'd be delighted if you and your daughter could both come to tea tomorrow. I shall be having an interesting group of friends over, who you'll both enjoy."

* * *

Outside, the Lorraine sky was weighted down with lead, a uniform, deadly gray. Inside the warehouse, Charles felt an odd claustrophobia, as though the walls were caving in on him, but he realized that it was just nerves . . . he was quite literally shaking inside.

Pierre Legrand paused and wiped the sweat from his creased brow. The manager of the munitions plant was the person Charles had earmarked to help him accomplish his task. Legrand was bulky and tough, with a soul to match. Charles had known him for years, since he himself had started in the personnel department of Fayard Industries and Legrand had been a junior foreman in one of the finishing mills. They'd come together because of their single-minded ambition, which each had immediately detected in the other. Two men of violently divergent backgrounds—Pierre's father had been a miner in one of the nearby coal mines, a devoutly Catholic father of nine—Charles and Pierre Legrand had nevertheless formed an instant, unspoken bond of mutual recognition. And though this hardly constituted a friendship, it was the basis for a mutual sense of trust that, over the years, had deepened with respect.

Pierre Legrand was no-nonsense. He'd worked his way up the ranks until becoming manager of the finishing mill, and when war had broken out, the munitions plant. He made Charles think that Armand Fayard must have been this sort of man in his younger

days. For Legrand was only a few years older than Charles himself
—no more than forty-five, at most.

"The boys put these three crates together," Legrand now said to
Charles, in his lilting Lorraine accent. The French inhabitants of
Lorraine were galled at the German takeover. They felt themselves
French through and through and, although accustomed to being
perennially subjected to a tug-of-war between Germany and
France, had never allied their hearts with the former.

Charles bent down and looked through the first crate. It contained several stacks of neatly packed guns. "I had to be very
careful," Legrand added. "I picked boys I'd known from childhood—the ones whose families have known my family. Four of
them, all trustworthy, all patriotic, and all as closemouthed as
me."

"Good," Charles said, and their eyes met. "My boys are handpicked too," he said softly. "My son, Alex, and his best friend.
They've got the truck waiting some miles down the road, hidden
behind an abandoned mine shaft."

"We'll bring them the crates after dark," Pierre told him. "I
never figured you for a risk taker, Monsieur de Rochefleur," he
commented, shaking his head and chuckling. "And risky business
is exactly what we're dealing with. The *Boches* have men on guard
inside the plant, but the worst are our own, the collaborationists.
They're ready to turn their brothers in to the Nazis, and are always
on the lookout."

Charles felt an incredible exhilaration. The operation was going
to work, and he had masterminded it! Under the eyes of the enemy
. . . He remembered Amelia as she had taken his hands and
gently raised them to her lips. "Be careful" was all she had whispered, but to him it meant *I love you*. An *I love you* that had sent
him on his way, like the wind at his back. France had rejected his
citizenship, but he would rid her of its occupants—for Amelia's
sake, to make *her* safe.

Because *she* wasn't Swiss and was, as an Austrian Jew, in greater
danger than any Frenchman in Paris.

I wonder if she's finished with the Alatini woman, he thought,
afraid for the first time that day.

* * *

In the residential district of Auteuil, in the rue Mallet-Stevens,
an imposing wall hid the Alatini property from the curious eyes of
passersby. Amelia paused for a moment outside the door and

pulled the veil from her small hat down to protect her face. Next to her, Christina tugged on her embroidered sweater and looked down at her black pumps, her knee-length skirt showing off shapely calves in rayon stockings. It was sinful to even *think* of silk stockings during the war, but today it was also important to look "proper," and very *Seizième*. The Sixteenth Arrondissement was where the debutantes lived, the stylish upper-class girls with whom Christina went to school.

Together the two women pushed open the massive door that stood inside the wall. To their surprise, they found themselves staring at a small white castle, standing in retreat beyond a manicured lawn in which a graceful fountain spouted cascades of water. A sinuous pebbled path crossed the lawn to the mansion, and Amelia and her daughter, arm in arm, took this path to their destination.

Amelia rang the doorbell, and a uniformed maid answered. "I'm Madame Habig," Amelia said.

"Madame is expecting you." The servant girl led the way into a charming Louis XVI drawing room, in which a number of other people were already seated, balancing teacups on their laps.

An attractive young blonde in her early thirties walked up to them. The maid said simply, "This is Madame Habig."

The blonde, who had sparkling light blue eyes, murmured, "I'm Régine Alatini. And I'm glad you could come. Please, sit down. You'll have to excuse us, but we could obtain no cookies. The shortage, you know . . ."

"Naturally," Amelia demurred.

Few of the guests were talking. Madame Alatini went to a magnificent silver teapot and poured a cup of very watery tea for Amelia, then one for Christina. She apologized for not having any cream to offer. Christina accepted a sliver of lemon; Amelia shook her head. Denying their Viennese sweet tooth, both politely refused sugar, which was sold by ration cards as a rare luxury. Their pleasant hostess waved them to a love seat, and whispered to them that they were going to have to wait.

Then the pretty Régine Alatini approached an older gentleman, and bent toward him. He rose and followed her into another room. Nobody moved. Christina, uncomfortable in this most elegant of waiting rooms, began to count heads. "There are nine people ahead of us," she said, sotto voce, to her mother.

Amelia tried to smile, but her mouth was dry. She sipped some tea and looked around. Christina was fingering the embroidery on her sweater, lost in thought, and Amelia wondered at the unfairness of her daughter's youth, contrasted to her own. Although at sixteen she, too, had been caught in a war—but an altogether different sort of war.

That morning one of their neighbors at the hotel had been visited by some Gestapo officers. A nice Jewish man, to whom she and Tina had politely nodded whenever they'd encountered him on the staircase. The Gestapo had come and taken him with them. Christina had seen the Jewish man, dignified in his navy blue suit, wedged between two of the Nazi officers. Later, one of the hotel cashiers had remarked, "They've taken a couple of Jewish people I know away. Where do you suppose they take them?"

Amelia didn't know. Nobody knew.

Régine Alatini reentered the room and went up to an old lady and her middle-aged daughter. Ten minutes later she returned and beckoned to a stylish woman in her fifties. A handsome man Amelia's age, with dark hair and dark eyes, smiled at her and tipped his hat. She smiled back, but pulled the veil automatically down over her eyes. And when Madame Alatini reappeared, it was to this man that she made a subtle sign. He rose, bowing slightly toward Amelia, and followed their hostess out of the drawing room.

Amelia found herself thinking of Charles. Charles, who had gone on his first mission to the munitions factory along with Alexis. *I hope they're both all right,* she thought, fervently closing her eyes.

"Madame Habig." Régine Alatini was standing at her elbow. Amelia and Christina rose in unison. From the opposite side of the room a dark little man set down his teacup and went ahead of them into the next room. Régine Alatini held the door open and allowed her guests to pass through, then followed them and shut the door.

They were standing in a small piano room, with a card table set out in the middle, four chairs around it. The dark man pulled out a chair for Amelia, then sat down himself. "I'm Jean Malvin," he said pleasantly, holding out his hand. "And I have everything ready for you . . . Madame Hautois. Madame Andrée Hautois, born in Villabella in Normandy, of Catholic parents. Put your signature here for me, please."

He was holding out a legal document, which Amelia recognized as a forged identity card. There was no perforation marked *J*. No sign of an alien birth within the Reich. An enormous relief swept over Amelia, and, with trembling fingers, she signed *Andrée Hautois* over the official-looking stamp.

"I've called your daughter 'Cécile,' to retain the original initials," Malvin explained as Christina took her mother's place and signed over the stamp on her own card. "So often, when the *Boches* come unexpectedly into someone's residence, they look for monogrammed pieces to catch discrepancies. So we always try to make up a name with matching initials."

"You're very kind," Amelia murmured. "But how much do I owe you for all of this?"

Malvin smiled and shook his head. "I've already been paid by Monsieur de Rochefleur."

He stood up. Madame Alatini moved forward graciously, and held out her hand. "I'm glad we could be of help," she stated. Then she opened another door, motioned the women through it, and closed it gently behind them.

Amelia and Christina were standing in a long hallway, and miraculously the same young maid who had let them in reappeared to escort them out the front door. Mother and daughter walked out onto the graveled path, fresh air lifting Amelia's veil from her nose. An orange dusk had fallen over the green lawn and turned the fountain to a burnished bronze.

"Mama," Christina whispered.

Amelia's glance followed her daughter's discreet gaze. Coming toward the house was a small group of men in imposing black uniforms. "They're Gestapo," she said tonelessly. Then, trying to keep the panic from her voice, she whispered, "Walk, Tina. Walk normally."

Amelia Habig squared her shoulders and placed an arm around her daughter. The Gestapo officers were barely a yard away from her now. In the sunset they appeared grotesque, dark and ominous. She kept walking, the girl synchronizing her steps to hers, hypnotically.

Now they were less than a foot away. Amelia smiled at them, the bright smile of a socialite on her way home from a tea party. She felt sure that her heart had stopped beating.

The first officer touched his hat, and stepped back. "Madame . . ." His eyes were coal black, unreadable. Was he going to arrest them right here, or would he first ask to see their identification? Amelia's hands fumbled over the clasp of her bag. She kept smiling, her smile freezing into a painful mask . . . summoning a courage she hadn't drawn on since the night of her rape, in Vienna. Her stomach was tied in knots.

The officer raised his eyebrows, looking the two women over quizzically. The picture they projected was of two well-bred ladies waiting politely to be dismissed, like children from the table. All at once he sighed, and, making a half turn toward his men, he barked out: *"Geschwind!"*

And suddenly the small group was parting, the officers falling in line to the left and right of the graveled path, making way for her and Christina to pass through. Amelia inclined her head graciously, and thanked them with her smile, unable to speak. But no one called after them. The only sounds the women heard were their own feet on the small pebbles, and the sound of the retreating Germans.

Amelia and Christina kept walking until they reached the heavy door set inside the wall, and then they both turned around, like Lot's wife unable to resist the temptation. The little maid was just letting the Gestapo officers into the beautiful white castle.

In the street, safely away from the Alatini household and its Nazi intruders, Amelia Habig burst into tears.

One of the women she'd met through the WIZO told Amelia the news several days later. "Did you have your card made at Régine Alatini's?" Sylvie Loeb asked her curiously. And when Amelia nodded, Sylvie filled in the blanks. "Four days ago, at six-thirty P.M., a group of Gestapo officers came to the door and took everyone inside the house. Children, servants, men and women. The Alatinis have been deported. . . ."

There it was, that dreaded word: *deported.* It meant "removed," "done away with." Taken God only knew where. And Régine Alatini, so helpful and generous, hadn't even been Jewish.

"Why are your hands trembling so?" Sylvie was asking. "This sort of thing is beginning to happen all around Paris, more and more often. Each time I run into a friend, I wonder if we'll ever meet again. . . . We're being hunted down, Amelia, and I'm afraid to go out into the street anymore."

* * *

Alexis felt a thrill of exhilaration as he watched the noon sun covering the countryside with gold dust. Since the previous night, he had hardly been able to contain his excitement. He and François Durand had been awakened by the arrival of Pierre Legrand and his four musclemen bearing four large crates packed with munitions for the underground Resistance. His father had been there, too, a strange figure in his evening suit of fine nubbed silk, hardly ruffled even at this midnight hour, always the patrician.

Supervised by Charles and aided by Pierre, the men loaded the crates into the back of the truck. And then Charles walked up to Alexis and François and wished them luck. Alex found himself staring into his father's eyes, and for a moment both men felt embarrassed, awkward. Charles touched Alexis on the shoulder, and the barest smile creased his face. "Take care, son," he whispered, and blinked his eyes rapidly, considering, perhaps, whether to give Alexis a hug. And Alexis himself hesitated, moving forward just when Charles had already stepped back. And then Charles turned away and joined his men, and Alexis remained by the side of the truck, staring confusedly into the pitch-black night.

This was the first time the young man remembered Charles's ever calling him "son."

Later, when the first clear signs of dawn had risen over the abandoned mine shaft, he and François busied themselves camouflaging the munitions. Battered orange crates, filled with rusty kitchen appliances and battered toys, were used to cover the cases of rifles, small explosives, and machine guns. Several old suitcases bulging with secondhand women's clothing surrounded shopping bags overflowing with tin pots and pans dubiously endowed with mismatched lids. Pleased with themselves, the two young men closed their truck, and François, who had memorized the map of Nancy, drove off whistling.

"The idea is to look so normal as to seem inconspicuous," he told Alexis. But for Alex, masquerading as an itinerant peddler felt anything but normal.

At twenty-five, François seemed to possess all the glamorous accoutrements of modern-day knighthood. He had fought in Spain, and later, although his dream of flying had been denied and he had been sent to "rot" behind the Maginot Line, he had participated in the war. François acted like a big brother to Alexis, but he had always recognized the younger man's eagerness to learn, as well as his extraordinary mind and valor. They genuinely liked each other, appreciating the very differences that had first attracted them to the other. No one but François would have known how to wend his way through a strange, hostile city alive with vigilant German soldiers at every street corner . . . just as François alone possessed friends in every nook and cranny of the country, spies and messengers for the underground.

Alexis slept awhile, and some hours later, as they neared the Langres Plateau south of Nancy and a little northeast of where they were headed, they stopped and had a brief lunch. Then Alexis took the wheel and François, in spite of the July sunlight that might have blinded another man, rolled up his sleeves, unbuttoned his shirt down to his chest, and went to sleep in the passenger seat.

At last Alex reached the Côte d'Or, the area of Burgundy just south of the plateau. Fields stretched on either side of the truck, and he tried to remember which way to go into the mountains to the west. The Morvan mountain area was hot and damp, and Alexis, already bathed in perspiration, wondered how much longer it would be until they reached the safety of the mountain woods, which would be cooler than this open territory.

Hidden in the mountain regions, the underground Resistance network was flourishing, but the problem would be to avoid the Germans. Just southwest of Dijon, the line of demarcation had been drawn between the occupied zone, in which they were now driving, and the free zone below.

The Resistance was accustomed to playing hide-and-seek with the Nazis. Alexis was not.

*   *   *

The previous evening, as soon as Pierre Legrand's key had unlocked the doors of the warehouse to let him and Charles out into the open air, the two men were accosted by a German lieutenant. He was young, blond, and very Teutonic, his blue eyes piercing Charles as he clicked his heels and saluted. "Herr de Rochefleur?"

"Yes?" Charles felt unnerved. The four crates stood ready behind the warehouse door, he and Pierre only inches away from the telltale signs of their clandestine transaction. *How did the Germans know that he was here, in Nancy?*

"General von Quistorp would like you to attend a dinner party at his house tonight," the young man stated, in perfect French. It sounded more like a summons than an invitation. Baron Kurt Von Quistorp was in command of the German troops in Lorraine, a worthy old general who had distinguished himself in the Great War and now, because of a leg injury, had been relegated to this supervisory post in the recaptured province.

"The general will be expecting you at seven-thirty, for cocktails," the lieutenant pronounced. Then, half smiling at Charles's sudden dismay as he looked down at his creased pants and rolled-up shirt sleeves, the young officer added, "And he instructed me to reassure you that the occasion will be quite informal."

Saluting once again, the lieutenant made an about-face and departed. Charles and Pierre stared at each other, dumbfounded. "They know our every step before we take it," Pierre informed his superior. "This is going to be some kind of test."

Charles's nostrils quivered, and he inclined his head. "Very well, then . . . so be it. I am not afraid."

Pierre Legrand's eyebrows shot up the barest fraction. But his response was firm. "I'll be here tonight at twelve-thirty, with my men."

*   *   *

Arabella Fayard sat up in her sumptuous boudoir of polished ebony and ivory. She stretched and yawned, then slid out of bed and walked over to the vanity, a magnificent piece of furniture adorned with carved panels of *pietra dura* painted to depict delicate landscapes. She flicked on the small light adjacent to the mirror, and began to scrutinize her face.

She was forty-seven years old this summer. And it showed, this late at night, when nothing protected the small dry lines and the slight sagging of her cheeks from her own severe observation. The roots of her hair were gray, though the rest was wavy and blond, as it had once been all the way through. She was no longer such a prize for a man . . . for any man but Armand, who, between his advanced age and the aftereffects of his stroke, was hardly a man at all as far as *she* was concerned.

It was so boring to spend the summer in Paris! Arabella hated summers anyway. They served as an unpleasant reminder of Cologne, when Charles had sent her away. Arabella hated Charles, and yet she spent undue amounts of time daydreaming about their years together, their sexual games, their laughter, their teasing. Had she loved him? Perhaps. She hated him for having ended her sexuality, because after him she hadn't felt like a complete woman, and had seen herself as aging and unattractive.

Nobody in Paris mentioned Amelia Habig much these days. Surely, as an Austrian Jew, that woman had to stay in hiding. Arabella wondered whether, in fact, she had been thrown over by Charles for the "Viennese nightingale." Charles wasn't the kind of man who lived well without a good woman in his back pocket . . . and Anne simply didn't count.

Arabella had picked up the telephone a few days ago, and over-heard a sotto voce conversation: it was Armand, telling someone that Charles would be in Nancy later that week. And so today she hadn't been able to resist, and had placed a call to La Folie. In the middle of the afternoon, Anne usually went on errands. Had she answered, Arabella would have hung up.

"I'm calling for Monsieur Tréclis," she lied when the butler answered the phone. "I was wondering whether Monsieur de Rochefleur had returned home yet, and whether I might expect him to drop some papers at our office tomorrow afternoon."

"Monsieur isn't in town, madame, and I'm not certain when to expect them back."

Them? Arabella swallowed, and asked: "Madame is with Monsieur . . . ?"

A discreet cough. "No, Monsieur Alexis went with Monsieur. But Madame will be home at five o'clock. Perhaps she could return your call?"

"It's all right," Arabella replied quickly. "It won't be necessary to disturb her."

Hanging up, Arabella chewed her inner cheek pensively. So they'd *both* gone. . . . Somehow, if father and son had left together, knowing how little Charles appreciated his son, it stood to reason that Armand had sent them. Armand liked that boy, and respected him. I'm going to find out what they're all up to, she thought, narrowing her lips. If it takes spying on Armand's conversations, it will be well worth it. I'll have something to do during this long summer. If Charles de Rochefleur has forgotten me, I certainly have not forgotten *him*! Whatever strange business Charles may be involved in, he will live to regret the way he threw me out of his room, and out of his life!

* * *

Baron General Kurt von Quistorp resembled a white rat. His skin was translucent, his hair totally white and slick, hugging his scalp like a stocking, and his eyes were bloodshot and lashless, like a rat's red eyes. His body was short and squat, and that evening, in full regimental regalia, he tried to dominate his audience by virtue of his rank . . . for, in stature, he stood far short of the other men in the room.

Charles, in his pearl-gray silk suit, was the only male civilian present. He let his eyes roam over the beautiful reception room, filled with fine French antiques, and felt a moment of pure anger and hatred. They had no right to appropriate the mayor's residence, and turn it into a German men's club! Had they done the same with Amelia's house, and his aunt Barbara's in Vienna? Old von Quistorp was drinking champagne . . . French champagne, of course. They took whatever France most valued and used it for their own amusement.

In the corner, a beautiful young woman in a clinging red gown stood smoking a cigarette, chatting with the young lieutenant who had delivered Charles his invitation. They even used the women! For one brief moment, his mind's eye imagined SS officers raping Amelia in front of Tina, and his blood pressure rose. Like any invader, they simply did as they pleased.

"I'm told that you speak fluent German, Herr de Rochefleur," von Quistorp said. He took a small round of pâté de foie gras from a crystal tray being passed around by a butler in white tails. Gingerly, he brought the hors d'oeuvre to his nose and sniffed it, then deigned to pop it into his large mouth.

"My father was from Munich," Charles replied, smoothly switching to German. "And I was reared in Switzerland."

"I know, I know." Von Quistorp smiled, showing pieces of pâté between his two front teeth. "The de Rochefleur family is well known to the Führer." Which meant, of course, that they had a file on him that detailed everything from Wilhelm's suicide to Anne's miscarriage. And it underscored one fact: that, Swiss or not, he was a Jew. "Well known throughout the world," von Quistorp added. "An oligarchy of cousins marrying cousins . . ."

"Have you been pleased with the quality of merchandise we have been turning over to you, sir?" Charles asked. Better to have things clarified right away than to waste time on other half-formulated threats veiled as amenities. Why had the old fox brought him out here tonight?

"Not only pleased . . . The Führer is delighted. Fayard Industries produces excellent steel products and armaments. But tell me, Herr de Rochefleur, isn't it strange that Armand Fayard should be sending *you,* personally, to check this fact out?"

Charles smiled, and accepted a second coupe of champagne from the butler. "Not really. You may not know Fayard, but he's a thorough man, and he trusts few of his employees. I am here to verify the products we have been shipping out, and to check the invoices, item by item, to make sure the foremen aren't cheating us. Cheating *you,* by making you pay for missing pieces—and cheating *us,* by clouding up our credibility with *you.*"

General von Quistorp smiled, but his eyes remained impassive. "So, Armand Fayard believes in the future of the Reich?"

Charles Lévy–de Rochefleur nodded gravely. "Indeed. Like many French industrialists, he saw at once that the threat was Russia, not the Führer. Germany will not rob France of its industrial potential. Indeed, you will help to develop it. But Stalin would mow down men like Fayard, and appropriate all." He looked the general in the eye. "Did you know that Fayard has been supporting the Enskilda Bank, and the SKF, its ball bearings trust, all along?"

"And *you,* Herr de Rochefleur? You have taken your wife's property to Switzerland, away from us. You do not trust us, perhaps?"

Charles smiled. "I am a Swiss citizen. Switzerland was good to me, and now I'd like to reciprocate. I would have moved the headquarters of the Crédit Industriel long before, had I been in control. Because you see, Herr General, like you, I am a chauvinist, placing the interests of my own country above all other concerns."

They had reached a stalemate of sorts. And so von Quistorp swallowed his champagne and regarded Charles with the look of a very hungry rat eyeing a piece of cheese—Swiss cheese. "I'm glad that Armand Fayard places so much trust in you, Herr de Rochefleur," he remarked, his words as smooth as velvet. "Because if we find a single rifle missing from our orders, we shall know whom to contact. Pierre Legrand alone is not big enough to attempt to swindle the Third Reich!"

Charles looked down at the small man in front of him and answered, equally softly, "Pierre Legrand is loyal to Monsieur Fayard, and so are we all. And Monsieur Fayard dines regularly with Ambassador Abetz in Paris. Don't worry, Herr General . . . we are all your trusted servants, and the Führer's."

Later that night, still in his silk suit, Charles met Legrand and cautioned him before setting off with the crates for Alexis's truck. "The accountant is one of ours," Legrand assured him. "But I'll make sure he keeps his eyes wide open." Then they joined the four steelworkers and brought the munitions over to the waiting truck.

* * *

Charles sat in Legrand's office, chewing on the end of a pencil, musing. Alexis and François had left early that morning. They were traveling no more than two hundred miles at most, taking into account unforeseen detours and winding side roads. Their drive would be long only because of the sudden stops and starts they were forced to make while hiding as a German jeep rolled by, or a patrol marched in the distance. Alex had been excited, even thrilled, at the idea of smuggling those few crates of arms to the Resistance. And if the effort succeeded, they would return each month to accomplish similar missions.

If the effort succeeded . . . It *had* to succeed. Charles owed this much to Anne. He'd married her so that her son might be born in good standing. He owed it to her that her son stayed alive.

And he owed Amelia something too: the better part of himself, which, for so many years, he had attempted to bury behind his anger and greed. The Germans had no right to be in France, had no right to annex Austria "just like that," killing Amelia's brother, her mother, and raping *her*. No one had that right. And suddenly, his old resentment of the French nation disintegrated, like sugar in hot tea, melted down by the passion of his righteous anger toward the Nazi invader. Yes, Herr General, he thought grimly: we are a family of cousins, and if at times we have been known to throw the glove down before one another, *against a common enemy, we act as one.*

* * *

Alexis felt a jolt of adrenaline pass through him. No more than a hundred yards ahead was a truckful of Nazi soldiers. Where had they come from? How was it possible that he hadn't spotted them?

Next to him, François was tugging on his sparse mustache. "They came from over there," he said, indicating a place to their left where the mountain road disappeared around a corner. A small tuck in the road that Alexis hadn't foreseen. *What now?*

"There's no retreat for us," Alexis whispered fearfully.

They were in the middle of a beautiful green forest, fertile with trees and moss and coolness—what he'd been dreaming of earlier. On his lap, François held a hand-scrawled map bearing the approximate whereabouts of the underground group that would soon be expecting their delivery. They had warned him about the close vigilance the Nazis kept in the Morvan, because it was so close to the free zone and also because several Resistance groups (de Gaulle's people as well as communist groups that had joined the underground) hid there as their base of operations. Hiding in the hills was the easiest way to avoid detection . . . but here, it had become especially dangerous.

"We don't move," François muttered. "Because we *can't*. It's too late! So we play innocent. Just pray the whole platoon doesn't search the truck."

Alexis held his breath and waited. The German truck approached. It was painted the colors of the German army, with huge swastikas outlined on its fenders. Almost nose to nose with the young men's old truck, it came to an abrupt halt, and a helmeted captain emerged, rifle in hand. He approached the driver's window, which Alexis had lowered to let in some air.

"Your papers!" the German barked. "Both of you!"

The rifle butt was resting inside the truck, centimeters away from Alexis's chest. But François was taking over. He inclined his head toward the captain, winking at him with all the nonchalance of a country boy. And his nimble fingers extracted the false identity cards from the wallet on the seat and he handed them over to the Nazi.

"*Vichy?*" the captain asked. "What are you fellows doing in these hills?"

"It's a long story, sir." François sighed. "My brother got lost around Dijon. I was sleeping. We've been all over, peddling our goods, and I was tired. Jean doesn't understand directions."

"That's an absurd story that doesn't hold together," the captain said. "Show me what 'goods' you're talking about!"

"Sure." François opened his door in the blink of an eye, and jumped to the ground with the light-footed agility of a monkey. The captain moved to join him at the back of the truck. Alexis turned off the ignition and climbed down but to what end . . . ?

"Those rich refugee bastards don't give us our money's worth, do they, brother?" François was saying. Alexis thought: *That's it, he's telling me something*—only, *what exactly*? François had flung the door wide open and was displaying his wares with a casual flip of the hand. "Not bad, eh?"

And all at once, Alexis understood. The truck door, at the back, was positioned at exactly the proper angle for nothing to be visible to the occupants of the German vehicle beyond. Had François's gesture been either too gentle or too strong, the door would have opened at a different angle, giving the Germans a clear view of the action among the three men staring at boxes filled with decrepit-looking pots and pans, clothing, toys, and other sad remnants.

The captain threw one disgusted look at this sorry display, and opened his mouth to speak. But in one smooth, unexpected move,

Alexis, who hadn't until then said a single word, jumped forward, clamping one hand over the Nazi's mouth while jabbing him in the ribs with a hunting knife. The young man's strength and power matched the officer's, but the German had been taken by surprise, and Alexis and François now possessed the advantage.

It was François who spoke, in a savage whisper: "Tell your jackasses to move on without you," he ordered. "If you don't, I'll blow your brains out." A small pistol was poised at the captain's temple, and François was smiling broadly. "We want you to tell us who tipped you off."

Sweating, the captain said tersely, "Anonymous. From Versailles headquarters."

"If you say one wrong word, I'll kill you," Alexis whispered in German. "Just tell them to wait for you at the bottom of the hill. Don't walk, Captain: just talk, loud and clear. It's your life."

But it's ours too, he thought, wondering why he hadn't yet felt the anguish of terror.

The Nazi nodded. Jabbing the knife closer to his ribs and keeping a strong hold on his chest, Alexis allowed his fingers to part over the man's lips. The captain called out, "Go! They're just peddler boys! Go down to the bottom of the hill and wait for me. I'm going to look through these bags and all this shit."

Though no one could see behind the door, Alexis could see from his side, and he winked at his friend. Someone was getting out of the truck, and François began to draw back the pistol's hammer at the captain's temple. An involuntary tremor passed through the man, and he shouted, "Get back! I said, go to the bottom of the hill! I can handle this alone!"

No one's going to believe this, Alexis thought. His men will suspect foul play and come after us within seconds. But the man who had gotten out was shrugging, and climbing back inside the truck. "Now, stick your head in here, as if you're really looking through things!" François hissed.

Their hostage played the part. And so the truckful of Nazis saw their commanding officer, his head hidden by a bag of women's nightshirts, leaning into the back of the peddlers' truck. Somebody laughed. Then the enemy vehicle moved down the hill, and slowly Alexis began to feel his arms, his legs, his body thrilling back to life as safety seemed more certain.

"Hurry the hell up!" François was shouting at him. "We have a couple of minutes, you fool!"

It took them less than that to tie up and gag their hostage, and to stuff him tightly between two crates of tinware and a huge, over-stuffed suitcase. They slammed shut the back door of the truck and, as Alexis stood guard outside, François ran down the hill as fast as he could.

Below them, the German truck was trying to round a precarious bend, a boulder blocking the driver's way. François hurled a gre-nade and ran quickly back to where Alex stood watching. To-gether, they saw the Nazi truck exploding into flame, and, almost as quickly, men darting out of the woods to put out the fire.

The next few minutes went by like a lifetime, crammed full of sequences that overlapped one another in haphazard succession. Suddenly the forest was alive with men, and one of them was yelling, "Are you trying to set the whole goddamned wood on fire?"

Alexis was trembling from head to toe, but François was laugh-ing, throwing his arms around the furious, sweat-drenched man. "Hey, Gilles, we brought you your stuff," he told him, and then they were hugging each other like children.

Alexis felt the tears on his cheeks; but still he was too dazed to react. The entire panorama appeared disjointed and separated from his senses. And then someone thumped him on the back, and he heard François crying, "We made it, buddy! And we delivered our guys a live one, to boot!"

Then he heard Gilles warning, "But we're going to have to move our setup farther up. If there's been a tip-off from Paris, then somebody's found out about our operation. Next time, we might not be so lucky. . . ."

CHAPTER XIX

Rue de la Pompe was a pleasant, winding street in the Sixteenth Arrondissement of Paris. One could walk northwest to the Bois de Boulogne, or southeast to the Eiffel Tower and the gardens of the Trocadéro, with its Palais de Chaillot built for the Paris Exhibition of 1937 and encompassing the twin museums of Man and the Navy.

At number 81, one passed through a grilled gate into a cool walkway, where a dozen town houses stood arranged in a semicircle around flower beds and a green lawn. One forgot that Paris existed just a breath away. The complex, named Villa Herran, was protected by a lacework of tree limbs stretching out from behind the town houses, making sure the sun would never scorch their elegant sandstone façades.

At number 12, Villa Herran, ensconced at the back of the complex, lived Andrée and Cécile Hautois, a mother and daughter from Normandy. The neighbors said that Madame Hautois possessed at least one parent of Alsatian origin. This explained the tiniest trace of an accent in her cultured, melodic voice. The women were beautiful: tall, willowy, with dark hair and strange eyes of a peacock blue, and the delicate profiles of Dresden figurines. They were both quiet and reserved, and everybody liked them, although few had ever exchanged more than a word or two with them since they had purchased their villa in the summer of 1941.

Paris was undergoing a rigorous springtime, this year of 1942, because the Germans had tightened their rein and were making life even more difficult for the French. The shortage in raw materials was more prevalent than the year before, and the winter had been freezing due to lack of coal, which the Germans had appropriated for their own use. The Nazis were feeling the pressure of a now uncertain future, and as a result were resorting to crueler and more desperate measures.

Their Russian campaign was not faring well, and in December 1941, the United States had thrown its lot in with the Allies and declared war on the Axis powers. France was beginning to regain hope, and its underground Resistance was causing more and more damage to the enraged occupants. As a result, the Germans were retaliating with brutal treatment of the "enslaved" French. The Vichy government in the free zone no longer behaved autonomously, for the Germans had removed Admiral Darlan and placed their own protégé, Pierre Laval, at the head of the government, leaving old Pétain as nothing more than a figurehead.

This spring of 1942, in occupied France, the Jews lived under a constant threat of deportation. Along with the perforated identity card, a Jew had to sew a yellow Star of David to his clothing, with the black word *Juif* delineated over it. A Jew was not allowed to go to the cinema, the theater, or any restaurant, even a simple café, and could not own either a telephone or a radio.

When an air-raid siren sounded, Jews were not allowed in the streets: the Germans would simply comb the area for people wearing the yellow star and take them away. And in the métro, they were only permitted to ride in the rear car of the train.

The worst restriction against the Jews was over food. They were not allowed into a number of stores, and otherwise were only permitted to shop for food between 3:00 and 4:00 P.M. Yet if one arrived any later than 11:00 A.M., no foodstuffs were left: not bread, sausage, carrots, or the white beets that had become a Parisian staple, could be obtained.

The general population of Paris closed its eyes, in defiance of the Occupation authorities. Brave gentiles rode in the rear cars of the métro, out of solidarity, and many storekeepers encouraged Jewish housewives to drop off their shopping bags in the morning; then, when time permitted, these kind vendors would place into the bags whatever happened to be on the market that day, paying themselves with the money they found in the purse at the bottom; and, promptly at 3:00 P.M., the Jews would pick up their groceries and take them home.

Mesdames Hautois did not wear any Stars of David; they queued for bread and foodstuffs early in the morning, like everyone else; but they avoided the métro, and kept to themselves. Twice a week a maid came to clean their town house, and several evenings a gentleman, blond, good-looking, and terribly Aryan of feature, would come around for a visit. Some said that it was this gentleman who had purchased the house for the Hautois ladies. But nobody knew for sure, and after an initial curiosity, the aristocratic inhabitants of the exclusive Villa Herran complex began to lose interest in their newest neighbors. The Hautois were neither extravagant nor conspicuous, and it seemed pointless to indulge in speculation on their behalf.

Amelia and Christina began to breathe more freely in the privacy of their town house.

* * *

It was June again, and the garden at La Folie had blossomed into colors that enveloped one's senses as they rose to meet the eye: verdant greens in the trees and the trellised arbor; corals, yellows, whites, and all the varieties of red that came to mind, in the flower beds and the rosebushes. Charles had said to Anne the previous week: "Poor Tina hasn't smelled a breath of fresh air in years. I'd like it if you invited her to spend a few days with us here." As though Tina Habig had been a member of the dispossessed, when, in fact, the stone house in the rue de la Pompe was impressive, even if restrained in its decor.

Why did Charles feel compassion for Amelia's daughter, if not for the fact that she happened to be *her daughter.* He is forcing her on me, Anne thought resentfully. But at least he had had the good taste not to order me to invite Amelia!

* * *

For the first time in years, Alexis felt as if somebody was listening to him. It wasn't the same as talking to François—the two of them had shared so many experiences, and their politics were in such close synchronicity, that neither drank in the other's words anymore.

But now, strolling through the garden with Christina Habig, Alexis had the strange impression of expanding upward and outward, unafraid.

She was intelligent, and she was quiet. She listened. And he had told her more, far more, than he'd ever intended. About the Morvan, and about all the other times he and François had been back there, to the underground to deliver guns, explosives, and small arms.

"Nobody ever gets suspicious, seeing a strange truck lurking around the plant in Nancy?" Tina asked.

"We try to be resourceful. We hide the truck behind abandoned buildings, or the old mine shaft. But it's so gratifying to know we're *doing something* to help the men in the Maquis!"

"How often do you go?"

"Twice a month. And we've had a lot of close calls. German patrols . . ." He stopped, his mind drifting off. She gently pressed his arm, and said nothing, allowing him the privacy of his memories.

Now he guided her toward the gazebo. "Do you remember how we came out here, years ago, and had our first conversation? You were only thirteen then, and I was your age. . . ."

She blushed, unexpectedly, and looked down. "You told me about your parents. About how hard it was to be alone. About your father."

Alexis sighed. "Well, at least *that* hasn't changed."

Christina bit her lower lip. "A human being is like a diamond, Alex. From one angle he may appear flawed, while from the other . . . Cousin Charles has always shown us so much care—my mother and me, that is."

Intrigued, Alexis asked, "Really? So there's a vulnerable side to the old man?"

She laughed. "I like him. Since we left Austria, no one but Cousin Charles has tried to help us. He comes to see us all the time. We look forward to it, Mama and I. He brings us little goodies—dried fruits, things to eat you can't buy on the regular market. And he sits and talks to us, the way you and I are talking now. We sit in our living room and drink that horrible chicory coffee, and just chat. About everything and nothing. It's almost"—she hesitated, embarrassed—"it's almost like being a regular family. I've sometimes wished . . . well, that he were *my* father. It's been so long since I had a father—I've almost forgotten the one I had!"

Alexis smiled, but his smile was singularly bitter. With infinitely delicate fingers, he lifted Christina's chin. "You see?" he told her gently. "I told you then, four years ago, that time would heal some of the pain."

Her eyes, blue like her mother's, were probing his face. "But it hasn't healed yours, Alex."

And they looked at each other, a long and penetrating gaze. Slowly, but with the strength of forethought, Alexis Lévy–de Rochefleur cupped Christina Habig's face into his hands, and bent down to part her lips with his own.

He didn't close his eyes until she had wound her arms around his neck, and allowed his tongue to find hers, yielding rapturously to the thrill of their first kiss. Her body felt soft and supple in his arms, and when he pulled her toward him, she responded by uttering a little cry that delighted him to the very core of his being.

From an upstairs window, Charles saw Anne's son kiss Amelia's daughter, and a sudden red fury swelled inside him. Amelia and Tina were *his* business, no one else's! And though he could not understand it himself, he felt their kiss as a personal violation, an affront. For an unspoken pact had formed between Charles and the Habig women: More than he and Anne, and Alexis, he and Amelia and Tina had developed a real closeness. The Habig women had belonged to *him* since the day Charles moved them into their residence at number 12, Villa Herran.

Alexis, damn him, had intruded on the only part of his life that was his alone, that he had grown to treasure.

* * *

There was an uncanny resemblance between Madame Robert Stern and Jeanne Netter, Anne thought, giving her attention to the young woman seated opposite her on the sofa. Lucie Stern had Jeanne's oval face; her wide blue eyes; the same sweet smile, similar blond, upswept hair and the feminine gestures that had at one time so endeared Jeanne to the members of her beloved WIZO.

Yet Jeanne Netter had sorely disillusioned her former friends. Her conversion to Catholicism had profoundly shattered her friends' belief in the integrity of their president. Now the WIZO had disbanded, because Jews in Paris, even prominent ones, had been forced out of the public eye. Most had left the occupied zone while it was still possible. Others, like Amelia, lived in retreat, using false identity cards. But not the wife of Robert Stern, the distinguished Zionist leader.

"I'd like to ask you something, Anne," Lucie now ventured. "Why have you remained in the occupied zone? A Swiss citizen by marriage, surely you would be safer in Switzerland!"

There was something fervently appealing to Anne about Madame Stern. And for so long now, since her discovery that Charles had bought the brooch for Amelia, there had been *no one to confide in.* She made up her mind, and looked directly into Lucie's eyes.

"My husband is involved in something," she said, her heart beating rapidly. "It has to do with the underground, and with Armand Fayard. More than that, I couldn't tell you. But . . ." Her eyes moistened, and she continued. "Alexis, my son, is in it with Charles. I don't ask, and neither of them has volunteered to tell me anything. But that's why we're still here." Then, as if she had just mentioned an inconsequential charity ball, or some casual gossip, she tossed off, "Anyway, we're Swiss, and so far, the Swiss passport has overridden the fact that we're Jews. We're not required to wear the star, you see."

Lucie smiled. Her smile had the compassion Anne had once read in Jeanne's.

"My dear Anne," Lucie said, her voice all at once full of entreaty. "Please listen to me. *The Jews of Paris are in desperate straits!* Almost every night, the Gestapo has been going through apartment buildings and houses, rounding up the Jews they can still find and sending them off to Drancy."

"Drancy?"

"It's a collection camp. Oh, Anne . . . the stories that have come back to us are incredible! From this place, they are sending the Jews to Poland and no one has ever heard a further word from their deported relatives! *We are being rounded up and killed off,* Anne! And that's why I've come to you, my dear."

"I don't understand . . ." she demurred nervously. *Drancy.* She'd been hearing this name more and more, recently, from Alexis, from the underground radio.

"You will. Anne, some of our people have been luckier than others. They've managed to temporarily escape detection during a raid. But the key word here is *temporarily.* For once the Gestapo is on to someone, they're bound to return. We need to form an underground network to give refuge to these people, and I thought that, well, since La Folie is so spacious, and you have the Swiss passport, this would be an ideal halfway house, or temporary refuge, for some of these people until we can find them a permanent residence in a tiny village away from here."

Anne felt the blood rushing to her temples. "Lucie, I . . ." A vision of Charles's face haunted her inner vision. He was a Jew in spite of himself, a Jew who'd never felt Jewish a day in his life. Whatever he was doing on behalf of the underground, she knew that he was doing it to please Fayard, or perhaps in some vague patriotic attempt to help the Free French. But *not on behalf of the Jewish people.* Anne held few illusions at this point in her life, and her husband's views had grown clearer and clearer to her as the years had passed. She still loved Charles—oh, *how fiercely* she loved him! But her love was no longer tinged by any hint of hero-worship.

"Lucie," Anne murmured, embarrassed. "Charles isn't a Zion-ist. And this is his house, as well as mine. I couldn't do that, even if, in my heart, I totally support what you are about to do!" Her eyes were glistening and her fingers trembled as she played with the tassel on her belt.

Lucie's blue eyes drilled into her, all at once relentless. "Anne Levy, I don't care whether your elegant Swiss husband has made every effort to hide his original surname behind your innocuously French 'de Rochefleur'! You are a Jew, and you have here a roof and many rooms to put at the disposal of men, women, and chil-dren who, without your help, will be sent to their deaths! Is *this* why you once joined the WIZO? To put *their deaths* on your con-science? Or are you going to tell Monsieur de Rochefleur that, willing or not, you are going to help your own people?"

Silence hung heavy in the room as the two women sat staring at each other, Lucie as shocked as Anne by her own words. Finally Anne whispered: "I'll help. Of course I'll help."

Madame Stern reached over and embraced her.

* * *

Anne had never imagined herself capable of engineering such a complicated affair.

The first hideaway had been rather simple: Yadzia Mouchkate. The legal age for arresting and deporting Jews was between fifteen and fifty-five. Madame Mouchkate, Anne decided, had perhaps reached the limit, perhaps not. She was a small Polish lady dressed in mourning clothes. "I've been a widow for twenty years," she hesitantly explained to Anne in her accented French.

She arrived with Lucie Stern, who quickly explained what had happened. Madame Mouchkate had gone to visit a friend in Passy —near where Amelia and Christina lived—and had arrived just as the Gestapo had been taking her friend away. Her friend had looked right through her, as if not knowing her, and had thus spared her from being taken too. But Madame Mouchkate had become afraid and had made contact with the Sterns . . . and here she was.

"In a few weeks, we'll come back for her," Lucie assured Anne. "But in the meantime, the Nazis would never think to look for her so far from where she's registered. That's in the Boulevard Murat —way over near the Place de la Porte de Saint-Cloud."

Anne smiled and grasped Yadzia Mouchkate's hands, which
were frozen, even though it was July and humidly hot both outside
and in. Afterward, when she had settled Madame Mouchkate into
the guest wing, telling her that under no circumstances was she to
make the slightest noise or to appear outside unless she heard three
rapid knocks on her door, Anne hurried into the kitchen, where
Marie Goujon was busy preparing soup.

"We have a problem," Anne announced nervously.

The old cook wiped her hands on her clean apron, and came
over. "Madame needn't be afraid," she murmured. Then, suspi-
ciously, "Does it have anything to do with the *Boches*?"

"Yes. And with Monsieur." She paused, gazing at her old servant and trying to decide whether she could trust her. She'd given
her word to Lucie without really having thought things through
. . . and without having had the slightest intention of leveling
with Charles about this matter. He would never understand, and
he would have forced her to go back on her promise.

Anne had no choice. She *had* to trust the Goujons.

"There's a woman here," she said slowly. "A refugee. We're
going to have to hide her for a short while, until Madame Stern can
find her a permanent place to live."

Marie's old peasant face creased with compassion. "A *Jewish*
woman?"

Anne nodded. The question of religion had never come up between her family and her servants. She wondered if they had even
realized that the de Rochefleurs were of the Mosaic faith. Now, ill
at ease, she waited, remembering old Russian peasant women who
had thought that Jews were born with horns, and were related to
the devil. But Marie said, very gently, "Madame needn't worry."

"You don't seem to understand, Marie," Anne cut in. "She's
registered in Paris, in the Saint-Cloud district! How are we going to
get food for her *here*?"

The old cook shrugged. "Simple, Madame. Aristide will just
have to go into town and do her shopping for her. Not every day,
but often enough. And this brings up another question: I think it's
high time Madame stopped being more royalist than the king and
let us buy food on the black market! Madame thinks it's very noble
to stick to one's allotted rations, but Monsieur Alexis is twenty-one
now, and has lost his special *J.3* privileges. Anyone who can afford
it is buying on the side! We're going to be needing all the food we

can lay our hands on, if Madame intends to hide anyone
else. . . ."

And this was how, much to their surprise, Charles and Alexis
began to eat real meals again. Tiny portions, but of what luxurious
quality! Chicken broth with noodles, which Alexis had not tasted
since the beginning of the Occupation, and Charles had eaten only
out of town or in other rich men's homes. Real white bread, with
real butter, not animal grease or lard. Meat, in a rich stew, and
white beans. And, finally, fruit. The Germans had prepurchased all
the fruit off the trees, and it was only with the utmost discretion
that the farmers sold to the black marketeers, who brought their
loot back to the city in the dead of night, selling it to particulars,
such as Goujon, for exorbitant prices. Had the Germans caught
any of the participants of this clandestine operation, they would all
have been summarily deported.

Alexis pushed his food away, the first time it was presented to
him. He watched his father eating heartily, and his mother nib-
bling nervously. Something was afoot, and so he said nothing, re-
serving his indignation for later, when he was alone with his
mother. After the meal, he went to her boudoir to confront her.

"Why are we eating this way, Mama?" he asked her quietly.

It was the first time her son had come to her in a long, long time.
They were alone, and Anne suddenly felt afraid . . . afraid to lose
him again. She sighed, and said in exasperation, "You're such a
moralist, Alexis! Why is it you young people feel it's your divine
right to judge everything your parents do?"

"*I'm* not the moralist," he countered. "It was *you* who decided,
long ago, that we should eat no differently from anyone else. I'd
just like you to explain what's changed your mind."

And so, looking at him earnestly, she told him. About Lucie
Stern, about Yadzia Mouchkate, about the Goujons who were
helping. And, most of all, she told him, fearfully, that Charles was
not to be apprised of any of this. At the end of her speech, Alexis
smiled. It was the first genuine smile she had received from him
since the day he had learned of his supposed heart problem.

"I love you, Mother," he said to her, and then he kissed her,
holding her very close. Anne dissolved into tears against his chest,
and knew at that very moment that she had done the right thing by
going along with Madame Stern.

*   *   *

The second time Lucie Stern came, she brought two people. Anne was going over the household accounts in the study downstairs when Goujon knocked with his usual delicacy, and, sticking his head inside the room, announced in a softly modulated voice: "Madame Stern is here. I have put *them* in the gallery. . . ."

Anne caught the plural *them,* and thought: Lucie is exaggerating! Where on earth does she suppose I can fit more people? For, though Madame Stern had promised to find permanent lodgings as soon as possible for Madame Mouchkate, the Polish refugee had by this time been hiding in the guest quarters for three weeks.

In the gallery, she found her friend and a strange couple. "Anne, dear," Lucie said, "I'd like to present to you Madame Xenia Chatzky, and Mr. Moïse Rabinkov." The man was in his early fifties, small of stature and thin of frame, with a long face, bright black eyes, a sparse head of hair, and bad teeth—hardly an appealing specimen, Anne thought. On the other hand, Madame Chatzky, about forty-two, was blond, with fine, aristocratic features: a slender, pointed nose, slanted eyes with long, curling lashes, and the elegant figure of a lady born and bred.

"How do you do," Anne said, sitting down. She was filled with questions, but she stilled them, waiting.

Lucie then told her a strange story. The two people she had brought both came from Russia. Mr. Rabinkov was a dealer in secondhand jewelry who had married in the city of Riga and emigrated to Paris during the revolution. There, his wife had lost her mind and hurled herself out of the window of their apartment. Alone and desperate, Rabinkov had moved to a residential hotel near the Champ-de-Mars, on the Boulevard de Grenelle—a modest place mostly inhabited by blue-collar workers, but clean enough and convenient for moving about town to meet his customers.

Xenia Chatzky had studied chemistry in Moscow, and had been married to two men. The first had died early in the marriage, and the second, a professor of philosophy, had left her to move to Chile to take over a chair at the University of Santiago. Although not legally divorced, his wife had moved to Paris by herself and had started a small business manufacturing beaded evening bags, which she had sold, before the war, to exclusive boutiques. Someone introduced her to Mr. Rabinkov, who had befriended her and encouraged her to rent a room in his hotel. Hers had been on the fourth floor, his on the fifth.

But it so happened that just last night, the Gestapo had raided their hotel. They had swept through the first three floors, looking for Jews, and now Madame Chatzky and Mr. Rabinkov were afraid that they might return and go through the remaining three stories. Lucie had brought them both to Anne, after having new identification cards made for each of them.

"We'll have to put them in with Madame Mouchkate," Anne said. "But the problem is, either Mr. Rabinkov will have to sleep on the love seat in the small sitting room, or . . . he'll have to share Madame Chatzky's room." Blushing, she added, quickly, "But, of course, there are two beds in that room—"

"That may be just as well," Lucie declared. "The man who made their cards was in a hurry, and thought he'd make life easier for himself if he turned them into husband and wife. So, from 'Moïse Rabinkov,' he invented 'Michel Robin,' and from 'Xenia,' such a typically Russian name, he was only able to come up with 'Xavière.' Anything with the monogram *C* will have to be explained away due to their very recent marriage."

Anne frowned slightly and for a moment was silent. Finally she sighed, and stood up. "When you're trying to save your skin," she said to Xenia Chatzky, "no one is going to observe formalities. You'll sleep in the second guest bedroom, and we needn't tell the servants or Madame Mouchkate the truth—that you aren't really married, that is."

"Darling," Lucie Stern told her, "nobody likes how we've come to live. *Nobody!* But the fact is, there is no room left now for old-fashioned decorum."

Anne nodded. How times were changing, she thought wryly. But none of this mattered. She was more concerned about how she was going to hide three people now, instead of one, from Charles. To her, he loomed a far more immediate menace than the pale remembrance of the two German officers who had come, a year and a half before, to requisition La Folie, and who had been disarmed by seeing *Mein Kampf* in her hand.

It was Alexis who somehow found a solution to the dilemma at hand.

Twice a week old Aristide Goujon had been taking the train into town and queuing to buy sausage, sugar, gas, dairy products, and bread for Yadzia Mouchkate (whose brand-new identity card now spelled out the name "Yolande Monot.") He had been going to the Porte de Saint-Cloud, where the poor woman was still registered; now he simply traveled southeast to the area below the Eiffel

Tower, in the La Motte-Picquet district adjacent to the Boulevard de Grenelle, where the Robins—Madame Chatzky and Monsieur Rabinkov—had been registered.

But the de Rochefleur butler was an old man, and the lines were long. Several times already, Charles had remarked how Goujon, contrary to his usual routine, had forgotten to polish the silver, or had left the lights on in the study, wasting electricity. Humiliated, the exhausted Goujon wrung his hands, saying nothing, his thin lips twisting into a grimace of acute distress. Anne's eyes had flown to his, apologetic. But inside their hazel irises the old maître d'hôtel had read only fear, and her plea not to give up on the duties he had undertaken to help the three refugees.

Alexis understood everything at a single glance. After dinner, he had announced to his mother in private that henceforth, to alleviate Goujon's load, he himself would take on the Robins' shopping.

"Don't worry," he assured her. "I'll find time off from my summer job. I'm sure Monsieur Fayard will let me go."

What he did not say was that this would give him an excuse to drop in on his cousins, Amelia and Christina. Tina had just finished her penultimate year of high school, and was waiting for the results of her first baccalaureate examination. If she passed, she would be admitted to her final year, crowned by the grueling second baccalaureate without which no French student could enter a university. But she was on holiday now, and her days were free.

The rue de la Pompe was close enough to the La Motte-Picquet area for the young man to walk over and share a cup of watered-down tea with her after shopping for Madame Chatzky and Monsieur Rabinkov.

All that remained would be to explain his twice a week delinquency from work to his father, and to Armand Fayard.

* * *

"You're asking me for time off, but you're not telling me why," the old steelman commented from his leather armchair. "What it sounds like to me is an assignation with a member of the female sex."

Alexis brought his hand up to his lips, to hide a smile. "Well, sir," he said. "It's something like that. . . ."

The chess board stood between them like a field of armed warriors. Alexis moved a white rook forward to capture one of Fayard's black bishops, and the old man's eyebrows rose. With amusement, perhaps, Alexis thought: but hardly with surprise. Very little under the sun surprised *that* old fox. . . .

"You let me do that on purpose," the young man chided his boss. Their eyes met, and held each other's stare, intent and in strange communion. Armand Fayard was seventy-six years old, Alexis twenty-one. Yet they read each other openly and with a trust that had existed almost from the start . . . a trust, Alexis thought with wonder and awe, that he had never felt toward Charles, nor his father toward him.

"But tell me why I should let you out of the office to see this young lady," Fayard demanded. "Working hours are not for flirting with your paramour. Your time is valuable to me."

Alexis regarded him for a moment. "My time is valuable to you in Nancy, and in the Morvan," he commented lightly. "This is the first time I've ever asked for something in return."

Armand Fayard sighed heavily. "Is she worth it, son? Or is it just a . . . sexual peccadillo?"

Alexis felt the blood rushing to his cheeks. "Monsieur Fayard," he said, all at once earnest and direct. "It's nothing sexual at all. It's . . . my cousin, Christina Habig. I think I'm—well, I like her an awful lot."

Fayard's brows rose again, and he nodded, pursing his lips. His eyes seemed unfocused and dreamy, as though, for some reason, the mention of Christina's name had sent him back in time, to another Christina, or another Habig. A little surprised, Alexis inquired, "Do you know my cousin, sir?"

"I once knew of her mother, a long time ago," Armand Fayard replied, his fingers suddenly frail over the beautifully carved ebony queen he had started to caress in absentminded fashion. "And she broke quite a few hearts, as I recall. . . ."

Then, abruptly, Armand Fayard moved his queen toward Alexis's rook, and flicked the latter roughly to the side. "Check, and mate. You can't get away, my boy. I've got you cornered."

Neither had seen the door to Fayard's office silently opening. But as Alexis rose he felt someone behind him, and turned to face her. He had smelled the rich musk of her perfume, and now, seeing her again after a number of years, he felt taken aback by her sudden proximity. "Good afternoon, Madame Fayard," he said politely.

She was exquisite in a black cotton skirt that molded her figure, and a white tailored blouse that showed off her bustline. Her platinum hair was topped by a wide-brimmed summer hat trimmed with black ribbon, and her black and white pumps added the final touch of style to turn her into a fashion model from the glossy pages of a prewar magazine.

"Do you remember young de Rochefleur, Arabella?" Armand said conversationally, making an expansive introduction with his hand. "He's beating me at chess now, regularly. But not today!"

"It takes quite a man to beat my husband at anything," Arabella stated, smiling. She was standing beside Alexis now, and he felt almost overpowered by the closeness of her body. He remembered his first impression of her: that she and his father might have been having an affair. And though it had made Alexis angry, he also recalled sensing something else . . . that this woman, this sophisticated female, had *liked him too*. Or had this merely been wishful thinking on the part of the seventeen-year-old boy?

"Leave Alex alone, Bella," old man Fayard cut in, amusement in his voice. "He's in love, and rushing off to his beloved. So for God's sake, get out of his way!"

Why was it that she replied, quite acidly, " '*In love?*' Isn't that a little trite, even for one so young?" Later, Alexis would repeat this line to himself, wondering why her eyes had seized him like a cat's, causing his steps to slow down at the door while he remained watching her, mesmerized.

She was an *old woman,* older than his mother, and Christina was young, fresh, and trusting. Alexis sighed, wondering why it was that in life, nothing was ever fair or predictable. Why had he not met a woman like that, but *available,* not married to the man he most esteemed in the entire world. And why had he not met such a woman before falling in love with Christina Habig?

Arabella was saying to her husband, "So, you've taken on another de Rochefleur? They seem to fascinate you, don't they?"

But Armand's eyes held little humor as he answered her. "This 'fascination' seems to run in our family," he said dryly.

CHAPTER XX

In the month of June 1942, only weeks after Alexis had first kissed her, Christina took her baccalaureate examination. A single year remained until she graduated from the private girls' day school she had been attending. But now she was on summer hiatus, and had time on her hands.

She had grown into a lovely young woman, with pronounced cheekbones, translucent skin, and almond-shaped eyes, like Amelia's a deep peacock-blue. Now that July was almost over, she discovered that her entire existence was revolving around visits from Alexis.

She did the marketing for her mother, and visited an occasional friend. Her mother was afraid to let her socialize with girls whose families were not personally known to her—for who could trust anybody's integrity, these days? But mostly the young girl waited for Alexis to come from his summer job at Fayard Industries. He only visited twice a week, on Tuesdays and Fridays, but on the other days Christina daydreamed about him, sitting for hours by the window, ostensibly sewing or reading a novel, her mind always wandering back to Alexis.

Why didn't Cousin Charlie approve? One evening last week he had stopped by to spend time with her mother just as Christina and Alexis were returning from a trip to the grocery for the Robins. Alexis had warned her to say nothing of this to his father, and so they'd pretended to be coming in from a casual stroll in the Bois de Boulogne.

Charles de Rochefleur was drinking tea with her mother, in the drawing room. Christina had been very glad to see him, and her face had brightened. But she hesitated and did not embrace him, for she saw the stony expression on his handsome face. Charles stared at Alexis and demanded, his voice unexpectedly hard, "What are *you* doing here?"

Alex handled the situation with great aplomb, although she felt him wince and take the words as a personal blow. "I just came to visit Tina," he replied mildly. "Monsieur Fayard gave me some time off."

"Really?"

Finally father and son had run into each other *here,* in the rue de la Pompe. Christina's mother rose, in a swift, sudden motion, alarm on her face. Placing a gentle hand on Alexis's shoulder, she turned to Charles and said, very softly: "Alex has been of invaluable support to Tina. I've been so grateful for his attentiveness, for his caring. So few of our friends know where to find us, and it's been lonely for *her,* especially. . . ."

But Charles ignored her. Marching over to the two young people, he addressed Alexis. Charles's face was crimson. "The Habigs are none of your concern," he told him bluntly, his voice piercingly cold. "From now on, I expect you to stay away from here, and not to try to see Tina again."

Horrified, the young girl sprang forward, tears filling her eyes. She cried out: "But *why,* Cousin Charles? We've done nothing wrong! Don't take Alex away from us—*please* don't. . . ."

"Isn't my daughter good enough for your son?" Amelia demanded, her tone suddenly angry, though her voice was low. And she gave Charles a look of hurt and outrage that made him turn aside, overcome.

Alexis took Amelia's hand and squeezed it, and answered for Charles. "You didn't understand, but *I did.* It's the other way around, I'm afraid: *I'm* the one who's not good enough, Cousin Amelia. But it doesn't matter. Unless you personally forbid me to come here, I shan't stop my visits. Tina and I have nothing to hide: we're good friends, and besides, I'm twenty-one and old enough to come and go as I please, Father."

Christina was proud of him, and her face flushed with joy. He had stood up for what he believed, for what he wanted. But was that the only emotion he felt when he was with her? *Friendship?*

But, in the kitchen, while they stood waiting for the kettle to boil, Alex suddenly grabbed Christina and kissed her, pushing her against the cupboard and plunging his tongue way inside her mouth, with a fierce passion that took her completely by surprise. And that kiss was certainly not one of pure friendship. . . .

* * *

One day, Madame Mouchkate shyly told Anne about Vera Tversky. The Tverskys, originally from Uman in Podolia, were extremely rich and lived in the Boulevard Exelmans in the Sixteenth Arrondissement. "Vera used to take piano lessons from me, and we became friends," Yadzia Mouchkate explained. "Now she's sent me this note through Lucie Stern that if someone will come to her house every Tuesday, she will give him a whole stick of butter, a good slab of white bread, and either beans, sugar, or cheese, for me."

Madame Mouchkate was embarrassed, wondering whether an additional trip to Madame Tversky would be ill-received by her gracious hostess. But Anne nodded understandingly, and said, "My son will go. He stops in to see our cousins twice a week when he picks up groceries for the Robins." Nobody ever referred to Xenia Chatzky and Moïse Rabinkov as anything other than "Monsieur and Madame Robin," although poor Madame Chatzky, Anne guessed, wasn't overly pleased by this turn of events, never having entertained the slightest notion of marrying the devout little Jew from Riga.

Anne had taken the custom of visiting with her "hideaways" almost every afternoon. She liked to practice her native Russian with the Robins; and Madame Mouchkate, always self-effacing and trembling with fear, filled her with pity. Once in a while she allowed them to take a brief walk inside their part of the garden enclosure, when she knew that Charles was far removed in his Paris office. In the beginning Anne had fervently prayed that Lucie Stern would find them all a permanent place to live as soon as possible, but as time went by, she had come to enjoy their presence, and even to hope that they would stay at La Folie. Yadzia had been there for nearly two months, the Robins for a little longer than one.

For the first time in many years, Anne de Rochefleur felt that there was a purpose in her life, people who depended on her care, who trusted her to keep them safe. She was important to someone other than her son, who, self-sufficient and strong-willed, loved her as young men tend to love their mothers . . . from a distance created by the generational and gender gaps that separated them.

Alexis found Vera Tversky quite charming; she was around his mother's age, of medium height, slender, with dark eyes and a small, upturned nose, a pretty woman. Mr. Tversky was an elegant, dapper man, older than his wife whom he blindly worshiped. They had a nine-year-old son, Léo, who was more than moderately retarded.

The last Tuesday in July, Alexis had first stopped by to pick up Yadzia Mouchkate's special rations, and Vera Tversky served him a late lunch of fresh noodles, bread and butter, and fruits. He had learned that one should ask no questions of anyone, during these strange days of the Nazi Occupation, and since Madame Mouchkate had assured him that the Tverskys were not collaborators, he had merely wondered what profession Monsieur might be practicing, to enable him to purchase such expensive foodstuffs on the black market.

But since the Tverskys volunteered no explanation, he accepted their lunch at face value, and the next time, brought along Christina, who didn't often get the opportunity to eat such fine meals.

Madame Tversky was very talkative, and she liked to complain. Léo, her son, had robbed her of a fine career as an artist, she confided in Alexis and Christina. The child was rambunctious, and had reached the mental level of a five-year-old, at best. He irritated his mother, but Christina's heart went out to him, and she tried to invent games for him that he might follow without too great an effort.

Unexpectedly thankful, Madame Tversky gave her a job to do. "Since you're in the middle of your summer vacation," she proposed, "why don't you take these pairs of my stockings home with you and darn them for me? I can't stand to do it, and I'm sure a young girl like you would enjoy the chance to earn some extra money."

Then, to Christina's amazement, Vera Tversky handed her a canvas bag and pulled out about fifteen pairs of ladies' stockings. All were of the softest silk. "I'll have more for you when you bring these back," she announced, patting the young girl on the shoulder. Where had the Tverskys come up with the money for such unheard-of luxury?

But Vera Tversky confided in Alexis that she and her husband were growing more and more worried about the Germans. They had been moving their personal effects to the tiny maid's room they owned on the seventh floor, to hide there in case the times became yet more dangerous and the Gestapo came to arrest them. The janitor, richly bribed by Monsieur, had promised never to reveal their secret hideaway. Madame took Alexis and Christina upstairs,

and showed them two folding beds, some slipcovers, a Bunsen
burner and a few liters of paraffin for it, plus some crockery and
several pots and pans.

The second week in August, when the young people arrived for
lunch, Vera Tversky explained to them, "We're sleeping upstairs
now, since raids always occur during the night. And should they
come for us, our janitor will take the Gestapo to our empty flat,
and tell them we have run away somewhere. What do you think?"

"As long as you feel you can trust this man," Alexis remarked,
"then your plan is a good one."

But the Tversky mystery continued to keep him and Christina
guessing. Who were these people, and where did their fortune
come from?

"I guess it doesn't really matter," Tina shrugged. "They're Jews,
just like us, afraid of being deported." Nothing else held any significance beyond this point of survival.

* * *

Anne hadn't been able to go to sleep, and, tossing and turning in
her bed, had finally risen and slipped on a housecoat. In August the
nights were stiflingly hot, and she walked downstairs and into the
garden, hoping to still her disquieting thoughts.

Amelia and Charles. The image of the two of them, making love,
kept haunting her. She visualized it at the most unexpected moments, and then she would start to hate her cousin once again, with
renewed rancor and pain. Yet, oddly, she couldn't hate *Charles. He
had always loved Amelia—he couldn't help the affair.* But Amelia
was a woman, and it was up to the woman to set her boundaries
and act decently.

Anne looked up at the beautiful stone mansion that had been her
home for twenty-five years. A quarter of a century. She held no
illusions: Charles also loved the house, and a large part of his
reason for marrying her had been because of La Folie. Yet, when
Anne was young, she had wished for only a single dream to come
true: that Charles Lévy might marry her, *for whatever reason.* And
he had, hadn't he?

All at once a strange smell wafted down to her in the soft night
breeze. It seemed to come from the guest wing, and, alarmed, she
looked up. A red flame seemed to be delineated in the window of
the Robins' bedroom, a flame that danced in the moonlight.

It can't be, Anne thought, panic-stricken. Then the window
opened, and she heard anguished cries: Madame Mouchkate's

voice! Anne picked up the long skirt of her housecoat and rushed
into the house, through the entryway into the smaller wing of the
building. She tore up the staircase, out of breath. As she raced
through the door to the little sitting room, she saw, aghast, that the
curtains were indeed on fire in the Robins' room. She ran in, bump-
ing into Xenia, who was running out, carrying a small pail to fill
with water. "Moïse fell asleep in front of the window," Xenia
Chatzky told her breathlessly. "His pipe was still lit and his newspaper caught on fire."

Yadzia Mouchkate was throwing more water on the singed drapery. Anne went into the sitting room, and returned with a tall,
wide crystal vase, which she filled with water from the bathroom.
Then the three women busied themselves trying to extinguish the
small fire, and after a few frantic minutes it was Yadzia who succeeded, hurling her bedspread over the flames and quelling the
conflagration.

Their faces drenched with perspiration, Anne, Yadzia, and Xenia collapsed on the latter's bed, and it was then, and only then,
that Anne noticed Moïse Rabinkov. His face a gray, ashen hue, he
lay huddled on his own twin bed, his jaw trembling. Furious, Anne
turned on him: "Why didn't you help us?" she cried. "Three
women, trying to fix the mess *you* started . . . ! What kind of a
man are you, anyway?"

But he simply stared at her, paralyzed with fear. He was saved
from Anne's outrage by the surprising entrance of Alexis, in his
pajamas, his hair tousled and uncombed. *"Quick!"* the young man
ordered. "Father's on his way up to check out the commotion. Get
Madame Mouchkate and the Robins out the back way, into the
garden, while I stall and tell him *I*'ve been staying here, to study
for my year-end finals!"

Guiltily, from below the windows in the small garden, Anne
tried to make out how her son had chosen to justify his occupancy
of the guest suite to Charles.

"I needed to be by myself," Alexis was explaining, the reasonable tone of his voice in total contrast to the fear and anxiety Anne
was feeling. "The exams are terribly difficult, Father, and I needed
to concentrate."

"Your room is plenty large enough," Charles countered furiously. "And why did you have to go behind our backs?"

"It was . . . well . . . there was more to it than just the
finals." Now Alexis's tone was apologetic, almost embarrassed.

"There was . . . someone I wanted to be with, alone, once in a while. Don't you understand, Father? A *woman*—just a waitress I know. Mama wouldn't have been too happy about it, so . . ."

"My guest suite is not a goddamned bordello!" Charles shouted.

"I'm sorry. It was careless, I know, to smoke so close to the window. I was . . . well, I suppose the strain of the exams had gotten to me. It won't happen again, Father, I promise."

"You'd better stay away from here!" Charles warned, but his voice reflected a measure of confusion and anger. The boy had thrown him off guard—for now, that is. But he couldn't help adding: "Next time you cross me, young man, I'm going to throw you out!"

Anne, suddenly cold, pulled her robe more tightly around her shivering body, and cast down her face.

* * *

The Tversky household was in a state of chaos when the two young people arrived. Christina felt herself breaking out in a cold sweat. Madame Tversky, her hands shaking, her face distraught and haggard, was throwing clothes haphazardly into an open suitcase. "They came!" she whispered. "They came!"

Quickly, Alexis crossed the room to a sideboard, and poured a jiggerful of cognac into a small snifter. He brought it over to Vera Tversky. "Here, drink this down. And tell us what exactly happened to unnerve you so."

In a quivering voice, Vera Tversky explained. At 5:00 A.M. she had been awakened by loud noises and realized that the janitor, whose palm her husband had so handsomely greased, was bringing the Gestapo directly to the door of their mansard room. When the key turned in the lock, she had jumped out of bed and hidden behind the door, which opened inward. The Germans hadn't seen her, but had grabbed her husband and taken him away, leaving the sleeping Léo in his bed.

"Léo is at school now," Madame Tversky said, nearly choking on her words. "One of his teachers promised to keep him with her for a few days. I was just throwing some of his things into that suitcase, to take to her for him."

"What about you?" Alexis demanded.

"I'll go somewhere, I guess," she answered vaguely.

"Where?" the young man insisted.

Her black eyes found his. "I have nowhere to go," she said simply.

"So you'll come home with me," Alexis told her. "You'll just have to go into hiding with the Robins and Madame Mouchkate. At least you don't smoke and aren't going to set the house on fire!" Madame Tversky, bewildered by these last words, burst into tears.

On the way to Saint-German-en-Laye, she turned to Alexis, her face ashen. "I have some things, important documents and some valuables I need. But they're in the cellar of my apartment building. Would you, Alexis, go and ask the janitor to let you in? They're things I've had since my childhood in Russia. . . ."

Alexis sighed. He could, at the moment, think of nothing worse than having to face the man who had turned in Monsieur Tversky. But Vera Tversky was devastated, and he had learned long ago, with his mother, that it was always better to give in to a woman approaching hysteria.

Thank God he was on his summer break and had no law school to rush to as soon as he awakened. "All right," he told her. "I'll go tomorrow morning."

* * *

The janitor recognized Alexis from his previous visits to the Tverskys' with Christina. "I'd like to go down to their cellar," the young man told him. "Would you take me?"

The janitor scratched his head. He was no more than twenty-five years old, dark like Alexis. "It's not that I won't take you there," he stammered. "But you know how the Gestapo seals off the apartments of those they've come to arrest. Come back tomorrow: I'll find a way to remove the seals, and you can take what you want. Afterward, I'll replace the seals the way they were."

Alexis felt himself stiffen. The man who had sold out the Tverskys was now asking him to return the following day, at a specific time. Was he going to call the Gestapo? Would Alexis find them waiting for him when he arrived the next morning?

As if sensing Alex's suspicions, the janitor looked away and said, "I had no choice, Monsieur de Rochefleur. I'm an Italian, and only French citizens are allowed to have jobs like mine. When the Gestapo put a gun to my head, I had to think of my wife and baby. Even if those *Boches* didn't pull the trigger, they might have looked through my papers—and I just can't afford to lose this job!"

Alexis couldn't answer. A man had been deported, his wife had taken refuge in the guest wing of La Folie, separated from her only child . . . and this man was speaking about a job.

"I'm risking my *own* job to come down here," Alex finally said.

"This very minute, my boss may be looking for me. But all right—I'll be back tomorrow. You'd better not be lying—and the seals had better be gone!"

That evening, when Alex came home, his mother told him that Lucie Stern had come for the Robins. She and her husband had found a place for them to stay out the war, not far from Paris, in the country. So only Yadzia Mouchkate remained, and a hysterical Vera Tversky. Anne had prevailed upon Lucie to get the latter false papers, and henceforth, his mother announced, Vera Tversky would live as "Valérie Trévin."

But what of Léo? "He won't be able to stay at his teacher's forever," Alexis said. "And he's severely retarded. It's been hard enough to keep three adults hidden from Papa. A retarded child is all we need. . . ."

They exchanged a single look that spoke for both of them. Then Anne sighed. "We'll have to take the risk. We've already come *this* far, haven't we, son? And sooner or later, the war has to end. . . ."

Apart from the bulk of what Vera Tversky claimed she "needed," and which Alexis was forced to carry home on the métro and then the train, the Tversky retrieval operation went off without a hitch. This time, the janitor was as good as his word and was standing in front of the Tversky cellar the following morning. Alexis simply went in, found Vera's things, packed them into a bag he had brought, and departed half an hour later. Then he stopped off at the Habigs' for a breakfast of sorts—a strange porridge composed of various cooked grains, which Amelia served him in her fine Meissen bowl, placing a steaming cup of chicory coffee in front of him.

After Amelia had left the two young people alone, Christina went over to sit near Alexis. "What's going to happen now?" she asked anxiously.

"Well, as far as the Tverskys are concerned, I'd like to ask a favor. Could *you* pick Léo up from his teacher's this afternoon? I'll stop off for him tonight after work. But if I take any more time off, Fayard will think that you and I are up to all sorts of mischief . . . and he may fire me."

Christina frowned, perplexed. " 'Mischief'? What are you talking about, Alex? What is it you've been telling that old man?"

But a wave of embarrassment swept over him, and he lowered his eyes. "Nothing," he told her. "Nothing at all."

Why was it that the hardest words to say were also the most simple? His *I love you* stuck in his throat with the porridge, and he gulped it down with a mouthful of hot chicory coffee, unable to face Christina.

* * *

Léo Tversky, like all little boys, liked to run up each set of stairs leading to an entryway along the road. His school for slow-learning children was on the rue du Ranelagh, not far from the rue de la Pompe. But because she was trying to avoid German patrols, Christina decided to make a detour through tiny side streets.

As they made their way through the streets, the boy would run up the steps of the houses, then wait for her to lift him down. He was heavy, but she had grown to care about him, and it cost her nothing but time to help him down. Besides, like many retarded children, he was stubborn and physically strong, and saying no would only have made things more difficult for her.

But when they reached the crossroad of the Chaussée de la Muette and Avenue Mozart, Christina admitted defeat. The inviting entrance of a subway stood beckoning to her. Her back was cramped from having lifted Léo up and down so many times along the way, and now she suggested to the little boy, "How about going the rest of the way by métro?"

To her surprise, Léo jumped for joy. "Great! My Mama never lets me go on the métro!"

And neither does mine, Christina thought wryly. But she was glad she had found such an easy solution to getting Léo home. And so, taking him by the hand, she walked down the stairs into the long corridor.

As usual, the subway was crowded. "You keep hold of my hand, no matter what," Christina admonished Léo. All she needed now would be to lose him as she struggled to find space among the crowd of commuters. But luck was on her side. They were able to climb into a car that, though full, at least afforded them sufficient room to stand side by side. Léo caused no trouble, his eyes filled with bewilderment over so many new faces.

At the very next station, Christina propelled him out the doorway. "So soon?" he asked, disappointed.

"It's just one stop," she replied. "And my mother will give us something to eat when we get home."

"Tonight, am I going to see my mama?" he questioned.

"That's right. Alexis is going to come and pick you up. I bet this is one of the most exciting days you've ever had, right, Léo?"

They emerged into the wide and beautiful Avenue Henri-Martin, which crossed, just a hundred yards or so to the west, the rue de la Pompe where the Habigs lived. But Christina was surprised to find this customarily busy street, usually filled with men and women walking to the Bois de Boulogne or the Trocadéro, completely empty. A tremor of nervousness passed through her.

Only two young policemen were standing on the opposite pavement. The August sunlight played with the sunglasses one of them was wearing, and Léo began to jump up and down. "Look, Tina!" he cried. "The cop has funny eyes like a beetle!"

To her horror, the little boy dropped her hand abruptly and started to run across the street. She ran after him. But the policemen had seen what happened, and one of them retrieved the boy from the middle of the road. They waited for her to catch up to them on the other side.

"You'd better be careful, miss," the one with the glasses told her. "If there hadn't been an alert, a car might have run your brother down."

His words hit Christina like a jab in the stomach. "An alert? I never heard the siren go off. . . ."

"We saw you coming out of the métro," the other policeman remarked. "Probably your train had just pulled in when it resounded, or the line would have stopped and you'd have guessed what was going on."

"Yes," she admitted. "Sometimes we've been stopped for over an hour in a métro train."

"You're lucky you aren't Jewish," the policeman with glasses said. "We pick out the Jews right away by the yellow stars on their clothes. And Jews aren't allowed to be in the streets during an air raid."

Christina nodded mutely. Now the question was, how to get away from these men and to her house. As she started to walk away, holding tightly to Léo's hand, she heard one of the policemen call to her. "Mademoiselle, you'd better show us your papers, just for the record."

Christina froze. Her hands shaking, she worked the catch on her bag, and extracted her identity card. It was the first time anyone in authority had ever asked to see it.

"*Cécile Hautois?*" the young policeman read. "Is that your name?"

She nodded. Next to her, Léo, bored, was starting to fidget.

The policemen were exchanging glances. Christina felt an urge to vomit. She had never been so frightened in her life. But the policeman wearing sunglasses handed back her papers, and said, "Next time, mademoiselle, make sure to have somebody do a decent job for you. A real card always gets signed first, and *then* the seal gets stamped on top. On yours, the signature's been placed *over* the stamp. And another thing—don't pick a tiny hole-in-the-wall in Normandy as your place of birth. That's always a reason for suspicion. Pick a large city: Nice, Marseilles. It's a safer bet."

Christina stood trembling, uncomprehending. "Aren't you going to arrest us?" she whispered.

The two men looked uncomfortable. "No. But we'd better not see you again in this neighborhood. If so, we'd have little choice. As it is, we've helped a number of Jews escape detection, and our superior has become distrustful."

Tears were welling up in Christina's eyes. "But . . . why are two good men like you doing such nasty work?" she asked. "It doesn't make sense. . . ."

"Because, mademoiselle, we're able to warn a lot of people like you, and save a number of lives. *Somebody* has to have this job—and better us than those who follow all the Nazi rules."

Impulsively, she threw her arms around the neck of the policeman closest to her. "God bless you," she murmured. "And God keep you alive."

Then, tightening her hold on Léo's hand, she began to run toward the rue de la Pompe. Only the kindness of these officers had kept her and the child away from Drancy.

When Alexis came to pick up the little boy, he found Christina in a strange state, her hands cold and trembling as she poured him his cup of tea. "What's wrong?" he demanded.

Looking away from him, she told him about the afternoon's incident. "I haven't said anything to Mama," she added. "I didn't want her to be alarmed."

"I want you to pack your bags and come home with me at once —all three of you," he commanded. "That policeman said you shouldn't stay in this neighborhood."

"No. I'm not going to go to La Folie. And neither is my mother." She looked away from him, suddenly miserable. Then, turning to face him, she added in a trembling voice, "Cousin Charles and my mother are lovers, Alexis! They've tried to hide it from me, but the way they feel about each other, I'd have to be blind not to see! And I think your mother knows about it. That's why we don't visit her anymore." With urgency underscoring her decision, she said, "There's no way on earth we'd move to La Folie!"

He took her by the shoulders. She could tell he was greatly disturbed, his face distorted by a sudden anger and dismay. "Tina! We're talking about *your life,* and your safety! *I don't give a damn* about family quarrels, and clandestine love affairs that may or may not be taking place! My mother's already saved the lives of four strangers and you think she wouldn't save her own cousins? *We're a family,* Christina! That's all that matters now!"

Her blue eyes were brimming with tears, and Alexis put his arms around her and drew her close. "Tina," he pleaded. "Don't make things any harder than they already are. . . ."

But to his amazement she pulled away from him, and regarded him with a determined expression. "It would be wrong to try to live together under one roof," she told him. "And I'm not even going to suggest it to Mama."

Enraged, Alexis turned away and marched into the living room. Amelia and Léo were standing in the hallway, waiting for him. With the barest trace of politeness, Alexis pecked Amelia on the cheek and grasped hold of Léo's hand. "Tell Tina I won't be coming round for a while," he announced, shortly. "The Robins aren't with us anymore, and won't be needing their rations. Goujon can pick up the rations for the Tverskys when he goes into town for Madame Mouchkate."

Then he and the boy walked out the door, not looking back.

* * *

Alexis picked up his glasses from the enormous leather-bound mahogany table in the law library of Fayard Industries. In front of him stood a load of court transcripts. Beyond the narrow windows of beveled glass, the September sky shone a timid mimosa yellow. Alexis stuck his wire-rimmed spectacles on his nose and sighed, diving back into his research.

François Durand, wandering in with a casebook under his arm, called out, "Hey, pal! Did you mend fences with that girl of yours?"

Alexis felt a flare-up of annoyance, and as his friend came over he shook his head. The last thing he wanted to do right now was to think about Tina. But François had other matters on his mind as well, and had only come in to look through a legal dictionary. After a few moments, the young man found what he'd been looking for, and wandered off.

François had long since graduated and been admitted to the bar. He was now a bona fide member of the law firm that handled the bulk of the casework for Fayard Industries. He came in regularly to do his research at the library and to meet with some of the junior executives of the firm. Although no one was pleased that most of the contracts came from Germans, Alexis felt that his friend had moved a long way off from three years before, when he had first met him as a law student. Now François, for all his communist bravura, was a member of the establishment.

And who am *I*? Alexis wondered, suddenly appalled. I'm neither a lawyer yet nor a real student. Half of me is still running off to the Morvan while the other half is busy taking care of things at La Folie.

He had a father who frankly disliked him—with whom, since the incident of the draperies in the guest wing, he'd been on the verge of out-and-out warfare. And his mother was unable, by herself, to infuse him with strength simply by loving him. She was good, but she wasn't *enough*. There was old man Fayard, of course. And there had been, for a time, Christina.

"Well," a voice broke into his thoughts. "What have we *here*, if not young Galahad daydreaming the afternoon away?"

Alexis started, and rose in embarrassment. How long had Arabella Fayard been standing over him, with that amused expression on her face? She was clothed today in rich fall colors: deep greens, and vibrant rusts of varying hues. Emeralds glimmered at her ears, and she wore a huge square emerald ring on her finger. "Madame," he said. "I—"

"That's all right, Alex. May I call you 'Alex'? That's what Armand calls you, isn't it? He does love you so."

What was it she'd come for? "I love him too," he replied simply. How much easier to admit this, rather than the complex tangle of his emotions toward Charles. Or his need for Tina, who hadn't needed *him*, in the final analysis.

They were quite alone in the law library. Arabella perched on the table itself, near Alexis's transcripts, balancing one stockinged leg on the edge of his chair. "Sit down," she told him kindly.

But now she was above him, and he couldn't help noticing that her silk blouse had come unbuttoned right where her cleavage began.

"Is there anything I can do for you?" he asked, somewhat ill at ease.

Arabella sighed, her breasts rising and falling. "My dear boy . . ." She had marvelous eyes, and she smelled of jasmine and heady musks, reminding Alex of a hothouse filled with exotic blooms. . . . Suddenly she stared at him and said, almost brutally, "How does it happen that such a nice boy has come from a man like *Charles*?"

Alexis colored. "I—I really wouldn't know how to answer that."

"Well, don't, then. I take it you and your father aren't close?"

How did she know? Had the old man picked up on it and told her? Or had his father? Alexis felt terribly uncomfortable, and wished she would leave. But instead she took out a long gold case, and opened it, offering him a cigarette. He lit hers for her, and took one for himself, just to be polite.

"It really doesn't matter at all," Arabella said with a shrug. "You know, Alex, some very handsome men are born with something lacking. It's as though they were nothing more than hollow shells . . . perfect on the outside, empty within. Haven't you noticed?"

He was beginning to understand. "My father doesn't talk much to me," he said. "You're right—we're hardly close at all, so I couldn't tell you much about him."

Arabella took a long drag on her cigarette, and blew it out in little circles of blue smoke. "*I* could tell *you*. . . . But better yet, why don't we stop this silly talk of Charles, who doesn't interest me in the least, and go out for a drink at the Ritz? It's not far from here, and I hardly think Armand would notice your absence for just three-quarters of a very lovely hour. . . ."

This time, she had succeeded in shocking him. Alexis's mouth opened, and he stood awkwardly searching for words—when suddenly, appearing from out of nowhere, Christina Habig entered the library. Arabella noticed the change in his expression, the quickening of his eyes . . . and for a moment, her face took on the hard look of a sphynx, coldly furious and judgmental. Her high heels clicked as she landed on her feet, a short exclamation point of a woman.

"Well?" she demanded loudly. "Are we going to go?"

Christina, in a simple blue tailored coat, was standing in the doorway, her eyes wide and frightened, her fingers nervously pulling off her soft kid gloves.

"I'm sorry, Madame Fayard," Alexis said courteously. "But I have work to turn in at the end of the day, and I can't be late."

Up went the small, firm chin, and Arabella's eyes narrowed to green slits. "I can only admire your perseverance, Alexis," she said to him, each word like vinegar dropped on a burning wound. "Your father will be proud of you *yet.*" And she walked away, nodding briefly in the direction of Christina, who moved aside to let her pass.

She stood fumbling with the buttons on her coat, trying not to look at him. Alex removed his glasses because of the sudden mist in his eyes, and for a moment touched the bridge of his nose. Finally he stood up, put his glasses back on, and asked, "How are you, Tina?"

She shook her head, unable to speak. He felt that the advantage was now lying in his court, and he picked up on it. "What may I do for you?" he asked formally, parodying his earlier words to Fayard's wife.

"Oh, Alex . . ." She blinked, and tears fell on her cheeks. "I just . . . I mean, I had to . . ."

"What, Christina?" Until now, he had never felt the urge to hurt anyone, except his father—and that only after twenty-one years of continued abuse. Why was it that he could remain so calm, so cold, and so remote with this girl for whom he'd felt so much, and who was standing there so miserably, hoping he would come toward her?

"I couldn't stand our being apart," she declared softly, coming toward him. Now she was standing very close, but still he couldn't make himself go to her.

"Tina, you're a sweet girl, and you're my cousin, after all. You're right, it *was* a stupid quarrel that we had, and we should remain friends, shouldn't we?"

"Is that all it ever was for you, Alex?" she accused him, her pretty face haggard with pain, her eyes brimming with tears.

Alex shook his head, sighing deeply. "No, of course, it was more than that! We both know it. But you said things that enraged me, things that made me feel that barriers existed between us. . . ." All at once he turned on her, a month of anger tumbling out of him. "I was so hurt!" he cried. "I wanted us to be together—to share something special, and *to hell* with other complications! What else really matters besides you and me?"

She smiled timidly. "Is that what you feel?" she whispered.

Then Alexis nodded, yielding at last, and took her in his arms. He felt her hot tears on his neck and the last of his resistance melted away. "You know I love you, Tina," he murmured. "And I only feel good when we're together."

He bent his face toward hers, and eagerly her lips encountered his as she pressed her body against his with all the ardor of her youth and emotion. At that very moment, as he felt her breasts crushed against his chest, her lips responding to his kiss, Alexis succumbed to a wave of wild exhilaration. *Christina belonged to him* wholeheartedly, and with her beside him, he felt empowered to conquer the world.

"Oh, Tina, Tina," he murmured, burying his face in her hair. "You don't know what you mean to me. . . ."

CHAPTER XXI

By November 1942, the German Reich no longer felt assured of its intended global conquest. In France, an increasing insecurity was making the Nazis grow meaner and more vicious, and, with their ardent collaborator Pierre Laval firmly entrenched in power in Vichy, they swept in and took over the free zone on November 11.

Two days after the takeover of Vichy France, Admiral Darlan, who had begun the years of occupation in support of the Nazis, committed the French fleet (inactive since 1940) into the fray on behalf of the British and the Americans. For the winds were blowing the sweet scent of victory toward the side of the Allies, and, ever the opportunist, Darlan wanted to make sure that his forces ended up on the winning side.

Later that month, the siege of Stalingrad was under way, and General von Paulus and his German forces were effectively being surrounded by the Russians. Rommel was suffering severe damage in North Africa and tension was building among the German High Command.

A resurgence of hope revitalized the occupied French, who now ardently prayed for the success of de Gaulle and Darlan. The Resistance movement surged with energy, more active than ever. And Alexis, with François Durand and several of their other friends from Fayard Industries, were making twice as many trips to Nancy and the Morvan area, bringing in fresh supplies that Charles and Pierre Legrand would discreetly funnel away from German orders for weapons.

Now the entire country was operating under Nazi rule. The newest show of German cruelty had been the abolishment of the age bracket beyond which Jews were protected from arrest and deportation. Old people and children were as likely to be seized as those between the ages of fifteen and fifty-five, and systematic roundups in Paris were proceeding with organized intensity.

At La Folie, Anne had just barely kept her husband from running headlong into Léo Tversky, who had taken it as his personal challenge to run away from his mother and Yadzia Mouchkate as often as he could manage. The retarded but energetic boy would scamper off to the kitchen, where he would take refuge behind Marie Goujon's ample skirts, begging for extra scraps of food.

With Alexis so frequently gone, it was to Anne that Vera Tversky turned to curry a favor. "There's a man in Paris, a Monsieur Billecocq," she told her hostess. "He's holding some money for me, which I'd like to have at hand in case Lucie Stern should find me and Léo a permanent place to live. Do you think you could go into Paris and get it from him?"

Anne hesitated. Alexis had told her of his mixed feelings about the Tversky affair. She hadn't liked the fact that Vera, for all her charm, and for all of Yadzia Mouchkate's assurances of her goodness of spirit, had risked Alexis's life by having him go to her cellar and deal with the janitor who had sold out her own husband to the Gestapo. Vera Tversky, who resented her child and complained at will about how Léo had ruined her existence, was a selfish, spoiled person.

Yet, if this Billecocq was holding her money, and Lucie did manage to come through with a hideaway, Vera would need her cash. Anne didn't like having to go into town to meet a strange man, but there was no one else Vera could trust. Anne accepted.

In order to be inconspicuous, she took the train into Paris, rather than ask Daniel to drive her. She did not want to run the risk of having the chauffeur disclose her little trip to Charles. Monsieur Billecocq lived near Vera Tversky's old apartment on the Boulevard Exelmans, and Anne had to take the métro to reach his sumptuous, high-ceilinged old town house. When she rang the bell, a servant let her into a small but elegantly furnished sitting room, where she waited for her host to arrive.

Monsieur René Billecocq was an old man with a headful of white, gleaming hair and the look of an aristocrat of the *ancien régime*. He kissed Anne's hand and inquired after the health of Madame Tversky and Léo. Anne was just wondering what the connection might be between her inmate and this gentleman, when Monsieur Billecocq said, delicately articulating his words, "Vera Tversky is my daughter."

Anne gazed at him, bewildered. "But . . . I thought she was Russian!"

Billecocq smiled, displaying impeccable false teeth. "My dear lady, one fact does not necessarily preclude the other. Vera was the result of a youthful peccadillo. I was once a talented pianist, and went to Russia to perform on tour. Vera's mother, a young aficionado of classical music from the city of Kiev, came to a recital . . . and the rest is history. I never knew I *had* a daughter until Vera arrived in Paris and contacted me. The papers she showed me —her date of birth, and the stories she told me about her mother— proved to me that she was telling the truth beyond any shadow of doubt, and that she was my child."

Monsieur Billecocq sighed. "You see, Vera's mother was Jewish. Of a very respectable family, but religious. They would never have accepted me, a devout Catholic, for a son-in-law. Besides, I never had the slightest intention of settling in Kiev." He smiled sweetly at Anne, and proceeded with his story. "But once I met Vera here in Paris, and learned that she and her Russian husband had arrived with few decent connections, I felt I owed it to her to help them in their new life. I helped to set up Igor—Monsieur Tversky—in the building contracting business, and I continued to help them once the Occupation began."

Anne was still puzzled. "But why didn't Vera go to *you*, then, when Igor Tversky was arrested and deported? You seem like an important man."

Billecocq licked his lips, genteelly embarrassed. "Vera may be Jewish, Madame, but I am not. To me, the powers-that-be have always been very good. . . ."

Anne took a deep breath, at last putting everything together: Monsieur Billecocq was a *collaborator.* A Nazi sympathizer. And while he had aided Vera Tversky on the side from time to time, he in no fashion wished to jeopardize his own position by openly coming to her rescue once her Jewish identity had been reported. He had not pushed fatherly obligation to the point of shielding her from the authorities.

Evidently, Vera Tversky understood all this quite clearly. But nevertheless she had sent Anne to confront this man who was on intimate terms with the German officials, without bothering to fill in any details as to who he was. Had Vera never considered the possibility of his betraying Anne's clandestine activities—or had she been completely sure that blood ties would mean more to this white-haired opportunist?

"Don't worry," Monsieur Billecocq reassured her, as if reading her mind. "I'm grateful for what you're doing for my daughter. If not for you, she might now be dead. I couldn't help what happened to Igor, but I certainly would do all in my power to preserve Vera's life."

Coming out of the luxurious town house, Anne de Rochefleur breathed the tension out of her body. This was the first time she had ever had a confrontation with an out-and-out, unashamed collaborator. He would keep Anne's secret *as long as the Tverskys remained at La Folie,* but not one minute longer. And so, much as she hated to do it, Anne resolved to ask Lucie Stern *not* to search for other lodgings for Billecocq's illegitimate daughter and her retarded son.

For better or for worse, Anne was going to be stuck with Vera Tversky and Léo for the remainder of the war.

* * *

Alexis had left home early that morning, in early December, kissing his mother quickly on the cheek and telling her not to worry. She still had little idea of what it was he was involved in; Charles had never clarified the issue, and neither had Alexis. Anne was now accustomed to living with two extremely private men who hoarded their affairs in the safely locked drawers of their minds and hearts.

She was feeling nervous at dinnertime, alone in the dining room with Charles. Goujon still set the table formally, with silver candelabra over a hand-embroidered tablecloth of Belgian lace. Anne felt the pain of sitting with the man she still so ardently desired, but who behaved toward her as a courteous but distant relation. They hadn't slept together for more than three years, and though Anne had never looked better—she had lost a great deal of weight—Charles had noticed no change. Or, if he had, he had certainly not reacted to it.

They concentrated on their dessert of bread pudding and filled the space between them with polite phrases and small talk. He was hiding his preoccupations from her, and she, naturally, could tell him nothing of her own: about Monsieur Billecocq, Alexis, Mesdames Tversky and Mouchkate, hidden in darkness in the guest wing.

A light frost had painted interesting landscapes over the outside of the windows of La Folie. Anne said, conversationally, "Alexis told me that Monsieur Fayard had offered him a position in the law firm that represents the Industries. He's going to take it, of course. But I had thought that perhaps when the war is over, he might want me to set him up in a practice of his own. He passed his bar exam with such flying colors!"

"He did very well," Charles conceded. Holding his long-stemmed crystal goblet to the candlelight, he turned to Goujon and remarked, "There's a spot here. Didn't you notice it?"

Anne felt her stomach turning, as it always did when Charles attacked the old butler. Her hands trembling, she rose unsteadily and said, "Shall we go for a walk in the garden, dear? With our fur coats on, it might be a pleasant distraction."

"If you'd like." He had finished his pudding and smiled at her. At least, she thought, he's going through the perfunctory motions of being a husband. With Alex, he won't even go through those of being a father.

Outside, bundled into warm overcoats, they walked arm in arm. Anne thought back to the summer, when Christina had come to visit and she had noticed the attraction between her and Alex. They were young, and she knew that Alex had continued to make visits to the Habigs at the Villa Herran. Anne wished that her own feelings weren't so complicated, and that she might like the girl, as she had promised herself to like whatever girl her son chose. If only circumstances were different . . .

Goujon was moving toward them, outlined by the single light she had allowed him to install to illumine the garden (paraffin was too rare these days for any waste). And behind him, to Anne's horror, she recognized the same two officers who had come to requisition La Folie in 1940, and who had backed off when they saw her holding a copy of *Mein Kampf*. *What were they doing here now?*

Charles, stiffening, moved forward, and as the small group approached he confronted them imperiously. "What's going on?" he demanded, taking the offensive.

Perhaps it was just a routine check and Charles would force them to leave. A man knew how to take charge when a woman didn't, Anne thought, trying not to panic. But the colonel, an ironic smile on his elegant Prussian face, approached her husband, his hand extended in a falsely congenial greeting. "How do you do, Monsieur de Rochefleur. Surely you can help settle a small question? Some of your neighbors have let it be known that now and then a child's cries can be heard coming from your garden." He furrowed his brow in apparent disbelief. "And, what was stranger yet, a woman's voice, calling out in *Yiddish*! I can't imagine," he added pleasantly, "that you and Madame here speak this absurd parody of our noble tongue. Am I correct . . . ?"

"*Are you crazy*, Colonel?" Charles cried, his genuine outrage freezing the German's insidious smile. "Why would anyone tell you such lies? My wife and I live here with our son, and our faithful servants. There are no children on these premises, nor does anyone in my family understand Yiddish! If you'd like to check the house"—his hand flew out angrily toward La Folie—"then go right ahead! But, as a citizen of neutral Switzerland, and one who is close to his ambassador, you can be certain that I shall report this breach of diplomatic understanding just as soon as you leave!"

The colonel cleared his throat. Charles waited for a reply, totally unafraid. His expression revealed quite clearly that he had not a single reason to be afraid of any search of the premises, but that, as a powerful Swiss citizen, he would not hesitate to create a scandal that would wreak havoc on the highest levels. And so, sighing, the colonel stepped back. "Very well, Monsieur de Rochefleur," he conceded. "You've won this round. I believe you. But should your family ever again be implicated in the slightest rumor, you can be certain we shall tear this venerable mansion down to the ground, to verify the accuracy of such a claim!"

Charles raised his brows. "I have no doubt you would," he replied. "But we shan't give you reason for such drastic action. We know the law, gentlemen, and we have no intention of breaking it."

Not until Goujon had closed the door of the gallery on the backs of the German officers did Charles turn to look at Anne. His eyes were cold and knowing. "And now, my dear wife, I think that I deserve a full explanation," he said, his fingers closing like a vise over her forearm.

Inside the den, in front of a miserly fire, she told him about the Jews she had hidden since the summer. She told him everything, her voice trembling, while she looked gravely at him. And he listened, white-faced, impassive, until she had finished her story.

"You realize, of course, Anne, that they will have to go, don't you?" Charles told her, his voice like ice water. "Tomorrow. I'll give them till tomorrow. Then you must call that Stern woman and demand that she pick them up—all three of them—and take them away. And if she doesn't . . ."

His phrase hung menacingly in the air. Anne could feel a swift series of tremors passing through her, but she tried to square her shoulders and return his stare. "Yes?" she whispered . . . "*if she doesn't . . .*"?"

"I'll kick them out into the street. I can't afford to be deported because of some strange Jews who mean nothing to me! Your ill-placed generosity—"

"*No,* Charles!" For the first time in many years, Anne dared to oppose him.

"What do you mean, *no?*" he demanded, his tone brutal and his face contorted with rage.

"I won't allow it," she stated simply. "Vera Tversky and her son, and Madame Mouchkate, the Polish lady, are here as my guests. By legal rights this house belongs to both of us, Charles. Take it, therefore, that these people are all living in my half. You can't, and you won't, throw them out."

"You would disobey me, Anne?" he questioned, shocked. "You would disregard twenty-two years of marriage, because of these three strangers?"

Her voice finally breaking, she said, "It is *you,* not I, who have chosen to disregard the decent boundaries of our nuptial agreement. It's *you* who has been keeping Amelia in Paris as your mistress, and who has broken not only your marital vows but the foundations upon which our family survived for centuries! I could forgive you almost anything, Charles—even Amelia—but I shall not forgive you your lack of honor, nor your inhumanity. You are a Jew, and we, the de Rochefleurs, have been proud to proclaim our faith from the days we were simple Blumenfels in Ulm! No, Charles, I repeat: I shall not let you send three people out into the streets, not now, and not until the Germans have, to the last man, retreated from Paris!"

Her hazel eyes shone with a determination he could not recall ever having read in them. His jaw dropped and, visibly shaken, he took a deep breath. Then he muttered, "Do what you will! But if you don't care to obey me, I'm going to spend the night somewhere else!"

And he stormed out, his footsteps falling in staccato sequence on the floor of the hallway beyond.

* * *

François maneuvered the truck around the bend at the end of the unused mine shaft a few miles from the factories of Fayard Industries. The winter sky was light gray, and mist clung to the chill air. On the passenger seat, Alexis shivered. "There's no place like Nancy to make you happier you don't have to live there, especially in winter," he commented, hugging himself to ward away the cold.

His friend raised an eyebrow, and grinned. "The law library at rue Cambon certainly is an inviting dream right now," he assented ruefully.

Ahead of them, the road looked open. François began to whistle. "Dry sausage for lunch?" he inquired.

But Alexis never had a chance to reply. Suddenly, from behind the shadow of a low, crumbling roadside wall, a group of figures in *feldgrau* sprang out, long rifles pointed at the truck. "*Shit!*" François muttered. "I'm going to gun it, what the hell!"

His foot slammed onto the accelerator pedal, and the truck dove forward. Alexis ducked low, and, sure enough, a discharge of bullets shattered the windshield and the window on his side. The truck was swerving madly, barely avoiding a tree standing forlornly at the next corner. And then, to Alexis's horror, the truck careened out of control and smashed headlong into a parked van. The truck came to a complete stop and Alexis, gingerly holding his dizzy head, turned to look at his friend.

François Durand had collapsed over the wheel, blood spattered on the dashboard in front of him. He was dead.

And in the next instant, Alexis Lévy–de Rochefleur felt that his own life was ending. He was vaguely aware of the Nazi soldiers dragging him out of the demolished truck, jamming their rifle butts in his ribs. He heard the Germans screaming something, which ordinarily he would have understood but which meant nothing to him now.

At that precise moment, all he could think of was that his Swiss passport—so contemptuously rejected when his father had handed it to him in 1940—was lying in his desk drawer at La Folie. Right now, to the Germans, he was nothing more than another member of the Resistance, caught red-handed with stolen armaments belonging to the Reich.

He thought of how he had barely brushed his lips against his mother's cheek the day before, telling her not to worry. And that he'd never asked Christina to marry him.

* * *

Amelia heard the pebble graze her bedroom window and jumped out of bed. *If it were the Gestapo, they would have rung the doorbell and demanded immediate admittance,* she told herself. It had to be someone who knew this was her bedroom.

She slipped into the velvet robe at the foot of her bed, and went to the window. Cautiously parting the curtains, she saw, to her surprise, Charles standing in his fur coat with a small bag in his hand. She dropped the curtain and ran down the stairs, opening the front door and turning on the light in the foyer.

As a greeting, he took her in his arms, burying his face in her hair. A sick dread was settling over her, and after a moment she gently disentangled herself. "Tell me what's happened."

He took a deep breath, avoiding the honesty in her eyes. "Oh, Meli, Meli," he murmured, using once more the tender nickname her brother had given her. "You must let me sleep here tonight."

Horrified, Amelia turned away, sinking her face into her hands. "But *why?*"

"Amelia," he told her softly, "it's all right. I'm sure she knows about us by now. And besides, I don't care anymore. We've had a terrible quarrel, and it's no longer worth it to me to preserve appearances to safeguard her emotions. Just let me sleep here, with you!"

She stood shaking her head, troubled and confused, and he came over to hold her. "Don't worry," he said, taking her by the hand and leading her gently up the staircase. "Stop thinking about Anne, and think about *us*. . . ."

Later, when she had closed the door to her bedroom and lit a candle on her nightstand, Charles removed the velvet robe and slipped the silk straps of her nightgown off her shoulders. She felt her nipples hardening as he touched her, and her whole body became a single electric wire, vibrating. With a mixture of decision and gentleness, Charles tilted her back onto the bed, and lay down beside her. She shivered, closing her eyes, wanting to feel his magic fingers as they explored her, his lips on her naked body. And then she reached out and drew him to her, wanting him inside her.

In the early dawn, when shimmering rays of pink and hazy blue slithered in through the curtains, she was lying on her side, watching him sleep. His features had the perfect chiseled grace evoked by Michelangelo and Cellini—and the peaceful expression of a child lost in dreams. And she thought: *He's right. I should trust what he says, and stop feeling guilty for a love that grows inside me with each passing day.* A love for which she and her daughter were risking their lives, each time they ventured out. . . .

* * *

Alexis stood squashed in the cattle car among almost a hundred men and women, all as scared as he was. At Drancy they will send me to wherever it is they deport Jews, he thought, and to arrive alive will mean certain extermination. No one he knew who had been deported had ever returned, or been heard of since.

Drancy was the point from which trains took loads of deportees eastward to the conquered territories of the Third Reich. Stories abounded about what happened to them once they reached their destination.

Next to him stood a thin, wiry man in his early thirties. He was dressed in workman's clothes, as was Alexis himself—warmly, for winter. But the suffocating heat created by this human compressor system had forced them each to squirm out of their outer layers. Alexis had noticed how much this man resembled François, and he tried not to look at him, to keep his emotions in check. *Death.* At all cost, it had to be avoided. Nothing else was significant now.

As fate would have it, however, the wiry man had every intention of making good use of their proximity. "How did they catch *you*?" his neighbor asked in a low voice. They were jammed together against the side of what, Alexis had noticed, was the next to last in a long line of cattle cars. "You in the Resistance, or did they get you in a raid?"

"Resistance." Alexis didn't feel like talking. A smell of human waste was beginning to spread, making him nauseous—an old man had defecated alongside them, perhaps out of fear, and several people had urinated: only a single bucket had been placed inside the wagon for such natural emergencies. Besides, he was attempting to concentrate on the layout of the wagon. Would anyone be able to squeeze out through the tiny slit of a window and make it to the roof? From there, it might be worthwhile to risk one's life and jump. . . .

"They caught me in an underground cell manufacturing some simple homemade grenades," the man informed Alexis. "My name's Roland, Roland Pêche. You?"

"Alexis Lévy." Somehow it seemed out of place, like name-dropping, to tell this fellow prisoner who exactly his family was. "I was smuggling arms out to the Maquis. They grabbed me in Nancy."

"I'm from Dijon."

After that, conversation ceased. An old woman had begun to moan. Alexis kept glancing toward the minuscule aperture—hardly worth calling a window—when suddenly he felt Roland Pêche's elbow in his ribs. "The safety valve on the bottom's the best way," the little man whispered. "If you're game, I'm game. But we'll need a tool to unscrew the damn thing."

Astounded, Alexis gazed down. The space in which one hundred people had been crowded together had originally been constructed to transport eight farmhorses or cows. He knew, from remembered bits of conversation with Charles, that when Charles had been designing for the firm of Meyer Frères, they had placed safety openings into the floors of boxcars. Not valves, actually, but small trapdoors that were securely screwed into the floor. In an emergency, they would come loose, leaving a hole large enough for a grown man to emerge, landing on the rail tracks below.

Roland was telling him that they should somehow open up one of these trapdoors and jump down—to a sure death crunched by the wheels of the next boxcar.

"We're just ahead of the caboose," Roland was explaining, his voice urgent. "If we wait till the train slows down, and if we're careful, we won't risk the wind's throwing us onto the rails themselves. We'll measure our jump and fall *between* the rails. But we'll need to work the trapdoor together, Alexis."

Early in his childhood, Alexis had discovered that no matter how dreadful life seemed to be, it could get worse. Being run over by a huge train would be one of the worst deaths imaginable—but death in a Nazi execution camp in Poland or Czechoslovakia might be slower and even more agonizing.

Alexis had always been strong and tautly muscled. He just *might* be able to control his body to withstand the certain gust of wind that would suck him out, and find himself safe between the rails and the crunch of the train's steel wheels.

His hand slipped into one of his pockets, and he felt the small penknife that was attached to the ring with the truck's keys. The Germans hadn't bothered to confiscate his personal effects, once he had been securely apprehended. This tiny knife would hardly have been useful in a hand-to-hand combat with the *Boches,* but perhaps it would work to unscrew the bolts of the trapdoor. . . .

"I'll do it," he said quickly, before his resolve had time to dissipate.

* * *

It was a rare occasion when the German ambassador, Otto Abetz, bothered to visit a Frenchman, unless it was accompanied by a full gala and the *ne plus ultra* of collaborationist Parisians were present. Otto Abetz was a handsome man, somewhat of a dandy, and a cultured individual married to a Frenchwoman—not, Arabella thought, a typical *Boche* with a robot's "Heil Hitler" response to everything.

But Armand Fayard wasn't just any Frenchman. He happened to be in control of a gigantic war tool—the armaments industry—and Abetz could not have held his head up in Berlin if he hadn't maintained proper relations with him.

In his massive bed in the marbled Renaissance room of his palace, the steel magnate reclined against a pile of pillows, his face ashen and sagging. Arabella noticed that the left side of his face now drooped beyond control. Armand appeared every one of his seventy-six years, although only days before, she realized with sudden shock, he had seemed his usual self, a mountain lion on the prowl.

"Monsieur Fayard," Abetz began, delicately lifting his teacup to his lips. "The entire affair is, shall we say, most awkward. General Baron von Quistorp insists that two young peddlers, who his men caught just outside an abandoned mine shaft on Fayard property, were not alone. How else would you explain their carrying arms from your own factory?"

Fayard took a shallow breath. "I'm not about to attempt any explanation, Herr Abetz. The tide is shifting among the French, and for all I know, many of my employees may well have turned into underground spies . . . or thieves."

"Von Quistorp apprehended Pierre Legrand, but he's had to let him go. Legrand's proclaimed innocence can't be proven one way or another, but I believe he can be more useful to us in his capacity as plant manager than somewhere . . . well, shall we say, on Polish territory."

"Legrand collaborated with you for three years," Fayard declared, sitting up straighter. "And the theft was on such a small scale—"

"Nevertheless, it puts us all in a bad light. It makes us mistrust one another. In fact, Monsieur Fayard, the reason I came to you is that General von Quistorp has asked me to arrest your vice-president, Charles de Rochefleur, who carries a Swiss passport and is therefore impregnable."

Arabella's ears were perking up. On the balls of her feet she inched forward, unnoticed by the German ambassador but observed from the corner of her husband's eye. Immediately she began to busy herself with the tea things near the alcove where the two men were speaking.

"Impregnable on one condition: that he not be in violation of the terms of his country's neutrality. If it could be shown that Charles de Rochefleur was passing arms to the French Resistance through these two seemingly insignificant young peddlers, then naturally I would have to go along with the general's demand, and seize and imprison your man."

"My dear Ambassador," Arabella interposed, breaking into the conversation for the first time as she came up with a tray of small cookies. "Charles works for my husband, that's all. He isn't really *his man,* as your words imply. My husband has displayed his loyalty toward the Reich in every possible manner, hasn't he? If de Rochefleur has committed a crime, then it has been, most evidently"—and her chin pointed to the sick man, who could hardly support his own weight on the pillows—"outside Armand's knowledge and without his consent."

"Madame, I meant no discourtesy," the German declared, standing and taking her hand, and raising it to his lips. "Of course we do not suspect Monsieur Fayard of the slightest wrongdoing. It is my obligation, however, to run a routine investigation of Charles de Rochefleur. You will have to understand. . . ."

Armand Fayard's eyes were shining brightly. "Herr Abetz, my vice-president is guilty of nothing but following each and every order issued to him. I am as certain of his loyalty as my wife appears to be of my own."

"Then you will not mind my poking my nose into his affairs, will you? To exonerate him while placating our good general in Nancy?"

From the doorway, a half-hour later, Abetz turned back and regarded Armand Fayard. "Oh, and I forgot—one good piece of news is that one of the peddler boys was shot to death by von Quistorp's men."

Fayard's face suddenly seemed to lose all countenance. He blinked, and for a moment both Arabella and the German ambassador stopped in their tracks, perplexed. *"Which one?"* Fayard asked.

Abetz uttered a civilized chuckle of apology. "I couldn't tell you," he replied, shaking his head. "But the other is right now on his way to Drancy." Abetz smiled, and added cheerfully, "I hope your health will take a better turn, dear Monsieur Fayard. My wife and I were counting on your presence at our next banquet."

"Don't worry," Arabella said to him. "We'll be there, hale and hearty!"

But as she led her guest down the long corridor, Arabella paused. Her hand, on Abetz's arm, tightened. "Armand is an old man," she murmured, her green eyes compassionate. "Don't count on his being as coherent as he may *appear*. There are vast lapses in his memory now, and . . . well, this de Rochefleur matter upsets me a great deal. And I can see that it's upset Armand."

"What do you mean, madame?"

His eyes were probing hers, and she shrugged. "Only that de Rochefleur, as I'm certain you know, is a *Jew*. And no Jew can possibly love Hitler. Charles has been out of town an awful lot these past few years . . . as has his son, Alexis. I wonder—might there not be a connection between those two peddlers and *Alexis de Rochefleur*? You know how young men like to take absurd risks, and this whole matter of the underground . . . You *did* mention that these peddlers were *young men?*" She made a charming gesture of pleased deduction, and added, "If I'm right, then obviously Charles would be in it as well, don't you suppose?"

"A family affair?" Abetz stood considering. He tilted his head to the side. "An intriguing notion, *gnädige Frau*, and well worth considering. But the problem is, of course, that investigations take time, and the Führer does not appreciate his officials' wasting it."

Arabella sighed, and nodded sympathetically. "Then if I were you, I would make my move as quickly as possible. Armand tends to idealize his employees, poor darling—you saw how quickly he stood up for de Rochefleur! However, if *I* were *you*, Herr Abetz, I would send my best squadron of men to his estate in Saint-Germain-en-Laye, and search the place from top to bottom. Who knows? If the de Rochefleur men are in this together, then certainly you will find a cache of armaments in the attic, won't you? And if they're not, the papers you are bound to come up with, looking through their personal files, will completely exonerate them." She batted her long lashes and added, "Which is what Armand and I both hope and pray for. . . ."

Abetz smiled once again. "You would have made the Führer an invaluable aide and right arm," he told her gallantly.

After letting the German ambassador out, Arabella pulled the massive front door shut and stood for a minute resting against it. Her cheeks were flushed, and as she closed her eyes, a voluptuous sigh emerged from the depths of her being.

"En garde, Messieurs de Rochefleur," she intoned in a singsong voice, rubbing her hands together.

* * *

"I'm very clever with my hands," Roland whispered to Alexis. "So, while I'm unscrewing this lid, you'll stand guard. This is a carful of old people—you and I are about the only young ones—and we don't want mass hysteria, or some old guy falling out while the train's racing full speed ahead."

Alexis passed him the penknife. Then, remembering his experiences on the Paris métro, he firmly elbowed their way to the place where, according to what he remembered of his father's descriptions, the safety panel had to be bolted into the metal floor.

Lithe and small-boned, Roland inched his way down to the floor, making a tiny space for himself to work, while Alexis pushed back a poor old man who groaned in pain. The boxcar was so small and crammed so full, it was difficult to find the screws and figure out how best to apply the penknife to loosen them.

Making grunting sounds, Roland succeeded in unscrewing one corner. They were numbed into silence by fear and the acute discomfort of their positions, and nobody spoke up to ask any questions. But Alexis noticed eyes—dozens of eyes, it seemed—riveted to his friend on all fours on the floor, working the second bolt to finally remove it.

An eternity later, Roland looked up. His face was dripping with perspiration, but he was grinning. Then, clearly but not loudly, he said, "Stand back!" to the people crowded closest to him, and lifted the top off the safety valve an inch or two. "We aren't ready yet," he explained to Alexis. "The train's going too fast. We'd be sucked out like refuse into a vacuum cleaner!"

"You boys aren't planning to *jump out,* are you?" a white-haired old woman asked fearfully.

"We're thinking it over," Alexis reassured her, smiling. She reminded him of his grandmother Yvonne, now so old and frail that sometimes the sight of her was painful.

When the train at length began to slow down, Roland waited until it had almost crept to a stop. Then he removed the lid. A gaping hole appeared, earth and rocks frantically rolling through on the other side, and a sudden rush of wind blew in.

Roland whispered, "I'll go first—you watch," and touched Alexis on the arm.

"Good luck," Alexis said softly. His heart was throbbing inside his throat. One wrong move, and Roland would be tossed a millimeter too close to the rails . . . and be crushed beyond recognition by the churning wheels of the caboose.

His newfound friend looked down, measured his move, and tried to hurl his body exactly through the center of the aperture. People gasped; a man screamed out. Alexis closed his eyes, telling himself not to think about whether Roland had made it or not. Soon enough, he'd be finding out. . . .

In a few seconds the train, which had slowed down approaching a railroad turnpike, would start up again at full speed, and his single chance of escaping Drancy, and whatever came next, would have passed him by.

Alexis jumped down and disappeared from sight.

CHAPTER XXII

When news reached Charles that Alexis and François had been caught, and that one had been killed and the other sent to Drancy, Charles felt too stunned to react. As Daniel drove him to Amelia's house, a kaleidoscope of memories assaulted him: Alexis at five, trying to spell *I love my father* for a birthday card; Alexis standing alone in his new school uniform on the platform of the train that would take him away to boarding school; Alexis maturing into manhood, and taking his first job at Fayard Industries. And finally, Alexis and his friend François Durand in their "peddlers' truck," excited and a little nervous about risking their lives for a free France.

Yet Charles had never loved him. He'd put up with the boy as part of the bargain he had struck with Alfred, before marrying Anne. And as little as he loved his wife, he had never left her, not even after finding out about their unwanted "tenants." Admittedly, he no longer kept up the pretense of being a decent and thoughtful husband—but he was still her husband, and it was therefore his human obligation to let her know about her son. But first he would fulfill another obligation, toward someone he loved a great deal more than his wife—Christina.

And right now he was going to have to face her with Alexis's death or certain deportation—for nobody knew which of the two young men had been killed and which one arrested.

But Christina simply wouldn't believe what Cousin Charles was telling her: that Alex might be dead. She stared, stony-faced, at her mother, who was crying unashamedly, and Cousin Charles, who had tried to comfort her as he explained what had occurred in Nancy.

"Alex would never let himself be caught," she said, shaking her head. "Alex is extremely smart, and extremely cautious. He would *know* if the Germans were lying in wait for him outside the truck's hiding place."

"Nobody can think of everything," Charles answered lamely, taken aback by the girl's stubborn defiance, by what could only be termed the single-mindedness of her feelings.

Then Christina stood up, her legs unexpectedly wobbly, her vision blurred. "Alex once told me he would do *anything* not to be sent to Drancy. And *he isn't dead.* I won't believe it until someone tells me they have seen his body! And if it's him they took away alive—then *he'll stay that way,* and come back!"

She turned and started to run up the stairs; then, suddenly, she wheeled around and cried, "I'm not going to let history repeat itself! But at least, Mama, you always had *me* . . . a part of Papa that was with you in the flesh! I never had the chance to be with Alexis . . . to be a woman to him! And I know that God wouldn't allow him to be taken—not this way, without there being *anything left. . . .*"

Her face distorted with tears, she ran upstairs before either Charles or Amelia was able to move.

* * *

Anne stood before the living room fireplace, shivering. Behind her, Charles paced the floor as he tried to think of what to do next. His hand reached out to touch his wife's shoulder, then retreated, almost timidly. She turned around at last, her hazel eyes bloodshot but dry, her face blotchy and red, and she cried, "*You don't really care!* What difference does Alex's death make in your existence, Charles? *You always hated him!*"

"That's not true," he answered lamely. "Anne, you don't mean this. It's just the grief inside you tearing you apart—"

"It's that I'm finally seeing who you are," she declared. "My son may be dead, Charles, and *you don't give a damn*! Well, maybe you're being more honest now than you've ever been. But don't try to comfort me—there is no comfort, nothing you can say! If my son isn't dead already, he will be soon. The Gestapo will murder him! Do you know, I hope he's dead! One quick bullet is a far less painful death than torture!"

And she marched out of the room, her gait unsteady but her head held high.

* * *

"Madame Habig is here to see Madame," Goujon declared, inclining his head with deference.

Anne was seated in the gallery, in her old bathrobe, so cold with shock and pain that Marie had had to cover her with a wool blanket, and place a hot water bottle under her feet. *Amelia? Here?* But she had no strength to speak, and no will to react. Only a sense of panic assailed her, and she wrung her hands.

Amelia came in, sober in a black wool suit, her hair hidden inside a black velvet beret. How beautiful she looked! This was the woman for whom Charles had sacrificed twenty-two years of marriage, and all Anne's devotion. Had that meant so little to him, by comparison?

"I'm sorry to intrude, Anne," Amelia said. "I realize I must be the *last* person you'd want to see . . . but I couldn't stay away." And she hastened toward Anne, falling to a crouched position by her cousin's chaise longue. Her hands reached for Anne's, clasping the frozen fingers tightly, tears dropping on the blanket.

Anne couldn't speak. Amelia's grief had taken her by surprise, further disorienting her. She hadn't expected such strong emotion, and yet . . . "You've got to let it out," Amelia was saying softly, moving up to embrace Anne. "Christina won't accept it, you know. She loves him too. . . . Oh, Annette, darling, we *all* love him! And we have to pray that Tina's right, that he isn't dead."

"I can't believe any of it," Anne found herself saying, her voice dull and detached, as though she were speaking in a dream. "I keep looking toward the hallway, expecting him to walk right in, calling for me."

Hearing herself, she burst into tears. Amelia held her tightly, rocking her back and forth like a small child. After a few minutes, Anne's hysterical sobbing subsided, and she sat back and examined her cousin. "Meli," she murmured, her voice weak and strained. "Why can't I hate you?"

Amelia took her lower lip between her teeth. For a moment she couldn't reply, overcome with shame. "Anne," she said at last, "I can't ask you to understand. If I were you, *I* might hate me. But you see, I love Charles with all the passion of my being and I can't leave him! Neither he nor I planned it this way. It just happened, and neither of us had the strength or the courage to stop our feelings. We did try . . . God knows, we tried."

"He always was in love with you, Amelia," Anne said. Her tone was neither bitter nor angry—just resigned. "I should have let him go to you when you came from Vienna. But even then, I loved him too much myself. I wanted him to care for me just enough not to leave me." Her hazel eyes met Amelia's, and she shook her head. "He never *did* leave me, did he, Meli? But what did that bring me? Only the continual awareness that I was the wrong woman, the one he was married to in name only. I held on for all the wrong reasons, and all the time I blamed you for his coldness and his lack of love. I never should have married him, because you can't force someone to fall in love with you, particularly when he's still in love with another woman."

They held each other, Amelia's hand gently caressing the nape of Anne's neck. "I'm sorry," Amelia whispered. "I truly am. . . ."

Anne's eyes filled with tears. "I'm sorry, too, for the wasted years in all our lives. But I'd give up everything I own for an assurance that Alex was all right. He's all that matters to me now, Amelia."

"I know, darling, I know." The two women remained silent, thinking of the young man. Anne was right: only Alexis's safety was important now.

Then, all at once, their communion was shattered. Aristide Goujon entered without knocking, his footsteps rapid and uneven. Simultaneously, the two women turned to regard him.

"Madame," the old maître d'hôtel announced, his breath coming in painful gulps. "Ten officers of the Gestapo are waiting for you in the vestibule." And as Anne's lips parted in dismay, he met her wild, haunted eyes and added, "They've brought along a warrant to search the entire premises, from top to bottom."

* * *

Alexis fell on the gravel, landing on his back. He felt bolts of pain shoot through his body. He flattened himself over the ground, closing his eyes to the train wheels inexorably clanging over the rails, inches from his head and body. The hellish noise reverberated through his cranium like echoes of devils' laughter, maddeningly loud.

The caboose was directly overhead now, and within seconds would be gone. The problem was to try to withstand the wind that churned all about him from the wheels and the impact of having fallen, and to keep it from buffeting him to one side or the other, to an instant demise.

After a while he became aware that the deafening noise of train machinery seemed to have diminished. With infinite caution, Alexis opened his eyes. Overhead lay a gray sky already dotted with a few timid stars, early arrivers on the nighttime scene. *The train had disappeared!*

Alexis turned on his side and looked behind him. The caboose was rounding a corner and moving off into the distance. *He was alive!* Adrenaline was flooding his body, and he could feel acute pain in his spine and one of his legs. His head felt like a balloon filled with water, sloshing from side to side. But he had survived his fall. . . .

Then it occurred to him that Roland must have landed ahead of him. There was just sufficient light in the sky to look around for him, judging that he must have fallen a hundred yards or so behind Alexis. But Roland, sprightlier and smaller, would already have picked himself up and hidden somewhere nearby, waiting for Alexis to join him. The question was, *where*?

Beyond the railroad tracks, to the east, stretched an enormous wasteland populated with an occasional bit of refuse, an empty tin or crushed pack of cigarettes signs of the railwaymen who checked the track each day. But toward the west there appeared to be a sharp drop—a hillside sloping down, with some sparse vegetation: some low bushes and a few tufts of dying winter grass. Alexis, unable to stand up, dragged himself over toward that side.

But something strange diverted his attention. Between the railing and the first bush lay an inanimate object he couldn't quite make out. Mesmerized, Alexis crawled over to it to see what it could be.

An arm, dismembered and bloody, stretched palm-up toward the sky.

Swallowing a sudden spurt of bile, Alexis turned his head back toward the track. And before losing consciousness, he saw what looked like the top of a skull crushed in, with gobs of white, gelatinous brain clinging to the steel rails.

Alexis Lévy–de Rochefleur felt himself yield to the attack of nausea overpowering his senses. Pinpoints of red exploded over his field of vision, then total darkness. His body collapsed and began to roll westward, somersaulting toward the bottom of the hill.

* * *

Like menacing black spiders, the Gestapo men pushed the three refugees with their rifle butts toward Anne, Amelia, and Aristide Goujon.

One of the younger officers said to the colonel, "We've searched the house from cellar to attic. No arms, no explosives, no armaments at all. But look what we *did* run into in the guest wing!"

The colonel frowned, regarding Anne. "Who are these people?" he demanded.

But it was the first officer who replied for her. "I already checked it out, sir. This woman claims to be the kid's mother. The older woman doesn't seem to be related. They showed me their identification cards, but there's something strange there. These three have obviously been living here, but they appear to be registered elsewhere, according to the cards they showed us!" He smirked and added, "They all look very Semitic to me, sir—not French at all, don't you agree?"

Anne's teeth had started to chatter. "I . . ."

The colonel smiled at her, his eyes remaining frozen in his parchment face. "Well, madame, we were told we might find arms in this house, illegally smuggled from a factory in Lorraine. But we had no idea we'd find a respectable Swiss neutral like yourself keeping a rooming house for Jews with false papers!"

"These people are here at my invitation," Anne said, her voice breaking.

"You are in violation of the terms of agreement with your government, madame. As a Swiss citizen, you were to obey the law of the land and instead, you've been shielding enemies of the Reich on your property! We have no choice but to arrest your entire household, in the name of the Führer!"

Anne shook her head in disbelief. Horrified, she turned to her cousin. Amelia's face was white and bloodless. Suddenly, Anne moved forward and, uttering a small cry, fell into Amelia's arms.

Amelia Habig stared fixedly at the Gestapo colonel, her chin raised in defiance above Anne's head on her bosom. "And *you,* madame?" the colonel asked with an ironic softness. "May I see your papers, to verify whether you are a member of this household too?"

She shook her head, seeing not *this* man, not these Gestapo officers, but other men in SS *feldgrau,* and the face of blond, imperious Karl von Stecher, who had once introduced her to Peter Habig and called himself her friend.

"My identity doesn't matter," she stated, tightening her arms around Anne. "Wherever you are taking these people, you can take me too. . . ."

* * *

It was early dawn when the two railwaymen came upon the unconscious form of the young man at the foot of the hillside. "Hey, Marcel!" the first one called in amazement. "Take a look at *this*!"

His companion bent down and knelt over the body. He grabbed a wrist and felt for a pulsebeat. "He's alive!" he cried. "Quick— let's take him somewhere. Must be a Jew, or some other kind of deportee who jumped off the roof of a boxcar or down from a safety valve!"

"Poor fellow," the first man said, picking Alexis gently up by his armpits, making sure that his head lay safely propped to one side. "Some jump that must have been."

"Looks as if he may have a couple of pretty badly broken bones," Marcel declared. "Let's take him to my sister's. If he's made it *this* far, we should at least help get him out of the way of any *Boches* making the rounds, reconnoitering the premises. . . ."

* * *

Holding each other tightly, the two cousins walked toward the front door—Amelia, proud; Anne, dazed and stricken with terror. Behind them, the three refugees had fallen into a deathly silence, the boy lodged between Madame Mouchkate and his mother. The Gestapo officers shoved their rifle butts into their backs.

Suddenly, at the threshold, Anne's slippered foot slid on the polished parquet floor and she uttered a sharp cry, falling toward Amelia. For a few seconds the little group remained frozen in place, watching Anne and Amelia slip to the floor. Then the lieutenant pointed his gun at the two women, beginning to shout. "What's going on? Trying to delay things here?"

"My cousin doesn't feel well," Amelia said, standing up and pulling Anne with her. "Look at her—she's been sick all day. I think she needs a glass of water to steady her."

"We have no time for that," the colonel snapped.

Behind them, old Yadzia Mouchkate had burst into hysterical sobbing. Léo started to whine. The young lieutenant aimed the barrel of his gun at him, barely an inch from his face, and shouted: *"You shut up!"*

But the gun only made the boy more frightened, and his whining became as strident as an off-key siren. The lieutenant, enraged, shoved his gun into the child's neck and, red-faced, yelled an insult in German. The boy kicked him, and the officer's finger pulled the trigger in reflex action. The gun went off. In front of the horrified group, the retarded boy's face splattered into bloody particles of skin, bone and brain in the air.

All this took less than a minute, but the result was pandemonium. Vera threw herself at the nearest officer, and Amelia jumped out to lodge herself between them, suddenly terrified that a mass shooting would take place if the Tversky woman tried to attack a member of the Gestapo.

In the next second, she felt a terrible jolt of pain. She never realized what had suddenly slashed the back of her head open, but it was the handle of a heavy rifle, swatted like a club to mow her down. Amelia Habig fell forward, the small velvet beret slipping off to reveal a wound oozing dark blood into her beautiful topknot of black hair.

Anne squirmed out of the colonel's grip and ran to where her cousin had fallen to the ground. She was sobbing hysterically. "You can't do this to us! You can't! We're an important family— we're de Rochefleurs! What are you trying to do to us all?"

The colonel stared down at her, his gun almost touching her forehead. "Get up!" he snapped angrily. "You saw what happens to rebellious Jews! It makes no difference *who* you are, madame—to us, you are all Jews, threatening the purity of the Aryan race!"

Anne looked up at him, her eyes brimming with hatred. "*Your* kind is threatening the purity of the *human race,*" she said, her voice reverberating in the paneled vestibule. And then, summoning all her ire, she spit into the colonel's face.

It was to be her last stance of courage. For, as the colonel raised a hand to wipe the saliva from his cheek, one of his younger henchmen aimed a rifle at Anne, and fired.

Anne de Rochefleur died instantly, the bullet piercing her chest to lodge in the back of her lung. Her blood seeped into Amelia's, merging into a crimson puddle on the parquet floor.

It was Aristide Goujon who, comforting his wife in the jail of the police station, found the words to express what they both were feeling. "Madame Anne died like a heroine," he said, tears welling in his rheumy old eyes. "And how like the de Rochefleurs, she and Madame Habig, perishing in a single moment, together . . . their blood mingling. . . ."

And then they were silent. The terror of their own destiny had not hit them yet; but the tragic murder of the child, and the vision of their beloved mistress and her beautiful Viennese cousin both killed on the floor of the house they had always thought of as theirs to protect and honor, loomed enormous and horrifying.

La Folie, they knew, would never be washed clean of the de Rochefleur blood that had been shed that day. Just as La Folie would never yield up the ghosts of the two women who had been killed in their prime, where once Napoleon had rested before venturing forth to win battles for France.

* * *

Alone in his dark, unlit office, Charles paced the floor. He wondered whether Anne would ever recover from the shock of the news about Alexis, and how their marriage would be affected. He had left her bereaved and angry, angrier than he'd ever seen her toward him. Because she'd always known he hadn't loved Alexis.

Damn him, Charles thought, slamming his fist into the palm of his left hand. Even now, dead or captured, that boy was causing problems. Charles wondered whose child he really was, and whether Anne, in the depths of her despair, was thinking of the man who had fathered her son.

Guiltily, he looked at his watch. It was already seven o'clock, and he'd avoided going home and facing her again. He'd have to offer additional solace and comfort, and the words lay strangling his vocal cords. Hypocrisy was difficult enough under normal circumstances, but when he had to muster feelings he didn't have, toward his own wife who could read the truth, wasn't it even worse for both parties?

Charles felt at loose ends, gnawed by an unusual sense of shame toward Anne. He was behaving despicably by avoiding her now. At least he should telephone and find out if she felt a bit better, and tell her that he'd been delayed by a pile of urgent correspondence. *I'll put her off,* he decided, *and then I'll go to the rue de la Pompe and inquire after Christina. Amelia will advise me how to act with Anne—she always knows exactly what to do in delicate situations that leave me baffled and confused.* Reaching for the telephone on his desk, he dialed his home number and waited for Goujon to pick up on the other end.

But the telephone kept ringing, and after a while Charles set the instrument back in its cradle.

Goujon never allowed it to ring more than three times. Therefore, if Goujon wasn't picking up, something had to be drastically wrong.

Charles searched through his memory, trying to recall the neighbors' name. The snobbish couple with the mansion up the street, who never quite knew how to behave toward him and Anne. What was their name? . . . Bonnier . . . That was it! *Bonnier!*

Charles dialed Information for Saint-Germain. He asked for a number for Monsieur Bonnier on the rue Lemierre.

After two rings, the Bonnier maid answered. Somewhat imperiously, Charles demanded to speak with Monsieur or Madame. The girl asked him who was calling, and he told her.

It was then that he heard her abrupt intake of breath. *"Monsieur de Rochefleur?* Oh, my God! You've got to get out of Paris! The *Boches* came in and swept through your house . . . and . . . and . . .". The voice was breaking. Charles could hear sobs.

"Tell me, my good woman, *what the hell is going on,"* he ordered, his heart pounding furiously.

"Oh, monsieur . . . it's simply too awful! They . . . they *shot Madame de Rochefleur* and also the Austrian lady who was visiting . . . the cousin! And they took everyone else away—all the Goujons! Afterward, Madame Bonnier and I went in the house and the vestibule was full of blood. It was the worst massacre I've ever seen . . . !"

But Charles had broken the connection, letting the receiver clatter to the floor. He could feel his entire body shaking, and his teeth chattering. But all that he could think of was that *it simply couldn't be true.*

Hours later, in the total darkness of night, he had still not moved. His hands lay frozen on his desk, and he kept hearing the Bonnier maid's words, none of which made the slightest sense. But somehow, of the catastrophe she had described, one phrase above all echoed in his brain: . . . *the Austrian lady who was visiting . . . the cousin.* Surely, *surely* she'd made a mistake, about that if not about the rest! He wasn't going to think any of it through until he determined where Amelia was, right now.

She *couldn't* have gone to La Folie, he reasoned. Not the way Anne felt about her! Why would she have done that? But even as he asked himself this question, he understood the answer. Anne, distraught, had needed help. Who but Amelia could have offered her a measure of comfort? Who but Amelia would have overlooked the hostility of her embittered cousin and gone to her arms outstretched, offering her her love and her faith?

Suddenly he felt terrible panic assaulting his senses, and he grabbed the telephone again, this time dialing Amelia's number.

Christina answered him on the first ring, her young voice anxious and scared. "Mama? Is that you?"

"No, darling, it's Cousin Charles," he said, trying not to frighten her with his own misgivings. "I was hoping your mother was at home. Isn't she there . . . ?"

Christina dissolved into tears. "I can't understand!" she cried. "Mama left hours ago to visit Cousin Anne at La Folie—only the phone doesn't answer there, and she didn't come home! It's not like her not to call and let me know what's going on—"

"Look," he cut in, his voice urgent and terse. "Make yourself some dinner and wait for me. I'm going to make a few important calls and then I'll be right over. Promise me you'll eat something, Tina?"

He couldn't make out her reply, because his heart had started to pound in his throat and at his temples, disorienting him. As the receiver went dead, Charles felt his eyes fill with tears.

How was any of this possible? The Bonnier maid told him that Amelia had been shot along with Anne. But Amelia couldn't be dead—he needed her too much, loved her too much, for anything to have torn her away. . . .

But the maid had also said to him, "Get out of Paris!" He'd call the Swiss ambassador, Walter Stucki, in Vichy, and beg him to come to Paris and find out what had happened. One of the advantages of being a de Rochefleur, he thought bitterly, was that diplomats always came running, even in times of war, even across frontiers, to serve their illustrious countrymen. Charles was considered an asset to the Swiss nation.

I won't think about Amelia or Anne, Charles swore as he brushed his tears away with a fierce motion of his hand. Stucki will clear things up, and until then he'd assume the Bonnier girl to be grossly mistaken, the mere recipient of a nasty rumor. *It can't be possible,* he assured himself. *Anne and Amelia can't be dead!*

* * *

Charles sat in the living room of the Swiss ambassador's suite at the Hotel George V, his face gray and drawn, the circles under his eyes purple and swollen. The Swiss diplomat stared at him from across a Louis XVI coffee table, but Charles didn't react, looking instead down at his hands, which were trembling out of control in his lap.

"Charles, Charles," Mr. Stucki murmured sympathetically. "Look, I know how you must feel about poor Anne's murder. . . ."

I wish I could find the proper words with which to offer comfort! But you're going to have to pull yourself together, no matter how empty and bereaved you feel. Our government needs your help, and you need to get out! I spoke with Armand Fayard yesterday morning, and he told me not to allow you to return to work—that the Gestapo has officers waiting to grab you outside the office! I have a means of protecting you, but you must pay attention and play your part. That's the main reason I came to Paris myself, as soon as I could arrange it."

Charles shook his head and pressed his hands to his temples. "Walter, why did this happen? Why did they do it?"

Stucki sighed. "Somebody in Otto Abetz's office called the Saint-Germain headquarters and suggested that in the attic of La Folie you were hiding armaments siphoned away from Fayard's Lorraine plant. My own informants tell me that Abetz visited Fayard not long ago, and following that visit, he became suspicious."

"Fayard would have taken our secret to his deathbed," Charles countered, shaking his head. "And why implicate *us*? It was a lie, anyway, Walter! I'd never have been fool enough to keep arms in my own house!"

"It sounds to me more like the vicious work of someone close enough to you and Fayard to have guessed at, or overheard, about your clandestine operation in Lorraine. But someone who wanted to nail *you in particular,* Charles—for whatever reason! And that's why now, you need to listen to me. Because if someone has gone to such lengths to cause you harm, then this individual isn't going to stop *until you have been killed or sent away!*"

"Who would hate me this much?" Charles wondered aloud.

"Does it really matter?" Stucki asked gently. "The point is, you're in mortal danger, and I'm trying to help."

But Charles had begun to weep, his shoulders heaving up and down. And he kept weeping, silently, until a measure of calm penetrated his being, and he was able to look up once more into Stucki's concerned face. "Tell me what you want from me," he said, his voice hoarse.

"There are about two thousand Swiss Jews still residing in France," the ambassador declared. "Our government is growing worried about them. We'll need someone important, someone like you, to organize two convoys to bring them back home. And as long as you're doing that, on top of your Swiss passport, you will be granted diplomatic immunity." He paused, and sighed. "But

Charles, you'll have to act fast! The Germans are becoming more evil every day, as their troops are dying at Stalingrad. Soon they'll be grabbing every Jew they can get their hands on, including ours, with no regard for their status as neutrals. Sweden, too, has decided to repatriate its Jewish citizens."

Charles dropped his head in his hands and was silent. Tactfully, the ambassador allowed his guest his moment of privacy.

Then, his voice very kind, he said, "I'm really awfully sorry about Anne. And after the recent news concerning your son . . . I can see how very deeply you must have loved her. Believe me, Charles, I wish there were something I could do."

Charles de Rochefleur lifted his head, and his eyes were burning with intensity. "There *is* something, Walter. You can make arrangements for me to take Christina, my cousin's daughter, with me and my mother. I can't leave her behind!"

The ambassador shook his head. "Charles, that will be almost impossible. The Germans will never want to grant an Austrian Jew an exit visa, and there'll be trouble at home as well. We sit surrounded by belligerent nations, and our small country has been unable to import any food. We've already let in several thousand refugee children from neighboring lands. How can I possibly go around so much red tape?"

"How can you *not,* Walter?" Charles countered simply.

The ambassador sighed once more, and held out his hand. "Charles, I can promise you that I will do my best. And we'll make every effort to locate your son. . . ."

Charles nodded wordlessly. He didn't have the strength to thank this kind man for his support. All he knew was that he would organize the convoys . . . in return for Christina's admission to Switzerland. That was all that mattered.

Because Tina was all he had left of Amelia.

* * *

On February 3, 1943, Christina Habig leaned out of the window of the train taking her to safety in Switzerland. Next to her, fragile and nervous, stood old Yvonne.

Charles had already sent the first thousand refugees home two days previously. Now, the remaining Swiss Jews were leaving France, fearing Nazi slaughter. But the eighteen-year-old girl gazed out at the rooftops of what had been her adopted country, and remembered a similar exodus, one step ahead of Hitler's cutthroats, five years before.

Only, that time, she and her mother had stood together by the window, waving good-bye to Vienna.

How was she ever going to survive, without Amelia?

And how would she survive if Alex weren't alive, *somewhere,* waiting for the end of the war to come and claim her?

The old woman beside her had lived a lifetime mostly on her own. She would understand, better than most, how it felt to have your beloved snatched from you at such an early age. But her aunt Yvonne had known what it was like to be a wife and a mother! Whereas Christina had never even slept with Alex . . . not once!

I should have found a way, she thought, her heart breaking and the tears finally spilling. I should have told you I would wait for you! Because, Alex de Rochefleur, *you will not die*! *You will come home to me!*

However long it took, Christina thought, she would think of him each day, willing him to cling to life. It was when you forgot, that a person really died. She had forgotten her father, as much as she had once loved him. And one day, even her mother's image would recede into a memory, ethereal and frail.

No, Alexis! Christina vowed. I will imagine you alive, every single day, until this horrid war is over and we can all come home. . . .

* * *

Armand Fayard's frail form rested against a mountain of crisp white down pillows, his face sagging, all color drained away. Only his bright black eyes testified to his virile past, and to a sharpness of mind that animated him even now.

Next to him, the neurologist, Dr. Pergola, stood admonishing Fayard's attorney, Maître Fernand Renard, to keep the interview to a few crucial minutes. "We can't risk your wearing him down any further," he cautioned.

"Go away, Pergola," Armand said hoarsely, shooing the doctor aside. "And keep my wife out, for God's sake!"

"I'll be right outside, Maître," Pergola said, and left the two men alone at last. Renard sat down on Fayard's bed, and for a moment the two old associates exchanged a long look. Then Fayard spoke, his voice reduced to a raspy whisper.

"Fernand, I can't fight any longer. To tell you the truth, if the boy were here, I'd have given one last push for his sake. But the way things are . . ." He cleared his throat, and continued. "Last night, I wrote a codicil to my existing will. Nothing in the world will convince me that Alex is dead! But I am not going to last out the war, and Charles has gone to Geneva, and so I need your help, urgently."

"You have it, Armand. You know that."

"Good." Fayard's beady eyes, like powerful magnets, stayed riveted to his solicitor's attentive face, and he proceeded. "A few months ago I thought it wise to advise you that Alexis de Rochefleur is in fact *my son*. I have always loved him, and he's returned my affection a thousandfold. And so I want to die in peace, knowing that whatever happens after my death, he would receive what rightfully should belong to him: my life's work, the network of companies that bear my name." When Renard nodded, he continued: "I've appointed Charles executor of my will. See to it, will you, that he receives it? I have your copy here, Fernand, and you can verify the provisions I've made. Fayard Industries will go to my son, Alexis de Rochefleur, unless, of course, he is dead. If he's alive, then he'll turn up, won't he, and claim what's his? Charles has reared him as his own child. I'm sure, once the Allies have won the war, Charles will return to Paris and move mountains to find Alex."

The old man closed his eyes wearily, and when he opened them again, Renard saw they were moist. But still, Fayard continued: "Until then, I want your firm to manage Fayard Industries under the close supervision of Charles de Rochefleur, who will act as chairman in absentia. He's always been a faithful friend, and a most excellent business associate. You will send mail to him in Switzerland for his approval and signature, twice a week, by diplomatic courier. Arrange it through Walter Stucki, the Swiss ambassador—surely you two will find a way to work this out. If Alex doesn't come home . . . well then, Fernand, of course the board will elect Charles permanent chairman, and chief executive officer." He coughed, then said, "Arabella will be taken care of. For the moment, you must take charge of this, but after the war, Alexis or Charles will take on the responsibility. I hope to God it's going to be Alexis . . . my only child."

"I'll be praying for him," the attorney declared. Taking Fayard's hand, he held it warmly. "About the codicil: It's fair, and it's legal. I shall see to it that Charles receives his copy in Geneva . . . although I hope we shan't have to act on it for a long time to come, old friend."

"Cut the sentimental nonsense, Fernand," the steelman coun-

tered brusquely. "I'll be buried before the fortnight is over, and
that's why it was essential that I see you now."

* * *

The young man awakened, his head swimming with pain, and
the room reeled around him. Nauseous, he lay back on a cushion,
and closed his eyes. "Easy does it," a voice cautioned him. "Your
right leg's broken in two pieces and you've suffered some kind of
concussion. What's your name?"

He didn't know. A terrible sense of panic assailed him, and he
felt the total hopelessness of his situation: *He had no idea of his
identity!* Opening his eyes, he tried once more to look around him.
Perhaps that would help him to know who he was. But all he could
see was that he was in a small, mansarded room, with paint chip-
ping on the ceiling.

The old woman sitting beside him asked gently, "You don't remember who you are, sonny?"

Sonny. A vague memory floated up to him of a woman with
bobbed brown hair and shining hazel eyes. *His mother.* He was
somebody's son. Yet that still didn't help. He tried to shake his
head, but it hurt too much, and so he gave up.

He felt a cool, wet cloth being applied to his forehead. And then
he felt nothing anymore, for he had fallen once again into a deep
blackness where reality did not exist.

Later . . . how much later? . . . he stirred again. Through the
small window he could see blue slate roofs, on an even line with the
window. He was on the top floor of a building.

The old woman at his side said, "Your fever's gone down. Are
you Jewish?"

Jewish: That meant something, didn't it? "Yes," he replied hesitantly. "I think so. . . ."

"Then I can't call the doctor," the woman demurred. "I've bandaged you myself, and the boys that found you tried to set your
leg. Does it hurt a lot?"

He felt like weeping. Who the hell *was* he, and how had he
gotten here? Licking his lips, he asked in a tremulous voice: "Madame, please tell me where I am, and who you are. That may help
me to remember what happened."

"The railwaymen that found you said you probably jumped
from a train in motion, on its way to Drancy. You were close to
Paris when that happened, and you spent one night with a relative
of one of the railwaymen. Then, the next day, they brought you to

me. I'm an old friend of Marcel's mother, and they knew I've helped those good Resistance fellows whenever I could . . . hiding a package here and there for them, delivering messages . . . that sort of thing. But never anything like a fugitive with a broken leg and complete amnesia!"

"Where are we?"

"In Paris, the rue Cambronne, in the Fifteenth Arrondissement. You a Parisian?"

Bewildered, he shrugged. "I'm not sure." And then he drifted off into sleep once more.

His dream was chaotic and jumbled. He was living in a beautiful old house, with a garden and a white gazebo. The woman with the bobbed hair and hazel eyes was talking to him. She was touching his forehead, lovingly, asking, "Does it hurt? Does it hurt?"

And then the image ended and was abruptly replaced by a blond man with a trim mustache—a very handsome middle-aged man, with blue eyes. Elegant and aloof. There was an old man there, too, with close-cropped white hair and sharp black eyes, and one side of his face was sagging. The old man was saying, "Come now, Charles! Let the boy make his move! It's *his turn, not yours!*" And the young man realized that the three of them were in some sort of office—an enormous room with a huge desk, and on the desk, a chess set.

He bolted awake, the dream still vivid. *Charles!* Who had those men been? But his heart was pumping with excitement, and he thought that if only he could figure out the answer, he'd have a clue . . . several clues . . . as to who he was!

Much later as the old woman was spoon feeding him, she told him, "You're going to be all right. I've changed your bandage and the swelling's gone down. You must be one brave boy. You in the Resistance?"

Now *here* was a word that immediately clicked. His mouth was full, but his eyes told her that she had struck gold. She smiled, revealing a silver tooth. "Good! At least we've got *something. . . .*"

In gratitude, he pressed her hand tremulously, his eyes welling up.

That night he had another dream. He was kissing a girl, a beautiful young girl, with eyes that were amazing: almond-shaped, and of a deep blue. She had soft black hair, and a tall, lithe body. And she was murmuring, "I'll never let you go, Alex—never, never!"

He awakened, with goose bumps. And when the old woman came in the next morning, he cried out, on a wave of excitement: "My name is *Alex*. I know a blond man named *Charles*, and I can play *chess*. My mother lives in a large house with a garden and a gazebo. . . ."

"Well," she told him. "That's what I call progress!"

It wasn't until weeks later, when she had finally unbandaged his head and he was able to sit up and hobble to the window on his one good leg, that more of the puzzle pieces came together. Until then, he had more or less understood that the kind old woman was the janitor of an apartment building, and that she had hidden him in a maid's room on the seventh floor. Paris was occupied by the Germans, who were Nazis, and French people had to use ration cards to obtain food. She was sharing her meager supply with him.

"How does one say thank you for something this overwhelming?" he asked her one evening.

"My boy, you don't. You just get well! And when you're well, and the war is over, just come and pay a visit to old Grandma Bourdin, in her janitor's quarters on the first floor. It makes me feel good to be helping one of our courageous young men. . . ."

Then one day he asked her to tell him her story, and she did. She had married a carpenter and had come to Paris as a young bride. After that he lost the plot line, because she had pronounced the magic word *Nancy*. She had been the daughter of a steelworker in Nancy, in Lorraine—had he ever been there?

A torrent of images assailed him at once, mostly of a young man collapsed at the wheel of a truck, and of Nazis arresting *him*. The name *François* flashed through his head. He shared it with her excitedly. And so she probed farther: Why had he been in Nancy? Did he know anyone there? What sort of business had he been involved in?

"Something about your own life fit, I think," he said. "The steel mills. . . ." He knew that she'd be bound to hit on it eventually, but now he felt a renewed sense of urgency. She was going to lead him to a discovery of his identity—he was sure of it!

She smiled, and touched his head gingerly, so as not to hurt his concussion. "Well, you're obviously not a millworker. You're an educated boy, refined even—a gentleman. Let's see, I was telling you about the mills . . ."

"Who owns them?" he asked abruptly.

"Well, it was a man called Fayard—big, powerful man, controlled the whole steel industry. But in my day—"

"*That's it!*" he exclaimed, elated. "*Armand Fayard!* He was my friend—my dear old friend! My God, Grandma Bourdin, if we could somehow find Fayard, he'd be able to fill in the missing pieces! I can't remember everything, but I can definitely remember *him,* and I know he'd help me right away! How can we get a message to him, do you suppose?"

But she sat looking down at her hands, suddenly ashen-faced. "Alex," she told him softly. "I'd go to him myself, if I could. But it's not possible. You see, I heard on the radio that Fayard passed away just a few days ago. . . ."

He sat staring at her, tears in his eyes. "Fayard is *dead?*" A terrible sense of loss came over him, and he struggled to pull something out of it—some additional clue. He knew that he had felt close to this man Fayard, and, all at once, images merged and his mind came alive with the certainty of having found his identity: *Alexis de Rochefleur!* He knew it was his name, and suddenly *he knew who he was*—or rather, who he had been. Chills went up and down his body. *He remembered!*

"*I know who I am!*" he cried. "Isn't it wonderful, Grandma Bourdin? I'm Alexis de Rochefleur, my father is Charles, my mother's Anne . . . and I'm in love with my second cousin, Christina. I'm a lawyer, and I've done a lot of work for the Resistance—and the *Boches* nabbed me in Nancy, your native city!"

"Then I shall find out what has happened to your family," the old woman said. "And now, my boy, sleep a while longer."

A few days later she came to his bedside and confessed that she had gone to the offices of Fayard Industries, to see if anyone there might tell her something about her young patient. He sat up excitedly, but she shook her head and suddenly started to cry. Appalled, he reached out and grabbed her arm, asking her what she'd found out that was so dreadful.

She told him she had learned a great deal about Alexis de Rochefleur. That his mother had been killed by the Nazis, and his father had fled to Switzerland. That the family home—some sumptuous mansion in one of the suburbs—had been requisitioned by the Germans. All this had happened recently, over the past three months . . . a time that seemed to coincide with Monsieur Fayard's final stroke.

"If you are Alexis, then, my dear child, a lot of tragedy has occurred in your absence. I almost hope you're wrong, and that you're someone else."

It was extremely difficult not to break down, and to keep his tears inside. But he shook his head, and she understood, from his gesture of despair, that he had put the pieces back in order. For him, there was no doubt left that he was, indeed, the ill-fated Alexis de Rochefleur.

As she pulled the short, homemade curtains closed, he asked softly, "And Christina? My cousin Amelia? Did anybody tell you what's become of *them?*"

Madame Bourdin's shoulders rose and fell, resignedly. "That girl I spoke to didn't mention those names," she said to him. "But one thing she *did* tell me was that Monsieur Charles, the man you dreamed about, is definitely your father. And that he took everyone that was left in the family along with him to Switzerland, to wait out the war."

Alexis closed his eyes, relief sweeping over him. Charles would not have left Amelia and Tina behind—of this he could be sure. "At least, I haven't lost *her,*" he said, all at once overcome with the enormity of all he *had* lost. And, completely exhausted, he lay back and fell asleep at once, dreaming of François and his mother, and of Armand Fayard.

In his dream the war was over, and his mother was young again. She was sitting in the garden of La Folie, chatting with him and his friend François, her voice charming and light.

Someone else was approaching from the house. In the dream, Alexis could feel his own heart lifting with a strong, reassuring gladness. The man raised his hand in greeting, and Alexis recognized Armand Fayard.

His mother was murmuring something, but suddenly her words were no longer important. All that mattered was that *they were all here.*

CHAPTER XXIII

The arrangement suited Charles. Every Tuesday and Friday he would go to a discreet conference room on the second floor of the Geneva City Hall, where a diplomatic courier on Walter Stucki's payroll would bring him a fresh batch of correspondence from Armand Fayard's office in Paris.

Fayard himself had organized the setup. This way, Charles could most ably manage the steel company from the safety of Switzerland.

Since he'd arrived in Geneva, the Swiss authorities had been bending over backward in gratitude for his having supervised the Jewish exodus from Paris. It helped, of course, that back in 1940 he'd transferred the headquarters of the Crédit Industriel to the comely Swiss city. For that made him unquestionably one of its most wealthy inhabitants.

He was immensely rich, and highly regarded. But, he thought, anger and bitterness surging through his veins, what good was it to have achieved all this *now*, when Amelia was dead? A terrible grief overcame him, and he steadied his hold on the back railing of the luxurious elevator bringing him to his biweekly meeting place. Now, when Anne no longer stood between them, when he controlled a worldwide banking empire, he was unable to marry the woman he had always loved and yearned for. The woman with whom he would have wanted to share his newfound glory. Especially with Fayard on his deathbed, and the promise of even greater power once he inherited the bulk of Fayard Industries!

I've lost her, Charles thought, but at least I have Christina. She is my inheritance from Amelia . . . the daughter I wish she'd been able to give me. Soon I shall have to find her a husband, but not for a while. For now, I shall live with the illusion that she is my daughter, and we shall help each other to get over the burning pain of losing Amelia.

If only the girl would stop thinking of that goddamned Alexis!

Alexis . . . whose fate was as yet undetermined, the matter of his whereabouts and of his very existence still unresolved. Charles stepped out of the elevator and into the long hallway, seething with annoyance, as he always did when he remembered that Anne's son had yet to be heard from. The news Charles hoped to hear was a confirmation of Alexis's death. Unless this could be definitely proven, Charles would have to wait a number of years until he could have the boy declared legally dead. Years in which he himself would have to remain no more than *acting* chairman of the Crédit Industriel, which Alexis would have inherited according to Alfred's will, upon Anne's demise.

All his life Charles had been *waiting*. Waiting, in his youth, to find a way of regaining his family home by wresting it away from Alfred; waiting for Amelia to fall in love with him; waiting for something to happen to Anne, leaving him free to marry his beloved; and now, finally, *waiting for confirmation of* Alexis's death, in order to stay at the head of an empire his own grandfather had founded.

And there was something else Charles was forced to wait for: revenge. Ever since he'd spoken to Stucki at the Hotel George V, Charles had known the truth about that terrible day when the Gestapo had burst into La Folie and murdered Amelia and Anne. Stucki had brought him all the clues, but, like a fool, Charles had overlooked the obvious conclusion. It hadn't been till later, on the train bearing him to Geneva, that he had digested Stucki's information: Someone had tipped off Otto Abetz, the German ambassador, about his and Alexis's involvement in the underground. Someone who'd wanted to destroy Charles, no matter what. Without implicating Fayard himself in the process. And that person could only have been *Arabella*—Arabella, who hated him for having ended their affair, and who could have learned all there was to know about clandestine operations put into motion from her husband's sickbed. . . .

Arabella, sure as the steel in Armand Fayard's foundries, had ordered Charles's execution. Only she'd misfired, and he hadn't been caught. Amelia and Anne had been killed instead, his house confiscated and his servants imprisoned. Charles did have a plan for evening the score with Arabella, but with the Nazis still in control of Paris, and Fayard still alive, he could do nothing more than plan.

At least, where Fayard Industries is concerned, I won't have to wait much longer, he thought with sudden hunger. He'd loved that old man and wished him back to health—but after the last stroke, Charles had realized that the game was over: there was no way Fayard would survive the year. And so, after an initial period of chastising himself for building his own future on his mentor's ashes, Charles had accepted reality and *waited yet again*—this time, for the announcement of Fayard's demise.

Charles would have his vengeance, and he would have his empire, an empire so vast, it would encompass industry and high finance: steel factories, mills, mines and international banks. If he waited patiently enough, the odds would turn in his favor, and Alexis and Arabella would both be finished off. If only Amelia had survived to be his wife. . . .

The minute he crossed the threshold into the small conference room, Charles realized that something had occurred. The Swiss courier, Hans Kepler, stood up at once, and walked over to him. "I'm sorry, Monsieur de Rochefleur—so terribly sorry! Monsieur Fayard's attorney, Fernand Renard, met me in Paris yesterday and told me that Armand Fayard had passed away three nights ago."

As much as he'd expected this, the news shocked Charles. Sitting down, he could feel his heart hammering. Armand Fayard had acted as a father to him. His kindness had been topped only by the superb way he had trained Charles to execute and manage the huge steel enterprise. "Did he—did he suffer?" he questioned.

"No. He went to sleep and never awakened. Madame Fayard and the butler found him that way in the morning."

"I see." Charles remained lost in thought. Stunned, he could not quite digest the secondary significance of Fayard's death: that as of now, *he, Charles, owned everything*! But at last he reacted. "Did Renard give you anything?" he demanded. "Some kind of official document?"

The courier hurried to his briefcase, apologetic. "Yes, yes, of course! There were a number of highly important papers, because it seems that Monsieur Fayard had named *you* to be executor of his estate. Here, let me see—"

"It's all right, Kepler," Charles interrupted him. "Leave the whole batch on the table, and I'll go through everything when you leave. I'll be able to put things in their proper order. Don't be concerned." Because he wanted Kepler gone, that he might savor his first moment as head of the Fayard dynasty by himself. *Without witness.*

With deferential gratitude, Hans Kepler bowed in acknowledgment, and hastened toward the door. "All right, Monsieur de Rochefleur—and thank you. Oh, by the way, Madame Fayard sends her regards," he added, turning to give Charles a most quizzical look. "She came in while Renard and I were still doing business and asked me to convey to you her . . . 'congratulations.' "

Charles's lips parted. "I thought this very strange, on the part of a grieving widow," Hans Kepler declared, shaking his head. Then the courier left the room.

Alone at last, Charles attacked the pile of documents with trembling fingers. Among them lay the key to his destiny . . . the proclamation of his inauguration as head of the Fayard empire. *The king is dead; long live the king!* he thought, wondering if crown princes, hearing their fathers had just died, shared his sense of exhilaration mixed with sadness.

He felt gratitude toward Fayard, above all. Fayard had discovered him, taken him under his wing, given him every opportunity to benefit from his wisdom and tutelage—and now, as a final gift, he was handing Charles the keys to the kingdom he had ruled for so many years.

Ah! Here was the letter notifying him of the general terms of the will, signed by Armand himself. Hardly breathing in his eagerness to devour its words, Charles set it aside to look for the will itself. It was there, inside a leather binder—pages and pages of typewritten forms, with a codicil. Now he could sit down and read the letter, and later, at his leisure, he'd go through the entire document in the comfort of his own office.

Charles chose a wide-backed armchair by the window, and sat down. Armand had begun quite as Charles had expected: praising his devotion, speaking of their many years of close friendship and understanding. But suddenly Charles froze. "I can't believe this," he muttered aloud, standing up to hold the letter to the direct light of the sun shining through the windowpanes. And then, again: *"I can't believe this!"*

Armand Fayard had written:

My dear Charles, I must now beg you to forgive me for breaking open your own life, and revealing a secret that will surely shatter you. For this, I am deeply sorry.

Had Anne been alive, I think she would never have allowed me to tell you the truth, but all the years you and I spent together, the issue of my silence weighed heavy inside my heart. For the sake of our friendship, I owe you an explanation. And for the sake of Alexis, I must speak out. His future is at stake, and it is more important than any other question—including your opinion of me, and even your opinion of Anne. *He is all that matters.*

Charles, when Anne married you, she was already pregnant. What she never told you, out of consideration for her son, was that *I was his father.* I can understand her feelings. She loved you passionately, and wanted you to accept Alex as your own. She wanted her son to have the father of her choice, not of true fact. Because Anne and I shared no love affair, Charles: our moment together was nothing more than one brief evening, born of loneliness and fear on her part, and, on mine, the passing fancy of an older man for a young woman's purity and waking desirability.

I behaved like a middle-aged scoundrel, and for this, I still feel shame. But Alexis exists, Charles, and he is my son. Now that I am dying, I want you to continue to do what you have done since he was born: to act as his father. For I am not attempting to take him away from you. Were I not dying, I would leave things as they were. But, since I am on my deathbed, I must spell out what I wish to be done. *Alex is alive, Charles—I know it!* Find him—and then, execute this will.

According to the codicil you will receive from Fernand Renard, Alexis will inherit Fayard Industries. He is eminently suited for such a responsibility, mainly thanks to the excellent upbringing you and Anne gave him. But he is still young, Charles, and will need every bit of guidance you can offer him.

I trust that, being a man of good heart, you will not hold his parentage against Alexis. Let us say that he has had two fathers: one, who reared him and will remain his father always; and the other, biological, who has loved him from a distance for many years, and who in no way wishes to interfere in his relationship with his first, legal father. I bless you both—you, who have shown me the devotion of a true friend, and he, who is everything I ever hoped for in a son.

With·these words I take my leave of you, dear Charles, embracing you with all my affection and gratitude.

The signature, "Armand Fayard," was as familiar to Charles as his own—and yet, staring at it, Charles felt such horror that he could barely make it out. *Alexis—Fayard's son?* It seemed too incredible to believe, almost as incredible as the fact that *Fayard was leaving everything to that bastard!* He, Charles, was to receive nothing, while Alexis was coming away with the entire bulk of Fayard Industries!

Charles fell heavily into his chair, his hand shaking. Not since Amelia had sent him back his engagement ring had he felt so shocked and betrayed. He'd loved Armand Fayard . . . loved him, toiled and sweated beside him, given him his best years and his clearest vision. And, as recompense, Fayard had completely overlooked him.

In itself, this fact would have been enough to destroy Charles. But, as a fatal blow, he'd given everything to Alexis—Anne's son, whom Charles had hated all his life. *Fayard's son! I've been rearing Fayard's goddamned son,* Charles thought, suddenly breaking into an absurd bark of laughter. For the ultimate irony lay in the fact that, to demonstrate his gratitude for having reared his son, Armand Fayard had totally passed *Charles* by, leaving everything to *the person Charles most hated in the world*!

Taking hold of his emotions, Charles set the letter down over the pile of correspondence and the will. He had to think this through. Alexis was lost, perhaps dead. Maybe he'd never show up, and if he didn't, Charles would inherit Fayard Industries after all. Hadn't Charles been hoping for news of Alex's death, to ensure him his chairmanship of the Crédit Industriel?

Alexis was either dead, or captured by the Nazis. In either case, Charles reasoned, he might as well be presumed dead. No one survived the Nazi tortures! He took a deep breath, opened his own attaché case, and placed the sheaf of papers inside. Then he snapped it shut and pulled down on the lapels of his jacket, to spruce up his appearance. *The boy was dead.*

Now that Charles knew Alexis's identity, it was easier to admit his hatred of Anne's son. For the ridiculous charade Charles had played all these years, at Anne's bequest, could fall away like the dead skin off a molting lizard. He'd never hated his own son: he'd hated *Fayard's bastard*. And he, Charles Lévy–de Rochefleur, would once and for all cease worrying over the possibility of the boy's survival. The odds were dead against it.

* * *

Christina Habig found Geneva pleasant enough. It was certainly a pretty city. Bordering the lake were the rue du Rhône and the parallel rues Basses, and behind them rose a craggy little mountain called the Cité, dotted with houses and crowned with Saint Peter's Cathedral. Narrow streets wound their way steeply to the very top, on which stood City Hall. On its other side, a wide avenue fell sharply to a public park, the Jardin des Bastions, where she and her aunt Yvonne liked to stroll together.

Across the park was the Corraterie, Geneva's equivalent to the rue du Faubourg Saint-Honoré, marked by its elegant stores. And round the mountain lay the Rhône River and the lake. Christina, accustomed to taking civilized walks in Vienna, found it a healthy pastime to wander through the walkways of Geneva.

Charles had purchased a sumptuous apartment in Champel, which, in earlier times, had been a wooded hillside in the far reaches of Geneva. Chalets had been built among the trees, walls erected between properties. The roads were unpaved, bordered by hedges and tall trees. Many denizens of Geneva proper had frankly considered it the country and built summer homes on its slopes.

But now all this had changed, and Champel was an elegant neighborhood of Geneva. The adorable chalets had been demolished, and with them, the trees. But the streets were large, open to the sun, with pleasant sidewalks, and the houses were four or five stories high. Cyclists loved to ride down the asphalted slopes, to the consternation of nannies and governesses taking their charges out for their daily walks.

Christina was eighteen this February of 1943.

Her old aunt Yvonne was still, at seventy-one, an ardent lover of nature and a painter—and the two women spent many an hour by Yvonne's easel facing Lake Geneva. But it was Charles to whom Christina now clung, Charles whose constant affection gave her comfort and steadiness. Christina knew that to him she had become the living image of Amelia, and the young girl was touched by the extent to which he had loved her mother. She responded wholeheartedly, and with gratitude.

Yet, Christina was not happy. The pain of losing Amelia

throbbed like an unhealed wound, making her break into tears at the strangest moments: eating an ice cream, climbing a hill, hearing a joke, she would suddenly want to share this with her mother —only, Amelia wasn't there. And, on a very conscious level, she grieved for Alexis, missing him at each turn of the road. She clung to the thought that somewhere, he was still alive. She had no choice but to believe this or, she knew, she would fall apart and lose her reason for living.

Finding her in tears as she looked out over the hillside of Champel, Charles had come up behind her and started speaking. "Don't, sweetheart! Don't do this—it does neither of us any good! Your mother's death was the worst thing that ever happened in my life, but you must remember, we have each other. You're like a daughter to me, Tina. We owe it to Amelia to make a home together, to stay close, you and I. . . ."

"This time I wasn't thinking of Mama," she whispered, turning to face him. "I was thinking of Alex."

She felt him stiffen. Then he said, "We must all come to terms with the fact that Alexis is dead, Tina. Had he been alive, we would have gotten word."

She turned to him, and he was startled by the fire in her eyes. "*How?* The war is still going on, the frontier isn't open, and there are no regular mail routes between here and France—"

Charles sighed. "One day you will forget Alexis," he said to her, trying to be gentle. "There will be other men, other loves."

Her eyes captured him with the blaze of their intensity. "Nobody ever replaced Mama for *you,*" she pointed out quietly. "You loved her all the years of your adult life."

He couldn't face the honesty of her emotion. But, once again, Charles de Rochefleur, who hadn't prayed in years, prayed—with a fierceness that flamed through him—for rapid confirmation of Anne's son's death.

*   *   *

Alexis sat up, gingerly touching his bad leg. A dizzy spell washed over him, and he had to recline in the comfortable plush armchair. Madame Bourdin bent over him and felt his perspiring forehead. "Don't you move," she admonished. "You're still weak, and I won't leave you alone unless you promise to be good."

He smiled at her, his eyes moistening. "How kind you are. Grandma Bourdin, you're the only one I have now, do you know that? Without you where would I be?"

But then his dark eyes clouded. "I've got to locate Maître Fernand Renard," he said with determination. "He was legal counsel for Armand Fayard and would have news of my family in Switzerland. Christina will be anxious to hear from me."

The old woman shrugged, and held her hands palms-out in front of him. "I'll just have to return to the Fayard offices. That nice girl at the reception desk—the one who gave me all the background on you, Alex—*she*'ll know where to find this attorney Renard. And then I'll go to his house and tell him you're alive. He'll help you, dear. He'll get word to your father in Switzerland . . . and to that Christina of yours." She was smiling at him, with that special tenderness of a seasoned old citizen toward a young one in the throes of romantic love.

* * *

At the front door of the Fayard Industries headquarters, Lise Bourdin was greeted by two uniformed officers of the Gestapo. "Your papers, please!" one of them demanded.

The old woman felt herself go limp. She looked through her pocketbook and extricated her identification card, and handed it to the man. He examined it and passed it to his companion. "You have business with Fayard Industries?" the first officer demanded, his tone harsh and curt.

"No, it's personal, monsieur."

His eyes sharpened. "You know anyone called 'Rochefleur'? Alexis or Charles?"

Madame Bourdin's teeth started to chatter. She shook her head. "Never heard the name?" the second man pressed her.

"No, I'm sorry," Lise Bourdin stated. "I was just dropping by to chat with my niece. She works at the reception desk."

"You'll have to visit her at home," the first man informed her. "Since this morning, the only people allowed in the Fayard offices are those cleared by Ambassador Abetz's office. I'm sorry."

"Thank you," the old woman murmured, and turned away.

"They're on the lookout for you, dear," she told Alexis later that day. "They wouldn't even let me inside. I think they'll be posted outside every place you might go, so we'll have to be doubly careful. We don't want any suspicious neighbors asking questions about who you are."

As he opened his mouth to answer her, she shook her head. "Now I realize just who I've been harboring in my little room. A real *de Rochefleur*. No wonder they're eager to find you, young man. You aren't just an everyday Parisian—you're an important person!"

But he stayed her with a motion of his hand. "No, Grandma Bourdin—I'm just Alex, the boy you've mended and put back together, who owes you his life." His face reflected intense sorrow and longing, and he turned his head as he spoke.

"So we'll have to forget about getting word out to anyone," he whispered. "I can be safe only if no one knows I'm here—alive."

*   *   *

Springtime in Geneva might have made almost anyone forget a war was still raging outside Switzerland—but not Christina Habig. It was already her second Geneva spring, and instead of alleviating her misery, the verdant renaissance of buds and tiny leaves, the burst of color on the hillside as multitudes of crocuses bloomed, only sharpened her sense of loneliness.

She was standing on a marble terrace in a white piqué dress, looking out dreamily toward the shimmering expanse of the lake. Behind her, a reception was taking place, and strains of music from a discreet chamber orchestra wafted out.

The tall young man next to her moved closer, balancing a plate of hors d'oeuvre in one hand and a champagne glass in the other. He had pleasant, even features, green eyes, and wavy brown hair, and his afternoon suit had been specially confectioned on Savile Row. Yet Christina didn't look at him, even when he spoke, his tone urgent and pleading.

"You know I've fallen in love with you," he was telling her. "I'm twenty-five years old, my father and your cousin are in business together, and when I turn thirty, I'm to become senior vice-president at my father's bank. Why won't you marry me, Christina?"

She finally turned, her face troubled. "I'm flattered, Robert, truly flattered. But how could I marry you when I'm in love with someone else? And how could Cousin Charlie expect it of me, when the one I'm in love with is *his own son*? Doesn't anybody care about Alex anymore?"

The young man sighed. "My father says Alexis de Rochefleur is surely dead. Christina, do you want to stay single all your life, waiting like Penelope for a Ulysses who will never come home? You've got to wake up to reality! And if you don't love me now, you'll learn to love me. I'll make you a good husband! You'll see— in time, you'll forget there ever was another man in your life!"

Bright red spots sprang out on her cheekbones, and she cried out angrily, "Robert Dreyfus, I'm losing patience with you! The answer is no, as it was last week, and the week before! I won't think about marrying anyone—not until the war is over and I can find Alexis, myself, if I have to!"

And, her vision blurring with tears, she ran back inside the house.

* * *

In rapid succession, the days of August 1944 went by in the heat of expectation, the hopes of the Parisians rising first timidly, then in mounting crescendo. It appeared that after four years of siege, Paris would finally be rid of its occupiers. *The nightmare was about to end.*

And so, like a badly spliced newsreel, each day brought a fresh supply of false rumors and happy announcements, as the Germans evacuated the French capital to make room for the impending Allied takeover.

Sunday, August 20, 1944

In their small janitor's flat, Alexis de Rochefleur and Lise Bourdin tried to catch bits of news over the BBC. The announcer claimed that the Germans would leave the city by midnight, for the Americans were barely three miles outside the Porte de Saint-Cloud, and would be there the following day. The Red Cross had freed fifteen hundred prisoners at the deportation camp of Drancy.

With evening came a fresh, cool breeze. A loudspeaker blasted through the streets, claiming that the Germans had agreed not to shoot the people they had recently arrested but to give them the same status as prisoners of war. In return, the French Provisional Government had promised to allow the fleeing Nazis free passage through the roads leading to Compiègne and Versailles.

"I thought all the *Boches* had already left," Alexis said. "That was the agreement, wasn't it?"

"Agreements with those pigs don't mean a thing! I saw eight truckloads of them driving by this afternoon," his old friend informed him. "And there was fighting in the streets between the Germans and our boys."

Alexis's eyes brightened, but she placed a cautionary hand on his forearm. "You're not going out there," she warned him severely. "You're a cripple, Alexis de Rochefleur. And right now the last person our fellows need hanging on their coattails is a limping hero of the Resistance. Time enough for that later on. . . ."

Tuesday, August 22

So, after his valiant efforts in the Morvan, he was to be reduced to listening to rumors brought in by an old woman. Alexis felt restless and angry in his helpless condition (his right leg had been improperly set and he walked with a severe limp). All he seemed good for was helping Madame Bourdin sew up the remains of an old red scarf, a white handkerchief, and a blue pillowcase into a crude flag.

All day, the question had lingered: *Would the Allies be here today?* But they hadn't yet entered the city. "I didn't see any *Boches* today," Lise Bourdin stated, snapping off a thread with her front teeth. But they had heard that fighting had occurred in the rue de la Pompe, where Amelia and Christina had lived, and in the Place Victor-Hugo, Place de Clichy, and Cité areas.

The Germans had taken back the police headquarters, as well as the city hall. And they brought back fifteen "tigers," huge tanks with cannon. "They're laughing in our faces," Alexis remarked, infuriated. "Four days in a row they've been ordered to leave the city by midnight!"

A neighbor tapped on the door and told Madame Bourdin that the Americans had arrived at the Porte d'Orléans; but she refused to let him in. "Who knows?" she murmured uneasily. "Anyone might turn out to be an informer, and the Germans, knowing they've been beaten, are more vicious than ever!"

Wednesday, August 23

The Parisians were weary. Nervous tension had finally worn them down. No one felt the courage to go out: most of the stores were closed, and there was nothing to do. Alexis and Lise played double solitaire, and she told him stories of her youth that she thought she had forgotten.

She brought back four newspapers, which heralded good tidings. *Why, then, hadn't the Allies penetrated inside Paris?* "Do you know," the old woman told him, "from Lyon you can travel in three different directions—to the ocean, the Mediterranean and the Alps—and you won't find a single German left along any of those roads?"

Thursday, August 24

During the night, it rained. And in the morning the population awakened energized and ready for more good news. General

Leclerc was at the Porte d'Italie and would be in Paris by noon; no, he was at the Porte d'Orléans and would make his entrance at five that afternoon. The Americans, it seemed, wanted to let de Gaulle enter the city first, passing through the Arc de Triomphe at the head of his troops—but de Gaulle was in Rennes, and no one knew where the French army of Normandy was.

Alexis, hidden in the small apartment, heard cannon fire all through the day.

Lise brought him copies of the newspapers *Le Figaro* and *France Libre,* which said that London, Quebec, and Montreal were decorated with flags, and that the British had wired congratulations to the French. The BBC announced that the French were already at Anthony, a southern suburb of Paris, and the Americans, at the rue d'Alésia inside the city!

* * *

Old Golle, the Fayard maître d'hôtel, opened the front door to two tall, portly French policemen. "We've come for Arabella Fayard," they declared. "Where is she?"

"Madame is having breakfast, gentlemen. I can't disturb her."

"Then I'm afraid we'll have to do it for you. Where is the lady having her breakfast, my good man?"

Appalled, Golle stepped back, unsure what to do next. The two policemen walked in and looked around the paneled vestibule, raising their brows, impressed. Then the first one said, "You'll have to go get her, old man, and right away."

She stood in the doorway, diminutive in her silk lounging robe, trimmed with lace and the soft marabou feathers she had always fancied, her small face clear of makeup and her blond hair pinned off her forehead. As she walked in the two men thought she was a thirty-year-old woman, but on closer inspection they saw myriad small lines webbed around her eyes and mouth, making her appear every one of her fifty years.

Still, she was a lady. The wife of a man who had long stood for the best and bravest their country had to offer.

"What may I do for you?" she demanded, half haughty, half solicitous. A gracious hostess accustomed to pleasing, but a snob unaccustomed to dealing with such riffraff as patrolmen of the Versailles police.

"You are to come with us, madame, right away. I'd advise you not to make a fuss, because if necessary we are prepared to carry you out by force."

"But you have no right!" old Golle sputtered, stepping between the two men and his mistress. "Do you know who you're talking to?"

The taller, heftier patrolman spoke up, looking past the old butler directly at the small blond Englishwoman. "Madame Fayard, you are responsible for the death of Mesdames Anne de Rochefleur and Amelia Habig, and for the deportation of three of their guests as well as their four servants. You were a traitor to Free France, a collaborator. We have evidence that it was you who told Ambassador Abetz in December 1942 that arms could be found inside Monsieur Charles de Rochefleur's estate, La Folie!"

Arabella's face, already pale, turned ashen. Golle was staring at her, horrified. "Come with us, madame," the second patrolman ordered, his voice all sarcastic politeness. "We have some old accounts to settle. . . ."

Outside, under the blazing sun, a crowd of Versailles citizens stood gathered together, watching eagerly. As the two policemen emerged from the superb Fayard mansion, Arabella between them in her lounging robe, an enormous cry arose: "Traitor! Cut off her hair! Cut the whore's hair!"

One of the policemen had brought a chair with him from inside the house. Terrified, Arabella cowered between them. "Wh-what are you going to do with me?" she asked.

The policemen grabbed her under the elbows. "Exactly what the people want," the first one said, smiling. "We're going to shave your head, like all the other female collaborators. Just be glad, madame, that your husband didn't live to know who you were!"

The crowd parted to let them through. They walked, Arabella's head hanging in fear and shame, to the whistles, catcalls, and insults of the mob that followed. They walked to the town square. And there, the two policemen set the chair down and forced Arabella to sit as hundreds of onlookers stared.

First came the scissors, shearing off her golden locks and leaving only short, bristly gray roots. Arabella's face was bathed in tears, and she could look at no one. Her ears had drowned out the crowd's hoots and derisive laughter. So Charles had won, after all. . . . He had gotten his revenge. After this public humiliation—where could she take refuge?

The policemen hadn't finished, however. Expectantly, the crowd waited. Out came the razor. Arabella felt its sharp blade against her scalp, and cried out. The mob burst into chants of mockery. A flashbulb went off. Arabella burst into tears.

As she stood up, her head totally shorn and shaved, she thought, hysterically: *I'll go back to England!* After this public branding ceremony, she'd never be able to appear in Parisian society again. And she raised her eyes to the multitude, searching to find one pair of sympathetic eyes . . . one friend, or, at the very least, someone undecided in his condemnation.

The first face she encountered, at the edge of the mob, was that of faithful old Golle, who had served her for thirty years. But his eyes showed her no mercy or compassion. He wasn't her servant anymore, but a Frenchman whose righteous anger and lust for vengeance had been provoked.

Yes, Arabella thought as a second flashbulb went off, momentarily blinding her, *I'll go back to Brighton, and settle there . . .*

* * *

The streets lay in total darkness, the gaslights unlit, for electricity was more sporadic than ever. That evening, August 24, Lise and Alexis jumped up from the dinner table to find out what the commotion was about. Lise pushed the window open, and cries of "Hip, hip, hurrah! *Vive la France!*" reached their ears like a blast of cool, invigorating air.

It was difficult to make out more than the general outline of people walking through the street, chanting. "Tonight, Grandma, even you won't be able to keep me out of this!" Alexis cried. And, grabbing the old woman's hand, he hobbled to the door and made his way into the street.

A group of enthusiastic Frenchmen, singing together, greeted them. Alexis and Lise pressed into the crowd, and he placed an arm around the old woman's shoulders, and hugged her. "God, this feels good," he whispered.

But suddenly, a man and a woman broke from the crowd and started to run off. Bewildered, Alexis craned his neck in the darkness, to make out what had scared the couple away. Just then a cry arose: "Watch out! The *SS!*"

In the stampede that ensued, Alexis was separated from Lise Bourdin, and pushed and shoved down onto the pavement, his bad leg giving out. In front of the apartment building, a small troop of Nazi SS soldiers marched up, their boots clicking on the concrete. Alexis remained on the ground, hoping no one would notice him until they were gone.

At last, they were rounding the corner of the street. Unsteadily, the young man stood up. But just as the SS soldiers were filing away, the last of them turned around for one final look of surveillance. And in that instant, Alexis knew he had been seen, his moving shadow spotted on the pavement.

Mustering all his flagging strength, he limped into a run, dragging his bad leg along behind him, just as the bullets started to fly. He reached the carriage entrance to Lise Bourdin's building and felt a tremendous pain in his left shoulder. He collapsed and his final thought was to fall toward the open doorway to the building.

And then darkness enveloped him.

Friday, August 25

Alexis awakened, his shoulder throbbing so badly, for a moment he was afraid he'd vomit from the pain. By Lise Bourdin's chipped sink, he saw a strange man in shirt sleeves washing his hands. The man turned and smiled at him. "You'll be all right," he said. "It's not a deep wound—not like your leg. But you'll have to miss the parade tomorrow, I'm afraid."

Through the pain, Alex felt excitement, and he attempted to sit up. "No, don't move," the doctor advised him, helping him back gently.

And then he saw Lise coming out of the kitchen, with a small tray and drinks. The old woman smiled, and nodded. "That's right, Alex: *they're here!*"

She sat down beside him, holding a cup of broth to his lips, and told him she'd been out to see them: tanks, military trucks, and motor-lorries, loaded with dirty, unshaven men, their tired eyes aglow. France's brave saviors. The crowd had greeted them with delirious shouts, young girls climbing on board to kiss the soldiers and throw flowers to them as they'd slowly rolled along the Avenue Mozart.

And he had missed everything.

Tired, weak, his shoulder throbbing, Alexis said to the doctor and his old friend: "You'll have to barricade the door if you expect I'll miss the parade tomorrow!" And then he closed his eyes, and slept.

Saturday, August 26

At 3:15 P.M., de Gaulle passed under the Arc de Triomphe, and a crowd of thousands along the Avenue des Champs-Elysées broke into the national anthem, the "Marseillaise." De Gaulle passed alone, on foot, and behind him one tank. Then came General Leclerc, also alone, and on foot. The crowd cheered and applauded, a tidal wave of enthusiasm and emotion.

And then it was over. The passage of the two generals and the ovation that had accompanied them had lasted six minutes—just that, but six unforgettable minutes. Still, troops were coming through, and groups of civilians. The public shouted, singing the "Marseillaise," "La Madelon," "God Save the King," and "Tipperary." The French people did not start to depart until after four o'clock, when Lise dragged an exhausted, limping, bandaged Alexis away from the sidewalk.

When the doctor came that night to check on his patient, he found Alexis in bed, delirious with a high fever. A young neighbor had given the wounded young man a ride on his bicycle, both to and from the Champs-Elysées, but the entire experience had been too much for him. "You can't blame the boy," Lise said to the doctor. "He's twenty-three and a hero of the Resistance. He deserved to be present at the liberation of Paris, don't you think?"

But already she felt herself begin to weep. For if Paris was free, how much longer would Alexis de Rochefleur remain in her care in the tiny flat? A de Rochefleur belonged with his own kind, in his mansion with gleaming antiques, and Alexis, as grateful and loving as he'd been toward her for almost two years, would soon forget Lise Bourdin.

Yet for a while, at least, he'd be forced to stay. His shoulder was wounded, and he'd be needing her till it was set and he could manage on his own.

* * *

Lise Bourdin waited on a hard-backed chair, her hands neatly folded in her lap. All around her in the large outer office, secretaries scurried to and from paper-littered desks, where young men of the Paris Liberation Committee stood in small groups conferring in low voices.

At length a man smelling vaguely of perspiration came up to her. "May I help you?"

She nodded, all at once made shy by the enormity of the work planned in this room. These men would be discussing how to wrest the remaining occupied areas of France from Hitler's forces. And here she was, with her small request—but how important a request it was, to Alexis!

Sensing her reticence, the young man motioned toward a small inner office. "Please, madame," he said, with an unexpected politeness that touched her. "We'll be more comfortable in there. My name's André Guiraud."

Away from the noise of typewriters and tittering laughter, of men's voices suddenly rising then falling, Lise withdrew the letter from her tattered bag. "Monsieur Guiraud," she said. "Since December 1942 I've been caring for a young man—a wounded hero of the Resistance, caught by the Nazis outside Nancy, who escaped from a cattle car on his way to a deportation camp. His family is Jewish. They've reestablished themselves in Switzerland, where, he tells me, his father set up the headquarters of their business. No one knows he's alive, and he's anxious to get news to them. Now that Paris is ours again, is there no way for you somehow to get this letter to the border town of Annemasse, where the mail to Geneva is functioning normally? His father's a prosperous financier. If he's in Geneva, as Alexis supposes, the Geneva postal office will forward the message to the proper address."

Guiraud's eyebrows shot up quizzically. "That's a mighty request, madame. We do, however, have intricate networks of men in our underground, and I imagine we could try to relay the letter to Annemasse. But you must tell your patient, at best it's a risky bet we're taking that it will reach his father. Who, may I ask, is your young guest?"

"His name is Alexis de Rochefleur," Lise replied, pride edging into her voice.

Guiraud smiled. "You've been keeping a de Rochefleur from the *Boches* for two years? I'm quite impressed, madame. . . ." Then, more seriously, he added, "But I'm making no promises. Our boys are working to reconquer our country, and personal correspondence has to assume a very low priority in the hierarchy of their mission."

"I understand," Lise said, holding out her hand. Guiraud took it in both of his, and shook it warmly.

"*Au revoir*, then, madame," he said to her. "And good luck to you both."

* * *

In his discreetly paneled office, Charles stared at the long sheets of notepaper for a moment, his fingers beginning to shake as he sat holding the letter. A glittering sun, the color of beaten egg yolk, was welcoming October just outside his window overlooking Lake Geneva. But Charles was shivering.

The letter had been delivered to him with his morning mail, an innocent-looking envelope mailed from Annemasse, only a few miles across the border, on the French side. True, the handwritten address had been somewhat incomplete: only his name, c/o the Crédit Industriel, Geneva. But when he had slit it open and pulled out its contents, a sudden chill had settled over him like a mantle of doom.

Alexis. The boy is alive. I should have known, Charles chastised himself. On a nearby wall table stood a small tray with sherries and liqueurs for his clients. He rose and unsteadily poured himself a snifterful of sharp cognac, and took a gulp. *Alexis was alive, and had located him.* For almost two years now, Charles had convinced himself that Anne's son had died, or else been deported to a camp in Poland.

Charles sat down, and began to read. Alexis had written to Christina, of course. There had never been any closeness between him and the boy, whereas between Alexis and the girl . . . Alexis's energetic handwriting mocked Charles with its vitality, but he examined each line carefully, as though to convince himself that this was not a hoax, a forgery.

"My darling Tina," Alexis had written:

> I pray to God this letter will reach you, as, for the past two years, I've prayed for your safety and well-being. So much has happened, golden girl, since that cold December morning when the Nazis grabbed me and killed my friend François, and I was put into a sealed cattle car crammed full of deportees on its way to Drancy. I escaped—the rest hardly matters. And, though wounded three times—twice in the leg and now, just a few days ago, in the shoulder—I've survived, and am all right.
>
> An elderly lady had been caring for me, hiding my presence from everyone, as the Gestapo had men stationed even outside the offices of Fayard Industries. I'm so glad you've escaped. I heard that my mother had been killed. And I never said good-bye to her! I keep reliving my last moments with her, and wondering if I should have behaved any differently . . . been any more loving or affectionate. One can never say 'I love you' too often to a beloved person. . . .

Of course, that's how I feel about you too: we never said good-bye, never made any lasting promises, and yet . . . I keep hoping that when this letter falls into your hands, you'll still be free and willing to consider me as your suitor.

You see, the reason I've survived, the reason I've stayed strong, has been because of you. Not a day has gone by that I haven't conjured up your face, your eyes, your smile, to keep me hoping. Christina—if you're free, *marry me.* I want us to have children together, to share a life forever. Don't let our love be washed away by time and distance, when, wherever you are, I can't continue without you to sustain me.

I love you— Alexis.

He had added as a postscript: "Kiss everyone for me: your mother, my father, and my grandma. When things begin to settle down and I can be sure you've received this, I'll send them a longer letter explaining everything that's happened to me."

Charles took another swallow of cognac and looked out over the limpid waters of the lake, colored bronze by the sun. He had to be honest: the issue of Alexis was highly complicated. There was the Crédit Industriel itself, which Charles had been managing. When the war ended, he had been planning to declare Alexis officially dead, and inherit the bank by default. With Alexis alive, the bank belonged to Anne's son, as Alfred's will had clearly defined. As well as half of La Folie—Anne's half.

I came so close, Charles thought, so close to finally recovering my patrimony, my just inheritance from my great-grandfather! It simply wouldn't be right for me to lose it all, *a second time,* to a twenty-three-year-old boy who isn't even my own son!

But the situation was even worse. There was Fayard Industries, which, more than the bank, should belong to Charles. He'd given his best years to Armand, and to the business. It had been his *life!* What right did Alexis have, by simple reason of one night of fumbling passion, to take all this away from Charles? *Fayard Industries is mine,* he thought fiercely. Just as it's up to me to decide who Christina marries. And there's no way in heaven I'll give Amelia's daughter to Alexis. . . .

Didn't he owe it out of common decency to the girl to send for her at once and give her the letter? *Alexis had written it to her,* and she'd cried herself to sleep night after night, rejecting Robert Dreyfus and several other perfectly decent prospects to save herself for him.

For a moment Charles wavered, his conscience twinging. Then he picked up his snifter, and gazed at it as a ray of sunlight splashed over its surface. A miracle had happened . . . a series of miracles, saving Alexis's life on several crucial occasions. Yet, with the war still breaking down France's economic system, most large French enterprises could hope for no more than a half-life existence at best. So there was little urgency for Charles to return to Paris until the end of the war. Unless Alexis rose up like a specter, to claim what was his. . . .

Charles needed a plan. Now that Paris was once again in French hands, Alexis would make his presence known and Fernand Renard would tell him about Fayard. And he already knew that the Crédit Industriel belonged to him. What was to prevent Alexis from attempting to cross the country and arriving here, in Geneva, to demand his inheritance and the girl he loved?

No, Charles determined: I'm going to tell her nothing about this letter. Instead I'll think of something to turn her away from Alexis once and for all. Something to end her love and free her to marry another man, quickly. Something to make Alexis afraid ever to show his face in Renard's office, or anywhere else in Paris where the de Rochefleurs are known.

All his life, Charles had been forced to use his resourcefulness to recapture what should by rights have been his without a struggle. This time, he wasn't going to lose. *The boy would be the one left on the outside, helplessly looking in without being able to touch.*

Charles took the sheet of paper and tore it in half, then into smaller shreds, then strode decisively to the small fireplace on the other side of the room. Crumpling the shreds of papers into a ball, he tossed it in, and lit a match to it. His hands behind his back, he watched as orange flames slowly turned Alexis's words into ashes.

* * *

Charles paced in front of Christina, his hands clasped behind his back. Abruptly, he turned to look at her. She was seated on the small love seat in his study, anxious with expectation and concern. "What is it, Cousin Charles?" she asked in a low voice. "Is it— Have you heard anything about Alex?"

He nodded, gravely. "I'm sorry, Tina. What I'm about to tell you is a terrible story. It's been a profound shock to me, as it will be to you, darling."

She stood up, her face alive with horror. "He isn't *dead*?" she cried.

Charles sighed, gazing out of the window before addressing her again. "Alex is alive," he stated, his tone hushed and saddened. "I only *wish* he were dead!"

"*What?*"

He shook his head, his eyes misting. "I haven't known how to present it to you," he said. "A few days ago I met with the diplomatic courier from Paris. He told me that Fernand Renard had received news, through some members of the Resistance who had known his own son in the underground, that Alexis was alive. But Alexis had turned collaborator, selling out his best friend, François Durand, to the Gestapo back in 1942."

"That's a lie!" Christina exclaimed. "How could Renard—how could *you*—believe something like that?"

Charles shook his head. "It's the truth, Tina. There are papers to prove it. Abetz himself hired Alexis to expose the whole Lorraine operation we were involved in, and the expeditions he and Durand had been taking to the Morvan area. How else do you explain that François is dead, and Alexis is hiding in Paris—as fine as ever? If the Gestapo had captured him, he'd be in a camp somewhere, not in Paris, right? *Whereas he's safe,* and has been for almost two years, left alone by an entire network of Nazis!"

"I'm sure he has an explanation for it," she countered staunchly.

"Renard checked everything out before confronting me with the facts. Christina—look at me, God damn it! Alexis is my *son*! Don't you believe I'd do anything to vindicate his name . . . to prove Renard wrong?"

"I'd like to speak to Maître Renard myself," she declared.

"Very well. But we aren't going to return to Paris until the end of the war. I want you to pull yourself together, as I had to. And to accept what happened. Alexis was never any good—only it took a war to bear me out!"

"You were always against him," she accused, but her voice was beginning to break. "Did Renard send you those papers, the ones that prove Alexis did—what you say?"

"Of course he did. Letters from Abetz to Alexis, intercepted by some of the men in the underground. They paint a very ugly picture. Do you really want to read all that, Tina? Isn't my word sufficient?"

For a moment she hesitated. Then, her chin trembling, she burst into tears, silent sobs that racked her whole body. Charles watched her weep, and remained motionless for a full minute, letting her grief overwhelm her. Finally, he went to her and let her weep in his arms.

"It's all right, baby," he murmured. "It's all right. . . . It's always better to be disillusioned *before* the wedding than after. Now you can freely consider any proposal that comes your way. You won't have Alexis's memory interfering anymore."

"I don't ever want to get married," she said, but as a reply he merely patted her on the head.

He had to admit that he was pleased with himself. If he'd successfully convinced Christina, the most loyal of Alexis's advocates, then convincing Renard and the rest of their Paris associates would be easy business. Alexis would never rear his head to fight this allegation of treachery, because he'd have no proof to offer in his own defense. And so he'd have to remain in retreat, to avoid the shame of facing all those who had once admired him. And to avoid prosecution by the Provisional Government as a traitor to Free France.

Then Charles would be able to have him declared dead within a matter of years, and be officially confirmed as the head of both the bank and the steel empire.

Besides, the boy had not the slightest idea that he was Armand Fayard's son and heir. None whatsoever.

* * *

In June 1945, a month after Adolf Hitler's suicide and the final capitulation of Germany, Christina Habig, on the arm of her cousin Charles, walked down the decorated aisle to the wedding *huppah* in Geneva's most elite temple. The *huppah* had been adorned with thousands of fresh flowers of every color, shape, and scent. All around them, the wealthiest members of Genevese society looked down on the beautiful bride, clothed in yards of hand-tooled Belgian lace inset with seed pearls, orange blossoms crowning her hair.

Christina's appearance was so spectacular that Charles heard the general intake of breath at her grand entrance, and only then did he finally allow himself to relax. He had done the right thing, and the young man waiting for her beneath the wedding flowers, had been the right choice.

Robert Dreyfus was an extremely wealthy man in his own right —the scion of a powerful Jewish banking empire with headquarters in Basel. He stood six feet tall, was twenty-six years old, and spoke French and German as well as a smattering of Italian and English. The perfect match for Christina: Amelia herself would have approved.

The twenty-year-old bride smiled, but beneath her wedding veil a mist blurred her vision so that she could distinguish none of the faces gazing down at her.

Robert was certainly the best of the young men her cousin had brought home to her as suitors. He loved her and he was tender and kind. He had given her a fur coat and a three-carat diamond ring as an engagement present, and his father would be setting a charming house at their disposal, complete with four servants. And after all, even if Geneva wasn't Paris or Vienna, it was a pleasant, civilized city populated with friendly people . . . and the best nursemaids for newborn babies.

But I don't love him, she thought. *I'm still in love with Alex, who betrayed his country, his family, and himself.*

She was no more able to shut off her feelings for Alexis than her mother had been in the matter of Charles. Was she doomed to love one man, *the wrong man,* while being married to another? *Charles was Alexis's father,* and her own dearest friend and relative. If he'd brought her the news about his own son, then she had to stop those nagging doubts. Charles would never have lied to her, especially not in a matter of such crucial importance.

Alex, she thought: *I'm never going to forgive you, wherever you are! For there is no excuse for betraying your own people!* And, shyly, she squeezed Robert's hand. He was going to try his hardest to make her happy: the least she owed him was to try to love him, just a little bit.

EPILOGUE

Checkmate

CHAPTER XXIV

Charles had to admit that Paris simply wasn't the same. The Germans were gone, but drastic food shortages still cramped the city. The métro worked, but at fifteen-minute intervals, and many of the stations were still shut down. Not many bus lines were in service, either. Even more appalling, however, was the taxi situation: drivers were only allowed to bring their customers to train stations and hospitals, and even then they were required to stop first at the local police station to report where they were headed.

But what upset him the most was La Folie. He had gone there immediately, even before visiting Fernand Renard at his law office. The entire residence was now occupied by strangers! An eccentric woman with two dogs lived on the second floor, and on the third, a refugee from Lille with her four daughters. The guest wing had become the home of a young couple recently rescued from the concentration camp at Bergen-Belsen.

Outraged, Charles Lévy–de Rochefleur had marched to the police station. Very calmly, the chief inspector informed him that not even for a member of the illustrious de Rochefleurs could he make an exception to the new law: all buildings occupied by Germans had been emptied and requisitioned, and filled with refugees. Unless one could find suitable lodgings elsewhere for the refugees, not even the rightful proprietor was allowed to evict them!

His beautiful home, filled to the rafters with strangers! Not one —but eight! And to aggravate the situation, no one in Paris had any domestics. Charles thought wrathfully that he would tell his secretary to sift through the entire city and its suburbs in search of any remaining Goujons—and, more important, in search of living quarters for the eight miserable intruders who he could not boot out.

Feeling almost overcome with frustration, he walked to the train station, remembering the days long ago when he had used his feet, the underground subway, *and* the train every single day.

Later, safely ensconced in Fernand Renard's law office, Charles allowed his story to spill out. How a young member of the Resistance, whose job had been to smuggle Jews into Switzerland, had found him in Geneva and told him what had happened to Alexis. How he had shown him letters from Otto Abetz, implicating his son—as well as replies from Alexis to Abetz. How, naturally, Charles still felt himself reeling from these disclosures. (For, while they both knew that Alexis was Armand Fayard's natural child, Fernand had to realize that Charles had reared him as his own, and still considered him so.)

But a skeptical Renard leaned forward, his eyes sharp as drills. "Charles, you can't mean this! I knew Alexis very well indeed—he worked for me, remember? Why, he was one of the most patriotic, courageous young men I ever knew!"

Charles inhaled deeply then opened his briefcase. He extracted a manila folder and silently passed it to the attorney. Then he sat back, exhaling, tension tying him in knots. *If it was going to work, it would work on Renard—and if not, the game was as much as lost.*

He'd paid the forger in Basel ten thousand Swiss francs for each of five letters: three from "Abetz," two from "Alexis." One night in Geneva he'd taken Hans Kepler out to dinner and stolen an unimportant invoice signed by the German ambassador from the courier's briefcase. It had been easy: while Kepler was away from the table, Charles had opened the case and found this simple invoice, which no one would ever have missed. Kepler never suspected a thing.

In the matter of Anne's son, he'd had no such problem: Charles possessed many pieces bearing the young man's handwriting. The forger had done a marvelous piece of work, and now the supreme test was presenting itself: Renard, Fayard's attorney, the only other person to know the contents of the steel magnate's will, had to believe that Alexis had betrayed the Resistance and collaborated with Occupation authorities.

When Renard had finished examining the documents, he pushed his steel-rimmed glasses to the top of his head and rubbed his eyes. Neither man spoke.

Then, not looking directly at Charles, Renard asked, "Do you have any idea where Alexis might be?"

Charles shook his head. "No one's heard from him in Saint-Germain. He hasn't come around to our house."

"Speaking of La Folie . . . I hear it's full," the attorney said, glad for a chance to shift the subject to a less painful topic. "But I know of a beautiful apartment in town, on the rue de la Convention, that could be yours for the time being, till your house is free. We could make all the arrangements while you're tying up your business in Geneva. Do you want to take a look at it while you're in Paris?"

"Why don't you have the office rent it for me?" Charles asked wearily. "I hardly know what's suitable and what isn't, these days. Without Anne, my life hasn't been the same . . . so what possible difference would my looking at a flat make? A flat's a flat. I'll take it!"

He rose to leave, and Renard went around his desk to meet him. Their hands clasped in friendship—a long, hard clasp. Then the attorney shook his head mournfully. "I'm so sorry, Charles. You'll never know *how* sorry. For you, of course—but also for my old associate, Armand, who had placed such faith in this young man. . . ."

"Who'd have thought any of this possible?" Charles intoned, his voice catching. And then abruptly he cleared his throat and adjusted the knot in his tie. "Thanks for handling the business of the apartment, Fernand. It means a lot to me."

The two men parted at the door. Not until he'd rounded the corner and was a safe distance from Renard's office window, did Charles alter his gait and begin to stride with vigor and enthusiasm on the cement pavement. *The hoax had worked!* Fernand Renard had been duped by the forgeries and thrown into bewildered acceptance of Charles's fantasy. Alexis, from now on, was a branded man—a despicable collaborator who had sold out his dearest friend and associate, François Durand, not to mention the country of his birth. And all, according to the excellent forgery, for the promise of a high position on Abetz's staff of French solicitors. *Alexis—a de Rochefleur and a Jew!*

* * *

"I went to the Fayard Industries offices," Lise Bourdin reported, trying not to meet Alexis's eager eyes. Instead, she turned her back and removed her hat, her coat, and her scarf.

On the sofa, the young man waited. Since August, 1944, he had been forced to live the life of an invalid, his shoulder and leg wounds painful reminders of his wartime experiences. After sixteen months, his health was still uncertain, and the doctor had warned Lise to keep him quietly at home until the Christmas season, when it would be all right to go back to work, although at first only on a part-time basis.

Going back to work . . . That meant getting his old job back at Fayard Industries. Why hadn't Tina ever answered his letter? Why had he still not heard from his father? Guiraud had let Lise know that the letter had reached Annemasse, and had been sent from there across the border to Geneva. Why, then, hadn't he heard from his family after more than a year?

"Lise," he said gently. "I know what a burden I've been, healing so slowly and unable to move around or work. You've been saving my life from the day you first laid eyes on me, and I owe you everything. But now it's time to stop, to think of yourself. It's cold outside, and you have better things to do than brave an erratic subway system to go to my old office."

"It's not that, Alexis." She coughed and walked over to him. Her plain old face was lined with age and concern. "It's that I heard the most terrible news! Oh, my God, it seems that each time I go to that dreadful place, I'm told awful things that will break your heart. . . ."

He reached out and touched her cheek. "Lise, you must tell me," he said firmly.

"The girls at the reception were all full of strange rumors—_that you collaborated with the Nazis!_ That Abetz bribed you. That you arranged for François to be shot, in return for which the Gestapo let you go free. They say that there are actual documents to prove this—which this Maître Renard, who was Fayard's lawyer, knows all about it. No one wants to admit he's known you, and everyone speaks of you like a traitor, Alex—_you,_ who risked your life so many times to save France!"

"What you say is impossible," Alexis retorted. "Impossible! Lise . . . you don't mean to tell me that _people believe this_? Not people who knew me—who knew what I stood for!"

The old woman sat down and started to weep. "Everyone believes it, Alexis. They say your father came to Paris, heartbroken, and that he's aged considerably. That he's planning to move back here all alone. The news of your 'treachery' appears to have destroyed him—"

"All this is nonsense," Alexis cut in. "All I have to do is show up and tell my side of the story. Come now, Lise—stop crying and tell me the rest. There's more, isn't there?"

She nodded. "Your cousin Amelia was killed with your mother. Christina went to Geneva with your grandmother, but, Alex—she's married now. She married a young Swiss banker . . . a Robert Dreyfus."

All at once, words failed him. He put his head in his hands and wept openly. The old woman bent over him, and finally he raised a tearstained face and whispered, "Lise . . . *why*?"

"Because she was told you had betrayed France," his old friend replied. "And your father says that if you show up now, he'll have to turn you in to the authorities. *What are you going to do?* What *can* you do to exonerate yourself?"

Alexis brushed his tears away with the back of his sleeve. Helpless and exhausted, he shrugged hopelessly. "If only I could find a witness," he said to her. "Someone who could have known what really happened to me."

"But they're all dead," Lise Bourdin reminded him. "François, and Roland, the fellow you jumped from the train with. Only the men who found you are alive, and they hardly count. The Nazis could have dumped you on that hillside according to plan, wounding you just to make the story more believable."

They stared at each other, suddenly struck with his impossible predicament. "Lise, if what you say is true, if everyone's convinced I'm really a traitor, then I'm going to have to leave Paris. Maybe I can find a small town where they need a lawyer. But I'll have to live under an assumed name, won't I?"

"Alexis, when I was a newlywed, before moving to Paris, I spent a year in Meaux, in the Seine-et-Marne department. It was a pretty little town, and we liked it well enough. We'll go there, if you like, until we can think of a better plan."

And as he opened his mouth in stupefaction, she stilled him by placing a gnarled hand on his arm. "You're the only family I have left, young man. And I'm not going to let you run off somewhere without me!"

* * *

Charles de Rochefleur glanced at his careful manicure and, on his left hand, the signet ring his grandfather had given him long ago. Soon, very soon, he would have La Folie back. The lady from Lille had found an apartment in town, and the young concentration camp victims had just leased a small flat in another part of

Saint-Germain. This left only the eccentric woman who currently occupied the floor that had once contained his room and Anne's beautiful bedroom.

It wasn't that he didn't like the large, elegant flat that Fayard's henchmen had found him at 2, rue de la Convention. But Charles didn't like the Fifteenth Arrondissement, which he found lacking in prestige and distinction. His associates kept telling him how lucky he had been to find such a wonderful apartment during these difficult times, when no one could locate decent living quarters, but he didn't feel comfortable in a place that was only temporary, that wasn't really *home.*

All his life, other apartments had felt like stepping-stones along the way to his final refuge, La Folie. He had felt at home only within its treasured walls, where he always believed he belonged.

Yet . . . had he ever truly "belonged" anywhere? Seated like this behind Armand Fayard's impressive desk, looking out of the beveled-glass windows his boss had especially ordered to soften the stark white walls and the modern upholstered furniture, Charles found himself all at once uncomfortable. He was seated there *by default.* Another man had built the steel empire, furnished it to please himself, and bequeathed it to his only child. Charles had been left out of the entire procedure.

For twenty years, Charles thought with a chill, *we have all lived a lie!* He had *not* been Fayard's protégé—*Alexis had*! Anne had hidden the truth from him, while playing the role of a devoted, adoring wife! He remembered her awkwardness the night of the Diaghilev ballet, in the spring of 1926, when they had run into the Fayards—and he, blind fool, had believed that the awkwardness had stemmed from the guilt and camouflage of *his own affair with Arabella*! Then there had been Anne's anger when he took Alexis into the city to meet Fayard for the first time, when the boy was seventeen. An unjustified anger, tinged with embarrassment and possibly shame. That Alexis had been turned down so quickly and summarily from the armed forces attested that someone of tremendous power and influence had been pulling strings at a time when the country was desperate for brave young volunteers.

Fayard had made love to Anne in May, 1920. Charles wished he could remember what had been happening to Anne that spring, but all he could recall was his own extraordinary meeting with Amelia, and his soaring hopes. No matter how he tried to rack his brain, Charles could find nothing else—no telltale episode, no outrageous moment—to explain how his shy young cousin, obviously a virgin and a wallflower, had been seduced by the middle-aged, virile, and very married steel magnate.

Charles Lévy–de Rochefleur thought, on a surge of bitterness, that he had never been anyone's first choice: not Amelia's, not Anne's, not Fayard's. His own father had set the precedent for the rejection and repudiation that would mark Charles's life in the forty-five years that had followed his suicide. Wilhelm Levy had killed himself without once considering that he was leaving behind a son who would be forced to bear the burden of his scandalous act.

No one ever forgave me for my father's suicide or for his leaving my mother poor and without a future. *Not even Anne,* he thought. Even Anne had not loved him enough to save herself for him, to bear him a child of his own.

He was the effective head of Fayard Industries and the chairman of the Crédit Industriel, which he had transferred back to Paris. He owned the palatial mansion he had coveted all his life, and had even hired new servants to prepare for restoring the premises. He drove a sleek Bentley Mark VI, and sat at dinners next to heads of state. Women—rich women, elegant actresses, heiresses, and widows—sent him perfumed notes and gold cigar boxes, begging for a single evening of his time as their escort. He was touted as France's foremost captain of industry—greater, far more powerful and influential a figure than Alfred, a mere banker, or Armand, an engineer, had ever hoped to be. He had combined their energies, their talents, their wealth, and welded them into a whole that should have made him proud, happy, and fulfilled. Yet—he wasn't. *Honesty was missing.*

Whenever he went to Geneva, the most beautiful young woman welcomed him with open arms, loving him like a father. Christina showered him with attention, tenderness, and gratitude. She believed he had saved her from the error of loving the wrong man—a traitor and a coward. Charles traveled to Switzerland to see her at least once a month, and in fact he was considering asking her husband, Robert, to move to Paris to help him manage the Crédit. Tina had filled the void of having lost Amelia—not completely, of course, for no one ever would—but her daughterly affection *had* given him a sense of "belonging." They were a family, weren't they?

Acutely uncomfortable, Charles picked up a silver letter opener, and fingered the blade. *Not one of his possessions had come to him honestly. Not even Christina.* He had manipulated her into marrying Robert Dreyfus by lying to her about Alexis. By right of justice, except for half of La Folie, *everything he "owned" should have belonged to Anne's son*—including Tina!

Charles had never been a religious man, but he remembered, suddenly, the young man he had once been. Bitter, yes; also angry at his father, at Alfred, at life. But honest, and proud. *A man of principles.* What was left of this young man? he asked himself. But the answer was too painful to accept, and so he rang the buzzer for his secretary. There was no time in his schedule for shame or for self-doubt. What counted was that he had everything he had ever wanted, and that he was no longer the dispossessed de Rochefleur. No man achieved a success like his without burying a few corpses along the way.

* * *

"The Grégoire Martin case is ready for your signature, Maître," Elodie said.

Alexis pushed his glasses above his forehead and looked at her. She was twenty-three, with a nondescript pretty face and soft auburn hair—and it was clear she was a little infatuated with him. Her eyes were downcast, and she was blushing under his scrutiny.

For two years now, he had been public defender in the city of Meaux, a town no different from any other provincial municipality. Its old buildings rose haphazardly through the countryside, and its inhabitants—peasants, working-class folk, and churchgoing bourgeoisie—minded their own business and trudged along the streets at an undistinguished pace. The men went off to work carrying lunchpails or imitation leather briefcases and, to Alexis, they all looked the same. You knew, even before they opened the door, that their living rooms would be equipped with nondescript mahogany furniture upholstered in harsh velveteen, and on each table would be a starched doily. A crucifix on the wall, a linoleum kitchen, and the decor would be complete.

Elodie Ginot, the mayor's niece, had worked for Alexis from the start. It had been understood that she came with the job. The rumor in town was that she'd run away with a local boy—a plumber's son—in her teens, and that she'd been sent somewhere to have a baby afterward. Now nobody would have her for his wife. Alexis thought the mayor hoped he hadn't heard the rumor or that, if he had, *he*'d be sophisticated enough to overlook a young girl's past.

This winter afternoon, the young man felt a stirring of compassion for this girl. "Elodie," Alexis said. "You don't really enjoy this job. Why don't you go to Paris and try something more interesting? Something in the world of fashion, perhaps? Meaux is an old people's town or, at best, a retreat for middle-aged couples set in their ways."

She turned even more scarlet. "But, Maître Bourdin"—he was living under Lise's name and everyone thought he was her grandson—"I'd be afraid! Paris is so large, so busy! I'd get lost my first hour there."

"Sit down," he told her gently. He moved the Martin file to the side of his desk, and examined her earnestly. "Life is a series of crazy jumps you take—that you have to take, or you'll feel cheated afterward! You can't stay here in Meaux and rot away, because when you were fifteen you fell in love with a young boy. We all make mistakes—but in Paris, people recognize this and there's less self-righteousness and judgment."

"You're from Paris, aren't you?" she asked, her green eyes fastening on him with interest.

He shifted uncomfortably in his chair, all at once acutely aware that both his knee and shoulder were throbbing. During the winter his shoulder hurt more often, though he could move it without trouble and the scar had faded to a thick white gash. He felt grateful to Lise for having forced him to see the best surgeon in town to have his leg reset. But the damp cold had a tendency to move right into his bad knee, and to send shooting pains up and down.

"Well, you are from Paris, aren't you?" she pressed him. "We've all wondered. . . ."

He knew they did: all the young girls he'd met, and their mothers. But no one dared to ask, and he volunteered nothing. He and Lise lived a retired existence in the small cottage they had rented in the better part of town, and accepted few local invitations. Yet, of course, Alexis's refinement had to have been noticed by one and all.

"I studied in Paris," he told her. "I know the city."

"Then, if it's such a marvelous place to live in—why did you leave?"

He'd hoped she wouldn't ask. But he'd opened this Pandora's box, and now he had to close it gracefully. So he thought things through and finally declared: "There was someone I . . . cared for. She married another man. I just couldn't . . . you know . . .

stay around after that. Within a certain world, Paris can be a con-
fining place, just like Meaux. We'd moved in the same circles and
I'd have been forced to see her at the theater, at art exhibits, at
other people's dinner parties. That sort of thing. . . ."

A vivid picture of Christina, as he had last seen her in a glossy
magazine, flashed into his mind. No matter how hard he tried, he
couldn't avoid hearing or reading about his family in the news. His
father's name was splashed all over the press, and even his grandmother, Yvonne, had received attention when a small gallery had
given her a one-woman show just last month. Now it was Christina's turn. His father had brought her husband in from Geneva to
help him manage the Crédit Industriel—which was *Alexis's own
bank,* for pity's sake! And now the young couple was heralded as
the toast of Parisian society: both so handsome and well-mannered,
and so *smiling* all the time.

In *L'Illustration,* she had been smiling into the camera, holding
her husband's arm in front of the Opera. And Alexis had felt a
wave of nausea and longing, thinking how much better-looking—
how much more finely chiseled—Robert Dreyfus's features were
than his own. *She'd forgotten him completely,* that much was obvious. And so, what he had told Elodie was part of the truth: He'd
never have been able to stand being that close to her, and having
her belong to someone else.

Elodie was blinking rapidly, to keep from weeping. "I know just
what you mean," she murmured. "Raoul was forced to leave
Meaux because of me. My uncle threatened his parents with a
lawsuit because I was a minor. You've heard the story, haven't you,
Maître Bourdin?"

Slowly, he nodded. "Yes, I have. And that's why I want you to
think about what I said. Paris isn't so frightening, Elodie. And
you're too pretty, and too nice, to be reminded every day that you
were a human being and gave in to a very normal desire."

She was surprised at the passion in his voice, and stared at him.
"You think it was normal? That I wasn't 'bad'?"

Alexis looked away, suddenly unable to fight his own melan-
choly. "No, Elodie, you weren't 'bad.' And a good man will turn
up one day soon who will think quite the opposite—that you were
brave and strong to give in to love. Every young couple should
explore their first love to the furthest and most exciting limits.
How else can you know if it's meant to last a lifetime?"

"Because your girlfriend didn't, did she? And you think, if she had . . ." Her sentence died, and she looked down at her hands, flushed and embarrassed. He was her employer, and she'd overstepped her limits!

But he was saying, "I've wondered, sometimes, if that might have made a difference. But then, Elodie, between us there were other problems besides physical intimacy." His eyes had hardened, frightening her with their intensity. "Go to Paris," he told her, and picked up the Martin file.

* * *

The long, elaborately dressed table stood surrounded by half a dozen embroidered Louis XVI chairs; a chandelier dropping crystal tears shimmered above, casting a medieval glow over the beveled ruby centerpiece engraved with a regal *D*. In her strapless gown of pomegranate taffeta, Christina surveyed the arrangement of exotic, out-of-season fruits on the sideboard, and closed her eyes.

"Everything looks perfect, and you look lovely."

Christina started, almost guiltily, and smiled at Robert. In his tuxedo, he cut an elegant figure. Her friends told her he was handsome, and wanted to know: *Is he sexy in bed?* She had to blush with embarrassment, not wanting to think about herself in bed with him. She always insisted that he turn off the light. Her friends would have found her ridiculously old-fashioned. In 1947, a woman of her age—twenty-two—was supposed to give herself up to the voluptuous pleasures of sex, but she just couldn't seem to feel anything.

Robert was placing his arms about her narrow waist, and she could smell his lemony after-shave as he kissed her in the crook of her neck. "Tina," he said. "Darling, we have an hour before our guests arrive. . . ."

She tried not to stiffen. "Rob, I'm already made up. My hair—"

"Just lie beside me?"

His voice sounded so soft, like a caress. He always wanted her to "lie beside him." And then . . . he'd touch her, and press against her. He was pressing against her now. Taking her by the hand to their bedroom.

In the darkness, she took her shoes off with the utmost care, laying them side by side meticulously. She felt numb, like a doll moved by someone else's manipulations. She could hear Robert breathing on the bed, urgently, and imagined his purple, engorged penis, ready to penetrate her—always ready, it seemed.

Finally, she had to turn to him and move toward his arms. "Darling, darling, I love you," he whispered, and started caressing her round, firm breasts. Without thinking, she pushed his hand aside.

Robert sat up, bewildered. "Tina? What's the matter?"

Immediately, guilt emerged, drowning out her own needs. "I'm sorry," she told him, tears edging into her voice. "It's just that I feel sore from playing tennis this morning."

"I'll be gentle, I promise." And he propped himself up on his elbow and bent down to lick the inside of her ear. Tiny butterfly licks that seemed, suddenly, like so many small daggers sent through her nerve endings.

The room was beginning to spin, and as he covered her lips with his own, she thought that she would suffocate. Her heart was beating so quickly that she was afraid she was about to faint. Weakly she shifted her body away from Robert's, on her side, and once more she regained her breath, and the dark shapes of objects in the room settled back into their proper spaces.

He was stroking her forehead, his voice concerned and tinged with sudden fear. "Tina, for God's sake! Aren't you feeling well?"

But instead of answering, she made a beeline for the bathroom, and burst into hysterical sobs over the marble sink.

* * *

Many years before the First World War, Baron Henri de Rochefleur had purchased a family vault at the Montparnasse Cemetery. It contained seventy-two spaces and was surmounted by a mausoleum of shining alabaster engraved with the de Rochefleur crest and noble initial. Henri and Alfred had both been put to rest there, although many other relatives (Guy, Jeannette, and the entire von Guttman clan) had died abroad, during times of turmoil.

Alexis thought about his mother often, and wondered if Charles had had the opportunity to give her a proper burial before fleeing to Geneva. Exactly five years had elapsed since he had been captured in Nancy—five years since his mother's murder. Every December, he would awaken chilled and anxious, remembering his friend François's death, and his own arrest and deportation. And he would think of Anne, his mother, whom he had loved, pitied, and respected, and whom he missed.

Every December, he would toy with the notion of sneaking into Paris during a workday and going to the vault at Montparnasse, to see whether she had been buried with her father and grandfather.

To try to say good-bye, and speak to her memory. Each year, of course, he rejected this idea and remained quietly in Meaux, afraid lest he be seen and recognized in the capital, and denounced to the authorities.

Why had it been different this year? Alexis, hugging his black wool coat around his shivering body, wended his way through the various vaults and mausoleums at Montparnasse, asking himself the question. His terrible loneliness had finally broken through the practicality of his fear—and here he was, reaching out to the only member of his family who, by virtue of her early demise, had not turned away from him.

A spray of mist hung in the air, turning the landscape to a muddy khaki hue. He could see the de Rochefleur monument up ahead, tall and white like a proud, haughty ghost, and he quickened his footsteps. Fog swirled around him, adding to the surreal quality of the surroundings. And suddenly he was at the entrance, awed and afraid that his mother's remains would not be inside . . . that the Nazis had scooped them up like garbage and dumped them off the face of the earth, scattering Anne de Rochefleur like particles of dust in the wind.

He stepped inside. And as he entered, he froze. A woman was kneeling by one of the tombs, her head bowed in meditation. She was wrapped in fur, and her head was swathed in a white silk kerchief—but even so, he recognized her right away. Of all the scenarios he'd imagined, this one hadn't played itself out. He'd forgotten, of course, that her mother had been killed along with his . . . and that Amelia, too, was a de Rochefleur, with a daughter to mourn her.

The young woman was raising her head, and pulling a handkerchief from her alligator handbag. She pressed it against her face. In the darkness of the mausoleum, Alexis watched her, mesmerized, impotent to turn and leave, although his brain was urging him to get out before she saw him.

Five years. Five years since he had seen her. Years in which he'd conjured up her image like a dream, caressing it as though it had been she. Now here she was, a few feet away, standing up, brushing dust from her boots and her mink coat, and he couldn't make his feet obey the impulse of his brain.

Slowly, thinking herself alone with her thoughts and memories, she patted her face and rubbed her gloved hands over her sleeves. And then she saw him. Her eyes grew enormous, her lips parted.

"Alex," she whispered, her voice as soft as a snowflake. "My God . . ."

He couldn't help himself, and so he rushed over, not thinking, his face naked with longing—all the old longing, plus the new, because *she was here,* at arm's reach. And just as he hugged her to his chest, she fell against him, her body suddenly shaking with sobs. Alexis kissed her head, touched her back with the hunger of feeling her alive in his arms. Then she pulled herself away and showed him her face, and he bent down and kissed her mouth, tasting the salt of her tears. "Tina, Tina," he murmured, speaking her name over and over to reassure himself he wasn't dreaming.

At last she drew back, and suddenly she looked away, embarrassed. He remembered: She was a married woman. Words had intruded. "You didn't believe that story, did you, Tina? Is that why you married that man?"

And now, with the eruption of his question, came the sense behind the words. The anger and the outrage. "Tina, look at me!" he cried. "Do you suppose for one single minute that I'd betray everything and everyone dear to me?"

Her voice trembling, she said, "I read the letters, Alex."

"What letters? I never wrote any incriminating letters! I never did anything dishonorable! It's a lousy, filthy rumor—"

Tears were falling down her cheeks. "No, Alex," she whispered. "It isn't just a rumor. I know your signature as well as my own! François was killed because you jockeyed for a position with the German ambassador! Oh, my God—*how could you have done that*? After all the work we did to help those refugees . . . after all the efforts your own mother made. . . . How could you?"

A strange feeling was creeping through him. "Where did you see these letters?" he demanded.

"Cousin Charles had them. He told me that Maître Renard had obtained them from someone in the underground. Oh, what does any of this matter? You betrayed yourself, Alexis, and you broke every sacred law in the book!"

Staring at her, he shook his head. "How far we've come, Christina, if you were able to believe a rumor and a forged signature. If your faith wavered before someone else's evidence! Because you never answered *my* letter, Tina, where I explained the whole story to you. I waited and waited for your reply, and it never came. Probably you'd already met your husband and simply couldn't be bothered to reply."

It was her turn to look at him with bewilderment. "I never received any letter from you," she told him. "And neither did your father. You disappeared and the next thing we saw were those letters you and Otto Abetz had written to each other."

"Don't you understand? *I never wrote them!* On my word, Christina, I never did! But I wrote to you, to tell you I loved you and wanted you to be my wife. I wrote you I'd been captured, rounded up by the Gestapo and sent to Drancy in a cattle car, and that I had escaped through a safety valve in the floor. That a kind old woman in the Fifteenth had taken me in, and patched me up. I gave you her address, and begged you to answer me there as soon as possible."

They were staring at each other, each one guarded and suspicious, afraid to believe. And then he said to her, "My father never doubted that I was a traitor, did he? It was he who turned you against me, wasn't it?"

Christina drew herself up, suddenly composed. "Alexis, Cousin Charles was so distraught that no one could speak to him for days. There was no 'convincing' to do! The letters were there: I read them. *What were any of us supposed to believe?* Who would have benefited by floating such a rumor? *No one, Alex—no one!*"

"Yes, there was one person," he said to her, his tone strangely calm. "You're forgetting the Crédit Industriel. It would have been mine, remember? By my grandfather's will!"

She shook her head, horrified. "I can't be hearing you correctly. You can't be . . . *accusing your own father?* You can't have stooped so low, Alex de Rochefleur! Please, tell me that I misunderstood you!"

Helpless, he shrugged, sadness taking over where hope had surged up. "Oh, Tina . . . Tina . . ."

"I can't speak anymore, Alexis," she whispered, her voice breaking. And she turned and ran out of the mausoleum, her sobs echoing in his head long after she had disappeared from sight.

He'd had her in his arms, he'd kissed and held her—and yet he hadn't managed to convince her of who he was. Either she'd never known him, or a devil had stepped between them and caused all of this to happen to separate them for good.

She was right: the notion of Charles's manipulating his own son's fate seemed too incredible to believe. And yet . . . who else had stood to gain by his, Alexis's destruction? *Who but his own father . . .*

If only I could find a witness, he thought for the millionth time. If only I knew where to look for one. . . .

CHAPTER XXV

Alexis and Lise sat in the tiny living room, a small, round woman seated in the rocking chair opposite them. Through the narrow windows, a brilliant May sun was pouring in, highlighting the dust over the black upright piano. The young man ran his fingers through his curly hair, feeling the tension gripping him like a tight steel band, and he repeated: "Marcel . . . has *passed away?*"

The plump woman sighed, her breasts rising and falling like twin down pillows. "It was a terrible railway accident," she told him. "They were both killed: my brother and his friend René." Then, wiping away a tear with the back of her hand, she asked, "Do you remember them at all? They brought you here in such a bad condition, after they found you at the bottom of the hill, that we feared you wouldn't survive."

"How can I ever thank you, madame?" Alexis said humbly. "You and your brother, and that other brave railwayman, René, saved my life." Turning to Lise, he took her hand and squeezed it affectionately. "And my dear friend here took over, gluing the broken pieces back together."

"Marianne," Lise Bourdin said, leaning forward earnestly. "The reason we came is because Alexis is desperate. He's been forced to live the past three years in Meaux, although his family is one of the most powerful in Paris. Alexis himself is the legal owner of an international bank! But a rumor is floating around that he was a collaborator—worse, an outright traitor. Someone wanted him removed from his family and his home. The only way he can clear his name is if he can find someone from the time he dropped down from the train, someone who could vouch for the authenticity of his story."

The other woman shook her head, perplexed. "Even my brother didn't see it happen. But wait—there *was* a strange coincidence! I remember that a month after we'd brought you Alexis, a woman I know on the other side of town told me that her husband, who used to work with Marcel on the railroad, had found another man who had apparently jumped down through a safety valve. A man from Dijon, who was hardly hurt at all—just a concussion and a few broken ribs! And all this took place around the same time that Alexis was here, in my house!"

His face suddenly flushed, Alexis said, "Roland Pêche, the man who jumped with me, was from Dijon. . . . But he was killed! *I saw parts of his body scattered near the tracks.*"

Lise Bourdin's sharp little eyes were gleaming. "Parts of a dismembered body don't always identify a man. You never examined the various remains, did you, Alex? *They might have belonged to anyone!* Don't you know that brave men tried to escape from cattle cars in many different ways back then, day after day? Who's to say that *that arm* you saw belonged to Roland Pêche . . . and not some other unfortunate individual?"

The three of them sat looking at one another—three pairs of eyes, luminous with hope. Then Alexis sprang up and hugged his old friend. "Lise," he said, "What do you say we take a little trip to Dijon?"

* * *

Christina Dreyfus stood by the window, silently surveying the scenery beyond. Through the burst of verdant chestnut trees she could see the Seine, gray-green-blue and slow, to her left the wide, beautiful bridge named after Tsar Alexander III. She had carefully selected the high-ceilinged, majestic apartment on the Quai d'Orsay, not far from the Ministry of Foreign Affairs. The boulevard's quiet, graceful elegance reminded her of Vienna—of her grandmother's house on the Ringstrasse, and of her parents' home in the medieval Old City. She found the Seine soothing to her restless nerves, a gentle reminder that life continued flowing on, like a river, no matter even when sudden storms turned its waters dark and choppy.

Slowly, she turned. She was standing in an exquisite living room, with walls of robin's-egg blue. Robert had praised her profusely for her decorating skills, but she had shrugged the compliment off. Didn't most women possess an inborn ability to choose patterns and color schemes?

Christina closed her eyes. An oppressive weight pushed against her chest, suffocating her, and she knew that if she was ever to breathe freely again, she would have to face reality.

Suddenly she walked away from the window, her step quickening as she crossed the room and reached the hallway. *It was now or never.*

* * *

Alexis rang the doorbell. The small, cobbled street behind him lay dappled in sunshine, but all he could think was: *Who will open the door?* Next to him, Lise adjusted her pillbox hat and straightened her posture. Both of them were nervous.

An old woman answered, sticking a rather sour face out from behind the half-opened door. "Yes . . . ?"

"Madame Pêche?" Alexis asked politely.

The woman's brow furrowed. "I don't know you, do I?"

"No," Alexis conceded, his heart knocking like a snare drum in his chest. "But I wonder if we might come in to talk to you for a moment. It's about—"

"I don't let strangers in, and I don't need subscriptions or vacuum cleaners," she cut in sharply.

"It's about Roland."

She had been about to close the door in their faces, but now she did a double take. "My son? What do you want with him?"

Alexis felt a rush of blood flow into his face. "Could we please come in?" he repeated. "I promise you, madame, we won't disturb you for more than a few minutes. And we wish your son no harm —no harm whatsoever. He and I . . . Well, if I could just explain, I'm sure you'll understand."

As an answer, she pulled open the door, stepping back to let them pass through.

* * *

Christina knocked on the door of the study, and opened it. Robert was sitting at his desk, leafing through investment brochures, and as she walked in, his face reflected pleasant surprise. "Tina. Come in! I didn't think you were still home. Weren't you and Monique Uzielli supposed to go to a matinée?"

"We were," she admitted. "But I canceled."

"You're not sick, are you, dear?"

She sighed. It was going to be so difficult. Things like this always were, she thought miserably, taking a seat across from the mahogany desk. "Robert," she said softly. "I desperately needed time to talk to you. I canceled Monique because this is more important. We can't go on this way!"

His face reflected bewilderment. "What do you mean?"

"Rob," she told him, a quiet urgency in her voice. "I tried to be honest with you when we married. I told you that I wasn't in love with you but that I'd try. Well, I have tried . . . but the truth is, I respect and esteem you, I like you. But I'm never going to fall in love with you, and the more we prolong this marriage, the more dishonest and dirty I feel."

His cheeks were ashen gray. "Christina, you can't mean that you want a divorce! I love you! We can work it out, darling, I know we can!" Reaching across the desk, he took her hands in his own, and continued, impassioned. "It doesn't matter if you're not 'in love.' That's all a lot of sentimental hogwash, really. Marriage is a way of life. It means getting along, putting up with each other, going out together, having a family and friends. What marriage do you know that was built on romantic love and is still working?"

She shook her head. "Robert, maybe that's how you feel, and maybe you're even right! The point is, we've been married almost three years, and I'm not happy. I'm not happy because something's missing, and that something is my own sense of emotional cleanliness . . . of honesty! I can't keep up day to day, thinking of you only as a dear friend, when to me, marriage has always represented a total merging of the soul, the body, and the heart! Call me a fool if you like, but I can't live this way any longer. And you deserve more! You deserve to find a wife who'll be passionately in love with you, who will jump at the chance to tumble into bed—not someone lukewarm like me, Robert!"

"But—"

She was starting to shake from head to toe. Standing up abruptly, she declared, "I'm not going to ask for anything, Robert. I'm going to leave the house, and you can tell people anything you want. I'll rent a small apartment, get a job. . . . It's time, really, that I took responsibility for my own life and stopped behaving like a spoiled princess everyone has to take care of."

He rose, too, but she began to back away. "Rob, *please* . . ." she whispered. "Please don't make this any harder! I really care about you, but it's simply *wrong,* that's all. It's living a lie!"

Then, to avoid his wounded eyes, she turned her back on him and walked quickly out of the study, never looking back, even when he called out her name.

* * *

The apartment was at the top of the staircase, on one of Dijon's back streets. Alexis rapped on the maroon door, then stood back, an unreal feeling creeping through him, as though he'd stepped outside himself and were watching a film in slow motion.

When the door swung open, a small, wiry, dark man looked up at him, squinting. Then all at once his ferret-like features lit into an expression of amazement and joy. "You're the Resistance chap that jumped down with me!" he exclaimed, throwing his arms wide open. Embracing Alexis, he cried, "I dreamed about you so often these past five and a half years, I could have picked you out of a crowd any day! But I thought you'd been killed in the fall. . . ."

"So did I, Roland," Alexis said softly, his voice catching. "So did I. . . ."

* * *

Fernand Renard pressed his spectacles over the bridge of his nose, and frowned at his secretary. "*Alexis de Rochefleur?* You're certain, Jean?"

"Quite certain, Maître. He's waiting outside with another man, and they claim it's urgent they see you right away."

The attorney shook his head from side to side. "This is incredible," he declared. And then, more decisively: "Usher them in!"

Two hours later, holding snifters of cognac in their hands, Roland Pêche and Alexis sat on Fernand Renard's leather couch. From his oversize armchair the attorney was regarding them with stunned fascination. "That was quite a story you boys told me," he remarked.

"Fernand, it's the absolute truth! And if you still doubt us, there's the woman that saved me, the railwayman's sister, who'll testify as to how her brother found me, and in what condition. Had the Nazis been trying to simulate a capture, they'd have treated me with greater care, don't you think? My leg was fractured in two places, I had a concussion, and I didn't regain consciousness until they'd moved me to the rue Cambronne, to Lise's."

Renard wiped his eyes, still shaking his head. "Alexis," he said, clearly moved. "You know you always were a favorite of mine. I couldn't believe the story of your defection, but there were documents . . . and I'm an attorney . . ."

"I understand," the young man cut in abruptly. "You found it easier to trust some papers than your own perception of human nature. . . . Be that as it may, Fernand, there's something you

could clear up for me. A while back I happened to see my cousin
Christina. She told me she had learned of my so-called treachery
from my father, but that he'd been informed of it through *you*! Is
that true?"

The lawyer creased his brow, and leaned forward. "That's
hardly how it happened," he replied. "She must have misunderstood Charles. *He* came to *me*, with documented proof! It was just
after the end of the war. He came to see me and said someone had
contacted him in Geneva. *I* had nothing to do with it, I assure
you!"

Alexis' face suddenly grew hard and cold, as though he had
drawn a steel mask over it. He rose and regarded Renard through
narrowed eyes. "That's interesting, isn't it, Fernand? I'll have to
think this information through." Then, crisply, he declared,
"We're going to have to proceed quickly and efficiently to exonerate me completely. And then, of course, I'll have to deal with my
father—and with the bank!"

But Fernand Renard was gazing at him with a new expression,
which Alexis couldn't figure out. "What else is there?" the young
man demanded.

Renard cleared his throat. "Alexis, now it's *my* turn to tell *you* a
story . . . as amazing a story as the one you told me. It's about
you, of course—and Armand Fayard. Listen to me, Alexis, and try
to understand, because your whole life is about to change as a
result of what I'm going to tell you. . . ."

Roland Pêche was standing up, awkwardly tugging at his tie.
"In that case, gentlemen, I don't think either of you will mind if I
run along. I have a train to catch, this evening."

Alexis gave the little man a quick hug. "We will see each other
again," he told him warmly. Then he patted his friend on the back
and released him.

When Roland had closed the door behind him, Alexis took his
seat again and looked intently at the attorney. "Tell me," he re-
quested, his entire body alive with curiosity. "Tell me about Armand Fayard. . . ."

* * *

Alexis wanted to be alone, and yet he couldn't leave, so completely had Renard's words stupefied him. Shaking his head, he
pressed his fingers to his eyes and sat that way silently for a few
minutes. An entire lifetime of pain, abuse, humiliation, inadequacy,
was giving way to remembered moments of pure joy, conviviality,

acceptance. Armand Fayard had really loved him, and suddenly it no longer mattered that Charles never had. Because Fayard had been his true father—not Charles.

Alexis felt light-headed and numb. He mumbled a farewell to Renard, and walked out into the June sunshine, toward the Place de la Concorde. Suddenly, without being conscious of how he had arrived there, he found himself in the middle of the Avenue des Champs-Elysées, at the corner of the Avenue de Marigny. He looked up at a tall, narrow building of white granite, and remembered that *this was where Christina worked.*

He'd read about her leaving her husband and joining a famous design firm. The separation of the perfect couple, Christina and Robert Dreyfus, had set the gossip magazines atwitter with stories. And yet Alexis had made no move toward her. Their encounter in the Rochefleur vault the previous winter had scarred him too deeply to attempt to approach her again.

But today, as Alexis stood in front of her workplace, he asked himself if perhaps he hadn't intended to come here all along. He might have walked up the rue du Faubourg Saint-Honoré, instead of coming this way, through the Place de la Concorde, and then he wouldn't have found himself standing here in front of the edifice housing her design workshop, the Atelier Jouffroy. Alexis hesitated only a few seconds before pushing open the front door and climbing the stairs to the third floor.

A silver plaque, decoratively engraved with the firm's name, told him he had arrived at the right place. He turned the door handle and entered a small waiting room paneled in coral silk and hung with carved mirrors. The older woman behind the desk said "May I help you?" and he asked if Madame Dreyfus was in today.

The woman disappeared down a corridor, and he sat down by a low coffee table of unvarnished wood. Magazines were strewn across it invitingly, but his heart was in his throat and he could hardly breathe. Maybe she was sick, and wouldn't come. And if she came . . . then what?

Her voice was the first thing he heard—her laughter, tinkling in the hallway. "Come now, Florence," she was saying. "Strange men don't come here in the middle of the day without giving their names. . . ."

"This one didn't seem to hear me, madame," the receptionist informed her.

And then she appeared, her pinned-up hair falling in wisps over her forehead, a work smock covering her dress. Her face held questions and a smile of welcome for the stranger who had shown up. But when she saw who it was, her smile vanished, and her cheeks paled. "Alex . . ."

The receptionist had tactfully removed herself, and now he approached her. "Tina, I must talk to you. Please come out with me, just for half an hour. . . ."

She frowned. "I'm not sure—" But he could see the vulnerable expression in her face, and it broke through his reserve.

"Look at me, Christina!" he cried. "I need you! Or don't you care at all about me anymore?"

She nodded quickly, grasping his hand and pressing it, and turned quickly on her heel. In a moment she reappeared, a light jacket tossed over her shoulders. "Let's go," she told him, her own voice breathless as the pulse pounded in her throat.

They walked, hand in hand, all the way to the Arc de Triomphe, talking. Or rather, he spoke, and she listened, filling his pauses with soft pressure from her fingers. She looked into his face and let him tell her everything. And then they sat down on a bench, and finally he put his head in his hands and broke out into sobs.

"All my life, Tina, I felt like a changeling—all my life, I felt that somehow *I didn't belong*! And now I know why," he cried.

In answer, she took him in her arms and held him close.

Hours later, when they realized that neither had eaten anything since breakfast, they wandered into a café and ordered steak and spaghetti-thin fries. He looked drained and exhausted.

"I don't know what to do," he told her.

"You'll go to Cousin Charles, and tell him that you know. And then you'll take what's yours."

"Why do you make it sound so simple?" he wondered. "Fayard Industries is a huge, monumental corporation! How do I just go in there and 'take what's mine'?"

She sighed, staring away from him into the distance. "Take it one step at a time, Alex. He isn't going to fight you, once he knows you know the truth. Once he speaks to Fernand Renard, he will realize that your story is corroborated by a chain of witnesses, from Roland, through Marianne, to Lise Bourdin."

"And what about *us*?" he dared to ask. "Is there any way . . . ?"

She smiled, picking up his hand from the table. "I've loved you forever," she said to him. "Since the day you took me horseback riding in Saint-Germain and told me that time would wash away my grief over my father. Tell me, Alexis," she asked. "What about Cousin Charles? How long will I feel grief over *him?*"

He shook his head, helpless to give an answer that made sense. Because since that morning, nothing in his life made sense anymore . . . although everything, suddenly, made more sense than ever.

Alexis leaned over the red-and-white-checked tablecloth, and took Christina's face in both his hands. Then, finally, he probed her lips with his, and parted them, like velvet roses, as if tasting her sweetness for the first time.

* * *

Charles Lévy–de Rochefleur had expected everything but this—and now, as he listened to Fernand Renard, his mind went back to all the years he had worked at Fayard Industries, imagining himself to be the heir apparent. Somehow, the Crédit Industriel mattered less to him: he hadn't set out to be a banker, hadn't spent twenty-two years of his life tied to its affairs, as he had at Fayard, helping to build the corporation into the powerful organization it was now.

"I'm sure Alexis will still want you to manage a large part of the company," the attorney was reassuring him. "Armand placed the utmost trust in you, Charles."

Later, when Renard had finally departed, Charles sat numbly behind Fayard's gigantic desk, a catatonic expression on his face. All his life, he'd dreamed of heading this steel company. All his life, he'd dreamed of being a captain of industry so powerful that heads of state would place him at their right hand. And now, the boy—Anne's son, his nemesis—was about to shatter this dream forever.

Even if he asks me to stay on, I won't, Charles thought bitterly. *I'll never work for him*—never! He still had his own stock in the Crédit Industriel, and that would be enough to live a life of comfort somewhere else.

I'll go to Geneva, he thought. I'll take Mother, and we'll go together. I'll ask Tina to come with us—

"Madame Dreyfus is here to see you," his secretary announced, sticking his head through the doorway.

"Madame Dreyfus!" Charles's face registered surprise, and, mechanically, he consulted his watch. It was lunchtime. Christina usually ate at work, a quick bite between assignments, and they

tended to meet for dinner or a cocktail after business hours. Why was she here *now*—without an appointment?

Pinpricks of apprehension raced up his spine. *Alexis!* This had to do with *him*. Christina had left Robert so abruptly, so unexpectedly, giving as her only reason that she wasn't in love with him and couldn't continue "the masquerade." *I can fool the whole world, Cousin Charlie,* she had explained. *But I can't fool myself.* But perhaps Alexis had been the real reason. . . .

Now she entered the office: tall, slim, in a frilled blue blouse and a long skirt of a darker, cobalt hue. He found her amazingly distinguished, yet simple, like her mother. Her hair had been neatly pinned into a chignon, and she had sapphire studs in her ears. Yet she seemed pale, drawn, and strangely distraught.

"I'm glad to see you, darling," he greeted her. "Do you feel like having lunch with me?"

She shook her head, unsmiling, and took a seat in one of the chairs across from his desk. "Cousin Charles," she said, and he was stunned by the coldness in her voice. "You know how much I always esteemed you. How much I loved you and was grateful to you. You know how much you meant to me . . ." Her voice broke, and she quickly looked down at her hands.

" 'Loved'? 'Esteemed'? What is all this, Tina? You're speaking in the past tense, for God's sake. What's happened?"

She burst into tears, and looked him in the eye. "You know damn well what's happened, Cousin Charles! *You lied about Alexis!* You fabricated the story of his betrayal! *He was never a traitor,* and you knew it all along! He has proof, you know, to corroborate what really happened to him, and now that he's able to move freely about Paris, he can have those documents you showed everyone displayed for what they are: elaborate forgeries!" She stood up, shaking, and leaned over the leather and iron table. "Why?" she whispered. Then, screaming, she repeated, *"Why?* Alexis would never have removed you from the bank, and certainly not from here. Why did you have to keep him from his inheritance and, worst of all, from the knowledge of who Armand had been?"

Charles's lips parted, but no sound emerged. Christina backed away, shaking her head. Her face was white, and her lips trembled. "Cousin Charles," she said, her voice uneven with emotion. *"I shall never speak to you again,* so long as I live! The damage you did will leave deep scars forever! *I married the wrong man,* because of your deception. And Alex—you almost ruined his *life* . . . *!*

You were never a father to him, all the years you pretended to be, but now at last he has a real father to remember: the man who loved him enough to show an interest in everything he did, who talked to him, gave him his professional training, and advised him how to be a man."

She inhaled deeply, then delivered her final message. "I'm glad you never tried to teach him *that*," she declared. "Because *you don't know what it takes to be a real man. . . .*"

With those final words, she ran from the room.

And Charles thought: *Now I've lost everything.*

EPILOGUE

———◆———

Charles stood by his bedroom window, surveying the garden behind La Folie, and thought about his life. This August 1, 1948, he was celebrating his fiftieth birthday, and he was alone. The garden was green and flowering, its latticed arbors hinting at romance and mystery, and he thought: Not for me, anymore. *My heart is dead.*

All his life, he had lived in fear: fear of poverty, fear of being robbed of his patrimony, fear of losing Amelia . . . fear of Alexis. But, most of all, *fear of the truth*. He and Anne, cousins, with a secret. He and Amelia, cousins, with a love that had to remain hidden. Had there ever been anything open, and honest, about his relations?

He thought about the children of this strange triangle, Alexis and Christina. That German general, in Nancy . . . what had his name been? Ah, yes, von Quistorp! He had branded the de Rochefleurs "an oligarchy of cousins marrying cousins." Tina and Alex wouldn't have disappointed him, for it was obvious they would marry as soon as her divorce came through.

In the meantime, the two young people were being seen together everywhere. Charles read about them in the magazine column, because Christina had kept her word and hadn't spoken to him since their confrontation in the Fayard office. How that hurt! Her silence, reminding him of his guilt and recalling to memory all the years when Amelia, too, had been out of his life, during her marriage to Peter Habig. . . .

Alexis hadn't done anything about his half of La Folie. His attorneys had repossessed the bank, and Fayard Industries—all very politely, with no hint of public scandal. And now the Bank of France had invited the twenty-seven-year-old man to sit on its board of directors. Financial magazines were featuring Alexis Fayard–de Rochefleur as the most interesting young mogul of the century. But he'd ignored the house. "After all," Renard had said to Charles, "it's been your home for years, and Alex wouldn't feel right about claiming his half now."

How typical, Charles thought bitterly: Alexis, man of principles, standing by what was "right" and "proper." Alexis, out of the generosity of his spirit, leaving him La Folie to dwell in alone and abandoned by all! The irony of this magnanimous gesture made Charles laugh: so the bastard—for that was what he was—had stripped him bare, but he had thrown him crumbs to look good in the eyes of his sycophants!

Alexis and Tina weren't living together yet. It wouldn't have been "right" or "proper," until they could be legally married. Alexis would make sure to preserve the appearances, to stave off the rumormongers. Alexis always knew just what to do to look immaculate of heart and mind. . . .

And that was why everybody always loved Alexis. That was why he had inherited everything—the bank, and half of La Folie from Alfred, the steelworks from Armand—and why Christina had left Charles's sinking ship and stepped on board the spanking new deck of the S.S. Alexis. Anne's son had snipped away the last flower in Charles's landscape: his beloved Tina, Amelia's unspoken bequest to him. The last tangible link to her part in his life.

How spectacular the garden looked, on this afternoon of his fiftieth birthday! The gazebo glimmered in the sunlight; the rosebushes spread their glory into coral, red, and pink blossoms that caught at his heart. Charles sighed, and suddenly he understood. All his life, he'd loved this house, so much so that he hadn't left Paris after all, not even when Alexis's lawyers had taken everything away from him—everything he had ever loved, wanted, and worked for. He had remained here, because he felt that *his life had begun at La Folie.*

His life was going to end at La Folie, in the house of his forefathers. Charles glanced down at his signet ring, with the crest of the rock and the flower, and thought about how complicated life became when human beings wrapped themselves in lies, and tampered with the destinies of others.

He was going to simplify his own, right now, on his birthday. Charles walked to the bureau and unlocked his secret drawer, and drew out the gun.

And all at once his fear slipped away. *He had no other choice but to pull the trigger,* and face his own truth.

Special Offer
Buy a Dell Book
For only 50¢.

Now you can have Dell's Readers Service Listing filled with hundreds of titles. Plus, take advantage of our unique and exciting bonus book offer which gives you the opportunity to purchase a Dell book for *only 50¢.* Here's how!

Just order any five books at the regular price. Then choose any other single book listed (up to $5.95 value) for just 50¢. Use the coupon below to send for Dell's Readers Service Listing of titles today!

DELL READERS SERVICE LISTING
P.O. Box 1045, South Holland, IL. 60473

Ms./Mrs./Mr. _____

Address _____

City/State_____ Zip _____

DFCA - 6/88